T0304831

# A CRANE
# AMONG WOLVES

## ALSO BY JUNE HUR

*The Silence of Bones*
*The Forest of Stolen Girls*
*The Red Palace*

# A CRANE
## AMONG
# WOLVES

JUNE HUR

WILDFIRE

First published in 2024 by Wildfire
An imprint of Headline Publishing Group Limited

3

Cataloguing in Publication Data is available from the British Library

Hardback ISBN 978 1 0354 2086 5
Trade Paperback ISBN 978 1 0354 2087 2

Offset in 12.97/18.94 pt Garamond Premier Pro by Jouve (UK), Milton Keynes

Printed and bound in Great Britain by Clays Ltd, Elcograf S.p.A.

Headline's policy is to use papers that are natural, renewable and recyclable
products and made from wood grown in well-managed forests and other
controlled sources. The logging and manufacturing processes are expected to
conform to the environmental regulations of the country of origin.

HEADLINE PUBLISHING GROUP
An Hachette UK Company
Carmelite House
50 Victoria Embankment
London EC4Y 0DZ

The authorised representative in the EEA is Hachette Ireland, 8 Castlecourt
Centre, Dublin 15, D15 XTP3, Ireland (email: info@hbgi.ie)

www.headline.co.uk
www.hachette.co.uk

To those who have dared to be a beacon of light
in the bleakest of moments

# AUTHOR'S NOTE

King Yeonsan (deposed name: Yeonsangun/ 연산군) ruled from 1495 to 1506 and was considered the worst tyrant in Korean history. Supposedly, he ruled decently for the first nine years of his reign, but in 1504—after learning of how his mother had been executed—he went on a revenge spree that began the bloodiest purge of his reign.

Emboldened by the absolute power he held, Yeonsan began committing widespread atrocities—stealing land from the people to turn into his personal hunting grounds, executing his own family members, murdering government officials in the cruelest ways, and kidnapping and enslaving women from every province.

I believe it's important to tell history as it is, with all its violence and corruption, and so I did not shy away from the realities of Yeonsan's reign. His crimes were so numerous, though, that I couldn't mention them all in the story. But for the ones I did, I'd like to offer the following content warnings: rape (mentioned), sexual abuse, misogyny, kidnapping women and girls, sex trafficking, incest (mentioned), violence, murder, animal cruelty, suicide (mentioned), infanticide (mentioned), psychological trauma, panic attacks.

# 1

# ISEUL

July 1506

*Never travel beyond Mount Samak.*

Halmeoni's words echoed in my ears, the memory of her warning tugging at me to turn back. But I could not; I had come too far. Pine needles scratched my face as I pressed through the forest, disregarding my blistered feet and blood-drenched sandals. My legs felt numb, not used to trekking for days over rocky slopes, steep ravines, and rushing rivers.

*Iseul-ah*, Grandmother's voice tugged again. *You must stay away.*

Wrenching my cloak from a tangle of branches, I hobbled down the narrow path and paused before a tower erected like a gravestone at the edge of the forest glade. Etched into the granite were the words:

TRESPASSERS WILL BE EXECUTED.

The damned king. The territory beyond had once been home to tens of thousands of people, until King Yeonsan had evicted them, turning this half of Gyeonggi Province—from the town of Yongin all the way to Gimpo, Pocheon, and Yangpyeong—into his personal hunting grounds.

"Heavens curse him," I snarled, stomping out into the open.

The sky was heavy with rain clouds, the air thick with humidity. Up ahead was a road that cut through grassland. And past the veil of mist, lush green mountains loomed, quiet observers who must have witnessed dozens of men, women, and children wander into this wilderness—and never escape it. I might die out here, too, if I let my focus slip even for a moment.

I ran a finger under my tight, sweat-drenched collar.

If I lost my way out here, there would be no one to give me directions. I couldn't make a single wrong turn.

Rummaging through my travel sack, I snatched up my ink-drawn map, studying it for the hundredth time. The route I was to take wound through abandoned rice paddies and demolished villages, over small mountains, and through valleys, then along the Han River, and at last to the fortress gates of the capital. The journey was a long one, and I was growing impatient. Suyeon needed me. She was waiting for me there, and I was her only way home.

"You had better wait for me, Older Sister," I rasped, continuing down the dusty road. "I am almost there."

Older Sister and I had faced horrors before—when royal soldiers killed our parents, and we'd escaped to Grandmother's home before we could be exiled to an island far away. Grief had strained our already waning bond, rendering us mere strangers living beneath Grandmother's roof, our interactions reduced to husks, of mumbled remarks and cutting glares. How shocked Grandmother must have been when she discovered my note, declaring that I'd left to find my missing sister.

I was shocked myself.

When my heart was far from Suyeon, I had seen her as a sister who was burdened by me and who carried herself with the irritating air of an afflicted martyr. But my heart had clung close to the memories of her during the past three frightening days. I no longer saw a sibling I resented but the girl our parents had adored, the cherished child whom Mother had conceived after eight long years of waiting. And once born, Mother and Father had showered her with an abundance of love, treasuring her as if she were worth more than a dozen sons. I had cherished her, too, when we were younger. She possessed a natural silliness and would entertain me until I broke out into squeals of laughter. She would also assemble scraps of material, fashioning them into whimsical puppets, performing enchanting tales of folklore to me, her delighted audience. I had laughed a great deal as a child because of her.

This sister of mine was gone.

*Do not die, Older Sister. Stay alive. You must.*

I forbade myself from resting, except to pause briefly by a trickling stream. I hadn't eaten since the morning—I'd packed enough for only two days, not three. Scooping up handfuls of water, I drank until my stomach felt heavy, the hunger less excruciating. Then I washed the sweat and grime and tears from my face. Leaning my weight against a rock, I lifted myself back onto my feet, and I was once more on the road.

I passed by a rag doll, an abandoned sandal, a leafy plant erupting from a crack in the road.

The eerie quiet chilled my skin as I stood before a town, as hollowed as a bone. Weeds crawled over shadowy huts, devouring walls and roofs. The streets that had once bustled with crowds, filled with voices and merriment, were now deserted. Families, neighbors, friends—they were all gone. They had either escaped the province in time or remained to guard their homes, only to be slaughtered by the king and his army.

I wondered if their ghosts were watching me now.

*Why are you here?* I imagined them asking. *This is forbidden territory.*

The truth was too unbearable to face. I tried to beat it aside, but as I trudged on, my mind sank into the memory of three days ago. I was once again the heartless and self-centered Iseul, the younger sister who could not stand to be under the same roof as her older sister.

I had run out of the hut after a dreadful argument with her, and it had been my fault. It was always my fault. *I cannot bear her*, I had snarled, even as guilt had plagued my conscience. *I wish she had died instead of Mother, instead of Father!*

I hadn't meant it, truly, but as though my thoughts had summoned him, King Yeonsan had prowled into our village. The treacherous king who kidnapped women as his pastime—the one who stole the married and the betrothed, the noble daughters and the untouchables alike. He did not discriminate. And my sister, who must have followed me out, was as lovely as an azalea in full bloom.

I had no doubt in my mind that His Majesty had taken her.

"Halmeoni," I whispered, the ghost town now behind me. Raindrops spotted the dusty road, and the mist shrouded the distant mountains in white. "I will find Suyeon. And I won't return home until I do."

I trudged through the rain, my head angled against the torrent, and walked until the night thinned into an early-morning gray. Beyond exhausted, I wanted to drop to the ground and curl up. By midafternoon, I finally saw a hamlet in the near distance. No weeds were crawling over the huts. Instead, the roofs were thick with golden straw thatching, the clay walls smooth and unblemished. A bell tolled somewhere in the town, followed by the sound of scurrying footsteps and creaking wagon wheels.

The sounds of life.

I pulled out my jangot, an overcoat I'd once worn over my head as a veil. I wore it now, not out of fashionable etiquette, but to conceal my face. I did not wish to be seen—or remembered. I was a fugitive, and a village did not always mean safety. I clutched tight to the sides of my cloak, clamped the travel sack under my arm, and focused on my steps. *Put one foot ahead of the next*, I told myself, determined not to collapse. As I entered the hamlet, out of the corner of my eye, I noticed handbills pasted onto public walls. The same handbill had been plastered around Grandmother's village. I'd read it over so many times I could recite it by memory.

THE KING DULY INSTRUCTS THE PEOPLE

A KILLER IS ON THE LOOSE.

PERSUADE ONE ANOTHER TO SEARCH FOR THE

CULPRIT—

I tensed, looking up as a woman and her ox-drawn wagon appeared down the dirt path, the wooden wheels turning precariously on their axles. She stopped to hold my stare, and I knew what she saw: a grim-faced girl with her chin perpetually raised, bearing the haughtiness of a yangban aristocrat, yet garbed in a dirty silk dress.

"Excuse me," I rasped, my voice scratched from disuse, "but would you point me to the inn? If there is one here."

Without a word, the woman pointed vaguely down another path then continued on her way, leading her ox and cart along.

I followed her direction and soon found myself before a long, thatched-roof establishment with a spacious yard spotted with travelers. Clutching my veil tighter, I studied the strange faces. *No one can be trusted*, the past two years whispered into my mind. *No place is safe.* I pulled the jangot higher over my head, to ensure that if anyone were to look, they would see only a pair of eyes, dark with a warning: *Stay away from me.*

I took in a sharp breath, squared my shoulders, then stalked into the bustling yard where some merchants were unloading their goods. Two children washed their faces on the veranda that wrapped around the inn. Weary travelers ate and quietly conversed. Steam billowed from the kitchen, and I took in the mouthwatering scent of soybean broth.

My stomach twisted; my head swayed. Suddenly, the exhaustion of the three-day journey struck me hard. My knees buckled, and I stumbled backward, the earth tilting beneath me until a strong hand gripped my arm.

"Careful." It was a female voice.

My hazy vision cleared and focused on a young woman who

looked to be no older than I. Adorning her head like a crown was a fashionable gache wig, glossy black hair braided into thick plaits and arranged in coils atop her head. Her eyes were just as black, and sparkling, too. A scar ran down from her right eyebrow.

"A traveler has arrived . . ." She tilted her head to the side, as though the heavy wig were as light as a feather. "And it appears my guest has come from afar."

"Yes," I croaked, then cleared my throat. "I am from—" *Chuncheon.* Instead, I gave her the name of another nearby town.

"Hmm." She examined my dress, my bloody sandals, then her gaze locked onto mine. "You went through the forbidden territory, did you not?"

"Here one comes for a warm meal and shelter from the rain," I said stiffly, "not for an interrogation."

"Rest assured, I shan't tell anyone," she whispered, then gazed off into the distance—perhaps beyond the road, the reed field, to the stone tower. "All who travel through that half of Gyeonggi Province look as though they've journeyed through the underworld," she murmured. "I've seen the look in their eyes. In my own father's eyes." She let out a little breath, and a smile reappeared on her lips. "Are you in need of room and board?"

I needed to rest. Desperately. "I am . . ."

"Then you have come to the perfect place," she said, and chivalrously offered me an arm. "My inn will take good care of you."

"I can walk on my own, thank you," I bit out. But when I tried, my knees wobbled and I unintentionally reached for her. I tried to pull away at once, but she stubbornly held my arm.

"You look like you'll faint at any moment."

Shoulders tense, I let her help me as I staggered farther into the innyard then sat down on a raised platform where three other travelers were hunched over low-legged tables, wolfing down stew. A fourth man, wearing a straw hat, nursed his bloody fist. I dragged my weight around and settled before an empty table, holding the edge to keep myself steady against the growing dizziness.

"Wait here!" the innkeeper chirped. "I shall bring you a most hearty meal."

I blinked hard, wishing the light-headedness would go away, hoping I wouldn't pass out in the company of strangers—including the innkeeper. Her kindness was too sweet, too suspicious. I slipped out my map, flipped it to the back, and stared at the face of my sister, which I'd drawn in ink. "Stay alive, Older Sister," I whispered to the drawing, "and I will, too." Her delicate eyes stared back at me, her calm and graceful expression—

The back of my neck prickled. Someone was peering over my shoulder.

I quickly folded the sketch and glanced up to see the smiling innkeeper. She proceeded to unload a steaming bowl of boiled herbs. Not a single chunk of meat to be found. It wasn't the sort of hearty meal I had grown up with, but I'd learned these past two years that more than half the kingdom survived on what could be foraged in the mountains.

"So," she said, "what brought you here to Hanyang?"

"Why do you wish to know?" I asked, my voice clipped.

"I like to know who my guests are. You are searching for someone?"

"No."

"You drew that?" she asked, gesturing toward the paper in my hand.

"Yes."

"The boy in the picture looks too young to be your father."

"It is a *woman*," I snapped.

She let out a most obnoxious laugh. "I jest! Is she your sister, then?"

"Even if she were"—I stuffed the sketch back into my travel sack—"it should be no concern of yours, ajumma."

"'Ajumma'?" The amusement in her eyes brightened. "I am neither a middle-aged woman nor am I married. In truth, I have no interest in ever marrying, even though I do have quite the line of suitors, if I do say so myself." She paused, as though waiting for me to laugh. When I did not, she continued. "I am only nineteen. Come, you look at me with daggers in your eyes. I only wish to help. You've come searching for your sister, and you can't be more than eighteen."

I was seventeen.

"Do you not have anyone to accompany you in your search? A father? A mother?"

They were both dead. And I had no patience for nosiness. I cut her a glare, preparing to say something biting. But then it occurred to me that while her curiosity was relentless, it also posed an opportunity. Innkeepers could be storehouses of information, of gossip. And what I lacked was knowledge of the capital, of how to get to my sister.

"You crossed King Yeonsan's hunting grounds, risked your life by doing so," she spoke in a whisper, seemingly unaffected by my reserve, "and you are here near the capital. Did she run away—?"

"No, madam," I said coolly, watching her closely. "She was taken from our village three days ago."

The innkeeper sighed. "You too."

Here was my chance. "You know of others?"

She cast a glance around. No one was in hearing distance except a man across from me, but she seemed to pay him no heed. "Many. The hamlet has even installed a bell, which is rung when the king is to pass through, to warn the young women who dwell here. That is, what remains of them. I have not seen a girl my age in months."

"The king passes through this village himself?"

She nodded.

We both fell quiet, and I noticed then that the straw-hatted man across from me was eavesdropping. He had stilled, no longer dabbing a cloth against his bloody knuckles. He also wore a straw cloak—though the rain had long stopped—and the brim of his hat was lowered over his face, offering me only a glimpse of his bearded and middle-aged complexion.

"How . . ." I dug my nails into my palm. This was dangerous, the question I was about to ask. A question that could lead to my imprisonment and execution. *Trust no one*, I had told myself, yet in this moment, I had no alternative—there was no one else to rely on. "Would there be some way that I might see my sister?" I dropped my voice as low as possible, glancing at our eavesdropper. "Just to speak with her, to hold her hand. Nothing more."

The innkeeper chewed on her lower lip as she gazed past me at the man, then a look gleamed under her slender brows. "Did you know, when the king goes hunting, he takes his courtesans—"

I bristled. "You mean the girls he's *stolen*."

"—he takes hundreds of his most favored courtesans to accompany him," she continued, ignoring my interjection. "I'm sure His Majesty wouldn't notice if one girl went missing. For a moment." Quickly she added, aware that this kingdom abounded with spies, "Just to hold your sister's hand, as you said. That cannot be treasonous, I should think. The king forbids husbands from ever meeting their wives, but His Majesty has made no mention of sisters . . ."

It took a moment for her words to register, and the barest flicker of hope drifted through me. "When . . ." I swallowed, trying to steady my voice. "When does His Majesty go hunting?"

"In the summer, often." The innkeeper propped the tray against her waist. "You must have heard the village bell ring when you arrived here."

Following her gaze, I glanced behind me. A dark thread of movement crawled over the distant hill, red flags billowing under the blazing sun. I swiped an oily strand of my hair away, then quickly buried my hands in my skirt to hide their trembling.

"The king keeps his women close," came a male voice, so gruff and commanding that I flinched. It was the eavesdropper, the brim of his straw hat still lowered, his face an ominous shadow. "And some of the finest swordsmen and archers guard His Majesty . . . *and* his women."

The innkeeper and I both stared at him.

Nonchalantly, he continued to nurse his bloody fist as he said, "To attempt to steal your sister right under His Majesty's nose will result in both your deaths. You won't even get close enough to touch her before you're shot dead with an arrow."

"I did not say I would steal her," I said calmly, even as cold gathered in my chest. This man could be a royal spy. "I simply wish to see her."

"Your love for your sister is admirable, but I have seen this love drive countless men to their demise. I would beware, if I were you."

"That is Wonsik ajusshi," the innkeeper whispered. "He is like the guardian of this inn, always fighting off cutthroats and thieves, so I would heed his advice." She then waved her hand with a flourish, as though to sweep aside my anguished look. "Do not look so downcast," she said too merrily. "So long as your sister lives, there will always be a way back to her." With that, she turned and walked off, taking with her the trace of hope I'd felt.

My gaze dragged back to the dark cloud of the king's approaching procession, and my stomach clenched around the awful thought that my entire journey may have been futile. That I was helpless and that my sister was gone, forever.

"Nangja," Wonsik interrupted my gloomy thoughts, addressing me as a young maiden. He slipped the bloody cloth away, and while he examined the cuts on his knuckles, he said, "Eat your meal." He flexed his fingers, testing. "You cannot journey back home on an empty stomach."

"I will not be returning home." I nevertheless picked up my wooden utensil and shoved spoonful after spoonful of soup into my mouth. "Not without seeing my sister."

The eavesdropper continued to examine me, then he left his table and retired to his room.

I picked up the bowl and gulped down the remaining broth.

I wiped my mouth with the corner of my sleeve, then stared into the empty bowl. I had nothing, absolutely nothing, to help my sister with; I did not have the strength and power of a military general, nor the cunning of a great strategist. I was simply Iseul. A troublemaker. A blemish on my sister's life.

"Madam Yul!" a panicked voice erupted. "Madam Yul!"

Everyone at the inn perked to attention, lifting their heads. I, too, glanced around, then I caught sight of a lanky youth dressed oddly—in a bright red robe and golden sash band. He came charging into the yard, then bolted straight toward the innkeeper.

"A murder! Right outside the village," he gasped, his face ashen. "And I overheard the village elder say that he'd reported it to the capital police bureau. The village elder thinks Nameless Flower has struck again. That means this is the twelfth victim!"

*Nameless Flower.*

That was the sobriquet the populace had given to the anonymous killer at large somewhere in the kingdom, the one who had murdered government officials, each of them one of King Yeonsan's sympathizers. Others referred to the killer as "The Guardian," for he would steal rice from the wealthy and leave it at the home of starving peasants. *Nameless Flower.* His name now ricocheted inside my skull as the two conversed in hurried whispers.

"Could it be a coincidence?" the innkeeper asked. "That Nameless Flower struck this very day—when the king is to pass through with his hunting party?"

"I don't think it a coincidence at all."

Madam Yul ran a nervous hand along her throat.

"The village elder doesn't want the king to see the crime scene, so he's moved the corpse into the reed field," the young man said, growing paler by the moment. "The elder fears that His Majesty will light this hamlet on fire in outrage if his hunting day is marred."

I had no interest in the killer anymore.

I half rose, meaning to retreat to my room, but the innkeeper hadn't pointed out where I could stay. As I turned to interrupt their conversation, I noticed another handbill fluttering on the public wall.

THE KING DULY INSTRUCTS THE PEOPLE A KILLER IS ON THE LOOSE.

On the day soldiers had first posted this handbill on public walls, I'd wandered out of Grandmother's home to read it. I should have hidden in the hut—it was dangerous for a convict's daughter to roam a village full of soldiers, but I'd ventured out nevertheless.

PERSUADE ONE ANOTHER TO COME FORWARD WITH INFORMATION REGARDING THE KILLING OF GOVERNMENT OFFICIAL IM, AMONG THE TEN OTHERS. HE WAS FOUND DEAD, A BLOODY MESSAGE THAT SLANDERED HIS MOST GRACIOUS MAJESTY SMEARED ACROSS HIS ROBE. ANYONE WHO RENDERS MERITORIOUS SERVICE WILL BE OFFERED A GRAND REWARD.

"Grand reward," I whispered bitterly.

Those two words had cast a spell over me the day I'd first read them. I had stayed out too long, fantasizing about what the king could give my family if I'd found useful information. I had imagined a life once more surrounded by the safe and secure mansion walls, perfumed by an immaculate garden, and endowed with servants who would come running to tend my every need. My life would finally return to normal, to the perpetual state of comfort and ennui where my utmost concern would be the condition of my nails, the paleness of my skin, and whom I'd be arranged to marry. On my return to our thatched-roof mud house, I had felt a glimmer of hope I'd not felt in a long while, only for it to be dashed away by my sister.

*Do not be stupid. No one will save us*, she'd rebuked me, *especially not the king.*

Our clashing had spiraled into vicious words that had sent me hurtling out of the hut two days later.

I pressed my fingers into my eyelids, wishing I could turn time around. I wished that I'd never left the hut, that I had never laid my eyes on those two words. *Grand reward* . . .

An odd floating sensation hovered along the outer reaches of my consciousness. Distant thoughts, gathering like clouds, and then they were gone. I frowned, searching for whatever it was I'd lost. But before I could grasp it, the innkeeper rushed across the yard.

"Uncle Wonsik!" She rapped on the latticed door; it was the room where the straw-hatted eavesdropper had retired to. "Samchon!"

When the door slid open, she spoke low-voiced into the shadows, "I think the killer you're looking for has struck again."

After a quiet moment, the man lumbered out of his room in his straw hat, drawing himself up to his full height. He was tall, broad-shouldered, and athletically built. A humid wind billowed by, lifting his straw cloak just enough to reveal a sword strapped onto his back. The scabbard was glossy black, heavily decorated with gold—he was no commoner.

"The messenger told me the corpse was relocated deep within the reed field," Madam Yul explained. "There is a bloody pathway marked by all the dragging, so we will not miss it."

"I need to speak with the village elder first. Where is he?"

"North of the field, from what Yeongho told me."

In that moment, I understood what I needed to do. Fear wavered through me, but I beat the hesitation aside and dug my nails into my palm. King Yeonsan was offering a grand reward. If I could catch the killer, then perhaps—just perhaps—His Majesty would return to me the sister I had wronged.

I'd do anything the king decreed, absolutely anything at all, to see Older Sister one last time.

# 2

# DAEHYUN

At Prince Daehyun's birth, the shaman prophesied that he would be put to death this year. He did not know the hour or the day, but one thing he was resolved to make true: He would not die at the hands of his half brother, the king. He was determined to trick the heavens, if needed, to live long enough to carry out one act.

Treason.

"Little brother," Yeonsan drawled as he sat proudly on his steed, holding the reins with one lazy hand, "I had a dream last night."

"Did you, indeed?" Daehyun replied, riding alongside the king. "Was it a fortuitous dream, jeonha?"

"It was a nightmare. Or perhaps a dark omen . . ."

Daehyun waited while the sun beat down on him and His Majesty's hunting party, scorching them as they traveled through a hamlet. Government officials huffed and complained among themselves while high-ranking royal concubines flapped their wide sleeves, outraged by the heat. And then there was row after row of captives, the stolen women with faces shadowed with grief. But Daehyun remained still on his horse, his gaze fixed on the villagers prostrated on the ground, trembling with their heads bowed.

"I dreamed that a brother of mine stole my dragon robe and sat on my throne while I still lived." Yeonsan glanced at him, a black patch tied over his right eye, the one perpetually infected. "Have you ever coveted the throne?"

Daehyun donned his well-practiced mask, widening his eyes and sliding an innocent note into his voice. "*Never*, jeonha. I am the former king's bastard. How could I ever presume to dream of the throne?"

It was partly true. He had never coveted the throne—even if he had, he was illegitimate and held no sway over the government. But he did covet power. Enough power to defy the cruel grip of fate. He refused to be ripped apart like the others, or beaten to death by Yeonsan's fists, or exhumed after death to have his skeleton crushed, forever denied a proper afterlife. He wanted the power to wipe the grin off King Yeonsan's face and to see him cower as those he loved had cowered before His Majesty.

"The heavens mandated you as king, jeonha," Daehyun continued, filling his voice with reverence, "so how *dare* anyone dream of changing the will of the heavens? I may be an ant in your eyes, jeonha, but I am an upright ant."

"An upright ant," the king repeated. "Then what am I to you, little brother?"

"You are the ruler of the sun and moon, the mountains, and the ten thousand rivers." Daehyun spoke loud enough that a few villagers raised their heads, and he knew what they saw, for it was what everyone in the royal court saw: a sycophant.

"Everything belongs to you, jeonha," Daehyun pressed on, looking away.

Yeonsan let out a great laugh. He sat taller on his horse, and the sun gleamed off his silk hunting robe and winked off the gilded crown that encased his topknot. "You are my favorite brother, and yet I'm not sure that I know you." His Majesty's smile sharpened. "You are a trickster, through and through. One never knows what you are truly thinking, or whether you can be trusted. I suppose only time will tell who you really are—and whether I was a fool to favor you at all."

*Who I really am?* He cast a glance back at Hyukjin, the royal guard riding a few rows behind. It was a question his longtime friend often inquired of him. *"Where has he gone, the Daehyun we both knew? And who is this man before us now, so cold and hollowed out?"*

Daehyun knew the precise date he had lost himself: The twentieth of the third lunar month, two years ago. The day of his foster mother's death.

"And time will show, jeonha," Daehyun replied in a smooth voice, "that I am indeed an upright ant."

The burning of the sun finally cooled, the oppressive heat of the open ground easing away as they entered a shadow-engulfed forest. Sunlight peeked through the darkness in spears of gold, illuminating patches of earth and the tense faces of His Majesty's entourage. Daehyun felt his own shoulders tighten as Yeonsan rode ahead with his personal guard. Would the king suggest another game? His Majesty often did during his excursions, and the games always ended in at least one death.

"Jeonha," came the nervous voice of another prince. "The heat is overwhelming today. Please take care of your body, and do not exert too much strength. You oughtn't stay out too long in this weather—"

"*Quiet*," the king ordered.

Everyone halted.

At the head of the party, Yeonsan sat pompously on his mount. He stretched out his arm, hand open in the gesture for silence and stillness. Leaves rustled; twigs cracked. In the distance, a doe and her fawn broke from cover, ambling out of the thicket to drink water by a stream.

Daehyun could feel His Majesty's grin chilling the forest air—the same grin that had split the tyrant's face while staring down at Royal Consort Jeong, the woman who had taken Daehyun in as her own child. He could see her now, her still corpse with a sack over her head, her life drained out in a rivulet of blood.

Sweat broke over his brow. *Banish the memory*, Daehyun urged himself. *Do not dwell on it.*

It took a few moments to recompose himself. With a smile secured on his face, he turned his focus back on Yeonsan. His Majesty had raised his bow, fixed his arrow, and now lined up his shot at the doe. The creature lifted her head quickly, as though sensing something unpleasant; her ears twitched, then she and her fawn darted back toward the trees.

*Run*, Lady Jeong had whispered on the eve of the king's bloody purge. *The king will kill us all—*

The arrow pierced through the forest, whistling with ferocious speed. It struck its mark with a horrible thud; the doe collapsed, its body hitting dirt. There came no cry, not even a whimper.

*Smile*, he commanded himself.

He forced his lips into a rigid arch as drums were struck, instruments played to celebrate the king's excellent hunting skill. The frightened fawn darted and disappeared beyond the thicket, an orphan now.

"'Tis a fine day for hunting!" Yeonsan announced, beaming. "Would you not all agree?"

"Yes, jeonha," the entire entourage replied in synchrony, "a very splendid day." Heads bowed in subservience. The shoulders of government officials sagged under the weight of the humiliating shineonpae His Majesty had forced everyone to wear, a small plaque tied around their necks with writing inscribed:

A MOUTH IS A DOOR THAT BRINGS IN DISASTER.

A TONGUE IS A SWORD THAT CUTS OFF A HEAD.

A BODY WILL BE IN PEACE

AS LONG AS ITS MOUTH IS CLOSED

AND ITS TONGUE IS DEEP WITHIN.

The king stretched his arms out wide, his silk sleeves billowing in the forest breeze, as he turned to the crowd of princes huddled on their horses. "My brothers, I am in an excellent mood!" A look of thrill glinted in his one eye. "Let us play a game, shall we?"

Daehyun gripped the reins tight, preparing himself.

"Prepare your bows and arrows, princes. Any of you who returns by sundown with no carcass shall be executed." A ferocious grin stretched across His Majesty's teeth. "Let the hunt begin!"

# 3

# ISEUL

Tattered clouds billowed across the blue sky, and the reed field rattled around me as I stood still, my cloak pressed to my nose. A dead body lay curled at my feet. I could not tell whether he was fifteen or fifty. His face was all bones, his skin stretched taut from starvation. A mane of black hair hung loose down his shoulders.

I glanced around, wondering if that swordsman was still speaking with the village elder. I hoped he stayed longer. Twisting a reed from its stalk, I poked the corpse then brushed his hair aside. It was clear how he had died—a blade to the throat. And there was a red flower resting on his chest, like every victim before him, along with a bloody message smeared onto his robe.

*Your Majesty, you think you are clever,*
*but you are a fool.*
*A drunk fool who dances with his concubines,*
*while his people starve.*
*You and your sympathizers will fall;*
*it is only a matter of time.*
*For when I move, I shall fall like a thunderbolt.*

The scent of death swelled in the summer heat, so pungent I could hardly breathe. I would have fled if not for my determination to find my sister through whatever means, even if it meant searching for Nameless Flower on my own.

"How does one even track down a murderer?" I whispered to myself.

Folding the reed to make it sturdier, I pushed aside his robe and noticed his left hand clenched into a fist. Something yellow peaked from between his fingers. Grimacing, I placed my travel sack to the side and reached out with my bare hand, hesitated, then finally pried open the blood-encrusted fingers one by one. Something rolled out.

Two beads—one red and one yellow.

I looked closer. They were smooth wax beads, with a single hole running through both. I wanted to examine them further but heard footsteps approaching behind me. Quickly, I slipped the red bead into my jolitmal; I had worn my breastband particularly tight for the journey—there was no worry of the bead falling out.

"The police will not be pleased with the village elder," came a voice, and I straightened to see Wonsik and Madam Yul entering the reed field. "When they learn he moved the corpse from the crime scene..." Our gazes locked over the swaying grass, and he paused.

"How is it," he spoke slowly, once he was near, "that you are here?"

I stood straighter. "I overheard the directions."

"And . . . *why* are you here?"

"I am here, ajusshi, because I wish to be here."

A long stare later, he heaved out a weary breath and said, "These days, the younger generation lack in virtue, such as respecting one's elder."

"Aigoo, samchon." Yul elbowed her uncle. "You speak like an old fart. You have but recently turned forty."

Under his heavy brow, Wonsik stared at us both as though we were burdensome children. "There is no time for determining my antiquity. Stay silent, the both of you, and touch nothing."

My fingertips fluttered over the bead tucked inside my breastband. "Might I ask why *you* are here, sir? Are you with the police?"

When Wonsik offered no response, Yul leaned in and whispered, "Wonsik-samchon used to work for the Uigeumbu, investigating cases of treason."

I froze. Officers serving the State Tribunal . . . they were the ones who executed my parents.

I took a retreating step back, then nearly tripped over my travel sack. I picked it up, holding it tight against my chest. "When did he resign from that office?"

"Two years ago."

"Two years ago *when?*"

A frown flinched across her brow, then her smile returned. "In the spring."

My shoulders eased. The officials had invaded my home in the autumn. Wonsik could not have been involved, then.

"Well, you must tell her, samchon!" Yul called out, and I was grateful for the deflection. "Tell her about the scariest case you ever undertook."

Wonsik continued to examine the dead man, ignoring us.

Yul didn't seem bothered by his silence. "The most frightful case Wonsik-samchon ever told me about was the Dead Garden case."

I decided to indulge her. "The Dead Garden?"

"A while ago, Wonsik-samchon learned that a mother was buried in her own garden, and tiny animal bones were buried in the ground as well. It turned out the violent husband—a retired royal guard—killed her." She shuddered dramatically. "Oh, I've thought of a far more frightening incident: the Missing Head case. My uncle was once chasing a traitor when he discovered him inside a palanquin, headless. And his head was later discovered under someone's desk—"

Yul continued to chatter on with ill-disguised thrill, but I watched Wonsik now, noticing the way his shoulders tensed. He had finally noticed the small, round bead, the yellow one I had left behind. He tugged at his short beard, looking deep in thought—a troubling thought, for his brows weighed over his eyes.

"Have you found something?" I asked, curious to know the bead's significance.

"I recognize this victim," he said, mentioning nothing about the bead. Odd. "This twelfth victim is Young Master Baek; he is the eighteen-year-old son of the king's close aide. He recently passed his exam and was bestowed a position in the government." He proceeded to examine the top of the corpse's head, the back, the throat, and even the ears and nostrils. "The young master went missing while traveling through a forest three weeks ago. He had two attendants with him; one was killed on the spot, and the other was wounded but managed to escape as far as Jamsil Village before perishing."

"Is Jamsil Village far away?" I asked.

"At least an hour's walk. Hanyang would have been closer."

I imagined a wounded servant running; it was nightfall. Fear pounded in his chest, he was unable to breathe, the sky spinning above him. *We must find our way to Grandmother's house,* a whisper intruded into my imagination, and another memory took hold of me: Older Sister and I gripping each other's hands, escaping the soldiers who had murdered Mother and Father.

I blinked, and the shadows vanished.

"I wonder—" My voice shook; I cleared my throat to steady it. "I wonder why the servant ran to another village so far away, rather than running to Hanyang, where the medical office is situated."

Wonsik looked over his shoulder as if reevaluating me and seemed to weigh my question with great consideration. "If you were stabbed, to where would you run?"

"Not to where, but to whom," I whispered. "I would run to someone I trusted, someone who would wish me no ill."

He nodded. "Perhaps the servant ran toward a loved one, then. A loved one who lives in Jamsil." He turned to continue his examination of the corpse, taking notes in his journal with a degree of precise detail and quantitative exactitude that reminded me of the scribes I had seen serve my magistrate father. "How is it that you are so calm when faced with a dead man?"

After witnessing Mother's and Father's deaths, little frightened me. "Are the dead not a common sight in this kingdom?"

He pursed his lips, nodding. Then he asked, "You've traveled from afar in search of your sister, yet you stand there wondering about this dead man. Why are you here, nangja?"

"It should be no concern of yours—"

"She *truly* fancies that line," Yul said, her eyes gleaming with amusement. "She already used it once on me, samchon."

My dislike for the innkeeper sharpened. But the irritation slid away, replaced by a flutter of panic as Wonsik spoke, his voice dark with concern.

"Are you, perchance, searching for the killer to ask the king for your sister? As a reward?"

"I'm not sure what you mean—"

"So I am right."

A chill coursed through me. He had deduced my innermost thoughts. "You presume to know me when you know *nothing* at all."

"You are right. I know nothing—aside from the fact that you belong to the yangban aristocracy," he murmured as he continued his examination. "Your parents are deceased, and you are a fugitive of some sort. But, indeed, I know nothing at all."

Another blow, but this time the shock was numbing. "Have...have we met before? You make these assumptions with such assurance."

"It is obvious, is it not? You have an air of self-importance about you—I can tell by the way you hold your head, the way you walk—and your hands, they have not known a day of labor, pale and uncalloused as they are. You wear a silk dress, when only yangban aristocrats are permitted to wear silk, yet I can also see by the state of the fabric that you have fallen on hard times. And you crossed the forbidden territory without accompaniment, which leads me to believe that you are quite alone, with no one to turn to. I would surmise that your family name is shrouded in either scandal or something of an illegal nature, for you had not a single friend or family member to turn to. I settled for 'fugitive' by the way you use your jangot to excessively hide your face, and by the way you are always looking over your shoulder—as though you are afraid of being recognized. But as you say . . . all mere assumptions."

I stood petrified, watching his every move, half afraid he would drag me to the authorities. But he remained calm, and after a stretch of time, the sight of him preoccupied with the corpse blunted the sharp edge of my panic. He seemed absolutely uninterested in me.

"Whatever the case." Wonsik rose to his feet, and I flinched back. "Making a bargain with the king is a foolhardy notion, but you don't strike me as the kind who'll heed advice."

"Begging your pardon?" I gaped at him. No one had dared to speak to me in such a manner, except for my sister. "It seems like a perfectly reasonable plan to me. The king offered a grand reward—"

"At the least, I hope you'll first ensure that your sister is even in the capital before proceeding. Did you see her among the king's entourage?"

"No . . ." My voice still quavered. "Where do the king's women reside?"

"In Wongaksa Temple, which is close to Gyeongbok Palace, but it is so heavily guarded it is impossible to enter. There is another way to see her. Nearly every day, almost without fail, the king brings his courtesans to entertain him at the Sungyungwan Royal Academy. It should be easy to spot your sister over the walls."

Wonsik circled the corpse again, then crouched on the other side. "I know for myself," he said steadily, "because my daughter was there."

*Was.* And by Yul's reaction—chewing on her lower lip and glancing away—I supposed his daughter was dead. I suddenly felt sorry for this man but shook aside the emotion. I had sworn to myself after Mother's and Father's deaths that I would never again open my heart to anyone.

"And you, ajusshi?" I said, pointedly changing the topic. "Are you investigating for the reward, too?"

"I've been helping someone find the killer. And the one I am assisting has no interest in the reward."

*Thank goodness,* I thought. Perhaps I could shadow Wonsik, then, and claim the reward for myself.

"Then what *does* the person wish for?" I asked. "The one you are assisting."

"All I can say is that the killer is causing more chaos than good in the capital." He waved at me to draw near. "Come. If you wish to find the killer, you cannot stand at a distance. You must examine for yourself and not allow your view to be obscured by the smoke of a stranger's examination."

I stepped forward and stared. All I saw was a horrifying corpse.

Wonsik indicated various parts of the body. "Based on the wounds, and the stiffness of the limbs, I can tell he died at dawn today. Your turn. Tell me what you see."

"My turn?"

"You said you wished to find the killer."

Yul nudged me forward. I moved to the other side of the victim, and glancing at Wonsik out of the corner of my eye, I finally lowered myself onto my haunches. I looked at the back of the victim's head. From far away, when Wonsik had been examining it, I'd seen only hair. But now I saw the hair and scalp crusted with dried blood. "He was struck in the head?"

"Yes. And that wound looks weeks old."

"So it must have occurred when he was kidnapped." My gaze drifted to the bloody wound across his throat. "But this is the wound that killed him."

"I will not bore you with the details, but he was confined somewhere, left to starve for weeks," Wonsik deduced, "and just before his death, he was killed while he still breathed."

"Being starved to death is the worst fate." Yul shuddered. "The absolute worst."

Ignoring her, I said, "How can you tell all this, ajusshi?"

"Evidence is always before us; it is more a matter of whether we notice it." Wonsik clapped the dirt off his robe. "In fact, the truth is often in the most trivial of details—"

Our conversation was cut short by the sound of hooves—a dark cloud of riders was approaching quickly.

"Keep your eyes open," Wonsik said. "The killer often returns to the crime scene."

We watched, and slowly the silhouette formed into that of a corps of uniformed riders, all garbed in red.

"It is the State Tribunal officials," Wonsik murmured, then glanced at me. "They are sent when the king orders an investigation into a specific case. Cases that usually deal with treason."

"I know," I whispered. I knew too well.

*Always stay hidden, Iseul-ah.* I took a step back, Older Sister's warning pricking at my thoughts. *We must live as though we are dead. We must live as though we never existed.*

The wind blew against my face, now utterly bare. The

jangot must have slipped off in my distraction—it hung off my shoulder, held around my neck by a ribbon. I quickly reaffixed it over my head as I walked off.

"Where are you going?" Yul called out.

A forest lined the edge of this field. At once I ducked my head under the billowing reeds and ran for the tree line.

Lush trees rose around me, enclosing me in a shadowland where only thin streams of light penetrated the gloom. I hurried deeper into the forest, pausing now and then at odd sounds, ghostly echoes reverberating through the air. I hurried past more trees when I heard it again, clearer this time: distant male voices, flushed with panicked desperation, and the wild galloping of hooves.

*Hide.*

My pulse quickened.

*Hide. Hide now.*

Hiking up my skirt, I climbed up a ravine and hurried down a narrow dirt path. A horse burst from the thicket right before me. I stumbled behind a tree, staring up at the rider. Fear made a pale mask of his face as he rode away with a bloody rabbit in his grip.

I clutched my travel sack tighter and ran, past a moss-covered boulder, through tangles of branches, then hobbled along a trickling stream. When I could barely take another step, I stood still, straining my ears. Nothing. I seemed to be far enough away from whatever had scared the hunter so.

Heaving out a sigh, I set down my travel sack and dropped to my knees before the stream. I glanced around one more time, then cupped fresh water and rinsed off the unbearable heat. I reached for another scoop, but paused, staring at my reflection, tinged red in the waning light. She looked afraid, the girl staring back at me, and lonely.

I beat down the feelings. "Hold yourself together, Hwang Iseul," I whispered to myself. I splashed my face with water until the coolness had washed away my nerves, steadying me.

Leaves stirred.

Panic lurched me to my feet, and I slipped between trees, tucking myself behind a thicket of plants. I crouched low and stared through the leaves.

Horse hooves tramped against the earth. Approaching, nearer and nearer.

My arms tightened around my knees. *Please leave*, every heartbeat in me begged. *Please leave me alone.*

Into a reddish-gold beam, another young man appeared with a bow and arrow, at least twenty paces away from me. He sat tall on his saddle, and his silvery blue robe glowed like moonstone, molding to his lean yet powerfully built figure. And his eyes, his dark eyes—they appeared as keen as a falcon's.

I let out a small breath.

Suddenly, his gaze swiveled around. I clamped my hands over my mouth, my thundering heart quaking as I begged the heavens to turn the man away. But in one smooth motion, he notched his arrow to the bow and swung it my way. A gasp of terror caught in my throat. I scrambled backward; the leaves shook around me as my back slammed up against a tree—

The ferocious whistling of an arrow headed straight my way.

*This cannot be happening.* My mind raced. *This cannot be—*

A powerful force knocked me back, blazing pain consuming me whole. I wanted to scream but bit my tongue. Blood gushed and filled my mouth. There was an arrow above my left shoulder, embedded deep in the trunk, and when I looked closer—to my utter horror—I saw a shred of my skin caught on the arrowhead. Tearing my gaze away, I tried to rise to my feet as the hunter approached. But my jacket was pinned to the tree.

*Do not die*, Mother's voice urged, and with it, the sensation of her fierce grip around my hand. *No matter what, you must both survive and take care of each other. You have no one else.*

I grabbed my jacket with a white-knuckle grip, and after three attempts that left my face drenched in tears and sweat, I managed to rip myself free. Fire oozed down my shoulder. I tried to stop the bleeding when the leaves stirred before me, pushed aside by a sleek bow, opening onto the young man. He stared down at me, and in his expression was the face of privilege—cruel, indifferent, and cold.

"Get *away*!" I screamed, hysterical now. My fingers tightened around a rock, and I uncoiled, lunging forward. *Smash his face then run, smash his face then run!* Hands raised, I struck, but my arm would not budge. His steely grip had locked around my wrist.

"Drop the rock," he ordered.

"Let me go!"

His grip tightened, so mean and biting the weapon slipped from my hand.

"Wh-what will you do?" I whispered, gritting my teeth against the tremor. "*Kill* me?"

His gaze was dark and impenetrable. "Should I?"

A new set of hooves approached. Without removing his stare from me, he shoved me back down into the foliage. "Stay there," he ordered. "Do not move if you wish to live."

I crumpled to the ground, the leaves closing in around me.

Blinking away the tears, I peered through the branches, looking for an escape route.

Instead, I saw a royal guard riding over.

"Prince Daehyun," the guard called out, "the king has ordered everyone's return."

Prince Daehyun . . . I had overheard his name whispered between my parents, of how he had endured cruelty and was infamously cruel in return.

"The king murdered a dozen people while you were out hunting," the guard said.

Prince Daehyun stilled. "A *dozen*?"

"Trespassers were rounded up and used for military target practice. We had to aim for the fruits placed atop their heads." He sighed, rubbing his temple. "Only I and a few others succeeded."

Muttering something under his breath, the prince withdrew, riding away with the guard. After a few agonizing moments, I finally staggered to my feet, sweat washing down my face as pain tore through me. The dizzying forest tilted beneath my feet, but I hobbled forward, glaring at the rock that had dropped from my hand.

How I despised the throne and everything it stood for.

The king had taken everything from me, and the prince was no better. He had held my life in his hands as easily and carelessly as if I were nothing at all.

*I should have bashed in his head.* The thought seethed in me as I bent down, trembling, to pick up the rock, its sharp edge biting my fingers.

If our paths ever crossed again, I was determined to make the prince bleed.

# 4

# DAEHYUN

**Blood filled his mouth. His** head still rang, struck twice with the hilt of a sword.

"Little brother," came King Yeonsan's silken voice, "you could not shoot a single creature for me?"

Daehyun stayed kneeling, grabbing his robe tight to hide his slight tremor. "I am no expert archer like you, jeonha."

Yeonsan let out a sharp laugh, then the air grew cold as a snarl slid into his voice. "Court ladies whisper, and they have seen you practice. You hit your target every time without fail." His Majesty's blade touched his throat. "Who are you trying to fool, little brother?"

Daehyun tensed, his mind split in two directions. The king appeared irked enough to kill him, and there was the girl. She could be bleeding to death, an innocent life taken by him.

He needed to find her.

He could not become his brother—

"Let me think of how I shall kill you . . ." The blade pressed closer, and he felt blood dribble down his throat. "Shall I have you quartered, and send your severed limbs to all four corners of this kingdom?" The king turned to the rest of his hunting party. "Do you think this punishment is appropriate?"

Heads bobbled like puppets. "Yes, jeonha," the officials acquiesced.

"So you would kill me . . . ," Daehyun said quietly, "your favored brother and most loyal servant?"

"Most loyal, you?" the king scoffed. "A snake is more loyal than you are."

"Jeonha, am I not the little brother who grieved with you when it was prohibited to mourn Deposed Queen Yun's death anniversary? Did I not prepare a memorial banquet for your mother and weep bitterly before it?" The king turned pale, his one eye turning red, tears burning at the rim. The name of his mother had always served as Daehyun's shield. "Such vile snakes surround you, jeonha, and you would kill *me*? The Milwicheong Prison is bursting with criminals who harbored treason in their hearts. Surely, jeonha . . . surely I am more loyal than all of them."

The malice in Yeonsan's voice eased. "I cannot tell with you: How much of you is true, and how much is a lie?"

"Let me prove my loyalty to you then, jeonha." Daehyun slid a note of desperation into his voice, and when the blade's pressure eased, he latched onto the opportunity. "Is loyalty not proved by what we are willing to do? I'll kill anything for you. Send me out again and I swear I'll return with a carcass. The sun has not yet fully set."

"I suppose you are right." Then a thought tugged at the corner of the king's lips. "You would kill anything . . ." His Majesty sheathed his sword, looked around, and paused at a fixed point ahead. "Or anyone?"

Daehyun looked up and saw the crowd. He had never killed a person before, yet he could already feel the warmth of blood on his hands, dripping into his conscience—

*Stop.*

He had to numb it all. The fear, the dread.

*There are more pressing concerns than the fate of a single human life*, he tried to convince himself.

"Or anyone, jeonha," Daehyun whispered.

The king grabbed an arrow, then tossed it before Daehyun. "Loyalty is proved by what you are willing to lose. Kill him for me." His Majesty pointed.

Daehyun looked—and his gaze landed on his own horse, a gift from Father.

His stomach turned, a cold sensation tightening his chest as soldiers grabbed hold of the reins, stilling the great beast. The horse was his only warm memory of his father, more precious to him than all the king's riches.

As the last rays of sunlight withdrew, he notched the arrow and drew back the bowstring, aiming directly at the creature's chest, at the strong heart beating under the velvety black coat.

Jeong-Hui, that was his horse's name.

*Jeong.* Right, proper, correct.

*Hui.* Bright, splendid, glorious.

He gritted his teeth, silencing his apology.

He released the arrow just as the horse shifted, the iron head sinking into the right eye. A terrible scream erupted as Jeong-Hui toppled to the ground, thrashing and dragging himself around with his forelimbs, knocking aside the soldiers.

Daehyun rushed forward. Taking out his sword, he plunged it into Jeong-Hui. Blood gushed down his wrist. Then with all his might, Daehyun carved the blade through the creature to strike the heart, to quicken his death. Finally, the horse lay on the blood-drenched earth, legs still twitching as though desperate to cling to life.

He stepped back, his hands shaking terribly. The slippery blade dropped from his grip. There was only silence now. The eyes of everyone were on him.

"You did well, little brother," Yeonsan murmured from the shadows. "You may live another day, for you make me feel less alone in this kingdom."

The forest reeked of blood, and soon the hunting party retreated from the site. But Daehyun lingered, staring down at his now-still horse, then at his hands. He had never seen so much blood.

His legs staggered of their own accord, taking him toward the forest. He needed a shovel. He could not leave his horse unburied—

A memory froze him. His attention snapped northward. The girl.

*"Damn it."*

He bolted down the trail, stumbling through the forest until he arrived at the spot he had last seen her. But when he pushed aside the leaves, he found no one. She was gone, and in her place was an arrow, still embedded in the trunk.

He pulled the bloody metal point free, and dread flooded him in a surge of ice water, at first chest deep, and then he was drowning in it. *You will become like the king,* his dying brother had warned, *if you play His Majesty's games. He will make you cruel and heartless. He needs the monstrosity in others to hide the one in himself. Do not descend into his darkness.*

Daehyun finally tore his gaze up, searching for the girl's trail.

"Daegam," came Hyukjin's worried voice. Daehyun had barely noticed his friend's approach. "What are you doing here—?"

"Go to innkeeper Yul." Daehyun gripped the arrow tight, his gaze pausing on a white sack abandoned by the stream. "Bring shovels and a few strong men; there is a horse to bury. And send word to Wonsik—there is a girl I must find."

# 5

# ISEUL

**The thorny woodland coiled around** me until I finally stumbled out into a clearing. The unbearable pain cut me loose from my body, and I was floating somewhere high in the evening sky, looking down at myself still holding the rock as I hobbled through the pale gold reeds, then down a dusty road, and finally into the innyard. Everyone had retired for the night, and I was desperate to lie down—but Madam Yul had not yet given me a room.

At the back of the yard was a kitchen, and steam was rising from a pot of simmering stew; someone had to be nearby. I dragged myself toward it. In the darkness beyond, I heard footsteps. I followed the sound and saw the innkeeper's silhouette, her face and red lips illuminated by the lantern she held.

"Madam," I barely managed to whimper.

She did not hear me and disappeared inside a storage hut isolated in shadows. When I followed her in, I froze. Emptiness yawned around me. There were only a low table used for ancestral worship and a folding screen opened against the back wall.

Another wave of pain struck me. I swayed and clutched the

doorframe for support, blinking hard in an attempt to make sense of the empty hut. My attention snagged on a smudge on the folding screen. It looked like blood—old blood.

*Am I hallucinating?* Then I heard metal clanking beyond the screen. I pushed it aside and found a door.

*What in heavens . . .*

Ever so quietly, I nudged the door, which opened onto nothing but darkness at first. Then my eyes adjusted; slowly, very slowly, the darkness took shape before my eyes, into the silhouette of Yul, who seemed to be inspecting her inventory. She lifted the lantern light, and my blood chilled. Deadly sharp sickles were secured against the walls. Bundles of arrows filled large onggi pots. Bows hung from the ceiling beam, along with weapon holders. And crates upon crates were stacked on the ground, holding stashes of swords shining in the light.

My heart pounded as I made my way out, careful not to knock anything down. What need could an innkeeper possibly have for such an armory? I hurried across the yard, and when I turned to glance at the storage hut again, I bumped into a broom that went clattering onto the stone steps.

"Damn it!" I hissed.

Yul burst out of the hut. "Who's there?" She raised her lantern, and the light came sweeping out onto me. Her eyes widened. "You! I wondered where you had gone!"

"I—" My voice wavered, the shock of what I had witnessed still pounding in my chest. My fingers were digging into the rock. I set it down now under Yul's intense stare. "I am in need of a room."

"And a physician, too, clearly. You are covered in blood."

Gently holding my elbow, she led me to the main hut, a long, thatched-roofed establishment with doors marching down the veranda. She stopped at the first door, which opened onto a small and neat room.

"I should notify Wonsik that you are well; he went off looking for you," she said as she helped me settle in, laying out a sleeping mat and blanket and lighting a candle. "What happened?"

"I had an accident in the forest. But I can take care of myself—"

"I know, your life is none of my affair. Even if you are bleeding to death."

"I am not bleeding to death—"

"But see here. So long as you dwell in this inn of mine, your affairs are my affairs," she said. "Every traveler I take in is like family to me. Wait here. I will return shortly."

I massaged my temples. An innkeeper who smiled too often and who also stored an armory . . . she was giving me a headache.

When Madam Yul returned, she carried with her binding material and two bowls of what turned out to be salt water and a poultice. "One must learn how to tend to wounds when managing an inn, as there are no physicians or nurses in this hamlet," she chattered to me as she set everything out. She stepped out again and returned with something for me to drink, which I hesitantly accepted.

"As I said," she continued, "I treat my paying customers as I would my own family."

Reminded, I set the drink aside and reached for my travel sack to give my payment, but hesitated when my hand found empty air. Where had I left it?

Madam Yul tugged off my jacket. She applied salt water to the bloody groove of my wound, and I instantly recoiled, a bolt of pain knocking every thought from my skull.

"That *hurts*," I snapped, hand hovering over my throbbing shoulder.

"Do you want me to tend to your wound or not?" she asked, her voice sweet yet firm. "If you leave it as it is, you will likely die from an infection. And what good will a dead girl be to her sister?"

Reluctantly, I shuffled back to the young innkeeper, clenching my teeth as she continued to tend to my wound.

"What is your name?"

"My name . . ." I could not give her my birth name, Hwang Boyeon—the name by which authorities might know me. And I feared that if I gave her the name on my false identification document, I would not answer to it, and pique suspicion. "My name is Iseul."

Mother had never favored my official name, Boyeon, but she had submitted to her father-in-law's bidding. Then once I was born, Father had agreed with Mother that I looked nothing like a Boyeon. I, in fact, looked like a dewdrop. And so *Iseul*, the pet name they had given me, had remained with me for all my life.

My thoughts returned to my missing travel sack. I wiped the cold sweat from my brow. "I lost everything I brought with me," I confessed, staring fixedly at my clenched hands. "My bag held everything I owned."

A lull fell between us as she quietly wrapped the binding material around my arm and shoulder. I waited for the innkeeper to throw me out into the street. And of course she would. *No one can be trusted. No place is safe.*

"I must have *some* kind of payment."

My chest constricted. "I have nothing to give . . ."

Madam Yul helped me back into my short jacket. "Of course you do. So long as you can offer me some kind of service," she said without a begrudging note to her voice. "Consider this inn your home for as long as it takes to find your sister."

A tremor moved through me. "Y-you would let me stay then? Truly?"

"In dark times, every mother becomes your mother, every child your child, every sister your sister . . ." She picked up the coat strings of my jacket and tied them into a ribbon, closing the front. ". . . and every stranger-in-need a friend."

Her words played at my heartstrings, and a yearning I'd spent two years burying shuddered awake. I wanted friends. I wanted to laugh. I wanted to trust. But at once I beat those desires down again. Grabbing my drink, I occupied myself by taking sips of it as I reexamined Yul from under my lashes. The boisterous innkeeper offered me friendship, yet the gleam of a hundred sickles flashed through my mind. Surely, Madam Yul's red-lipped smiles hid something sinister. Surely she was not really a friend, but a liver-feasting gumiho in the guise of a young woman, waiting to sink her teeth into her next traveler.

"What kind of service do you need?" I asked slowly.

"Help me overthrow the king?" she said, grinning.

I nearly choked on the water. "*What?*"

"I jest!"

And there came her obnoxious laugh again; it grated on my nerves.

"I work at this inn alone," she continued. "This here"—she

pointed at the thick ripple of a scar over her brow—"is what shields me from becoming the king's next prey. Unfortunately for the servant who used to assist me . . . the king took her."

*Or did you kill her?* I shook my head, trying to ward off the image of that blood on the folding screen.

"So," she concluded, "in a few days, once you are somewhat recovered, you will assist me around here. Can you cook?"

"No."

"Do you know how to wash laundry?"

". . . No."

"What *do* you know how to do?" She grabbed my hand and examined it. "You are no noblewoman, yet possess the hands of one. Clearly, someone pampered you. Your sister?"

I flinched. My sister had labored for two years after our parents' passing, and I had let her, refusing to ruin my hands. *This was not the life I was destined for*, I had always said in protest.

"You are one of those little sisters, I see."

A burning knot formed in my throat. "What do you mean by that?"

"I must imagine your sister felt awfully lonely ever since your parents died," she continued, not answering my question. "I am guessing they are dead?" Before I could rebuke her for her remarks, she quickly asked, "Can you clean? You *do* wish to stay at this inn, do you not?"

I did. I gritted my teeth and swallowed down the hurt. "I think so. I will try."

Madam Yul released my hand. As she returned the bowls and binding material onto a tray, she said lightly, "If you are to stay in this hamlet, there are a few things to heed. When the bell rings, always hide. It is an alarm bell indicating that the king approaches. He plucks girls off our streets as one might pluck flowers off a field." She dropped her gaze now. "And you may notice strange activities and hear strange discussions about politics, but do not mind them. The travelers here love their game of janggi, so are ever strategizing among themselves, even when they are not playing. Whatever the case, focus on finding your sister. Is that clear?"

The shadows from the secret storage room drifted into my mind. "Of course," I said.

I woke up that night with a scream in my throat.

I had dreamed of my sister dragged into the darkness, where a shadow with fangs cut into her flesh. Guilt and self-loathing slid into my chest like a long needle. It was all my fault that she was in the palace, enduring unspeakable indignities. I fumbled for my travel sack before I remembered it was not there. I did not have the san-jo-in seeds I had brought with me, the dozen or so remaining from hundreds I had painstakingly collected over the months from dried jujubes.

The seeds were merely herbal medicine, yet to me, they became sacred promises when placed on my tongue. Promises that sleep would come, that I would find a moment of relief from this wretched life. But I had lost them all, along with my travel sack and everything in it. My hands trembled as I washed my face from a bowl of water, then cracked open the hanji-screened window and looked outside. It was still nighttime, and the chirping of crickets filled the hot and humid silence.

The pressure in my chest would not ease. *You, you are to blame. It was all your fault.*

If only I had obeyed my sister, who had only ever wanted to keep me safe. If I had, we would not have quarreled. If I had, I would never have gone out, leading her straight into the king's hands . . .

If only. If only.

I felt a pang in my heart as I tried and failed to recall a single day when Older Sister and I had *not* fought. How had we so drifted apart, Suyeon and I?

The ache deepened, and realization settled over me like a bone-chilling mist. Despite the cherished moments we once shared, a chasm had quietly widened between us, expanding year by year as our lives unfolded—hers, that of the dutiful eldest, and mine, that of the much-forgiven troublemaker.

I hadn't fully noticed this chasm until the day I rushed into her chamber, weeping in grief over the news that she was to be betrothed to a young man who lived afar and, after marriage, would be compelled to move to the far end of the kingdom to live with her in-laws. I'd felt truly devastated over this. But Suyeon had refused to even look at my tearful face, as though the sight of me repulsed her, and the whole time she had scrawled furiously into her journal. That night I had sneaked a peek into the book.

*I am tired of being the elder sister*, were the words within. *When I expressed my objection for the first time today, Father gave me such a look of disappointment that I felt my entire world tremble. Why does he only see my disobedience, and not my desperate love for him? To live near home, to be close enough to care for my parents in their old age—I wish I could cry, I wish I could fall apart as little sister often does, and still be loved and understood. But I cannot. My parents do not love me when I am weak, when I fail them, when I err. Who am I, if I am not the perfect daughter?*

My sister had written these words when she was fourteen years old, and I now felt her loneliness. Perhaps she had always felt this lonely.

When morning came, I felt beaten, in a sort of trance as I watched myself—a girl with shadows under her eyes and blood dried along her left arm. She struggled into a clean dress Madam Yul had provided, a white cotton jacket with a collar of midnight blue, and a skirt of the same hue. She threw a veil over her head and stepped out into the unwelcoming, early-morning gray. A wooden sign hung under the eaves reading, RED LANTERN INN.

I shuddered, and I was once more in my own body.

Tugging the veil low over my head, I staggered down the road, unsure of how to reach the Royal Academy in the capital. I was determined to look for Suyeon there. But there was no one around to ask. Then I heard a male voice singing and followed the sound to its source.

A small crowd of spectators surrounded a troupe of jesters. They wore masks as they performed a story about a wealthy government official and a lowly peasant. I had grown up watching these plays from over the black tiles of my mansion wall, fascinated by the stories that criticized the wealthy and brought joy to the common folk. I would always view these tales as I might distant mountains—as sheer entertainment, unable to relate to the suffering of others. But now their grief was my own. Hunger, loss, and humiliation. I had drunk from that bitter cup for the past two years.

In time, the performance came to a close, and the spectators dispersed. The jesters packed up, loading their instruments and masks onto a wagon, and I was still standing there, lost in memory.

"Are you waiting for someone?"

I startled at the rough Southern Jeolla dialect and looked to see a tanned and striking face. It was a young man carrying a narrow drum beneath his arm.

"No." I turned to leave.

"I know you. You're the new resident at the Red Lantern Inn, are you not?"

I looked at him again, then recognized his face. He was the one who had come running to Madam Yul with news of the murder.

"Where are you heading so early in the day?" he asked cheerfully.

I hesitated. "The capital. Which way is it?"

"We are heading there ourselves," the young man said, nodding at the group of performers. They were all men, tired but merry. They wore bright red robes and golden sash bands, and they walked with bamboo canes and straw shoes.

"Should we not accompany her?" he asked his fellows.

"She may follow, if she wishes," came a scratchy voice from the group. It was an elder with his white hair tied into a top-knot. "There's a killer on the loose. A young woman like yourself oughtn't be wandering alone."

"Thank you," I said stiffly. I did not trust myself to find my way to the capital with no map. "I would appreciate that."

Another conversation hummed farther ahead. "A killer is on the loose, and still, no one knows who he is."

"Have you been searching for the killer, too?" his companion asked. "I truly believe that the king will give us anything we want if we find this slayer."

"The king offers a promotion in status. I'm tired of living as a court jester. Tired to the gods-damned bone."

So these men were all court jesters, which were, in fact, part of the government—serving under the Bureau of Performance. They would be hired for events at mansions and the royal court.

An idea bubbled to mind as my heartbeat quickened.

"What is your name?" I asked the young man, a bit too eagerly.

"Yeongho," he answered.

"My name is Uijeongg," I lied. I couldn't resist asking the question. "You and the others are court jesters?"

"We are a traveling troupe, but we made the king laugh once, and so we have been performing at court whenever the king summons us."

"Have you ever performed for the king at the Royal Academy?" *Could you find a way to sneak me in?*

"Once or twice."

"Are you heading there now?"

"No, we are going to perform for a nobleman's hwangap celebration tonight."

Disappointment sank in my gut. I would have to resort to my original method of climbing over the wall. I might not leave the Royal Academy alive tonight. But there was no use looking for the killer, doing anything at all, if my sister was not even in the king's company.

As we set off down the road, Yeongho told me, "It isn't too far. The capital is about a half hour's walk. Do you think you can make it? Your . . . your sandals are bloody. I could piggyback you—"

"You will certainly not," I said, a bit too vehemently.

He raised his hands defensively, and the performers chuckled, whispering, "It seems we have taken in a wildcat."

Their conversations faded to the background as we reached the fortress, towering stone walls that enclosed Hanyang, the capital of Joseon. There was a crowd of people waiting to be permitted inside, and as I stood in line, I fidgeted with my skirt. I was supposed to be a thousand miles away in Jeju, exiled there along with what remained of Father's relatives. But my parents must have known—possibly since I was born—that the day would come when we would need to flee. They had prepared false identity documents for Older Sister and me, pushing the papers into our hands the day State Tribunal officers had invaded our home. I slipped out the document now from within my dress, the one thing I had not kept in my travel sack.

Once I arrived before the gate, a guard inspected my document, then waved me through. The sense of relief lasted but for a moment, for when I stepped into the city, the place did not match the glorious tales Father had shared with me. Instead, I felt as though I had stepped into a battle-torn wasteland.

Decapitated heads sat impaled on wooden pikes, eyes staring and tongues lolling. Police officers were busy scrubbing the public walls, trying to wash away the words of slander sprawled across in paint: *Damn the king! Damn the king! Damn the king!* The city was coated in a gloom cast by black smoke.

"You will grow accustomed to the sight of death," Yeongho murmured as he stepped over a corpse that lay ignored in the street. Then he cast a wry smile my way. "Welcome to the capital."

"Where is that smoke coming from?" I whispered.

I followed the troupe as they wound through the narrow and filthy roads, and finally Yeongho pointed eastward. In an open yard, books were being burned. Wagonful after wagonful of confiscated books were thrown into a great blazing fire. I watched the pages blacken and curl into ashes, the flames consuming the words like the king's fury over the land. I had seen this same scene two years ago, with the banning of eonmun—King Sejong's alphabet system that had so fascinated my sister. His Majesty had carried out this ban to suppress public slander. He had also had every literate man and woman submit four pieces of writing, to ensure that should anyone slander him, he could identify the writer.

"*The king has reinforced the ban on eonmun,*" Yeongho recited the words he must have memorized. "*Do not teach eonmun, and do not learn it. And those who are literate must report to the Hanseongbu Government office. Anyone who knows of neighbors who are literate but does not report it will be punished. And anyone who uses writing will be decapitated, and anyone who witnesses others but does not report it will be beaten a hundred times. Any books written in Hanguel or Gugyeol are to be destroyed.*"

I stared at the blazing fire as my throat ached. Tyranny billowed in the plume of black smoke, rising and rising, choking the heavens. Suyeon had stood by me when we had witnessed the first book burning, and she had watched in terror. She loved reading more than I.

"We live in a terrible time," Yeongho said. "An era when the truth is a crime. And there is nothing we can do about it—"

Suddenly, he gripped my hand and pulled me aside as a group of officers prowled by. Crowds quickly dispersed, and a young woman's panic-filled scream rang in the air.

"Beware of officers in bloodred robes," Yeongho whispered, now holding both my hands with urgency in his eyes. "Those are chehongsa officers, in charge of kidnapping girls for the king." He cast me a quick, timid glance. "I've only met you, and yet . . . I don't want to see you hurt. You must hide, too."

His remark blew right past me. "I have no time to hide," I said, then looked past the severed heads and black smoke. "Which way is it to the Royal Academy?"

Yeongho stared at me. "You might as well ask me the directions to your own grave."

"I am not frightened of the grave," I muttered, watching as Yeongho scratched the back of his head with indecision. "But I am frightened of never seeing my sister again."

"You must love her very dearly."

My breath caught in my throat. *Love my sister?*

"You either love her or you don't. It is quite simple," Yeongho said after my prolonged silence.

The mere thought of loving anyone sent a dark, winged creature swooping through my soul, and panic rumbled in my bones: *Those you love always die.*

I shook my head, and while staring at the ground, I murmured, "Whether I love my sister or not, it doesn't matter. I am going to bring her home. I am going to find Suyeon."

# 6

# DAEHYUN

"**Every day I feel as** though I am suffocating," Daehyun whispered. He stood before the shelves of the royal library, his jaw locked as he flipped through military literature. "Should he reign another year, I will undoubtedly lose my sanity."

"It is not only you," Hyukjin replied quietly, glancing around to ensure they were alone. "I have spoken with other royal guards over drinks. I can tell you this—we all share the same thoughts. The soldiers, their hearts have left the king long ago. They are all waiting for change to occur. But everyone is too afraid to admit it."

They both tensed as footsteps crunched outside.

"Who knew that one day our courage would be so tested . . ." Hyukjin cracked open the window, watching until the patrolling guards disappeared. "Remember the time we explored the forest and discovered an abandoned hut? It became our command post. We would spend hours here reading *Romance of the Three Kingdoms*. We played military games, and remember how we swore to each other, 'We two—Prince Daehyun and Soldier Min—though of different families, swear brotherhood, and promise mutual help to one end. We will rescue each other in difficulty—'"

"We will aid each other in danger..." The words slipped from Daehyun before he could stop it. He shook his head. "That was long ago."

"We swear to serve the state and save the people," Hyukjin pressed on. "We ask not the same day of birth, but we seek to die together."

"It was child's play," Daehyun said, his voice strained. Once, he had cared—for the lives of the people, for the soul of the kingdom itself. And once, he had even believed himself capable of goodness and honor. But now he glanced down at his hands, the blood washed away yet he could still feel its stain. "All of it was child's play..." He sighed. "What did you wish to speak with me about?"

"I cannot stay long; my sister wishes to see me." Hyukjin turned to him. "I spoke with Wonsik this morning. He has been acting strangely ever since Nameless Flower appeared."

"Do you doubt his loyalty?"

"Of course not."

"We would have perished at the age of eleven, then again at age twelve, fourteen, and sixteen if not for his intervention."

"How could I forget the first incident?" Hyukjin let out a humorless laugh. "Death by bee stings, if not for the investigator. He is as loyal to us as we are to him."

They had disturbed a log hive in the deep mountains, and Wonsik—nearby, searching for the missing prince—had nearly died from using his body as their shield. Both Daehyun and Hyukjin had sat by the investigator's bedside for days after, assisting the physician in removing the countless stingers.

"As I was saying, I spoke with Wonsik. He says we must find

a government official to spearhead the—" Glancing around, he dropped his voice low. "The Great Event. He says it is bound to fail if we attempt to lead it."

"I am of the same mind as him."

"Indeed?" Hyukjin looked rather disappointed. "You understand, once our elders take over, we will be pushed into the shadows."

"Those who are closest to the king wield the most power," Daehyun murmured, glancing beyond the open shelves. They were still alone. "We are in need of such men and their influence, for we have none. But here is where my two concerns arise. First, we must find an official to lead, yet whom can we trust when no official trusts me? Second, Nameless Flower continues to kill off potential allies."

A group of government officials entered, their brows clouded as they grumbled something about the king's taxes. They faltered at the sight of Daehyun. Hyukjin had melted into the shadows, tucked into the space between the wall and shelf.

"D-daegam," the officials stuttered, then exchanged glances among themselves. "Begging your pardon."

Donning the mask of a bored prince, Daehyun returned his gaze to the book, but his attention remained pinned on the men. No matter where he went around the palace, around the capital, everyone whispered in contempt about the king. Yet no one dared to betray His Majesty. It was a tricky game, attempting to find someone willing to risk all to dethrone King Yeonsan.

"I forgot to tell you," Hyukjin said, once they were alone again. "Wonsik informed me of something that might interest you."

Daehyun snapped the book shut, reached to return it onto the shelf, then tensed as Hyukjin whispered:

"The girl you were looking for. He has found her. She is not dead."

# 7

# ISEUL

**Yeongho stood before me, both** of us tucked behind a massive
tree, its branches spread high above us in a shimmering green.
He had finally agreed to help me enter the Royal Academy,
and I wondered if it was solely because he found my face
pleasing.

"Two guards are stationed at the gate," Yeongho whispered,
"and more are stationed around the academy. I will distract the
guards, give you enough time to climb"—he pointed—"over
there. That is the lowest point in the academy wall. It shouldn't
be too difficult to scale. Understood?"

I nodded. "Do any of the captured girls ever escape?"

"Do you want the truth?"

"Yes."

"One girl managed to escape with her father, but they didn't
get past the fortress gate. The king placed the entire capital on
lockdown to recapture her. Another girl ran away with her family to the mountains to hide, but they were all found one by
one and killed. There is no escape, and to even attempt one will
result in bloodshed. So I hope you are not planning to flee with
your sister. You'll need a better plan."

"I have another plan," I whispered. "I simply want to see her today."

"Good. Go over that wall." He twirled his finger, as though whirling my imaginary figure over the barrier. "Once you're on the other side, you will see an establishment with a sign that reads 'servant hall.' There should be a few uniforms within to help you blend in. From there, you will have to pass through two guarded gates. One in the west, then a second in the south, which will take you to the main courtyard where the king hosts his parties."

"Do you think the king is there right now?"

"When the king is not hunting, he is almost always debauching at the Royal Academy."

I studied the suspiciously helpful jester. His face was turned away, offering only a crescent of his strongly carved features. His large ears added a mischievous charm to his otherwise manly veneer.

"How do you know all this?" I asked.

"I scouted the academy whenever I had the chance to perform, so I know this place well. Families sometimes pay me to get them in to see their wives and daughters."

"I have nothing to pay you with. I have lost everything—"

"I do not want payment from you."

"Then . . . why are you helping me?"

He straightened, then glanced over his shoulder. "Give me your story. That is what I want."

I blinked. "Begging your pardon?"

"A good story will feed me through the winter, and I think you have one. A pretty girl searching for her beloved older sister . . . that would wring a few tears out of my audience." He let out a sigh at my expression. "You look bewildered. The life of a jester is a miserable one, you see. The Bureau of Performance barely feeds us. So we perform in villages whenever we can to earn a few extra coins. If I can find a good story and have it performed . . . As I said, a good story could feed the troupe for months."

"My story . . ." I cast a nervous glance at the wall, the one I was to climb over. Time was slipping away. I hung my cloak on a low branch. "I need to leave now."

"Of course, of course." Yeongho waved his hand. "You are staying at the Red Lantern Inn. Expect to see me soon for the story you owe me." Before I could protest, he touched my wrist. "Remember. Once inside, do not move in haste. Be like the mountain. Move silently and cautiously."

With that, he was off, rushing toward the guards. "The killer! He has struck again. Come quick, before he gets away!" The guards hesitated for the barest moment before yelling at him to stop as they chased after him, leaving the wall clear for me.

The moment had finally arrived. I might see her again, my sister.

Yeongho's words echoed. *You must love her very dearly.*

I had believed, once, that my greatest desire in life was that of prosperity. But Suyeon's absence had cast such a gloom over all my fantasies of returning to our old life, safely tucked within a mansion. Her absence had stripped me bare, down to the very sinew of my being, and I had no choice but to face the truth: I did love my sister. The same way I had loved my parents, the same love that had left me bedridden with grief and depression, the love that left me haunted and sleepless many nights still. More than ever, now, I was afraid of this love for her, afraid of the intolerable agony that came with loving anyone at all.

I touched Mother's ring hanging from my neck, drawing courage against my rising panic. "I will bring her home, eomonni."

With all the speed I could muster, I dashed toward the lowest point of the wall and leaped. Grabbing hold of the black tiles, I hoisted myself higher, struggling to even lift myself. My shoulder blazed with pain, the blood-clotted wound threatening to tear open. But I managed to hook my leg over the top. I landed on the other side, and memories of Older Sister followed me in.

Mother had told me that when I was an infant, Older Sister would crouch before the thick blanket upon which I lay, placing her small hand over my beating heart, and I would lock my pudgy arms and legs around her wrist, as though to anchor her against me forever.

I had clung to her in my younger days, watching and emulating her. I had learned to crawl and walk too soon for my mother's liking, determined to follow after my sister, who appeared to me like a butterfly flitting from one flower to the next. My dimpled, plump fingers would grab at everything she possessed. All her dresses had appeared the prettiest. All her hairpins had glittered like the sparkling of sunlit waves. And when I was older, I had followed the way she laughed, lips pressed tight, her chest shaking, eyes crinkled at the corners. I had even tried to read more books, hoping that in doing so I might come to think and speak like my learned and brilliant sister.

Then I had grown up.

"Focus," I whispered, trying to push past the dizzying memories. "Focus."

It was quiet here. Mountain mist billowed across the yard and crouched under flared eaves. I felt myself floating along with it, right into the building marked SERVANT HALL. Everything was a blur, but my legs were rushing, my hands scrambling, and soon I found a spare uniform—several, in fact—folded neatly within a chest. I shrugged into the turquoise blue jacket and deep blue skirt, the uniform loose enough to accommodate the dress I already wore. Then I stepped out.

I forced myself to walk calmly, steadily through both sets of gates as Yeongho had directed, passing by the guards, who barely noticed me, seeing only a harmless servant girl. As I stepped into the main courtyard, I froze.

A parade of women filled the open space. Hundreds of women were playing instruments and dancing at the center, long sleeves fluttering through the air. Hundreds upon hundreds of them arranged in rows. And the king gazed upon them while lounging before his banquet table. His head lolled from side to side, an intoxicated smirk curling his lips. *I have devoured these girls*, his satisfied expression seemed to whisper. *Their bones are ashes between my teeth.*

I moved from pillar to pillar, examining each face. No one looked familiar, and at the same time, every woman appeared the same. Their faces were all powdered white, their eyebrows shaped like willow leaves, lips painted the color of peach blossoms, and their eyes—their eyes were dark and empty pits. They reminded me of statues, all crafted to be identical, with no uniqueness, no soul.

*Please do not be here*, I prayed.

The longer I studied each woman, the more difficult it became to tell them apart. I might have passed by my sister without knowing it—

A flash of drifting hair caught the corner of my eye.

On instinct, I glanced back, and I spotted a tall young woman with a familiar birthmark on her temple. Her gaze was trained on the floor, her arms hanging limp by her side, and there was a look in her eyes I had never seen before. They seemed the eyes of a frightened yet weary girl clinging to the edge of a cliff, her grip slipping, finger by finger. The eyes of a girl who believed no one would come for her. That she was alone.

Suyeon. My Suyeon.

Hands trembling, I moved behind the row of women, picked up a pebble, and flicked it in her direction.

Nothing.

I took another pebble and cast it her way.

She turned slowly. A bruise the shape of a handprint wrapped around her throat.

*How could he—*

*How* dare *he—*

Pools of liquid fire burned in my chest. That was my sister, a girl raised by the most loving hands, a girl who had never been struck or even pinched, now bruised by violence. Hands trembling, I discreetly gestured for her to approach. As her gaze met mine, a momentary glimmer of recognition passed through them before her features stiffened into a pale and terrified mask.

*Older Sister!* I wanted to scream. *I am here!*

She gestured back at me, a small yet violent swish of her hand. *Leave!*

It was reckless, but I stepped out of the shadows and bowed before her. "My lady, you have been summoned," I said vaguely. The courtesans did not look twice my way, and surely, in a parade of over a thousand women, no one would notice Older Sister's brief absence.

"This way," I whispered as I took her arm and, with a firm tug, led her back the way I'd come. She resisted at first, then trailed me like a wilted flower, the way she neither followed nor pushed me away. Once we reached the gate, I thought the guard would let me pass, but he stopped us.

"Where is this courtesan going?" his voice boomed.

I faltered. "Where is she going . . . ?" I had not planned for this.

"The lavatory," my sister whispered. "Please, my stomach is hurting."

We offered the same excuse at the next guarded gate, and soon I was urging my sister across the courtyard to the Servant Hall, and there she stood, so quiet. She looked foreign, stranger-like, half cloaked in shadows.

"What are you doing here?" she whispered, sounding different, too. Colder. Detached. "Are you mad?"

"What do you think? I came to see you."

"Return home. And do not come looking for me again."

"What do you mean?" I cried.

"I am not returning home."

"What is the matter with you? How could you ever expect me to leave you here?"

Silence unraveled around us, and my dangling question suddenly appeared comical.

"How could I ever expect it?" she repeated, the lines of her face hardening. "We lived together for two years, and do you know I felt alone the entire time?"

"I am *sorry.*" My voice broke, my eyes stinging with tears. "And I will apologize ten thousand times over once I return you home—"

"No. You can and you must leave me behind." She twisted herself free from my grip. The remaining ounce of color drained from her, accentuating the angry purple bruise around her throat. And there was a distracting scent rising from her, of musk and salty skin, of overripe fruits and oppressive sweetness. "And even if you asked me to leave with you this very moment, I would not."

"Why are you saying this? Please. I have a plan—"

"I do not wish to hear it."

"Well, you *will* hear it! I refuse to have come all this way for naught. I will find the killer, the one King Yeonsan is searching for so desperately. And I will strike a bargain with the king. I am going to ask for you in return—"

"You are a mere girl. Nothing you do will bring me home," she said coolly. "There are over a thousand women here who wish to return home but cannot. This is the way of life for us. We are born to be devoured." Her gaze looked so faraway now, drifting further and further, until what stood before me was not my own sister but a shell. "It is fine. It is fine. This is our fate. We must be silent even when we are in pain; we must endure."

Her words lodged in my stomach, cold as a brick of ice. She was still alive, yet she stood before me like a woman murdered, as though the king, in making her his, had plunged a knife through her heart.

I reached out. "Older Sister—"

She flinched away from me. "Go."

Footsteps crunched outside the Servant Hall.

"You must leave now," the shell whispered. "Find Uncle Choi Ikjun. He may not be our uncle by blood relation, but he was closer to Father than any of his own brothers. He recognized me in court and helped me send a letter to Grandmother. He will find a way to return you home. Perhaps you will finally marry. You can still reclaim the life you always wanted, with a hundred servants at your beck and call."

The footsteps creaked down the hallway, advancing in our direction.

"Older Sister," I begged, "I am not leaving until you promise me this. Stay alive—"

"Hwang Boyeon!" She called me by my proper name only when in a fury. "Even if there was a chance that you'd keep your promise, I wouldn't want you to." She shoved me over to the back window and unlatched it. "Go, go now. I will never forgive you if you die. Forget about me, Iseul-ah."

She shoved me out the window, and I landed roughly in the dirt, just as the door slid open.

"What was that?" came a man's voice.

"N-nothing," my sister muttered.

"But I heard something—"

A bloodcurdling scream punctured the air, coming from beyond the Royal Academy walls.

"What is happening?" my sister whispered.

"Another arrest being made. No matter. I saw you rush off... Why are you here?"

I froze by the window, a feeling of dread coiled in my stomach; I peeked into the room. It was a middle-aged man dressed in the uniform of a government official. He reminded me of a maggot. So pale, so slimy.

"I will escort you back to the main courtyard," he said.

Older Sister nodded, hurrying toward the door, but before she made it outside, Maggot grabbed her waist. Brushing aside a strand of her hair, he leaned forward and whispered, "You look beautiful when you cry. No wonder the king wants you. And, to be sure, you ought to consider it an honor that he has shown you favor."

My sister kept her back straight, her chin held high, maintaining her perfect composure as ever. But now I noticed the slight tremor in her hand, the way her jaw was clenched, and I knew what she was feeling: han. The feeling of outrage, the vicious urge for vengeance to right the wrong, pierced by the acute pain and grief of knowing our overwhelming odds at ever claiming justice.

Older Sister gripped her fingers into a fist, and sweat beaded down her face as Maggot's lustful grin widened.

As Suyeon finally left with the man, I realized my hands, too, were curled into fists.

I climbed over the Royal Academy wall in a red daze. I wished to claw out Maggot's eyes. I stormed toward a crowd that had gathered around a screaming voice.

"I b-b-b-beg you!" the female voice wailed. It was the girl from earlier. A young woman who looked around my sister's age lay sprawled on the ground, scrambling away from a chehongsa officer in his bloodred uniform. "Let me go home! Let me go home to my mother!"

I meant to walk by, as I had always been taught to do before. Mother and Father had bade me ignore the cries that erupted from the other side of our mansion walls. Their desire for us had been to climb upward, as high as we could, away from the violence of life. Marriage had therefore been their primary concern. *Marriage is not a matter of love*, Mother and Father would often emphasize. *Love cannot shield you, my daughters, but a powerful family can. Always seek to align yourself to those with influence.* They must have always known that we were in danger of being crushed by the king's wrath.

Yet as I walked toward an alley, something sharp pricked me awake. Splintered wood from an abandoned cart; it had left a bleeding cut on my wrist as I'd brushed by.

*This is our fate*, came Older Sister's despondent words. *We must be silent even when we are in pain.*

I turned. Beyond the crowd, I glimpsed Older Sister again, as though she was the one lying on the ground—the purple bruise around her throat, her skin coated in the lustful stare of men, her eyes hollow and hopeless.

Something cracked in me.

I broke off a piece of wood from the cart, then rushed through the crowd. I kept shoving, shoving, shoving, until the human wall opened onto a red-robed officer. He was kneeling almost on top of the struggling girl, twisting her arms behind her back, tying her wrists together with rope.

"Let her go," I barely managed to choke out.

The officer grabbed the girl by her hair, lifting her up.

I was too dizzy to think straight. "I said leave her *alone*, you filthy boar!"

He turned to look.

I swung my arms as hard as I could.

The chipped wood ripped across skin; blood splattered across my own face.

I grabbed the girl and hauled her to her feet. "Run!"

I whirled around and raised the stick once again. The groaning officer looked up, his cheek torn and bleeding profusely. I could not move. My breath felt caught in the air.

"Inyeona!" the officer swore, drawing out his sword.

I flinched before death—then the spectators surged forward in a riot. Peasants grabbed the officer, twisted his arm around. Others grabbed any item they could find and threw it at him: stones and rotten vegetables. I looked around for the girl; she must have managed to escape.

"You need to run!" It was that jester, Yeongho, shoving me forward. "Get as far away as you can!"

Just as I had stumbled to the edge of the mob, a hand caught my wrist.

Everything happened so quick, nothing registered except a few sensations and sights—the hand around my wrist was calloused, and we were moving quickly, past the crowd, past more crowds, then shadows, narrow walls, dense with more people. Then solitude.

"How will you help your sister," came a familiar voice, "if you are dead?"

I blinked, and the face came into focus. It was the swordsman from the inn: Wonsik. And we were in a small, empty yard, surrounded by the backs of a few shops. Beyond, the sound of police whistles pierced through the market noise.

"Patrolmen infest the capital," he continued. "If you'd stayed a moment longer, you would have been arrested and executed tomorrow, without a trial."

My mouth opened, but I failed to find my voice. It all felt like a fever dream. I tried again, and at last asked, "Why are you here?"

"I went to attend a police interrogation, and Madam Yul said I might find you near the Royal Academy. You certainly drew attention to yourself." He tossed something soft into my arms; it was my jangot. "I found it nearby and recognized it."

"Why . . . ?" My voice nearly failed again. "Why were you looking for me?"

"Madam Yul begged me to make sure you were alive. She told me about your wound. An accident in the forest." He watched me steadily, and when I nodded, he said, "An accident that very much appeared like an injury by arrow, according to Yul."

"As I said, it was an accident—"

"Who shot you?"

An uneasy sensation unfurled in my chest. "No one," I said at first, reluctant to divulge the truth. But then I became curious. He was hiding something. "I mean, someone. A prince, I believe; but it happened all too fast."

He shook his head. "Well, steer clear of forests and princes. Put on your veil." Wonsik finally looked away, walking over to peer down the alley. "We cannot hide here forever. And I found your travel sack."

"*My* travel sack?"

"I will return it to you at the inn."

Eager to lay hands on my san-jo-in seeds, the promises of sleep, I quickly pulled the cloak over my head, wincing in pain as I did. "Did you find a bag of coins inside?" I asked, hoping to finally pay Madam Yul.

"No. When the bag was found, it appeared rummaged through."

My heart sank. My hands would soon know hard toil.

"Did you see her?" he asked, quietly now.

"Who?" My voice came out flat and cold.

"Your sister."

The mere mention of her pierced me like a knife. "I did."

"Reclaiming your sister from the king is no easy task, nangja. You will need friends."

"I have not come to the capital to make friends."

"You will not always be the wisest, nor the strongest, nor the bravest. That is why we need friends. They will guide you down the right path, no matter how dark it grows."

"Such friends do not exist," I snapped.

No friend had stood by Older Sister and me amid our growing troubles. Family might cleave to you in times of hardship, as my sister had, for we were bound by blood. But not friends. What reason had they to remain loyal? Friends fled in the midst of chaos, and I did not blame them.

"And when you find such a friend," Wonsik continued, lowering the brim of his straw hat, "you fight for them, and they will fight for you. But alone, you will not survive in the capital. Either defeat or death will crush you, and you will never bring your sister home."

# 8

# DAEHYUN

**The sun lay shrouded beyond** the palace walls. Pavilion roofs were silhouetted against the sky, and the wide eaves cast the deepest shadows, cloaking Daehyun as he hastened toward the main gate. After an uneventful audience with the king, he had lingered at the royal library, reading about coups of the past. But the hour was late. The curfew bell had struck, and soon no prince over the age of ten would be permitted within the palace walls, aside from the crown prince.

He was passing by a row of red-painted pillars when a guttural cry stopped him dead in his steps. He looked across the courtyard to see a figure looming over another. The king's silk red robe thrashed as he beat a motionless man, and the dragon emblem on His Majesty's back gleamed gold in the lantern light.

"Why did you not save her?" the king roared. "You are a royal physician! How dare you let her die?!"

His Majesty unsheathed a sword. The silhouettes of petrified palace attendants disappeared into the pavilions. Daehyun looked away, his limbs tensing as gruesome noises filled the night, of blade piercing flesh, of screaming and gurgling. No matter how many were killed within these walls, each time Daehyun still felt shock carve a gaping hole in his chest.

"L-little brother."

Daehyun's blood turned cold. At once, he tried to retreat, but he was backed up against a wall as the king charged toward him. His Majesty cupped Daehyun's face, the physician's blood hot on his cheeks. "Lady Seungpyeong is dead, little brother."

"Jeonha...," Daehyun whispered, fear straining his voice. "She was in perfectly good health a few days ago."

"Lady Seungpyeong was like a mother to me, and now she is dead." He was shaking, like a stray leaf in winter. "They say she died by suicide, but why would she do that? Only this morning I laid eyes upon her beautiful face. I told her, she is fifty and yet her beauty continues to startle me. Someone must have poisoned her."

"Poisoned?"

"The royal physician found a suspicious substance at the bottom of her tea bowl." The king whipped around and bellowed, "Eunuch Mun!"

A frail servant darted out from the shadows, sweat dripping down his pale face.

"Where is Investigator Gu?" the king growled. "Find him, tell him to come *now*. I will open an investigation into her death. I will rip the killer apart with my own hands!"

Daehyun stood frozen as the king staggered away into the dark, the eunuch scrambling alongside His Majesty. He remained still for a long time, blood dripping down his cheek, down his throat.

"*Daegam.*"

He flinched. It took a moment for his stare to fix upon a young palace servant peeping out from behind a pillar. It was Jiyu, a lowly musuri maid. He had occasionally sent her on discreet errands within the palace, and in return he had provided for her ill mother.

"*Daegam!*"

His legs would not move.

The girl glanced around, then like a mouse, she scurried over to his side.

"I wanted to tell you earlier, daegam—" She squeaked as leaves stirred behind them. A bird lurched off a branch and flapped away. She continued, trembling. "Royal Guard Min Hyukjin's sister requested a strange favor."

He could not find his voice. Stiffly, he pulled out a handkerchief and wiped the sides of his face, rubbing his cheeks raw.

"She asked m-me to send her brother a message—to procure medicine for her, and that if he should n-not, she would be punished for being d-disloyal. I warned him that it was forbidden to bring outside medicine into the palace, yet he did nevertheless. I thought you should know."

"What do I care about any of this?" Daehyun snapped.

"B-because . . ." She blinked quickly, glancing around once more. "Court Lady Sonhui tasked her b-brother with procuring kyungpo-buja for Lady Seungpyeong. And now Her Ladyship is dead."

Dread constricted his heart. Kyungpo-buja—the small purple flower was both a cure and a weapon. A remedy for pain if properly prepared . . . or a deadly poison for when one wished to kill without a trace.

What had Hyukjin entangled himself in?

# 9

# ISEUL

For the following five days, I could scarcely rise from my bed, and I was doted on like a fallen empress. A skilled physician from the capital came with a nurse to treat me and left Madam Yul with instructions on how to tend to my wound. She cleaned it daily, wrapping me with fresh binding material, and I realized she had spoken the truth; she did treat her customers like family. Because of all the care, the pain in my shoulder improved significantly. Then on the sixth day, Madam Yul woke me up at the break of dawn, when the scent of nighttime dew still moistened the air and clung to leaves in sparkling drops.

"I let you rest long enough. Time to earn your keep," she said cheerfully.

Bearing woven baskets and short-handled hoes, Yul and I climbed up a hilly forest, and I was heaving, trembling, while she marched up easily. She was singing a folk song that burst out from her chest. Once we were settled, she continued to sing as we scraped off tree bark and dug up mugwort roots.

"What is this for?" I asked.

Yul stopped singing to answer. "Chogeun mokpi. This will

be our coarse and miserable food. It will barely keep us alive, but we have little barley left for everyone."

The sharp hoe thwacked into the earth. Soil sprayed. Dirt filled my nails as I yanked out the tough roots.

"I usually make meals from what travelers trade in to earn their keep." She half spoke to herself, wiping her sweaty brow and leaving behind streaks of dirt on her face. "But there are so few travelers these days, with the roads cut off by the king's hunting grounds. And no one has anything to trade anyway. We are all taxed beyond our means; the king has turned rice paddies into his personal territory, and he has deprived the people of crops grown throughout the year. So we turned to foraging herbs. Then the king confiscated all that, hearing of how nutritious wild herbs were. Now we must survive on the bitter things of this earth until I can buy more barley." She tossed a bundle of bright green mugworts into her basket. "It will upset our stomachs and give us constipation."

"But at least we will not die," I whispered.

The work was laborious; my shoulders throbbed in agony. I pushed on, never pausing for breath, preferring the physical agony over the memory of my sister's empty gaze. But soon memories caught up, grabbing hold of my ankle and dragging me deep into the past.

I was four, breathing in the bright rays of sunshine, as Older Sister pushed me on the geunettuigi swing tied to a sturdy branch. Our laughter rippled through the summer air.

I was ten, the age when my sister and I began to drift apart, but she would always leave the last honey-fried biscuit for me.

I was fifteen, and my sister held me tight, pressing her hands over my ears so that I might not hear the screams of my parents.

A few months ago, I had turned seventeen. I had spent my days in Grandmother's hut, embroidering and bemoaning the lack of suitable men in the village, fully convinced that the only means of escaping our plight was through marriage. I would waste away the hours adorning my nails with crushed bongsunghwa flower paste, stubbornly refusing to soil my hands, and shirking my duty to assist Older Sister in the monthly chore of washing our menstrual cloths. She would return, trembling and chilled, to hang the cloths, only to remove them before dawn's first light . . .

The mere recollection made me want to peel my own skin off.

I glanced over at Madam Yul. Today, without the wig, the thick layer of face powder, and the red lip stain, she looked different. She appeared less like a liver-devouring gumiho and more like a girl my age, someone whom I might have called a friend.

"Do you have siblings?" I asked.

She continued to work as she answered, "I had a younger brother. Only a year younger than myself."

*Had.*

"We used to live in the part of Gyeonggi Province that is now the king's hunting grounds."

"You were evicted, then . . . ?"

"I took over my aunt's inn, and I thought the worst was over. But the worst is *never* over, is it?" She spoke so brightly, it unnerved me. "My brother ran back home; our mother's grave was there. He was determined to exhume her and rebury her elsewhere, but . . . he never made it out. Neither did my father, when he went searching for him. I think they were both caught ánd executed." As she thwacked the earth, the hoe looked deadly in her grip. She laughed an empty laugh. "At least I have no one to nag at me anymore. My ears would hurt from them always telling me to get married." She grinned, but her voice wavered. "Every morning they'd wag their chopsticks at me, telling me . . . telling me they never wanted to see me alone in this world. But I am not alone. I am never alone. I have my inn and Wonsik-samchon."

We continued to fill our baskets, and I quietly observed Yul throughout. Her smiles no longer looked so bright, though they stretched across her teeth to the same degree.

"*Yah.*" She gently nudged my side, and I looked at her agáin. She held out a plucked flower. "It is a honeysuckle. You drink the nectar like this."

I watched as she sucked the back of the yellow flower. Once, I would have smacked the flower away, disgusted. But I was famished, and I knew that the only meals awaiting me were bitter. I plucked off a honeysuckle and followed Yul's example. My heart brightened as the nectar perfumed my mouth with a honey-floral flavor.

"I grew up with this," Yul said. "Brother and I would spend the summer behind our hut sucking out the nectar every day because we were hungry."

After a dozen honeysuckles lay at my feet, I licked my lips and reached for more.

"Sometimes," Yul said, plucking a few and dropping them into my basket, "a little sweetness cheers the soul."

\* \* \*

I assisted Yul in preparing meals for the occupants of the Red Lantern Inn. There were ten guests in total, including a young mother of three; an old retired soldier who always carried around his game of janggi; and a poor, yet haughty scholar. They all conversed and bickered among themselves as though they were one large, disgruntled, meddling family. Watching them quietly, I ate the steamed herb roots and tree bark, but I tried to imagine I was eating something else. With each bitter and tough bite, I infused my tongue with the memory of soft clouds of white rice, flavored by spoonfuls of rich, milky bone broth, accentuated by the sharp crunch of spicy, pickled vegetables, or the jujube-sweet jeonyak, the jelly melting in my mouth. And when imagination failed, I preoccupied my mind by eavesdropping on the conversation humming from the corner of the yard.

"So this is what we know," the old soldier said, waiting for Wonsik to make his move on the wooden janggi board. "The first victim was Government Official Im. He was found in an alley, his head caved in by a heavy object."

A few onlookers had gathered around the game, and one spouted, "I'll wager the killer is a blacksmith. Used his hammer to break the skull. Maybe it is Pongdol. I have seen the way he works like a beast."

"Aigoo, aigoo, just because his son eloped with your daughter, you make him out to be a killer?" A second onlooker wagged his finger. "You be careful with your words, old man. We all want the reward, but we mustn't endanger the lives of innocent men."

"Who says Pongdol is *innocent*—?"

Grumbling and mockery followed.

The old soldier continued, "The government official was also found with a flower next to him. No message, only blood on his robe. It was from the second victim onward that Nameless Flower began leaving bloody messages, listing the king's offenses."

I scoffed quietly and took another bite of my meal, gnawing on the coarse bark. The killer would need to murder many more before he could finish writing out all the king's offenses.

"The twelfth victim was Young Master Baek," the old soldier murmured. "Son of the king's close aide. He, too, had a flower in his hand. But instead of writing out the king's offenses in blood, this time the killer wrote some kind of message. And Baek was starved until he looked like a dried fish, then murdered. I learned about this all during the public police interrogation—"

Wonsik nodded. "The next move is yours."

The old soldier leaned forward, examining the game board, and the onlookers leaned into the puffs of tobacco smoke with their advice.

I returned to my meal, reviewing the information I'd gleaned. The first victim had died from the crushing of his skull. The twelfth, starved then slaughtered. I bowed my head into my hand. My brain ached from overuse.

"I hear you are off to question a woman from Jamsil Village," the old soldier said. "Does it have to do with the investigation?"

Curious eyes turned to Wonsik, including mine. *Jamsil . . .* The name circled my thoughts. I had heard of this village before.

"You mean, Odeok? I heard her husband died while escorting the young master—"

"Will you be going with that royal guard? Min Hyukjin?" an onlooker chimed in. "Everyone is talking about that handsome young man. He was praised by the king for his good shot during the hunt, or so my daughter told me. *All* my daughters are talking about him. Always looking out for him, they are, when he rides by during the king's hunting parties. They say the king will promote him to his own personal guard one day."

Wonsik let out a weary sigh. "I doubt that day will come."

"Samchon!" Madam Yul called out. "Could you help me move a few clay pots?"

Wonsik stalked off, and an onlooker replaced him in the game. I stayed still. Thoughts flickered at the corner of my mind, but the lack of sleep made it difficult to think at all. I focused harder, and finally, the memories came together.

*If you were stabbed, to where would you run?* Wonsik had asked while we discussed the matter of the servant's death—the one who had accompanied the twelfth victim and had managed to run as far as Jamsil.

*I would run to someone I trusted, someone who would wish me no ill*, I had answered.

The servant witness had run to his wife.

Surely she had answers.

I crossed Han River by sneaking onto a crowded vessel, and throughout the crossing the sunlit water sparkled so bright that I was left with a slight headache when I reached Jamsil. Along the riverside, where reeds billowed, laundresses squatted on stones, washing their soiled outfits. The villagers had directed me here when I had asked them about a woman named Odeok.

I could almost hear my sister's voice scolding me: *You ought to wait for Wonsik. You have absolutely no idea what you are doing.*

I, indeed, had absolutely no idea, yet I could not trust Wonsik. He had known about Odeok, yet he had withheld the information from me, fully knowing that I, too, was searching for the killer. There was no guarantee he would share with me whatever intelligence he gathered from this woman.

"Excuse me, I am looking for a woman named Odeok."

The laundresses gestured down the riverbank to where a woman washed her laundry alone, apart from the rest. As I approached, I was struck by a sense of familiarity. The long face, the high cheekbones, and the shape of her nose all reminded me of Suyeon. The resemblance lasted only at a distance, but the sensation remained. And as I crouched next to the woman, I felt as though I were sitting next to my sister.

"*What*," she snapped.

Just as Older Sister would have. *Are you here to merely watch?* she would have added. *Or to help?*

Before, I would have sprung up to my feet, muttering unkind words before taking my leave. But I remained, feeling sad as I watched Odeok's calloused hands plunge into the river, dragging me through a current of remorse. I wished, so wished, that I had followed my sister on the many nights she had lugged laundry out into the wild to wash them discreetly. I wished I could have returned home with her, both our hands shaking and red from the icy river water. At least then our suffering, when shared, might have turned into fond memories.

"Let me help you," I said stiffly.

She eyed me. "What do you want?"

"You remind me of my sister."

Her brows lowered with bewilderment, but she neverthe-less pushed the basket of soiled garments my way. "I'll gladly accept help. That is one less garment for me to break my back over."

I took out a dress, dunked it into the water, and hesitantly began to rinse it.

"You do not know how to wash laundry, do you," she observed, staring at me.

"I was pampered," I explained.

"You were loved. Someone sacrificed their back and their hands for you—"

Unexpected tears gathered in the woman's eyes. "Why did I sacrifice for him?" she whispered, voice strained. Then she shook her head, gesturing at me to leave, and moved to sit down on a log nearby. I took a seat next to her. We remained quiet for another long stretch of time.

"Both my parents are dead, so I know something of your pain," I whispered, and when she frowned at me, I explained. "I heard what happened to him—your husband."

She lowered her gaze again.

"They were killed, too," I added. "But by a man who will never be caught. I hope, for you, though, they will find the killer and punish him."

She scoffed. "All I want is to thank the killer."

"Thank him?"

"He was a monster to me, my husband." Her breathing quickened, and a distant look glazed her eyes, as though she were staring far off—or at a hazy memory. "A monster killed by another monster."

I hated to pry, but I had no choice. "Did you see him, before his passing?"

"I did," she said after a pause. "A passerby noticed my husband on the ground and informed me of it—why am I telling you this?"

"And what did he say in reply?" I asked gently.

She massaged her forehead, staring fixedly ahead. "It made no sense," she mumbled to herself.

I waited, and as the moments passed, my back began to ache from sitting so stiffly. "Perhaps," I offered carefully, "I can be of help? If you share with me what he said, that is. Surely you must want to understand. It was his last few words, after all . . ."

For a moment, I wondered if she had even heard me, then she whispered, "'A tall shadow, half man, half wolf.' That is what he said. Hallucinating, he was."

The crunching of gravel alerted me, and I whirled around to look. Wonsik had arrived.

"Excuse me," I whispered, and rushed over to the old man. "What are you doing here?" I demanded.

He stared at me, arms folded across his chest. "I came to continue my line of inquiry . . . Though, it seems, you are here for that same reason." I waited for him to scold me, to declare that I was ruining his investigation, but instead, the corner of his lips twitched. Amusement. "And did you manage to learn anything?"

He was mocking me. He thought me incapable.

"Half man, half wolf," I blurted.

"Begging your pardon?"

"That is what the woman told me." I was divulging precious evidence, but such evidence was no use to me if I could not understand it. Perhaps Wonsik knew something. "Her husband, while dying, told her this. About the killer, I believe."

He stood straighter, levity disappeared, and he seemed to be examining my words carefully.

"You think he was wearing furs?" I asked. "Or the mask of a wolf? Why else would a human being appear to be *half wolf*?"

"The wife told you this?"

"Yes. Did you know already?"

He cleared his throat, looking uncomfortable. "No, she would share nothing with me. What made her open up to you? What . . . what strategy did you use?"

"I know how to hold a conversation," I said, glancing past the feathery reeds and across the Han River in the direction of the capital. There was one other task that required my effort today. "I will leave you to question her now. Perhaps you can find out what she meant by *half wolf*."

"I have no need to question her further, for she would not know what her husband meant by that," he said. He seemed content with the information I had given him. Perhaps it was significant.

Before I could pry further, he asked, "Are you returning to the inn? I will escort you—"

"I am going to the capital to visit a family member." I was, in fact, going to try to find my uncle, in the hopes that he could become a resource to me. Relying on my own wits would take me years to find the killer, and years my sister did not have. "Do you know of Government Official Choi? Choi Ikjun?"

Wonsik's heavy brows lowered. "You are looking for Official Choi? Why?"

"Do you or do you not know of such a man?" I asked pointedly.

"Of course I know of him. He oversees the government office in charge of military supplies, nearby in Yongsan. But he visits his home in the Northern District now and then, from what I know. His family lives in the capital."

"In the Northern District . . . Where, specifically?"

His frown slammed even lower. "No."

"No?"

"Stay away from the capital today. After what you did, there might be sketches of you plastered all over, and greedy eyes looking for a quick reward." He did not stop there, as though sensing my stubbornness. "That officer you attacked will take justice into his own hands. I know his sort. Chehongsa officers are cutthroats, the lot of them. They will not let a slight go unpunished, let alone an attack on their person by a mere girl."

Ignoring him, I stalked over to the boats lining the dock. "Could you take me to the other side of the river?" I asked one of the boatmen, who was languidly smoking his pipe. When he nodded, I stepped inside, my arms spread out on either side to keep my balance as the boat rocked under my feet.

Smoke curled from the boatman's mouth. "And my payment?"

"I will pay once you take me to the other side—"

Wonsik stopped the boat, holding it by the rope. The boatman tried to row away, muttering, but Wonsik flicked his cloak aside, revealing his sword. "This girl is a cheat," he said. My eyes widened. "She has not a single coin on her person. She will make you row her all the way there, then bolt."

The boatman sucked on his pipe, then gestured with his chin for me to leave. "Before I push you out," he added for good measure.

I cursed him, stormed out of the boat, and stalked past Wonsik. I would find someone else to take me to the other side, or perhaps find another crowded vessel to sneak onto.

Wonsik caught up to me in a few long strides. "You need to stop charging thoughtlessly through challenges. Sometimes you must learn to take your time and strategize. You are going to get yourself killed otherwise."

"I don't know how to do it any other way."

"So you really are serious—about finding the killer?"

"*Yes.*"

"Are you serious enough that you would learn from me?"

My steps slowed. "What?"

"You will not repeat foolhardy decisions like infiltrating the Royal Academy?"

"I came out alive."

He pinched the bridge of his nose. "It was sheer luck that you did." Then wearily, he added, "And take nothing from crime scenes next time—"

I halted my steps to glare up at him. "I took nothing, ajusshi."

He grunted. "I was observing you at the scene. You took one of the two beads. You, a girl who has no experience with investigations. Disturbing evidence only makes it even more difficult to find the killer. Which means he will kill more people."

I shrugged. "He may do as he wishes and kill half the kingdom, and I will not feel the worse for it." I meant it. All of Joseon could burn; my only desire was to be reunited with my sister. Then I paused, my thoughts narrowing around his remark. "Are the beads evidence?"

"In your brash haste to bring your sister home, do not bring harm to others. Do not trample and hide the truth. For I assure you, the killer will kill again, and one day it may be someone you wished you could have saved."

"Are the beads evidence?" I repeated, enunciating each word. "Tell me what you know, ajusshi."

He paused, casting one last look over me. I could imagine what he saw—a girl, as slight as a stray cat, standing so alone in a kingdom overrun by wolves. A heavy sigh escaped him.

"Ask yourself: How would it end up in the victim's hand? Why would this man cling to a mere bead even in death? The answer is quite simple."

Irritation flickered through me. "Tell me, ajusshi. Where is the bead from?"

"Make a deduction."

I clamped my lips shut, outraged.

"Pause and look around you," he pressed on. "Do not forget to notice the smaller things. Each day, try to notice if things have changed and remember how they were before. Doing this will improve your memory and your faculties of analysis." He crouched, picked up a stone, and tossed it to me. I barely caught it. "Hold on to the bead later, and examine it. And ask yourself why anyone would cling to a bead when he is being killed and while bleeding out."

He lowered the brim of his straw hat, but not before I caught a glimpse of his curiosity. "If you can figure out the answer to this, then you will know for yourself that you are observant enough to hunt a murderer."

# 10

# DAEHYUN

**Daehyun spent the night by** the latticed hanji screen, staring at the empty courtyard. He saw someone approaching quickly, and soon Hyukjin was announced in. Female attendants prepared a small table of late-night dessert—flavored glutinous rice and two bowls of sweet sikhye drinks swirling with pieces of rice.

"You have likely not eaten," Daehyun murmured. "Eat."

Hyukjin picked up the drink; his hands were shaking. He set the bowl back down. "All day, I sensed that I was being watched. Did you have someone follow me?"

Daehyun frowned. "No, I did not."

Hyukjin shook his head. "It is likely all in my mind."

"One cannot be too sure . . . When you leave, I will have one of my servants accompany you—"

"Y-you must have heard the news from a few days ago," Hyukjin interrupted, his expression growing frantic. "About Lady Seungpyeong's death."

"You procured kyungpo-buja for her."

"H-how did you—?"

"Our messenger girl. I have been searching for you ever since."

Hyukjin ran a hand over his haggard face. "I was so certain that no one would notice. It was supposed to be medicine."

The dread in his chest beat stronger, but Daehyun kept his voice steady as he asked, "Did Court Lady Sonhui kill her?"

"No. My sister came to me to confess all. Asked me for advice on how to escape the trouble she would be in—for having procured poison. I took leave from duty, feigning illness, and have tried to arrange a way to help my sister escape. But I am kept awake at night by the thought that perhaps . . . encouraging her escape might lead to her death. So I am here to ask you— what should we do?"

"Tell me everything. Leave nothing out."

"Lady Seungpyeong asked my sister to secretly procure kyungpo-buja, saying it was for Her Ladyship's aching limbs. My sister agreed to it—"

"Did it not occur to her the perilous nature of her undertaking?" Daehyun asked, his voice flat.

"Sonhui is simpleminded, as you know; the girl believes what she is told. Gods, up until she was twelve, she believed her dead mother was a heavenly maiden because of a story I had told her long ago! So why would she have doubted Lady Seungpyeong? If the old lady wished for medicine, then of course Sonhui would deliver it to her!"

Daehyun sighed, massaging his temples. "Proceed."

"Sonhui swore to me she did not know it would be used as poison. It was all a naive mistake. What do I do? My mind is a tangle of thoughts, and I—"

"Does she have any idea as to why Lady Seungpyeong might have wished to die?"

Hyukjin fell quiet, then covered his face with both hands. "She did. My *foolish* sister. She *never* should have entered the palace." He pressed his fingers into his eyes, continued to curse, then took in a deep breath and composed himself. "Sonhui told me of an odd incident. After a visit from the royal physician, Lady Seungpyeong had broken into tears, pleading with a chronicler not to record a shameful incident. But the chronicler is duty-bound to record all the palace goings-on and thus refused."

Daehyun sat straighter; his curiosity piqued. It was a chronicler's mandate to accurately collect information for the Draft History in an objective and dispassionate manner. No one was permitted to tamper with the material, not even the king himself. Not even a murderous tyrant. Chroniclers had died in their fight to preserve recorded history, and no amount of begging could sway them. Lady Seungpyeong must have known this, yet still she had pleaded, utterly terrified of her secret being unveiled for generations to come. But what secret was so abominable that she had chosen death?

"Well?" Daehyun said, his attention trained on his friend. "What was recorded?"

"She ... she had symptoms of pregnancy."

"But she is a widow. Whose child?"

Hyukjin grew pale as his jaw locked. "The king's."

Daehyun could only stare, unable to form a single word. A wave of disgust swept through him. Tyranny, murder, rape. He had thought it impossible for the king to sink into further depravity.

"Since I was a child, I heard rumors—" The words caught in

his throat, sharp as thistles. Daehyun took a sip of sikhye, stared into the bowl, then recomposed himself. "I heard rumors that King Yeonsan was wooing his aunt-in-law. I did not believe it then . . . He treated Lady Seungpyeong with lavish affection, but I thought it was because she reminded him of his own mother." He frowned. "But to be pregnant at fifty—is it even possible?"

"It is."

"No one else knows of Her Ladyship's pregnancy?"

"According to my sister, it is still a private matter."

"Gods, I have lost all my appetite." Daehyun folded his arm across his chest, staring down at the dessert. "You do under-stand, if your sister is caught for having procured kyungpo-buja, she will be executed."

"I know. I am at my wit's end, daegam."

"I will find a way to protect you, I promise. Who else knows about the procured poison?"

"No one else. I—I am sure of it."

"Your sister and all of Lady Seungpyeong's attendants will be interrogated under torture. Is Sonhui brave enough to with-stand that and stay silent?"

Hyukjin's voice broke. "The girl may be simple, but she is braver than both of us."

"No one will be the wiser, then, if she keeps her mouth shut. And you keep your mouth shut, too. From now on, you know *nothing.*"

Hyukjin sank forward, hunching over his drink. "Is there no other way? Perhaps I ought to run away with her. I would die ten thousand deaths to allow my sister to have a bright future."

"For her to run is to admit her guilt. The king would send an entire army after her."

"So she is trapped," Hyukjin whispered. "The godsdamned king needs to die."

"We are still waiting for an opportunity—" Daehyun tensed, realization dawning as he stared at his grief-ridden friend. "Wait . . ."

"This coup . . . I sometimes wonder whether it will occur at all." Hyukjin emptied his sweet drink in one swallow, then stared at it dissatisfied, as though wishing it were soju. "All we do is talk and dream. But nothing happens."

"Hyukjin-ah," Daehyun's voice rasped, "what say you to Deputy Commander Park?"

Hyukjin watched him steadily, his brows knitting with bewilderment. "He is the king's closest aide, daegam. He holds great power over the government, and he would never turn traitor."

"Opinions can be changed. As did Wonsik's."

"When we recruited him, he declined because he was worried for us both. He rebuked us for an entire day, and then he agreed to it only because I knelt and begged him," Hyukjin said. "But the deputy commander? What does he care for our lives? If we try to recruit him, he will have us executed instead—"

"What would you do, Hyukjin-ah," Daehyun said softly, his heart thundering, "if you learned that your sister was harassed by her nephew-in-law for years? What would you do if she then died by suicide because she was violated, resulting in a pregnancy?"

"I would kill this nephew. I would—" Hyukjin's face

drained of color, and a light shone bright in his widened eyes. "Lady Seungpyeong's brother is Deputy Commander Park."

"And I believe," Daehyun said, hope straining against his voice, "the deputy commander and his clan would not suffer such an offense in silence."

*General Jeong Jungbu, 1170.* Names and dates rushed through Daehyun's thoughts as he retired to his personal chamber. He had studied coups day and night, for he knew history was the wisest teacher. *General Yi Seong-gye, 1388. Prince Yi Bangwon, 1398. Prince Suyang, 1455.*

In all instances, the coups had succeeded because of their golden opportunity, among other factors. And as he and Hyukjin had discussed until an hour before dawn, they had wondered if their golden opportunity had truly arrived. Perhaps the truth behind Lady Seungpyeong's death would ignite enough anger to *finally* overthrow the king . . .

Daehyun must have fallen asleep, for he woke up with his head resting on his low-legged table. His chamber was drenched in the blue-gray of early-morning light, and there was an urgent voice outside his door.

"Daegam! Daegam!"

Daehyun straightened himself. "Come in."

His manservant tumbled in, muddy and out of breath. "Daegam, you sent me to accompany Royal Guard Hyukjin home," he said, his voice shaking. "And so I did. I watched until he returned to his residence, then I looked around the neighborhood to ensure that all was safe, and I was about to leave when I saw him race right out on horseback! I asked his personal servant where the master had gone off to. He looked frightened but would not say where!"

"Perhaps an urgent matter arose." Still, an uneasy sensation stirred at the pit of his stomach. Calmly, he prepared a message. "Send this to Wonsik."

# 11

# ISEUL

The following day passed by uneventfully, and without Wonsik to converse with, I had kept mostly to myself, reviewing all that I knew about Nameless Flower. By dinnertime, I could smell from my room the bitter scent of the meals prepared. Chogeun mokpi, Yul had called it—the coarse and miserable food relied on by the poor and desperate. Once, I would have refused to even eat a spoonful, but I knew now that to miss a single meal would result in debilitating weakness.

As I left my room, I nearly stepped on a book lying outside my door. The pages were bound by five stitches, the cover faded yellow. Picking it up and flipping it open, I found a note:

*The first thing you must learn is how to think like an investigator. We will discuss.*

*—Wonsik*

Annoyance twisted through me. Instead of offering me a short route to the truth, he was taking me the long way around, compelling me to discern the truth for myself. I had even tried to do what he had asked—I had spent the entire night holding on to the bead, asking myself why a dying man would cling to it, and the effort had resulted in nothing but frustration.

Sitting down before one of the tables out in the yard, I let out a huff and flipped through the book, titled *Muwonrok: The Treatise on Forensic Medicine*. The first chapter explored ways in which to prevent the unjustified death of a human being, relying on traditional knowledge and forensic investigation. The second listed all the causes of death, from common ones such as death by strangulation to death by stabbing, or more outlandish ways, such as death by lightning strike, by boiling water, by live burial, by tiger, and so on. My appetite had vanished by the time my meal arrived, and the thought of corpses filled my thoughts as I chewed on the bitter, overly tough mugwort mixed in soybean paste soup.

A shadow settled before me.

I looked up to see Yeongho. His entire troupe had gathered in the yard, clustered around a table where they sat rubbing their hands in anticipation of food.

"What are you doing here?" I asked.

"Madam Yul always feeds our troupe whenever we perform in this village." He plucked the book from my hand, flipping it aside to glance at the title. He arched a brow and let out a low whistle. "An intellect are you, reading such books out of amusement?"

"How could anyone find such a book amusing?" I said dryly. *My sister would have loved it.*

He snapped my book shut and set it down next to my empty bowl. Perching his elbow on my table, he leaned forward. "Well? I have come to collect your story."

"I do not want to talk about it."

He opened a golden pouch—the same color as his sash band—took a pinch of a white substance and ate it. "You owe me a story."

My stare returned to the pouch. "What is that?" I asked.

"It is limestone powder."

"That sounds terribly salty."

"Mother used it to make delicious confectionery for me." He smacked his lips together, then looked away as he murmured. "My mother is dead, too."

I stiffened.

"I assume both of your parents are dead, since you are roaming about alone," he continued. "Shall I tell you my story, then?"

"No."

"I was destined for a bright future, like many of us, until the one-eyed dragon—" he leaned in and dropped his voice "—that will be our moniker for *the king*—" he raised his voice again "—ruined our lives. I was devastated, nearly at the brink of death, when I was taken in by the troupe out of pity. The troupe, and this inn even, is a place for those like us."

I quirked an eyebrow. "Us?"

"Those who are without a home, without a family." He smiled, yet a painful note strained his voice. "And without a future."

"Without a future...," I whispered. No young person had any future in this kingdom. All that consumed our minds was whether we would even live to see tomorrow.

The *Muwonrok* pulled at my attention, and I continued to look at it as Yeongho and his troupe devoured their meals, then bid us good day. I watched the way the setting sun pooled over the cover, half in light, half in shadows. The book felt like Wonsik holding out his hand, his offer that I learn from him. That I trust him.

I flipped through it idly again, the sour scent of aged paper perfuming the air.

It was a tedious book, and half the time, utterly incomprehensible. I nevertheless continued with my reading and was a quarter of the way through it when I heard a great yawn from the street beyond the inn's gate. A farmer was returning home, pulling along his wagon. It was nearly nightfall, the last rays of light fading, rendering the pages difficult to read.

I returned to my room and lit a candle. Setting the book before me, I unplaited my hair and brushed through the locks, running the comb from my scalp all the way down to my waist. My hair, among my other vanities, was an indulgence I could not bring myself to abandon, even after the passing of both my parents. But tonight, I stopped at the fiftieth stroke.

*Let there be no resentment*, the book seemed to whisper, lying there in the shadow.

I tossed aside the brush, grabbed the book, and rushed out of my room. I walked down the veranda that wrapped around the inn, then settled myself close to the bright lantern hanging from the eaves. The sky was not yet completely dark, but a deep, washed-out gray.

I drew my long hair behind my shoulders, then flipped the book open again. I would do whatever it took to bring Suyeon home, even if it meant reading and memorizing the most dreary book I had ever perused.

A warm gust of wind billowed by, rustling the pages.

The sound of footsteps crunched across the innyard.

My dancing hair obscured my vision; I tucked the strands behind my ears and looked up.

My heart stuttered.

A young man strode across the innyard, moving with a grace that few men possessed. His hat was tilted to shield his face from the lantern light, and his tall figure was garbed in silk, inwoven with golden threads.

I set my book aside, and at my slight movement, he glanced my way. My breath caught. His falcon-sharp eyes sent a jolt of terror down my back.

I bolted to my feet and crossed the yard, away from my room that could easily be invaded, and into the kitchen, where I hoped to find Yul. She was not there. The kitchen was swamped in shadows and the dim glow of a burning furnace. I was utterly alone, and my limbs froze as I heard footsteps approaching.

*Stay alive*, Mother's words urged me, as the memory of his arrow rushed past my left ear, so loud that my knees buckled as I retreated deeper into the kitchen. *Stay alive, no matter what.*

My hands fumbled through the darkness and stopped at a kitchen knife. The blade glowed red in the furnace light, and Mother's blood dripped into my mind. Even as a crimson stream had dribbled from her mouth, she had continued to cry, *Stay alive. Stay alive.*

A hand touched my shoulder.

I whirled around. My knife hovered before his throat as I stared up into what felt like the endless night, for his expression was just as dark and impenetrable.

His fingers wrapped around my knife-holding hand, and my entire body stiffened with fear. "You are shaking. Have you ever killed a man before?"

"I will make you my first"—my damned voice trembled—"if you do not release me."

"It is nearly impossible to kill with a knife unless you know precisely where to stab. Either you bury the blade beneath my ribs and stab my heart, or . . ." He leaned forward, his face so close to mine, as he pressed the blade to his throat. "You cut me right where the blood flows."

"Daegam mocks me."

In one smooth motion, he gave my wrist a quick twist, disarming me easily. He kicked the knife away, and it went skidding out of the kitchen. I rushed for the entrance, but he blocked it with his body.

"This is the second time that I have had to disarm you," he murmured. "I hope this will not become the norm each time our paths cross."

"This will be our last."

"Will it?"

"What—" my voice rasped as I took a step back. "What do you want from me?"

"What are you doing here, away from home?"

"It is no concern of yours," I growled.

"You are right, it is no concern of mine . . ." His eyes were dark and intent. "But I admit—your presence here raises many questions, and I am, by nature, prone to curiosity. You traveled all the way here by a rudimentary map, crossed the king's hunting territory, to come to the capital." He placed on the kitchen table my map, opened and revealing the sketch. "I was informed that a young lady here had procured an arrow wound on the same day of our own incident." He picked up the map and flipped it around, staring down at my drawing. "Did you come for this girl? Your friend? No . . . your sister?"

My face and neck grew hot. I snatched the document and lowered my gaze to the floor.

"I say this out of kindness: You ought to consider your sister dead. You will never free her from the king."

His words slammed into my chest. "I will not," I snapped, as much to him as to myself. Hot tears rushed to my eyes, tingling my nose, but I kept my voice steady. "When someone you love is taken, you go into the den of the tiger. You go to the ends of the kingdom and across. You go to where they are. You find them—no matter the cost."

"So you will steal her from the king?"

"She is my sister!"

"Do as you wish," he murmured, turning to leave. "I will not stop you. Neither will I assist you."

I stood in the darkness, the meager light of the furnace dancing across the wall. *Of course you will not help me*, I thought, still shaking. *Why would you, when rumors claim you murdered your own flesh and blood?*

"Daegam," came a gruff voice outside. "What brings you here?"

I peered out from the shadowy kitchen, and my lips parted at the sight of Wonsik bowing to the prince with such reverence.

When he drew himself back up, I saw his face in the lantern light, the way his lashes remained lowered in submission, not daring to look into the face of a royal.

"Have you any intelligence on Min Hyukjin's whereabouts?" the prince asked.

"Not yet. I received your note. He did not arrive for his duty at the palace. And when I visited his residence, a servant informed me he had indeed rushed out at daybreak and did not return. He left this note behind. It was half burned."

Prince Daehyun looked at the note. "It is from his younger sister. She writes that she is running away from the palace . . . But it cannot be her. She was in the palace being interrogated this morning with the rest of the attendants. Who knew of their familial relationship?"

"He spoke of her often when she was with us three . . . And once, she sneaked out and came to the inn to meet him here. But more important, the note—it is the same handwriting as Nameless Flower's."

The prince at once tensed, and the man he had been inside the kitchen was no more. No studied casualness to his tone, the biting coldness to it gone. There was, instead, a warm depth of concern to his voice. He seemed like an entirely different person.

"So I followed his trail," Wonsik continued, "and the last person to see him was a farmer; the man saw Min Hyukjin riding into Mount Acha."

"Come," the prince whispered, "we must leave at once."

I watched as they took horses from the stable at the back of the inn, and they rode out with bows secured to their backs and cased arrows strapped to their horses. Once they were gone,

I walked toward my room, then paused. They were going to go find the killer, and if the killer was the only path to my sister, then I ought to accompany them as well.

As I rushed to the stable to borrow a horse, I knew I was being reckless, following those two men to Mount Acha. But risking my life was easier than sitting alone in the silence of my thoughts. For if I was not running, if I was not charging forward, I feared that self-loathing would corner me. And I refused to feel defeat when I had barely even begun.

# 12

# DAEHYUN

**Premonition closed in around him** like the mist that veiled the hills, ghostlike swirls in the wind. But he refused to believe that danger had befallen Hyukjin—his comrade, his confidant.

"The letter summoned Hyukjin to Mount Acha—but why there?" Daehyun shouted over the loud rustling of trees as they rode into the forest.

"He often travels across Mount Acha to visit his grandmother," Wonsik yelled back. "Perhaps he believed his sister was running back home!"

"But how could Nameless Flower know of this detail?"

"What I wish to know, daegam, is why lead Hyukjin there? And why today—?" Wonsik's thick brows knotted. "When does the king plan to go hunting?"

"Tomorrow. He will be going to Gwangneung Mountain, near Namjangju—" Ice trickled through his veins. "His Majesty and his hunting party would pass through Mount Acha."

"The killer has displayed only three patterns thus far. The bloody message, the flower . . . and leaving the bodies where the king could find—"

A silhouette moved beyond the thicket. Turning, Daehyun reached for an arrow as Wonsik raised a torch higher.

"Who goes there?" Wonsik called out.

A rider trotted forward, and the torchlight illuminated a delicate face, the high cheekbones littered with cuts from riding through the woods, a pair of distrustful eyes, and windswept hair. She sat straight, her chin raised, bearing the aura of an empress riding into war.

"The girl from the inn?" Disbelief punctured Daehyun's voice. "She followed us—did you know of this?"

"If I knew, I would have sent her back!" Wonsik called out over the whistling wind. "No matter. We ought to keep riding. A storm is on its way!"

When the girl rode forward, Daehyun steered his horse to block her. "Why are you here?"

"Wonsik promised to investigate with me. We are partners."

Daehyun shot Wonsik a glance. "Partners?"

Wonsik shifted on his saddle. "I offered to help her find the killer."

"Did you, indeed?" he said, voice brusque with irritation.

"We only wish to find Nameless Flower," Wonsik explained. "Let the girl deliver him to the king and claim the reward."

"What reward—" Daehyun paused. He turned to her. "You intend to ask the king for your sister, don't you?" He rode closer, to ensure that she heard his every word. "*Look at me*," he ordered. "You intend to bargain with the king himself?"

A muscle worked in her jaw. "I do."

He was truly amazed by the simplicity of her thoughts. "You

believe you can save your sister? With a bargain?" He shook his head. "Do you think a king who steals girls will listen to one, let alone honor a bargain with her?"

A flinch of doubt crossed her face. "If you can think of a better method, then please do—!"

"Wonsik, escort her to the nearest village." Daehyun gripped the reins tight, steering the creature around. "She will not be accompanying us. I forbid it—"

They all stilled at the sight of a lone horse roaming ahead. A posy of wilted flowers hung from the saddlebag, petals shuddering in the wind.

"That is Hyukjin's horse," Wonsik whispered.

"Split up," Daehyun said, lighting a torch for himself. "He may still be here."

He forgot about the girl as she rode off with Wonsik. He was on his own now, ducking away from thrashing branches. Leaves whirled, erasing all traces of hoofprints, all traces of his friend.

"Hyukjin-ah!" he called out, over and over, until his voice grew raw.

He rode as far as the low mountain peak, covered in large beds of rocks that he carefully navigated across. The night had grown so dark he could barely see the sparkle of the Han River and the lights of the capital. He continued along the mountain ridge until he caught sight of a piece of white fabric fluttering on a branch. Abruptly steering his horse, he followed the rocky trail downward until he reached a little clearing above a low cliff.

"Hyukjin!" he called out. "Hyukjin-ah—!"

A droplet of rain fell onto his cheek, then more fell in a

steady drip, drip, drip. The droplets felt peculiar, and so he touched his cheek. Dark red liquid glistened on his fingertips. His chest tightened as he raised the torch and looked up.

Bare feet dangled. Limbs swayed. Loosened hair drifted across the face.

*Breathe*, he told himself. *Breathe, Daehyun-ah.*

He inhaled, and the darkness rose until he was chest deep in a memory. The palace courtyard surrounded him, blood gleaming on the ground. His foster brothers were bludgeoning two women, anonymous women with sacks over their faces.

*Kill!* the king ordered. *Or be killed!*

*Breathe.*

Deeper, he sank into cold night. Clubs fell to the ground as his brothers staggered back, screaming. The women tied to the chairs were motionless. The sacks had been pulled off their heads. His mother's dead eyes stared at her sons, unblinking.

*Breathe.*

He couldn't. Death crept up his spine, over his shoulder, whispering in his ear: *You can never save those you love.* The whispering continued, drowning him as he stared at the corpse hanging from a tree.

The bare feet twitched in the air.

A bolt of cold shot through him. "Hyukjin-ah! I am coming!" He scrambled up the slope, toward the tree that stood at the cliff's edge with its sprawling roots. A rope was tied around the trunk. He still had time to save his friend. He was not too late. Not this time.

Racing forward, he grabbed the rope with one hand, and with the other hand he reached as far as he could. He reached until his hand skimmed Hyukjin's collar. Grabbed hold of it. He hauled his friend onto the cliff, and grabbing his dagger, he cut the noose free—

A deep, cheerful yell exploded, echoing in the shadows.

Daehyun snapped a glance over his shoulder. Had he imagined the sound? Wind whistled through leaves; trees were dancing all too merrily. Shadows merged and parted and swayed. There was no time to spare, though, and so Daehyun proceeded to cut the noose free even as the back of his neck prickled.

"You ruined my display," a voice slid up behind him.

Pain exploded behind Daehyun's eyes. Soil smashed into his face. He struggled to rise, his hand reaching across the earth toward his friend. But a shadow dug its foot under Hyukjin, and with one firm shove, kicked him off the precipice. Then it turned and swung a club.

Darkness overtook him.

# 13

# ISEUL

I urged my horse to a halt, craned my head to the side and listened. A stormy wind roared through the trees, night critters chirped, and a light rainfall swept through the forest. But I could have sworn I'd heard a muffled cry.

"Ajusshi?" I called out. My voice was swallowed in the sea of noises.

I had followed Wonsik after encountering the missing man's horse, only to find myself alone, as though I had taken a wrong turn in the shadows and had ridden elsewhere into a terrible nightmare. A world in which I was the only human soul in the sea of trees.

The wind whooshed by me, nearly knocking me off my horse.

"Steady there," a deep voice called out.

I turned, pushing aside my hair. Wonsik.

"Where did you go?" I yelled as I rode over to him.

"I wondered where you had gone myself. You were behind me one moment, gone the next."

"Where is the prince?"

"Come, we must find shelter!"

We tethered our horses and stumbled into a cave, and as the rain fell stronger, washing down the entrance, it was as though we had sneaked into a cavern behind a waterfall.

"I wonder how far the tunnel goes," I thought aloud as I ventured deeper, only to find the passageway blocked by a stack of rocks. Retreating, my gaze returned to Wonsik, who stood before the mouth of the cave, his silhouette a tense line.

"You are worrying about the prince," I said.

"It is my duty to protect him," he whispered. "His birth mother was distantly related to my wife, but as close as sisters could be. And when she gave birth to Prince Daehyun nineteen years ago, a shaman prophesied a death omen over him. I swore to watch over him ever since."

I had heard of his death omen. My parents, whenever speaking of him, had often referred to him as the "doomed prince." The prince who would die in the year of fire and tiger.

"If the prophecy is true, he would die this year," I said indifferently.

"And hence why I keep such close watch over him. I never believed in shamans and their superstitious words, but ever since Yeonsan turned to violence and depravity, we have all become a little uneasy."

"And if it were not for the promise, would you still protect him?"

"I would," Wonsik replied, a strange fondness in his voice.

"You would?" I stared, bewildered. *"Him?"*

"He is not quite what you think he is."

"Then what is he?"

"The prince was a kind-hearted child growing up. He used

to cry so frequently that his nickname became 'ulbo.' He would cry over everything, moved and wounded by all things. Then he stopped one day, two years ago. He stopped one emotion—overwhelming grief. But, you see, when you numb one feeling, you numb them all. He no longer feels things deeply; shame, anger, happiness, joy, gratitude—"

"Of course the prince changed," I murmured, remembering the tale I had overheard. "Anyone would change after committing murder, taking the life of one's own brothers."

"They were his foster brothers," Wonsik replied. "The two princes, Prince Anyang and Bongan, treated Daehyun-gun like their own family ... What rumors have you heard?"

I reached out and touched the damp cavern wall. "His two brothers were exiled after beating their mother to death."

"The king ordered it—the killing of their own mother."

"And the king also ordered Prince Daehyun to apprehend his brothers, who had run away. And Prince Daehyun did so. He hunted down his own family. This story is no secret. Everyone whispers of it."

"No wonder," he whispered.

"No wonder what, ajusshi?"

"If that is the story you believe, then it is no wonder that you look at Prince Daehyun the way you do." Wonsik settled on the cavern floor. "He is a monster in your eyes. In mine, he is simply a young man who has lost himself."

We both looked out at the cave entrance, gleaming from the rainfall.

"Rest," Wonsik said. "Travel is impossible in this weather—"

"About the bead," I said, taking it out and rolling it between my fingers, "I have followed your instructions, yet the answer continues to elude me. Can you not simply tell me?"

"Did you read the book I gave you?"

"Yes—it is tedious, and I have not come to the capital to be tutored. I have come to reunite with my sister."

"The title *Muwonrok* comes from *mu*, for 'elimination,' and *won*, for 'great sorrow,'" he explained, completely ignoring my frustration. "As stated by the title, the *Muwonrok* is a treatise on how to eliminate great sorrow among the people. I hope that in studying this book, you will also understand that there is nothing more important than a human life, for there is no punishment greater than death. If you are going to investigate with me, I cannot have you rashly leaping to conclusions and judgments, rushing off into reckless action. Great care must be exercised in the collecting and recording of evidence, for anything—even the absence thereof—could be critical in establishing the facts. If we are to work together, I thought you should know this."

I frowned at him, thrumming with impatience, and yet grudgingly grateful, for he was not obliged to assist me at all.

"Prepare your heart, nangja." His voice was gruff. "This investigation will be a battle against yourself. A battle against the voice that tells you to surrender to the darkness. So do not give in to hopelessness. Bring your sister home. I will do what I can to help, if you would trust me."

The last of my irritation melted away as his words seared into my mind, and I knew I would never forget his kind offer.

For the rest of the night, Wonsik kept his back turned, allowing me a semblance of privacy, and when first light peeked into the cave, my head spun from exhaustion. I had hardly slept.

"I found something, sir!" an unfamiliar voice shouted.

I jolted up, looking around for Wonsik. He was gone, along with his horse.

"The king will arrive soon; what should we do?"

*The king?* I stood still for a moment, then hurried after the noise and peered through the branches. A squad of royal guards stood before a bloody corpse covered in flies.

Pieces of their whispers reached me. "... it is him, Royal Guard Min... several stab wounds... neck broke from the fall..."

I looked above and saw a low cliff jutting out above them. Withdrawing into the thicket, I made my way up the slope of damp leaves, clinging to trees to keep from slipping. My heart thudded in my chest as I inched toward the cliff that overlooked the scene. Carefully, carefully, I held on to a tree and peered over the edge, down at the top of their military hats, their beaded chin straps swaying.

"So ... what should we do?" one asked, looking around.

"What do you mean?"

"Should we move the body? Do you recall the last time the king witnessed a corpse, he—" The guard sliced his hand across his throat. "But if we hide him, long enough for the king to pass through—"

"Are you mad? Investigator Gu will kill us if he finds out we touched a murder victim. We must not disturb anything."

I glanced beyond the group and noticed another guard. He was a tall young man with a ghastly pale face and dark, beady, and unblinking eyes, like those of a crow. Royal Guard Crow—as I had decided to call him—walked toward a small object, then he glanced at his fellow guards still whispering among themselves. He kicked it under a bush.

"Gunwu-yah!"

Crow flinched and glanced over his shoulder. "What?"

"Come look at this!"

Before I could wonder what it was, I heard the thunderous tramping of many hooves, and the king appeared with his hunting entourage. He spoke in a hissing whisper to his personal guard, too quiet for my ears. Tension stiffened my back as I took in the sight of the tyrant. So pale and lanky, with mild features, he did not look capable of destroying a kingdom. Then his lips stretched across his teeth, curling into a thin sneer, and those surrounding him shriveled with terror.

"Did he leave a flower again?" King Yeonsan raised his voice into a sharp blade. "Well? Answer me!"

"Y-y-yes, jeonha," one of the guards stuttered. "It was tucked into his s-s-sash belt."

"And he has left another message?" he hissed. "Read it to me."

"Jeonha—"

*"Read it!"*

A man shoved by the trembling guard, uniformed in a dark red robe. He halted before the corpse and read the bloody message:

> *"King Yeonsan is more of a thief than a king.*
> *His oppressive government is more feared than a tiger.*

*His Majesty has too many faults; do not be afraid to abandon him."*

Dead silence followed.

"Investigator Gu," the king said, and my attention snapped back to the man uniformed in red. The brim of his military hat was lowered, obscuring his face. "Nameless Flower attacked Royal Guard Min and left him in the middle of my route. They say you see everything, just like your mentor. Is this a coincidence, or did the killer know that I would pass through here?"

"It was intentional."

"How can you be so sure?"

"Everything appears staged, just for you, jeonha." At last, the investigator lifted his head, allowing me to catch a glimpse of his rugged features, and he looked to be no more than twenty-five. "Royal Guard Min was supposed to hang right there from that tree—"

I quickly ducked and remained curled as all eyes likely turned to the tree before me, to the rope still tied around the trunk. I had not noticed it before.

"But something must have occurred," Investigator Gu continued, "and the corpse was freed from the noose, shoved off the cliff. As you can see by this drag mark, the body was pulled from the bushes and left right here—on the path you would take, jeonha."

"But *how*?" the king bellowed.

I shifted to peer over the cliff again, watching as the king leaped down from his horse. Everyone in His Majesty's path shrunk away as he stalked over to Royal Guard Min's body. His lips curled as he began to pace. "How can this killer know that I was to ride out today? How could he know of my plans? I fully intended to go hunting in Gwangneung Mountain next week but changed my mind and decided to go this morning."

"When did you change your mind?" Investigator Gu asked.

"Two days ago."

"Then the killer was near you in those two days, jeonha."

A wave of panic rustled through the entourage as the king whirled around to stare at his party—his guards and soldiers, advisers and courtesans. Soon, I sensed, people would be pointing to the tree trunk, declaring that they had nothing to do with Royal Guard Min Hyukjin's death. I shifted again, slowly retreating from the cliff. Once I was far enough from being seen or heard, I straightened myself and dusted the soil off my dress.

I moved to leave, then my eyes fell upon the telltale signs etched into the mud before me: a trail left by something heavy being dragged. I followed the path that led me down a gentle slope and into a thicket of trees. It was then that I beheld a figure, drenched in crimson, slumped against the trunk of a nearby tree.

The prince.

"Daegam," I whispered. He didn't so much as stir.

I walked over and crouched before him, peering into his blood-streaked face. Was he dead?

"*Daegam*," I whispered again. At his prolonged stillness, I hesitantly pushed aside his collar and dared to touch the side of his neck. I felt nothing—was that even where the pulse lay? My fingers trailed gently across his skin, searching.

"You," came a whisper.

I startled, glancing up into a dark pair of eyes. "You are not dead."

"Disappointed?"

"Terribly." Rising to my feet, I took a step back. "What happened to you?"

He weakly gestured at me to return. "Give me your arm."

"I do not take kindly to being ordered about—"

"You dare disobey the orders of a prince?"

"What is a prince but a title?" I said brusquely, emboldened by spite and his helpless state. "What is a flower but a simple plant?"

"There is no time for such impertinence," he spoke through gritted teeth, wincing with each word. "Extend me your arm at once." When I took another step back, it must have dawned on him what I was thinking. I had no reason to save him. "I cannot be discovered here," he spoke slowly now, the sharpness gone from his voice, "or I shall become a suspect, and no one would doubt my guilt. After what happened to my family, everyone would believe that I had waited all this time to exact my revenge by becoming Nameless Flower."

"In short," I said, "if I leave you here, you will die."

"Yes," he rasped. "You would not let a prince die—"

"Yes, I would."

His face went ashen.

*Leave him now*, a voice in my head urged. But still, I could not make myself move.

"Please, wait—" A bead of sweat trickled down his bloodied temple. "What is your name?"

"Iseul," I said warily.

"Iseul," he whispered. "Help me, and in exchange, I will help you reunite with your sister. You have my word."

His offer sent a jolt through me. "How can I believe you?"

"You will have to trust me."

Trust *him*? Did he think me a fool? My thoughts came crashing to a halt when I glanced below. Soldiers swarmed the lower ground, moving upward toward the cliff. If they cast one look to the side, past the sparse lining of trees, they would surely see us.

"Damn," I whispered, and glanced at the prince. The man who had shot me and left me for dead. "If you stay very still, perhaps they will not find you."

"I will tell you my secret. A secret that would ensure my execution. Then you will know that I mean it—I *will* help bring your sister home."

I hesitated for a moment, but there was no time for indecision. I grabbed the prince, and with all my might, I heaved him up onto his feet, then pulled his arm around my shoulder. Pain flared down my back as my wound—the one *he* had inflicted—split open and bled.

"They are nearly out of sight," Daehyun whispered, but not a moment later, a soldier's bellow pierced the air. An arrow whistled by, splintering through leaves and branches.

"Run faster!" I hissed, grabbing his arm tight and anchoring him closer to me. "Before they catch us!"

# 14

# DAEHYUN

**They had barely escaped over** the mountain ridge and now they were completely alone.

"Where should we go?" Iseul gasped as they continued their journey.

"We will travel the long way around," Daehyun whispered, wincing with every step. "The mountain pass will be infested with the king's soldiers."

So they traveled deeper into the forbidden territory, weaving through the tangled forest, passing by skeletal villages. In the silence of their journey, Daehyun's mind finally returned to last night.

Hyukjin was dead.

Running a hand over his haggard face, Daehyun could feel the seams that held him together coming loose. Echoes of their childhood returned, tinkling with Hyukjin's laughter and grand declarations. *He lived to serve the kingdom, and he died—for what?*

A sharp ache dug into his chest, constraining his ribs until he could hardly breathe. *There are too many sorrows in life to feel each too deeply.* He could not slip, could not fall back into the despair he had felt when his family had died. The monthslong grief that had left him wretched. The overwhelming darkness.

The hours upon hours of torment. Weeping until his entire body ached. He could not go back to it. He gritted his teeth and refused to feel and waited for the numbing fog to roll in.

"You are hurting me."

He looked down; in his effort to stay afloat, his hand was around her wrist, gripping her with enough force to bruise.

He snatched his hand away. "Apologies."

As they passed a tree, he snapped its branch downward.

"You said you would share with me a most dangerous secret," she said. "What is it?"

He had many secrets, and he considered which to share with her, or whether he ought to simply fabricate one. As he calculated, he took a moment to consider her. Her hair fluttered wildly in the wind, her torn dress was stained with mud, yet no matter her disheveled appearance, she still bore the aura of a magistrate's daughter. Magistrate Hwang was her father, according to the identification document he'd discovered in her travel sack. She belonged to a prominent yangban family. He wondered what her connections were, whether she might be of any use to him.

"You said you would go into the den of a tiger for your sister," he said. "You would steal her from the king."

She avoided his gaze. "I am not sure that I did, daegam. And you did not give me an answer—"

"Would you betray the king, too, if that would lead you to your sister?" he asked. At her silence, he said, "You are quiet. Are you afraid of me?"

She looked at him, dead in the eyes. "Would *you* betray the king?"

He tensed under her probing gaze.

"You are quiet," she said, arching a brow. "Are you afraid of me, daegam?"

The corners of his lips twitched. Who was this girl? She belonged to yangban aristocracy, and thereby would have been raised with a Confucian upbringing, where the rules of obedience and submission were carefully instilled from a young age. Yet she behaved like a heathen. He knew he ought to despise her, but instead he was curious.

"Were you always like this?" he asked.

She narrowed her eyes. "Like what?"

"Rebellious."

"It is impossible not to be," she mumbled, half to herself. "One is imprisoned by a thousand rules as a woman, and no one will explain to me why such rules exist."

"Your parents were strict," he observed.

"Only to my sister. She always strove to be perfect, and her life looked dismal—" She stopped, then whispered, "Why am I telling you this?"

"And where are your mother and father?" he probed.

A muscle in her jaw worked, her lips still stubbornly clamped.

"You traveled all the way here by yourself," he continued, "perhaps because your sister is all you have now."

She looked at him, and he was surprised by how quick the rims of her eyes turned red. "It cannot be considered treasonous," she whispered, "or slanderous to state a fact. The king killed my father—he ruined my family. *Your* brother."

*We are the same*, he thought. "So you are completely alone in this kingdom. Are you not afraid?"

She raised her chin. "I am not completely alone. I have an uncle."

"And who is your uncle?" he muttered. "The local butcher?"

"Surely you must have heard of Government Official Choi Ikjun?" She quirked a brow. "From my memory, he is a government official of the second rank. I hear that is quite high."

"Choi Ikjun . . . ?" he whispered, and Iseul seemed pleased by his surprise. "Of the Chungju Choe clan?"

"Yes. So you know him—"

"That is Deputy Commander Park's closest friend."

"I don't follow."

He lifted his stare to Iseul. The image of her sharpened before him, the mountains blurring into the background. She was the one. The missing piece on the janggi board.

She stumbled. He reached out and caught her shoulders to steady her, but she let out a small gasp, flinching away from him. The color had drained from her face, her hand hovering over her shoulder—a hand wet with blood.

His own hand glistened red. "You are bleeding—" He stopped, realizing it was the same shoulder he had wounded with a careless arrow.

"Well? How will you help my sister out of the palace?" Her voice was sharp, her eyes fiery. Demanding. "You *promised*. I hope you have not forgotten—I hope you will not go back on your word."

"Seek revenge," he whispered. "Only then will you save your sister."

Her brow furrowed. "What . . . what do you mean?"

A twinkle in the darkness yonder interrupted them. A hut, sitting alone in the middle of a vast field.

"We must have wandered back out of the forbidden territory," he whispered, still staring at her shoulder as a sickening sense of remorse stirred in him. "Soon it will be full dark. We will have to seek shelter here for the night."

# 15

# ISEUL

White charm papers fluttered in the wind, strung around the hut, as though to keep out evil spirits. But as though ghosts had slipped in upon our entering the yard, the door slid open and the shaman appeared. "Who's there?" she called out.

"Where might the next village be, mudang-nim?" Daehyun inquired. "My wife and I injured ourselves on the journey, and we are in need of a place to rest for the night."

*Wife.* I would have scoffed at this, but the pain of a thousand brimstones burned through my shoulder. I could hardly think.

"The next village is a half day's travel away," the shaman rasped.

Daehyun looked at me, wearing the mask of a concerned husband, then he turned to the old woman again. "May we stay here tonight?"

"You may, but with payment of sort. Do you have anything edible? Dried fruits? Dried squid?"

Daehyun paid with coins, and she happily led us to a single room. A room so small that I backed up against the wall to avoid brushing into the prince. "Surely you do not expect me to sleep here with you," I remarked, casting him a swift glance.

His unease was evident as well. "I wouldn't dare shut my eyes in your company," he muttered, "lest you attack me with your blade—or rock." He then waved a hand. "Rest. I will return shortly then remain outside, on guard for the rest of the night."

I breathed with ease once he had left, then proceeded to examine the room. There were a low-legged table, neatly folded blankets, and a single bed mat in one corner. My exploration was cut short as the shaman arrived with a tray. There were two bowls of water and two washcloths. "For you and your husband."

I touched my shoulder, wincing. "Do you have fresh binding material?"

"Aigoo, I forgot. I will have your husband bring it to you."

"Where is the pri—the husband?"

"He went for a stroll, and I am not sure why he would at this hour." She waved her hand at the night sky, framed by the opened latticed window. "My hut is on the outskirts of the forbidden territory. A few steps in the wrong direction and he will find himself among soldiers."

Perhaps he had gone to survey the area . . .

"Could you inspect my wound? I worry it may be infected." I struggled out of my jeogori jacket, gritting my teeth to keep myself from whimpering. "And perhaps you would help me tend to it—"

She clucked her tongue. "You have a husband, ask him. What else are they good for?" And with that, she left.

"Curse it," I hissed, alone again. I slipped the straps of my skirt down over my breastband to access the bandage wrapped around my shoulder and underarm. I needed to wash my wound but was too afraid to even peel off the bandage.

The door slid open again, and I glanced up; the prince had

approached as silently as a panther and now stood before me at the entrance. A quiet look of shock hardened his features. I was too dizzy for embarrassment to even register.

He set the binding material down and at once stepped out. "I will wait outside." Once the door closed, he called in, "Perhaps you should leave the old binding material on," just as I tugged the bandage off. I felt fresh blood flowing. Washing down my arm. Panic rose in my chest.

"What happens if I don't?" I asked.

"The blood would have clotted, so if you peel off the binding material, it will bleed again—" He paused, then asked grimly, "You pulled off the bandage, didn't you?"

"Yes," I whimpered.

"Sh-shall I help?"

The sight of so much blood impaired my better judgment. "Yes."

Footsteps drew up behind me, and he pushed aside strands of my hair.

"Does it l-look awful?"

He let out a restrained sigh. "It does not appear to be too serious."

"Is it infected?"

"No. Once we return to the capital, you will receive proper treatment to ensure that it remains that way."

The fear of death eased away. Pain I could tolerate.

Sweat dripping down my skin, I stole a glance at our reflection in an old bronze mirror. We stood close, too close for comfort, and my muscles tensed with the need to leap away. But I forced myself to remain still under his hand, feeling his fingers move cautiously, as if he were afraid to further harm me—afraid to even touch me.

"Lift your arms," he murmured, once the wound was cleansed, "if you are able."

I complied, as I continued to watch him intently through the reflection. He began to wrap the long bandage around me and winced, holding his side as he worked his way around my torso. Despite his own wounds, he did not stop or falter until the last bit of the bandage was neatly secured.

"Finished," he breathed out in relief. He helped me into my jeogori jacket with a gentleness I hadn't thought him capable of, then he stepped away from me. "You ought to rest now. I will keep watch outside."

With those words, he strode over to the door, and I was most eager for him to leave. His presence drained the air from the room, left my skin feeling overly warm and tender. But as I gingerly touched the back of my shoulder, the pain was a burning pulse, a reminder of who suffered greater than I.

"Wait," I called out. "You ought to tend to yourself, too."

He paused in his steps, casting a wary glance my way.

"You cannot travel covered in so much blood. It would only draw attention to yourself."

He remained standing for a moment longer, then grudgingly moved across the room to where the fresh washcloth and bowl lay. He dipped the cloth into water and attempted to wipe the blood off the back of his head, but as he reached back, a look of pain splintered his expression. He lowered the washcloth onto a table, gritting his teeth as he held the side of his ribs.

"I could help you, if you wish," I offered.

Beads of sweat formed on his forehead as he struggled to regain his composure. It was then that I noticed it. His robe, the V of his neckline, revealed an angry red bruise, and I imagined there were more along his ribs.

"Let me help," I said quietly, picking up the washcloth and wetting it in the basin of water.

When he did not protest, I stood up on my tiptoes and dabbed at the back of his head, the back of his neck. "You never told me—who wounded you?"

A tremor crawled up along his back. His emotions were unraveling, and I could hear grief surfacing in his voice. "I watched him push Hyukjin off the cliff—" He shook his head, his back tensing as an eerie calm fell over him. "There is no use grieving for the dead," he whispered, as though to himself. "The dead are already gone."

"And we are left behind," I murmured to myself, dipping the cloth into water, twisting out the blood, "not knowing how to exist in this kingdom, a world where they have ceased to be."

Daehyun stilled, then looked back at me, and we held each other's gaze for the barest moment. I was the first to look away, rinsing out the rag again until he finally stared ahead once more. I continued to wipe the blood off his head.

"Is that how you felt when your sister disappeared?" he asked with such studied calm and coolness that I had no desire to answer.

"So … what is your secret?" I changed the subject. "You said you would share your secret with me."

"I was going to tell you in the morning, but perhaps it is better to tell you now …"

*Tell me your darkest one.* He owed me a lethal secret, one

terrible enough to be used as blackmail should he go back on his promise to bring my sister home. And if his secret was a mere confession about the last court lady he had seduced, then I would surely dump the entire bowl of blood-water over his head—

"I intend to commit treason," he said, straightening the collar of his robe.

My thoughts froze. The bloody rag dropped from my hand. I quickly picked it up again. "You are lying."

"I would not lie about this."

Water dripping onto the floor, I stood numbly holding the rag. "What . . . what kind of treason?"

He finally turned to face me again. "A coup."

*A coup . . . ?* My mind remained caught in a haze of shock. Several moments passed when finally his confession registered. *A coup!* "Why are you telling me *this* secret?" It suddenly occurred to me. "You are dragging me into an insurrection—"

"A banjeong," he said quietly. "If we succeed in changing the heavens, it will be called a banjeong. The restoration of our kingdom from King Yeonsan's treachery."

"And if you fail, it will be a mere banlan. A rebellion, the refusal to obey the will of heaven." I shook my head. "I have come to bring my sister home, not to overthrow a kingdom. If you think I will have any part in your games, you are wrong."

His gaze held mine. "You cannot carry out the first task without executing the latter. It is foolishness to think you can bargain with King Yeonsan."

He was not wrong. The thought of catching the killer within a reasonable timeline was daunting, and the thought of trying to bargain with the king was truly petrifying. "This might fail," I whispered. "But why are you committing"—I bit my lip, glancing at the screened door—"treason?"

When he did not respond, my curiosity doubled. "You speak of changing the heavens. You speak of saving this kingdom from Yeonsan's tyranny. They are such grand words. But I wonder, daegam, who is it you are saving this kingdom *for*?"

He glanced at me, his eyes expressionless as he uttered four cold words. "There is no one."

I blinked, confused. "There is no one? But surely you must be fighting for someone?"

"I will not pretend to be driven by honor. Should a coup occur, I will be among the first to be executed. I am disfavored by many officials, you see. But I wish to live."

I had expected a more glorious reason for one's desire to overthrow the king. I shook my head. "And who will lead this coup? Yourself? No one would join!"

"It will not be I," he said dryly, "and I will not bore you yet with an explanation. I give you until our return to the capital to decide—whether you will join us or not."

"Who is *us*?"

"Wonsik and Madam Yul and Hyuk—" His expression darkened. "The three of us."

"And if I refuse to join?"

"Then I suspect you will never see your sister again."

I suspected, too, that I would never live to see the next day if I refused.

The shaking would not cease, not even as the sky grew pitch dark outside, not even as I lay still for hours, staring at the screened door that bore the prince's lantern-lit silhouette, his figure rigid and on guard.

"A coup . . ." I was alone, yet found myself whispering the words, needing to taste them on my tongue.

It was startling to imagine—a kingdom no longer ruled by King Yeonsan. The past two years of his tyranny had felt endless, more like a decade. It seemed impossible. Everyone believed that the king was chosen by the will of heaven. Could it really be changed?

I sucked in a deep, nervous breath, then let it out slowly.

I did not expect to sleep, not when my thoughts were so crowded, but when I finally closed my eyes, I was swept away into the past. I dreamed of Mother, imagined her arms around me. My sister lying on the other side. Father quietly reading by candlelight on a low table.

*Moon, moon, bright moon . . .* Mother's voice sang a song, a familiar lullaby.

*With my gold axe, I will cut down the cinnamon tree*
*Trim it smooth with my jade axe*
*A house to build all thatched with straw*
*Rooms there shall be one, two, three*
*One for Suyeon*
*One for Iseul*
*One for me and my husband*
*May we live there a thousand years*
*Ten thousand years together—*

The singing cut off dead, and when I looked, I found myself lying in a pool of blood. Mother and Father and Suyeon lying with their arms sprawled open, eyes unblinking, and I was screaming. Horror and grief splintered through me, the agony intolerable.

*Seek revenge.* The memory of Daehyun's words greeted me in the dark as I finally opened my eyes, swollen from crying in my sleep. *Seek revenge. Only then will you save your sister.*

My eyes were still puffy when the sun rose. Moving my arms carefully, I rose to my feet, refreshed myself with the fresh bowl of water someone had brought in for me. I then stepped out and came to an abrupt halt.

A shadowy figure sat on the veranda, back straight and legs crossed, studying a book opened on a low-legged table. My eyes adjusted in the early-morning dimness, and I recognized Wonsik. He flipped a page, dipped a calligraphy brush into ink, then rolled up his sleeve as he wrote down a note. It was his investigative journal.

"How did you find us?" I asked.

He looked up. A deep shadow was cast over his face, yet I could hear the relief in his voice. "You are awake at last. I followed the markers left behind for me by the prince."

So that was why the prince had been purposely snapping branches. "Are we leaving now?" I asked.

"We will leave tomorrow," Wonsik said, returning his attention to the journal. "The king's guards still infest the entire western pass."

My thoughts moved within my mind as slow as a slug, then another memory shifted into focus: the prince's dangerous proposition. My chest constricted—the thought of a coup filled me like a thousand birds fluttering their wings in my chest. I collapsed onto the veranda next to Wonsik, staring ahead blankly.

"He told me," Wonsik said simply, turning a page.

Now I gaped at him. *He is part of it, too*, I remembered. "Everything? You do not look pleased."

"It is a perilous game the prince has lured you into. I was equally disapproving when Hyukjin persuaded Yul to join."

I glanced around, then lowered my voice. "Does your prince want to be king?"

"No. If one hopes to sway the majority government, it is best to choose the most obvious and least controversial candidate. The only other legitimate heir: Grand Prince Jinseong."

I nodded slowly. "Hopefully King Yeonsan does not kill the grand prince before the—the Great Event occurs."

"The king has kept him alive all these years, and I think he will continue to do so. The grand prince's mother, the Dowager Queen, is like a mother to His Majesty. And for that reason alone, the grand prince has not faced execution."

I nodded, then shook my head. A wave of anxiety struck me. "The probability of this event succeeding seems impossibly low. Besides you, ajusshi, we are all so young. Yul, Prince Daehyun, and I . . ."

"History moves its course, Young Mistress Iseul," he murmured, flipping the page of his journal. He took up his calligraphy brush again. "But it is the youth who point the current in its direction."

# 16

# DAEHYUN

Daehyun secured the saddle to his horse, recovered by Wonsik from the forest, then he paused at the sound of a door sliding open. Looking over his shoulder, he watched Iseul trudge out, with the shaman holding her with a steadying grip. The girl had changed into a clean white robe given to her by the older woman. She had not yet braided her hair, so it hung down her shoulders in a stream of black.

"You look like a vengeful ghost," he murmured, adjusting the seat.

"And you are the sort I would furiously haunt for all eternity," Iseul retorted.

He was too tired to form a response. When the girl arrived beside him, he held her waist and lifted her onto the saddle, disturbed by how light she was. He had heard the king took food from the people, and the cruelty of the king's greed struck him now. Iseul felt as brittle as a twig. Once seated behind her, Daehyun felt a strange new anger simmering in his chest—

"*Stop*," he ordered himself.

He did not want to care. Indifference was all that had kept him sane.

"Well?" Iseul called out. "Shall we go?"

Soon they were off, speeding across the grassland. He tried to keep his distance from the bundle of female nuisance before him, but it was impossible on a single saddle. Iseul wiggled and stretched and twisted around to look behind, nearly elbowing him once or twice. "Where is Wonsik?" she called out over the blast of wind.

"He rode ahead to scout for soldiers."

When they reached the Han River, shimmering under the sun, he reined the horse into a steady trot as they followed the river upstream. Within two hours, he spotted the main road in the distance, dotted with people heading toward the capital.

"Have you made up your mind?" he asked. "Regarding what we discussed?"

She stiffened. After a long pause, she said, "Why would I turn down your proposition? I have two paths that might lead to my sister now. My bargain with the king—and my bargain with you. One of them will hopefully lead back to her."

"So you will continue with that foolhardy notion?"

"I saw the king; I saw His Majesty's fury and humiliation. I'm certain he would trade my sister for Nameless Flower. He has a *thousand* women. He could spare *one*."

"But would you risk your life to find out?"

She swept her hair over her shoulder, and as she braided it, he tried not to notice the length of her neck. "People whisper that if there is ever a revolt, it will be the heartbroken husbands and fathers who take down the king."

"And the sisters," he whispered.

He watched the way her fingers curled into a fist, the way an angry flush crawled up her collar, along her neck.

"And the sisters," she affirmed, and then glanced back at him.

A strange sensation stirred in his chest as he held her gaze. Then he quickly looked away and spoke no more to her for the rest of their journey.

# 17

# ISEUL

"We live in a time when we must hide our innermost thoughts." Wonsik moved a janggi piece across the game board. "A time when speaking truthfully can result in our execution. It makes those like Nameless Flower all the more dangerous."

"And why is that?" I asked. We were sitting on the inn-yard platform, and I was trying not to move my left arm. We had returned from our fraught journey a few hours ago, and the travel had aggravated the wound.

"Nameless Flower kills without any surety. He targets king sympathizers, yet how can he know for certain where one's loyalty lies? That is how Min Hyukjin ended up dead—on the outside, all the killer saw was a man who was prized by the king for his military prowess. Nothing else." Wonsik nodded at me. "Make your move."

I stared down at the game board, welcoming any form of distraction from the ache.

"Do you have an idea of who the killer might be?" I asked, my finger hovering indecisively over the squares, then finally moving the soldier. "Investigator Gu, he is your former mentee?

I heard him say that the killer is likely a trusted adviser, or someone close to the king."

"And why does he think that?"

"Because the killer was aware of the king's hunting schedule."

"There are many who are closely acquainted to the king.
From princes and princesses to government officials and concubines. And then there are those intimate with the king's close
acquaintances. And we also have those who are close merely in
proximity to the king, from servants to entertainers to his thousand courtesans. Anyone can easily know the king's hunting
schedule. The net is too wide."

I sighed. "We will never find Nameless Flower."

"Of course we will," he said, too assuredly. "The truth is
often right before us. We simply need to know where to look.
And I have been so preoccupied of late, assisting the prince with
his plans, that I have not had much time to focus on the case."

"You have me now to assist, ajusshi."

He moved the chariot, then nodded at me.

I picked up the general, only to be stopped.

"The general—or as I like to think of him, the king—
cannot leave the fort. These four squares here are your palace."

Tapping my lips, I reexamined the pieces, trying to remember in which direction each one could move.

"And how shall you assist me with the investigation?"
Wonsik asked.

"Tell me what I ought to do, and I shall do it."

"Perhaps you might begin by learning the significance of the
bead."

"*You* are aware of its significance already, yet you will not tell me the answer," I said, rather imperiously. "My mind is already too preoccupied with concerns for my sister—"

Wonsik proceeded to overtake my piece, and with my every move, he overtook even more. As he continued to lecture me, I watched, helplessly, as my dynasty fell into shambles.

"Do not expect me to share what I know if you have no intention of even trying to find it for yourself. Such people, I have observed, have no genuine interest in the truth."

An irritated sigh and a bundle of sharp words gathered in my chest. Then I stopped. This was precisely what had led to my quarrel with Suyeon—my refusal to truly listen to her and to understand her concern, heart deep.

"I *am* interested in the truth," I said, finally glancing down at the pouch tied to my skirt string. "I simply—" This sounded awful, but I said the words anyway. "I am accustomed to being provided for."

Wonsik heaved out a sigh, then said in a gentler voice, "You are capable, though—more than you know. That is why you are here. You traveled all this way to find your sister. With that amount of stubbornness and grit, you have the capacity to find answers no matter how deep that truth is buried." He gazed at me with such intensity that, for a moment, I felt as though I were his own daughter sitting before him. "The ability to exercise your judgment is invaluable, especially during times when anxiety threatens to sweep you into a current of indecisions and dangerous conclusions."

I took the bead out of the pouch, then sat straight, poising myself in the manner of a compliant student. "I do not know where to even begin."

"It is quite simple. Sit with the bead and ask yourself: Where have I seen it before?"

"I have never seen it."

"Look at it."

I sat, staring. "It is a bead."

"What are beads used for?"

"For adornments?"

"What kind of adornments?" He watched me steadily.

"For . . ." My mind flipped through the pages of my memory, racing through all the beads I had encountered. "For necklaces and bracelets—prayer beads! Are these prayer beads? Used by Buddhist monks?"

"Do they look like prayer beads?"

"No," I murmured. "Prayer beads are smaller and made of wood."

Wonsik cleared the janggi board, slowly arranging the pieces on their squares as he watched the innyard crowd with farmers, military officials, and more. All come for a drink after a long day of work.

"Wade through the pool of your memory. Concentrate yourself on the details," Wonsik said. "Small details are infinitely more important than your general impression."

"You seem certain that I have seen this bead before."

"I am quite certain that you have. You simply need to discover it. The truth will wait for you, however long it takes." He pursed his lips. "In fact, I am reminded of the words of Confucius. *Heaven does not let the cause of truth perish.*"

The old retired soldier, to whom the janggi board belonged,

finally returned to the inn. And as he and Wonsik played a match, with a crowd gathering around them, I went off to the veranda, where I sat, tucking myself behind a pillar to avoid the glaring sunset.

*The truth is right before me.* I stared down at the bead, rolling it between my fingers as I searched my memory—as one might wade through the sea in search of a pearl. *It is impossible . . .*

The sky darkened. Lanterns hanging on eaves were lit. Yeongho appeared, smiled at me as he searched for his golden pouch, and, not finding it, ate his tasteless meal while the other jesters chatted about their performance at the royal court three days ago.

"We need more bawdy jokes." A performer rubbed his forehead. "If we fail to make the king laugh again, he will surely execute us."

I felt sorry for Yeongho and his troupe.

Once finished, Yeongho wiped his mouth and hurried up to the veranda, sliding open a door. In the room, Prince Daehyun was flipping through a book, the candlelight and shadows dancing across his chiseled face, tracing the haughty lines of his mouth and nose. He glanced up, and our gazes locked. The bead slipped from my fingers.

"Damn it," I whispered, trying to catch it.

The bead rolled across the veranda, dropped onto the dirt yard, only to be swept aside by a passing military officer, then kicked to the far end by a little boy. I hurried after it, and when I finally grabbed it, I found myself before a voluminous dark blue skirt.

"I truly wanted you to rest from your travels, and then you looked so preoccupied with whatever Wonsik was telling you," Yul's voice huffed. "But the evening crowd is endless!"

Tucking the bead away, I stood and found Yul precariously balancing four trays loaded with stews and wine bottles. I relieved her of one, as I had only one good arm to use. "Does Wonsik do this to you, too?" I asked as I served the meals alongside her. "Never tell you the answer because he wishes for you to find it yourself?"

"No. Well, I never *told* Wonsik I wished to investigate with him. You brought this upon yourself, Iseul-ah. You have awakened his pedagogical fervor. Now that I think of it . . ."

Her sentence hung midair, unfinished, as we rushed from table to table, serving and wiping away spills. Once the crowd thinned, Yul let out a dramatic sigh.

"What was I saying?" she murmured, while massaging her arm. "Oh yes. Now that I think of it, I suspect Wonsik misses training investigators at the State Tribunal, and you have become his project . . ." Her voice dwindled away again. Her gaze fixed on a young woman waving at her, sitting next to a drunk young man.

Yul nervously waved back, then whirled around. She pulled out a small bronze looking glass. "My rouge is all melted off!" she hissed as I followed her into her room. "Why she decided to marry that dirty boar is beyond me." She froze, then turned to face me. "I was so preoccupied with the rush I absolutely forgot!"

"Forgot?"

"I've been meaning to give you something all day long, but

that old fart was lecturing you, so I hadn't the opportunity to approach you."

"Give me what—?"

Yul stepped in close, wrapping her arms around me in a tight embrace. "Prince Daehyun told me everything, that you have joined the cause to overthrow the monster." She then held my hand, shaking it. "I am thrilled to have another woman in our circle. Working with only men was growing insufferable."

The warmth of her embrace lingered, seeping into my heart. Somewhere during my time at the Red Lantern, my determination to remain alone and friendless had crumbled. She must have noticed my glistening eyes, for she asked, "What is the matter?"

"Nothing. And how did you come to join?" I asked, trying to deflect. "What is your duty?"

"Hyukjin was a childhood friend, and he thought having an innkeeper in the circle would be of use. My inn is, after all, a storehouse of information. *And* a storehouse of weapons. I will show you our secret room later."

I already knew of that room. "Why are weapons being stored here, of all places?"

"Because I have the space. Because no one would expect it. And when weapons are brought in, no one would notice the crates, as merchants are frequent visitors of mine. Well, they used to be more frequent, before the roads were blocked off by the king's hunting grounds."

Memory of the crates of swords flashed through my mind. "Did you . . . steal them?"

"As I said, merchants are frequent visitors, and one is a trusted friend of mine. And that merchant is good friends with a blacksmith. We were able to arrange a deal. Hyukjin and Doaji spent the entire night unloading the crates—" Yul opened a decorated wooden case, crowded with porcelain cosmetic bottles, then looked around her room. "I wonder where I put my rouge."

"Who is Doaji?" I asked.

"Yeongho! It is the pet name Hyukjin gave him, but I should stop calling him that. What man wishes to be called a baby pig?" She opened a chest and took out a small, folded blanket. Something else dropped out. A dragon-shaped hairpin with a red pearl.

A quiet gasp escaped me. The hairpin was stunning, more exquisite than any I had ever owned—or even laid eyes upon. "Where did you get that?"

Quickly, Yul retrieved it. "An ajusshi gave it to me."

"*Gave* it to you?" I could not dampen my interest. "Is it an heirloom?"

Without looking at me, she proceeded to carefully tuck the pin deep inside the chest. "The ajusshi told me to pawn it in ten years, then use the money to get married and raise children. Though I never intend to get married. I have no interest in men or having children of my own."

I held the hairpin in my mind, the gold glinting off every corner of my thoughts. I knew everything about ornamental hairpins.

The binyeo pin was worn only by married women, and its material symbolized one's place in the world. Gold, silver, and jade were severely restricted to the elite, while commoners wore those made from wood or animal bones or horns.

"Symbols . . . ," I whispered, a thought hovering outside my mind, just out of reach.

"What is it?"

"There are rules governing what we can and cannot wear. Almost every article on our person indicates our status, from hairpins to *hat strings*." My hand rose to my throat, thrill rising with a realization. "Beaded hat strings are worn by nobles to indicate their status—as well as military officials—" My breath caught at my throat, and the gulf of my memory illuminated. I was at the cliff's edge once more, peering down at the royal guards examining Hyukjin's corpse. They wore military hats, and dangling in a long loop from one corner of the hat to the other was a beaded string. Wax beads that alternated in color— red, yellow, red, yellow, red, yellow.

"Red and yellow." I could barely speak. "The same color beads that were found at the crime scene."

"How eerie," Yul murmured, "you look precisely like Wonsik-samchon when revelation strikes him."

Ignoring her, I rushed out of the room, and as though the kingdom had slid under crystal glass, I found myself fascinated by the details. The blackwood of a woman's hairpin, the purple stain on a man's robe, the dust on a grandfather's knees. And there they were—the beads. Alternating yellow-red beads dangling from the hats of two police officers. They were hunched over a table, pouring themselves another bowl of liquor. And they were not royal guards.

As I pondered over this, a burly shadow fell by my side. I did not need to look to know who it was. "This wax bead . . . ," I said under my breath, my heart racing faster. "Nameless Flower is a military official."

"Not any military official," Wonsik said. "Remember what the widow told you when you interviewed her."

"Half man, half wolf. Her husband told her those words before he died . . ."

And then I finally understood what the dead witness had meant. Most military official hats were round at the top, but the hat of a royal guard had two feathers pointing up on either side. They could look just like a wolf's ears to an injured and terrified man.

"Nameless Flower is a royal guard."

"Or someone who wishes to be one," Wonsik replied. Then, gathering his hands behind his back, he looked at me. "So how does it feel, Young Mistress Iseul? How does it feel to find the truth for yourself?"

I glanced down at the bead resting in the palm of my hand. "Absolutely exhilarating," I whispered, feeling rather breathless.

The corner of Wonsik's eyes crinkled, then his amusement deepened into a great, rumbling chuckle. Before I knew it, I was laughing along. And for that brief moment, it truly seemed possible that all would be well in the end.

# 18

# DAEHYUN

Iseul's laughter rung outside, vibrant and bewitching. Daehyun caught himself listening, unable to speak or move, seized by curiosity.

"Daegam?"

Daehyun straightened himself, focusing on the young man before him. The court jester. "Min Hyukjin seemed to trust you. I hear he even gave you a pet name."

"Doaji!" A nervous smile flitted across Yeongho's mouth. "Of all the pet names he could have given me . . ."

"He would often remark upon your righteous spirit. Why is that?"

Yeongho's gaze brightened into that of an eager child. "When one is able to differentiate good from evil, it is impossible to accept the way things are."

"We all have the faculty to differentiate good from evil," Daehyun murmured. "But greed closes the eyes of some, turning people into wolves who throw all ethics and values to the wind." *You are a wolf*, the king's whisper slipped into his ear, *just as I am.* He poured himself another bowl of rice wine and downed it. "Hyukjin once tasked you to assist him in a discreet matter. Do you recall?"

"Indeed, daegam. He asked me to help him and Yul in the moving of some cargo."

"Do you know what it contained?"

Yeongho wiped his palm against his robe. "I overheard bits and pieces that day."

Daehyun examined the jester, calculating the likelihood that the young man knew—of their armory, of their plans. "Hyukjin told me about the performances. You and your troupe would risk your life to criticize the king?"

"I am a gwangdae. That is what I do. Risk my life to criticize the king and to bring joy to the people."

"From what I understand, you were taken in by the troupe a year ago."

"They rarely let me perform. I always change the lines, make things more elaborate. I have so much to say!" He spoke fast, and his Southern Jeolla dialect was so strong Daehyun could barely follow. "So I took it upon myself—if they are to let me stay with them, then I will at least provide them with stories. Stories feed them. A few times, government officials have paid me to spread gossip—"

"And before the troupe, what did you do?"

"Two years ago, the king demoted my father, stripped him of his wealth and rank. I hear the king demoted multitudes."

"He did, indeed."

"My family fell on hard times. Mother sold herself into servitude to provide for us. Then a year later, there was a plague outbreak—my parents died. I ran away, empty-handed. The troupe took me in out of pity."

"How good of them," Daehyun said blandly.

"Perhaps that is why my heart goes to Iseul," he murmured, snapping up Daehyun's attention. "She is alone, as I am. She may look unafraid, but truly, when I first met her, I thought to myself, 'Here is the loneliest girl I have ever seen.'"

Daehyun folded his arms. As reluctant as he was to recruit Yeongho, a man with an apparent fondness for Iseul, he was in need of a rallying figure to stir the hearts of the populace. One to provoke greater unrest and persuade the masses to embrace and join in the changing of the heavens. Only then would the tide of war be in their favor. "You mentioned a government official paid you to spread gossip. What kind of story did you spread?"

"That Concubine Jang Noksu is behind the king's horrible policy," Yeongho replied, politely filling up Daehyun's empty drinking bowl before filling up his own. "I overheard them talking, and they hoped to shift the blame off the king, for this was when rumors were spreading that Lee Jang-gon was planning a coup with other exiled officials. Normally, I would not care to assist in anything that would benefit the king. But I am convinced Jang Noksu practices black magic and has used it to possess the king—"

"Do you believe Lee Jang-gon will overthrow the king?" Daehyun asked.

"If he does not, I am sure *someone* will."

"Do you think so?"

"Well, it is inevitable, is it not, daegam?" Abruptly, Yeongho clamped a hand over his mouth. "I have a bad habit of saying whatever is on my mind."

"I am not here to cause you any trouble," Daehyun said, then withdrew a bag of coins. "Spread a story for me."

Yeongho snatched up the bag, and his eyes widened as he stared within. Then he looked at the prince. "What is the story?"

Lantern light filtered in through the latticed hanji screen, stamping the floor in a rectangle of gold. "It is a story about Lady Seungpyeong," he whispered. "It is a tragic tale of why she killed herself, and your task will be to stir up hatred against the king."

"But people already despise the king, daegam."

"Intensify it. Have the hatred be so overwhelming that people can no longer be silent, no longer still."

Yeongho's hands were now shaking. "Daegam, I have long waited for this moment, a moment when I can make a difference. I promise you." He looked up, his eyes gleaming bright. "I will not disappoint you."

# 19

# ISEUL

**Deep into the night,** I found myself sitting on the floor, examining the bead. My heart felt buoyant, riding on the wings of wonder and astonishment. There was a beauty to truth that I had never recognized before. It brought forth a memory—our family had once traveled through the deep mountains, and we had paused on our temple visit to watch a crane surrounded by a pack of hungry wolves. I had waited for the pack to tear it apart and devour it, only to be startled by the crane's formidable strength. The truth reminded me of that crane; the truth was strong. It held the courage to strike out, no matter how ferocious the oppression.

When the morning arrived, I was curled on the floor, still clutching the bead, my consciousness drifting along the borderland of a dream, one populated by trees and cranes and wolves.

"Iseul-ah, you slept in!" Yul called from outside my door, snapping my mind awake. "The morning crowd has arrived! Help me serve the meals!"

I dragged myself up and made myself decent. Yul could be heard rushing from table to table, but my vanity would not permit me to leave yet. I knelt before my bronze mirror, brushing my hair, then braiding it as I daydreamed of the wax bead's significance.

"Iseul!" Yul yelled.

Quickly smoothing out my dress, I stepped out—and collided with the prince. All thoughts of the investigation vanished, replaced by memories of the shaman's hut and my bare shoulders and his hands painstakingly avoiding contact. But Daehyun held me now, to keep me from tripping on the stairs, and his fingertips slipped along my arms as I stepped away.

"Good morning, Iseul." His voice was deep.

"Good day." I walked away, perhaps a bit too curtly.

A sudden shyness had come over me, and the shyness deepened into embarrassment as I felt the prince's eyes on me. I served the travelers, setting down bowls and cups, stew and rice wine splattering onto my skirt, my hair coming undone in the shuffling about. This was not the life I was meant to live. I suddenly wished Daehyun could see me as I had once been— dignified and clean, as delicate and poised as a pale flower. But the thought quickly vanished. I would gladly serve tables for the remainder of my days if it meant reuniting with my sister.

"Did you hear?"

My attention drifted to an old man who busily slurped his soup, then licked his lips and spoke on. "Nameless Flower has struck again."

I froze, as had the customers around me—spoons had stopped midair, bowls of wine paused before lips.

"Whom did he murder this time?" It was the prince's voice, sharp and menacing.

The old man waved a hand, flustered. "Not killed! I meant,

young man, that he has struck again with his acts of kindness. He left a bag of rice for the family next door to mine. Their son was dying from hunger." He clucked his tongue. "I am your elder; only a scoundrel would dare speak to me in such a rude manner!"

"Scoundrel?" the prince whispered, his voice icy, but a loud scoff interrupted him.

In the crowd stood the young mother of three, the traveler who had been staying at the inn since my arrival. "Nameless Flower is an imitator." She snatched up her chopsticks, picked up a fermented vegetable, and shoved it into her mouth. "My husband is Bandit Leader Hong. He was the first to steal from the yangban families to provide for the poor."

Everyone broke into whispers.

"*The* Bandit Leader Hong?"

"Did he not steal from King Yeonsan, too?"

"Hong was arrested six years ago!"

Finally, someone asked, "But are you not a widow?"

"Anyone imprisoned within the Milwicheong is as good as dead," the woman replied. "The king never frees traitors." Then proudly, she added, "He is the mawang there; that is what they call the most senior-ranking prisoner." She tilted her head haughtily. "And he has subordinates to keep him on the very top, and there are at least five *hundred* prisoners locked up there. And they all believe that *my* husband is the true guardian of the people, not that Nameless Flower—"

The young mother's speech was interrupted by the tolling of the village bell.

At once, the meals and tables were abandoned as customers

fled, and beyond the innyard, women disappeared into huts, windows and doors slamming shut behind them.

"King Yeonsan is near," Yul said, her voice as hard as ice. She slammed her tray down and wiped at the cosmetic powder on her face, revealing the full ripple of the scar over her brow. It was her shield against the king's preying interests. "The day that warning bell stops ringing, I will throw the most elaborate feast at my inn." Then she gestured at me before disappearing into the kitchen. "Iseul-ah, you had better follow me."

"Yul is right," Daehyun murmured, giving my elbow a gentle push. "You ought to hide."

"I want to see my sister," I whispered, setting down the bowls of stew. "I need to know she is still alive."

Daehyun caught my upper arm, and leaning close, his whisper brushed against my ear as he spoke in a low, warning tone. "Instead of risking your life to merely see her, risk your life to *free* her."

His remark struck a chord in me, and the impulse coiled within my limbs eased. The sight of Suyeon would have offered me some peace, but what mattered most was freeing her from King Yeonsan's hold.

"Very well," my voice wavered, unable to hide my grief. "Then tell me what I must do."

"We will find a safer place to speak. Follow me."

He took my hand and led me across the innyard, his grip gentle yet firm, guiding me through the back gate and down the winding village path. As we walked, he kept a watchful eye out, positioning himself close by my side as though to obscure me. It was only when we emerged into the open that I realized we had strayed far beyond the familiar boundaries of the village.

"Why are we leaving the inn?" I asked.

"There are too many people hiding in the rooms. Too many listening for the king; they might overhear us instead."

I continued to follow him, across a vast field and up a hill that was occupied by a lone tree. Its trunk was so wide that the two of us would have struggled to wrap our collective arms around it; its branches swept across the sky in waves of green. Beyond, the morning mist glided over acres of empty greenery.

It was the perfect place to speak of secrets. If anyone approached, we would spot them from miles away.

"What is it you wish to tell me?" I asked, glancing down at his hand, still on my wrist.

As though realizing his mistake, his hand recoiled, and he took a few steps back, retreating from me. His gaze drifted off into the distance, and a somber grimness settled over his brows. "If you agree to this, you must understand that you are entangling yourself in a perilous game. Wonsik asked that I emphasize this warning to you. Once you agree to this, there can be no turning back."

"Tell me what it is," I said, growing impatient.

A muscle worked in Daehyun's jaw. A mixture of relief and distress flickered in his eyes. "I wish for you to approach your uncle, Official Choi, when he returns from his travels in five days' time." He paused, watching me closely. "And find out for me his political stance. Whether he is for the king or against him."

I frowned. "Why my uncle?"

"He took care of the king's hunting grounds, but the king disliked his management, and so dropped him from second rank to ninth. He must surely have ill feelings toward the king. And if he becomes our ally, he may be able to help us persuade Deputy Commander Park Won Jong into joining our side."

"Who is that?"

"All you need to know is that the deputy has great influence in the government and that I possess a secret that might make him and his family seek vengeance against the king."

An uneasiness stirred in me, but I beat the feeling aside. My feelings did not matter. Only my sister's life did. "Very well, you may use me."

"Must you word it in that manner?" he muttered, looking ahead.

We remained standing quietly. Somehow, we had drifted close again, our shoulders nearly touching, and the gravity of his proposition weighed on me. A perilous game, indeed.

When the warm wind swept by, the leaves rustled as loud as waves on the seashore. I closed my eyes and could imagine us adrift in the middle of the sea, alone in the lulling dark. The waves lifting me up and down.

"I mean it," I whispered. "I will do whatever must be done to save my sister."

He glanced at me. "What is her name? Your sister."

"Hwang Suyeon. But she likely goes by her false name, Jonggeum."

Gradually, the king's hunting party came into view on the distant road, thousands upon thousands of soldiers. When I had seen them up close before, these men had loomed like giant, broad-shouldered beasts. But from this distance, they resembled tiny, insignificant ants, scarcely visible in the vastness of the landscape before us.

"Why does the king venture out accompanied by so many?" I asked.

"His hunting excursions are his means of flaunting his concubines and courtesans, as well as military exercises to keep his army battle-ready," Daehyun replied. "He trains his soldiers, for he is afraid."

"The treacherous, murderous king?" I shot him a frown. "Afraid?"

"Utterly terrified. He has grown paranoid since last year and has increased the guard of every palace gate by sixty. Soldiers are not even permitted to spin their swords or shoot arrows in the direction of the palace."

I paused, looking ahead at the contingent of figures all wearing fluttering pink dresses. There were hundreds of them, and hundreds more at the temple. At this thought, sadness settled in my chest. "What need has the king for a thousand courtesans? I cannot possibly imagine wanting a thousand husbands."

"Because rape—" He flicked an uneasy glance my way, as though afraid to offend my womanly sensibilities. But I did not shy away from the word. How could I when it was the reality my sister lived with? "Because rape is about power; it is never about desire or love," he answered quietly. "His Majesty is a power-hungry beast with a voracious hunger for more, and what better way to display that he reigns supreme than by taking what is precious to his own people?

"But the more women he devours," he continued, "the more starved he becomes. A thousand will not satiate him. And one day, should his dream come true, and he gains ten thousand . . . I fear he will only be hungrier than ever."

## 20

# DAEHYUN

**Daehyun found himself in the** palace two days later, watching as servants arranged the king's surasang, twelve dishes spread across three tables. All meals had been sampled for poison in the royal kitchen, but the king, in his paranoia, ordered his food be tasted once again. And thus the time-consuming procedure commenced.

A court lady nibbled and sipped her way down the main table, from the assortment of side dishes—grilled mountain ginseng, pan-fried meat delicacies, raw fish, pickled vegetables, cubed radish kimchi, whole cabbage kimchi seasoned with jeotgal, white kimchi, braised meat, boiled pork slices, fermented and salted seafood, salted fish—

Then she coughed.

Everyone tensed, including Daehyun. The king turned pale.

"B-begging your pardon." The court lady heaved for air. "A fish bone caught in my throat."

Once she re-collected herself, the young court lady moved to the small round table, sampled the red bean rice, scooped up a spoonful of the milky white bone broth, and chewed a bite of honey cookies and sweet rice puffs. She licked her lips, glanced at Daehyun, then shuffled over to the rectangular table of raw ingredients to be boiled in the sinseonllo hot pot. By the end of the sampling, she was still alive, staring nervously at Daehyun from under her lashes.

She likely wondered why he was here.

Daehyun wondered himself as he knelt across from the king.

"J-jeonha," a eunuch stuttered, after a long and tense moment. "Does the meal displease you? You have touched nothing—"

King Yeonsan grabbed his chopsticks and stabbed at his favorite plate of braised deer meat. Juice dribbled out. "I cannot sleep. I cannot think. I have wept until I passed out. Everywhere I go in this palace I am reminded of *her*." His voice broke, and his face grew red. "I cannot *bear* it! When do we leave these godsforsakened walls?"

"We leave for Kaesong City n-next month, jeonha," the eunuch replied shakily. "On the e-eighteenth."

Another stab into the meat chunk. "Deer tail is best dried in the shades of Buan County, but deer tails from Jeju Island are tasty, too." His Majesty spoke, his teeth grinding together. "As for deer tongues, the people of Hoeyang County excel at cooking them . . ." His white-knuckled grip trembled. "Even the sight of my most favored delicacy gives me no pleasure, because she is *dead*!"

He gave a violent shove, and the tables came toppling down, bowls and plates crashing to the ground. Court ladies scrambled back. Daehyun remained frozen before the king.

"And do you know why she is dead?" King Yeonsan's gaze shot to Daehyun. "Do you, little brother?"

"I do not, jeonha," he managed to whisper.

"Little brother." Yeonsan dragged himself onto his hands and knees, crawling over and grabbing Daehyun by the collar. "When I look at you these days, do you know what I feel?" A smile trembled across his lips. "Lust for your blood."

"Jeonha, I am unsure of what you mean . . ." Daehyun's mind raced, examining and reexamining everything he had done and said in the past few days. Somewhere, he had erred. "What have I done to lose your favor—"

A sharp pain struck his face.

"You *know* what you have done!" the king's voice rose as he raised his hand again. "Shall I kill you the way I killed your brothers? Shall I scatter your head and limbs across the kingdom as well?"

His brothers. Their heads. Daehyun grappled to stay above the memories, but another blow struck his face, and an explosion of panic submerged him.

*Breathe*, Daehyun told himself.

He dragged air into his lungs, but he was already drowning in dark waters. His brothers were tied up. They watched him from a ship, watched him as they disappeared into the fog. Carried off to a faraway island. Exiled.

*Breathe deeper.*

He sank deeper into the shadows, and the palace emerged. He was on his knees, too paralyzed to cry as he stared at his decapitated brothers. Their bodies buried on the island, their heads delivered to the king.

*Breathe. You must breathe.*

The chamber tilted, but he grabbed onto his knees and steadied himself.

"Little brother," the king whispered, still hovering before him, "tell me the truth. Did you have anything to do with Lady Seungpyeong's death?"

Daehyun blinked fast, trying to reorient himself. "I did not, jeonha."

"An apothecary testified that Min Hyukjin—*your* closest friend—had asked for kyungpo-buja. The very poison that killed Lady Seungpyeong." Yeonsan grabbed a fistful of Daehyun's robe, giving him a firm shake. "Min Hyukjin would not commit such a deed of his own accord. So who ordered him to kill Lady Seungpyeong? If not you, then who *did*? I have interrogated everyone, including his sister, and I cannot make sense of Her Ladyship's death! I refuse to believe that she killed herself, as some claim. Someone murdered her!"

Of course the king refused to believe the truth. He had abused Lady Seungpyeong to death.

"You know something. *Tell me*!" the king roared.

"C-court Lady Sonhui," Daehyun finally managed to say, his voice choking, "came to me on the night of Lady Seungpyeong's death."

Yeonsan glowered. "Hyukjin's sister? I have tortured her. She tells me nothing."

"She . . . ," Daehyun spoke slowly, allowing himself time to steady his mind. He had failed to save Hyukjin; he could not fail his sister, too. "She told me . . ."

"Told you *what*?!"

"She witnessed her brother lurking around Her Ladyship's residence, hours before Her Ladyship was poisoned . . . Sonhui saw her brother hide a white substance in Her Ladyship's chambers. He would not tell her what it was."

"Court Lady Sonhui told you all this?" Yeonsan growled.

"Sonhui believed her brother was involved in the murder. But I did not believe her; I warned her to keep silent." Before another blow could strike his face, Daehyun whispered the king's greatest fear, "But now I know she spoke the truth. Now I fear for your life even more, jeonha."

Yeonsan stilled. "What do you mean?"

"Did it not seem odd to you? Min Hyukjin died by the hands of Nameless Flower the very next day. What if... what if Nameless Flower is close to you, and he blackmailed Min Hyukjin into poisoning Lady Seungpyeong? Nameless Flower then killed Min Hyukjin, the liability. That is what I think, jeonha. That is why I fear for your life. Nameless Flower may be right before you—in plain sight."

King Yeonsan grew pale, and he appeared intoxicated with fear. Nameless Flower had indeed killed Hyukjin. And it was also true that the killing had occurred right after Lady Seungpyeong's death. It was not an outlandish assumption that the two events were connected.

"Investigator Gu told me as much, that the killer is someone near me. But why would Nameless Flower kill—" Yeonsan froze, his eyes widened. "He knew of my love for Lady Seungpyeong."

"It is Nameless Flower that you want," Daehyun whispered. "Please, jeonha, spare the girl. Hyukjin's sister had nothing to do with Her Ladyship's death."

King Yeonsan staggered to his feet, his arm raised in a weak gesture. "Eunuch Mun, have Investigator Gu summoned." Then he turned to Daehyun. "And you—*leave.*"

Bowing, Daehyun retreated from the chamber and found himself sweating profusely. When he reached an isolated courtyard, he vomited, leaning against the wall, unable to walk. He wanted to bury himself forever in the shadows, to block away all the horror and fear.

Gritting his teeth, Daehyun closed his eyes. He took in five deep breaths, imagined himself as a speck of a man alone on a snowy mountain, breathing in the numbing frost. Detachment spread across his heart, sealing away the vulnerabilities within. Indifferent and calm now, he made his way to the palace well. Maid Jiyu had not yet arrived, but as the sun dipped, she came scrambling around the corner with buckets—as she always did around this time. Soon royals and consorts would expect fresh pitchers of water with which to wash their faces. Jiyu set the buckets down when their gazes locked across the courtyard.

"Daegam!" she whispered, scurrying over to join him in the shadows. "My mother is healing well because of your benevolence."

"I am pleased to hear that," Daehyun replied, his voice as blank as the sky above. "There is something you must do for me."

"Of course, daegam—!" Her eyes went wide. "You are bleeding!"

"It is nothing." Daehyun wiped the blood off his split lip. "Go to Court Lady Sonhui. She is being held for interrogation, and I know you excel at slipping in and out of places without anyone knowing the better. Can you do that?"

"I can, daegam. What message shall I pass along?"

"Tell her that her brother is dead. Tell her to place all blame for Lady Seungpyeong's death on his shoulders. She will refuse, but you must convince her that there is no use protecting the dead. Once I manage to arrange a visit to the State Tribunal, I will speak to her myself and ensure that our stories corroborate."

"Is that all, daegam?"

Daehyun paused. "There was one more thing . . ." It took a moment to reach through the fog in his mind, and at last he arrived at what he sought. "She mentioned her sister's name."

"Begging your pardon, daegam?"

He glanced down at the maid. "Are you able to enter Wongaksa Temple?"

"I go there often to clean up. The temple never stays orderly with a thousand courtesans living there."

"Then I need you to find a particular courtesan for me. Her name is Suyeon, but she may also go by the name Jonggeum. Find her; there is a specific task you must carry out for me. And whatever you do, you must be discreet. No one else can learn of the task that I will entrust to you."

# 21

# ISEUL

**Formidable stone walls surrounded the** property. Dread pulsed at the base of my throat. *What if I fail?*

"Are you afraid?"

I swallowed. "Not at all, ajusshi."

"The prince and I will be nearby." Wonsik slipped a sheathed paedo into my hand. "It may be a decorative knife, but it is sharp enough to wound. Tie it onto your dress, as many young women do."

I glanced into the shadows of the alley cloaking the prince, who had kept his hat lowered all morning—but the brim had failed to hide the vicious bruises on his lips and along his jaw.

Looking back at Wonsik, I asked, "Why do I need this?"

"As a precaution, but I doubt you will need it. Otherwise, I would not send you in at all."

Tying the hanging tassel of the knife around my skirt, I watched as Wonsik left, and a fresh wave of nervousness rolled through me. My attention returned to the walled-in mansion. I took in a deep, steadying breath, then made my way over to the gate. Upon knocking, a manservant peered out.

"Is Official Choi in?" I asked quietly. "Inform him that his niece is here to speak with him."

The gatekeeper left to convey the message, then returned to escort me inside.

"This way." He guided me up a set of stairs that led to the Guest Hall, a long building with a flared roof held up by sturdy columns, and a dozen or so screened doors that marched along the terrace. Inside, I found myself in a vast and airy chamber decorated with lacquered furniture and delicate vases.

My uncle sat behind a low-legged table, watching me. He was as I remembered him to be the many times his family had visited our home—an unremarkable man with a round, pale face and a weak, lusterless gaze. His wispy beard twitched as I bowed deeply.

"Uncle," I whispered, kneeling before him. It was then that I noticed the janggi board spread out on his table. "It seems I have interrupted you in your game."

"I was playing with my son. Did you come discreetly?"

"I did."

"Hmm." He tapped his finger twice. "Your aunt is in the countryside, but if she were here, she would send you away at once. Considering you—" he glanced around, ensuring that we were alone "—are a convict, and you endanger our entire family."

I opened my mouth to apologize, but he spoke on. "I suspect you are here to find your sister? You understand she is now the king's property?"

"But—but I wish to bring her home."

He arched a brow. "Surprising. I did not think you the sort"—he waved a hand—"to brave such a mission."

I gripped my hands together. "You did not?"

"I've known you since your birth, and never once did I see affection between you and your sister. My strongest impression of you was when you were thirteen; Suyeon would not lend you her dress, and you cast a book at her, and the corner struck her so hard she bled. I was so stunned to see a girl strike her own sister over a trifle."

"Then I must try all the more," I whispered, my face warm, "to return her home, Uncle."

He twirled a game piece between his fingers, then bowed his head. "That is honorable of you. Admirable, even." He looked up. "You both have endured so much; I pray the heavens will be kind to you and grant you your wish . . ." He seemed lost in thought for a moment, then mumbled, "May your path to your sister be a smooth one." He moved to rise.

"Uncle," I hurried to say. He could not dismiss me yet. "I have a request—"

He settled back down on the floor mat, peering at me with dull eyes. "Do you know why your father was executed?"

The question had plagued me for two long years, but I hadn't expected him to bring it up so suddenly. "I think I do, but no one has confirmed my suspicion," I whispered. "Do you, Uncle?"

"Are you aware of the Literati Purge of 1504?"

"I am aware."

He explained it to me anyway. "The king executed the

government officials who had supported the execution of his mother. He even punished officials known simply to be present at the royal court at that time, for the crime of not preventing the actions of those who abused his mother." His gaze held me in an almost desperate, unwavering stare. "Your father," he said slowly, "was one of them; he had been visiting his cousin, a royal consort, and no one remembered he had been there. Not until someone divulged his secret to the king."

I lowered my gaze, picking at the skin around my nails. "I suspected this," I said, my voice shaking. "Father's execution occurred within the same month when other officials were being purged." Glancing up, my gaze rested on the janggi board.

"You look pale," Uncle murmured. "Shall I have a servant bring you a drink?"

"My parents are now gone, their lives taken by the king," I said, still staring at the game. Wonsik had told me the names of each piece. That one was a jol, and the duty of this foot soldier was to move forward or sideways to catch the opponent's piece. The jol was not permitted to move backward. I, too, forbade myself from retreating. "As you must imagine, Uncle," I proceeded, quietly, cautiously, "I cannot have the king take my sister, too."

"It will be impossible, getting her out of the palace."

"I have a plan."

"Do you?"

"I intend to bargain with the king," I said, and the plan seemed so ludicrous to me now in retrospect. "I will find the killer Nameless Flower and claim my sister as my reward."

He set down the game piece. "You? Find the killer? The king employs some of the brightest investigators in the kingdom and yet Nameless Flower continues to elude him."

"I need to try, and that is why I am here. Perhaps you could assist me with the investigation—"

"It is dangerous and futile. I think you should return home."

"And where is my home, Uncle?"

"You have a grandmother, do you not?"

"She only loves my sister. No one wants me. I belong nowhere." I swallowed hard, the words burning in my throat. "None of this would have happened, Uncle, if the king had not killed my mother and father. I would not be so miserable, if not for His Majesty."

"Hush, hush." He looked around. "What if the servants hear you?"

"Everyone thinks this! You think this, too, do you not, Uncle? The king *demoted* you."

His left eye twitched; his jaw locked. For a moment, he looked consumed—not in anger, but in remorse. "I spent my entire life to reach the second rank, yet how quickly I fell . . ." He looked up. "Hwang Boyeon, there is something I must tell you. I—" He shook his head, a look of fear now draining the color from his face. "You will not succeed in reuniting with your sister. Leave her, and start a new life. She would wish that."

The conversation was not going as I had planned. He was not expressing anger toward the king, as I had hoped.

I clenched my fingers tight, trying to hold down my impatience. But I could feel every shred of control unraveling, and as my stare bore into the janggi piece, my head filled with warnings.

*No, Iseul-ah.* Suyeon would say to me, if she were here. *Do not be reckless. Do not be foolish. You must bide your time.*

But time was not my friend. Every moment that passed, my sister was in the palace being eaten alive by a monster.

"Do you daydream like me, Uncle?" My voice cracked and trembled. "Do you?"

He frowned at me. "Are you crying?"

My hands shook as I reached out for the wooden janggi pieces. A set of red- and blue-engraved ones. Two opposing kings held court on either side, facing each other on the board.

"I daydream about what our life would have been like," I choked out, picking up the red king and placing him off the board, in the graveyard of the overtaken pieces, "if the king had not killed Mother and Father. Would my sister and I be back home, then? Would she have never known such misery? What would life be like"—I placed the blue king in the red territory—"if the king were no more?"

Uncle stared, then slowly his brows lowered. "Changing kings..." He studied me. "You switched the rulers..." Uncle pushed the janggi board aside, and his expression darkened. "You should be careful, Hwang Boyeon, about entertaining such thoughts."

"But I am safe to share it with you, am I not?"

He held my stare and whispered, "You are."

"Uncle... do you not think the heavens are displeased with the king?"

"I do," he whispered, then dropped his gaze. Twitches now

flickered all over his face. This man was nervous. "You ought to go now. Leave at once."

I stepped out of the mansion and stared blankly at Bugak Mountain looming over the capital. I closed my eyes a moment, letting out an unsteady sigh.

Uncle had said yes. He had said my treasonous thoughts were secure with him.

Did that also mean yes, he believed the king should be overthrown?

Shoulders tense, I staggered down the road. My mind lost in a daze, my knees wobbled and I held the wall.

I paused to collect myself, then continued down the street, wondering where Wonsik and the prince had gone. As I searched, my ears prickled as male voices whispered close behind, "I think it is her. The one you were looking for."

Before I could turn around, a hand grabbed my wrist. The brim of his hat was so lowered I could not recognize him at first.

"They are following you," came the prince's voice.

"Who is?"

"Do not turn," he ordered. "Act unaware."

We took a shortcut through an alley, then an explosion of noises greeted us as we entered the marketplace. We continued to weave through the crowd, our stride stiff and tense. And by the urgency of the prince's grip, I knew we were still being followed.

"Wonsik is going to distract them. On the count of three," he whispered, "we run from the officers. One . . ."

"Officers?" I whispered, confused.

"Two."

The prince's grip tightened around me as a commotion sounded from behind us, of pedestrians being shoved aside.

"*Three.*"

A loud crash splintered the air, and as we ran, I glanced behind. Dark feathers puffed into the air. Hens scattered out of their wooden cages, beating their wings against the crowd and a trio of flailing men in crimson uniforms. My blood froze over. Chehongsa officers. And one bore a gruesome scab across his face—the one I had struck with a sharp piece of wood.

With a fierce tug of my wrist, I was plunged into darkness, surrounded by mud walls. Clothes hanging on lines whipped my face. Another tug, and we were out in the open, and soon rushing through a shop, hanging silk swirling around us in a burst of colors. In no time at all, we were in another alley, but this time he was garbed in a different colored overcoat, and a jangot cloaked me. I touched the bright green silk. "When . . ." I heaved for air. "When did you take—"

His face taut, he pressed me up against the wall. "Why are they so intent on chasing *you*?"

"He's . . ." I pressed a hand to my thundering heart. "He's the one . . . I . . . injured."

"Gods. You attacked a chehongsa officer?" He glanced behind, then around. We were alone before a dead end. "I am curious to know who you were in your previous life, young mistress. Perhaps a member of a violent street gang?"

He was jesting, and the urgent grip on my wrist had loosened. Shaking myself free, I slumped against the wall, still trying to catch my breath. "We are safe now?"

"It would seem so." He joined me against the wall.

The sun had begun its descent, infusing the sky in rich shades of pink and purple. The moon hung above us, so faint as to appear translucent, and as I stared at its stillness, my own heart slackened and my breathing steadied.

"The curfew bell will ring soon," Daehyun said. "We will head north to my residence."

My eyes widened. "We shall?"

"Once the fortress gates lock for the night, there will be no way out. Wonsik will know to join us there."

A strange sensation gripped me, but before I could examine it, footsteps came down the alley. The prince and I exchanged glances. "Wonsik?" I mouthed, but then I heard a male voice inquire of someone, "Did you see a woman in a white dress come this way?" At once, I grabbed the prince's collar, pulling him so close every soft part of me pressed up against his solid chest. "We must pretend," I whispered, "that we are sweethearts—"

He reached for the jangot, tying two ribbons and thus securing the veil that covered me like a hooded cloak. Gentle hands then held my wrist. "Perhaps you might release my collar. You will appear less like you are strangling me."

"You jest? At this moment?" I whispered harshly, shooting a glance over his shoulder. No one yet. "They would take me to the king to be his plaything—does that amuse you?"

His expression darkened. "That will never happen."

"You have no weapon to fight them with."

"I have my title. And I will use it if I must."

My grip loosened, and I remembered to breathe again even as footsteps approached and a man appeared. At a glance, he was not a chehongsa officer, but clothed as a servant. Whoever he was, I could feel his stare boring into us. A minute passed, or perhaps ten; he was not leaving. My pulse quickened again. If Daehyun revealed his title, word might reach the king. The officers would claim they had attempted to seize me for His Majesty but had been obstructed by the prince—

Daehyun slid his hand beneath my veil; my mind went quiet. His hands brushed up the length of my arms, up the column of my throat, past the loosely tied veil ribbon, until he was cupping my face. He leaned in. His lashes dropped, his stare on my mouth, sending a jolt of tingles that curled my toes. For what seemed like a lifetime, we remained still, us two, inhaling and exhaling inches from each other.

"Where did she go?" the servant whispered, then hurried off.

We were safe now, and yet . . .

"Iseul . . ." His whisper grazed the curve of my ear. "Who gave you this sobriquet?"

"My parents," I murmured, my voice oddly raspy. "I . . . I reminded them of a dewdrop."

The sky had darkened, and he remained, broad-shouldered and tall, my chest pressing up against his with every nervous breath.

"You remind me more of a thorn."

I let out a scoff, then my pulse leaped as the great bell tolled.

"Curfew has begun," I pointed out.

"It has." The heat of his gaze remained on me, unwavering. His hands still cradled my cheeks.

"We should leave," I remarked.

Slowly, very slowly, his hands dropped away, and yet I could still feel the warmth of his touch, like the slightest burn.

"Come," he said, already walking ahead. His voice had regained its cool and imperious tone. "Keep close to me."

My heart beat at an odd, skipping pace as I followed him out of the alley and down the main road that was now illuminated by hanging lanterns. We turned on a narrow path that led into the Northern District, a cluster of neighboring mansions. It was silent here, as were we. We had not uttered a single word since leaving the market.

"The night has grown cool," I said conversationally. "It seems summer will come to an end soon."

He glanced at me, his expression shuttered, and we stood there in awkwardness for a few moments before continuing along the upward-sloping path. By the time we arrived before a mansion gate, the tension had grown so palpable that I could hardly breathe.

"Your home?" was all I managed to voice.

He nodded wordlessly, staring ahead.

My body grew warm as unwanted imaginings flickered at the back of my mind, but I chided myself at once. *Remember who he is, Hwang Iseul. He is the brother of the treacherous king. His family is the reason Mother and Father are dead.*

This reminder was enough to cool my blood, like a splash of freezing sea water. Finally, I felt calm enough to ask, "You said Wonsik will be joining us?"

Before he could reply, there came the steady clip-clop of hooves. We both turned to see the silhouette of a rider, and as he approached, a nearby lantern lifted the shadow and revealed his face.

"I had my manservant follow you, Niece." My uncle's eyes

narrowed as his stare rested on the prince. "A word with you, if I may, daegam."

Daehyun remained still for a moment longer, then called out his arrival. A servant rushed the doors open. "Show Official Choi to the Guest Hall," he ordered. "I will join him shortly."

When my uncle was led away, I stared wide-eyed at the prince. "What do we do?"

Daehyun let out a sigh, which almost sounded like defeat. "I will invite him to join our circle, and if he refuses, then your uncle must die."

My blood ran cold. "But it is my fault. I should have spoken more vaguely, but I was impatient—"

"It is not your fault. It is nearly impossible to speak vaguely of the matter."

"Please, do not harm him. He is family."

"If we let him live, you are in as much danger as I. And you are here to reunite with your sister—no matter the cost."

"I will *not* kill anyone."

"Iseul-ah, you have already committed to joining me; there is no turning back." He held my gaze, and sympathy warmed his eyes, if only for a moment. "The path we are to take will be littered with death. Freedom will always come at a cost."

# 22

# DAEHYUN

Daehyun held court in a shadowy chamber. Floor lanterns glowed, dancing on the shoulders of Official Choi, who sat kneeling in a posture of deference—a deference that was no more than courtesy.

"You know why I am here, daegam," Official Choi said, his stare fixated on the low-legged table between them. "It is you, is it not, who sent her my way?"

Daehyun remained silent, watching as Official Choi slipped out a small object and set it down. A wooden piece from a janggi board with a red engraving. It was the king, and His Majesty ruled the center of the table.

"Why would you plant such a dangerous notion in her?" Official Choi asked, his voice tense. "And do not claim to know nothing. I am quite sure of your influence behind her outrageous words."

Daehyun continued to examine the man before him. If the conversation spiraled in the wrong direction, he could easily bury it—along with the official's body. There was nothing to fear, yet dread coiled tight in his chest. He did not wish to harm the old man, if only because he was Iseul's uncle. She had lost more than enough family for one lifetime. "And I am sure that you will die if you do not join the cause."

The corner of Official Choi's lips twitched. "You are blackmailing me? That is unwise of you, I think."

"Not blackmail. A promise, for a rebellion *will* happen. It is inevitable, and when that day arrives, there is no guarantee you will not be mistaken for a king supporter and killed."

Official Choi remained still for a while, his lashes lowered, his cheeks pale. "I am curious . . . ," he said, flicking up the barest glance. "You say such a day is inevitable, daegam, yet for two years government officials have chosen self-preservation. They have chosen to wear those humiliating shineonpae plaques demanding their silence. Why would they change their minds now and risk their lives? I think even one's beliefs and values collapse under the weight of fear."

"The times are different now."

"Is it, indeed?"

"For two years the powerful and wealthy kept silent, for they felt removed from the king's treachery. But then the king decided to tax yangban aristocrats on their property and riches. Now, rumors are flooding in from all corners of the kingdom of disgruntled officials, as well as rumors of those planning coups. That is what has changed."

Official Choi remained tense, his expression guarded.

"It is clear that a catastrophe will happen soon," Daehyun pressed on. "The heavens have abandoned the king. It is time we abandon him, too."

"And whom would you place on the throne next?" he asked testily, suddenly taking on the air of a schoolmaster. "Yourself?"

"Grand Prince Jinseong. To place him on the throne would cause the least amount of contention, since he is already next in line."

Official Choi's gaze remained lowered, but this time Daehyun noticed something else. Under the man's lowered lashes, his pupils were shifting across the table as though he were carefully reading all the pieces on an invisible janggi board. *He is calculating the rewards and risks*, Daehyun realized. Official Choi was evaluating the possibility of a coup's victory, whether it was high enough to offset the dire consequence of failing.

"I have no army to mobilize," Daehyun said slowly, "but I know of one who does. Deputy Commander Park—your close friend, I believe."

"Park Won Jong?" Choi frowned. "He is the king's closest aide."

"More important, he is the brother of Lady Seungpyeong, who died by suicide."

"That is hearsay."

"She was impregnated by the king."

"I . . . I did hear rumors once, long ago. So she was indeed seduced—"

"Raped," Daehyun corrected.

Official Choi cleared his throat loudly, his discomfort clear. "It is all hearsay."

"You will find evidence of the crime in the Draft History. The chroniclers are officials with legal guarantees of independence. They have no reason to lie about the rape and pregnancy."

"Recorded for the ages . . ." Official Choi's voice trembled. "I had so wanted to believe it was mere gossip. Lady Seungpyeong was like a sister to me, too."

Daehyun balled his hand into a fist, to still the tremors. If he could not sway the man now, he feared he never would. "I wonder how your friend, Deputy Commander Park, would feel should he learn the truth behind his sister's death."

A storm gathered on Official Choi's brow. "Park Won Jong has deep connections to the military, but even if he raises up an army, it would still be greatly outnumbered. The king has over forty thousand soldiers in the capital alone."

"There is something else you ought to know," Daehyun said. "The king will be leaving for Kaesong City on the eighteenth of next month, and whenever His Majesty travels, he takes with him a large entourage. The capital will, therefore, be empty."

Official Choi shook his head. "The eighteenth is too soon. And even so, we would *still* be outnumbered." He heaved a deep sigh, and he set his hands on the ground, about to rise. "The probability of victory is too low. I cannot and will not take part in this—"

"Wait."

"Daegam, it is best that I leave—"

"Royal Guard Min Hyukjin once told me . . ." Daehyun gritted his teeth as grief unlocked itself. The shadow of Hyukjin's feet dangled in his mind. "He once told me about a conversation with the royal guards. He told me their hearts left the king long ago." His damned voice wavered, and he closed his eyes, waiting for indifference to seal every entryway into his heart.

"What are you telling me, daegam?"

Numbness returned at last, and his voice steadied. "The

king may have forty thousand soldiers. But a sword that has lost its heart for its master becomes but a useless object."

Official Choi blinked, blinked again, then an illuminating spark filled his eyes. "You are right," he whispered eagerly. "I have seen it each time I visited the palace. Hearts have indeed left the king." He reached out with a trembling hand and turned over the red king. "I will help you, daegam." Liquid fire pooled the gaze that met Daehyun's. "Let us move the heavens together."

# 23

# ISEUL

Official Choi's laughter echoed from deep within Guest Hall.

Heart pounding, I hurried up the short flight of steps onto the terrace. I whispered to Wonsik, who stood guarding the entrance, "Do you think he has agreed to join—?"

"Is that my niece?" came my uncle's voice from within, startling me. "Permit her to enter. I would like to speak to her, too."

Wonsik and I exchanged glances. He murmured, "Behave yourself," then slid open the double doors. At once, I walked in and was surprised to find Daehyun smiling in a quiet, subdued manner. It seemed he had received good news, yet I could not be too sure.

"Come in, my niece." Official Choi waved. "Have a seat."

I knelt next to him, my stare shifting from my uncle to the prince, then back to my uncle. Why did he look at me so? His eyes were twinkling with tears.

"Hwang Boyeon," my uncle said, his voice rasping. "Do you know that on your first birthday, relatives from afar arrived to crowd around your fortune-telling game of doljabi?"

I sat straighter, unsure of why he mentioned this.

"I watched as you were placed on a mat with several symbolic objects laid before you. You skipped the fruits, the sewing needle, and picked up a gold hairpin. It was your destiny to live a prosperous life. Perhaps that is your destiny yet."

"My destiny . . . ?"

"Should the heavens be moved, I swear to you—I swear upon my mother's grave—I will do all I can to have your father's honor restored. I will find you and your sister a worthy match in marriage." He clapped his hands, chuckling again. "For you, I have the perfect gentleman in mind, a young and handsome government official I know! What do you think?"

"That sounds . . . delightful," I said, my voice lackluster even to my own ears. I had dreamed of such a destiny, yet something about my uncle's tearful joy struck a discordant note in me. "I am so grateful, Uncle. I am so grateful that you care so much about our future—"

"It is my redemption," he whispered, as though to himself. "After all these years!"

The two gentlemen continued to converse, and when my uncle finally left, I barely noticed—and barely noticed Wonsik coming to my side, too preoccupied as I was turning over and over the one word my uncle had uttered: *redemption*. Redemption from what?

"You do not smile," came Daehyun's voice, almost brusquely. "Does it not delight you? You might marry a handsome young man."

Wonsik peered at me. "Marry?"

"That is of *no* importance at the moment," I said sourly, shrugging their attention away. "The discussion with my uncle, daegam. How did it fare?"

"It went well," Daehyun replied simply.

"And?" I waved my hand about. "Tell us *more.*"

"He has agreed to speak with Deputy Commander Park. And your uncle senses many more officials will be interested in joining, should the deputy agree to spearhead the Great Event."

"So that is good news," I said, feeling faint with relief.

"*Very* good news," Daehyun replied, then let out a humorless laugh. "If Min Hyukjin were alive, he would be weeping with joy."

"Daegam, I will do all I can to find Hyukjin's killer," Wonsik said solemnly.

"And you must find him soon," Daehyun said. "The Great Event is in danger of unraveling so long as Nameless Flower is on the loose. We know nothing of his plans—or whom he will strike next."

*To eradicate Nameless Flower*, I realized, *is to guard the coup leaders—and guard my path to Suyeon.*

"What is the next step with the investigation?" I asked Wonsik, determined to be of assistance. "Whom should we interview? What should we be looking for—?" I stopped, a thought brushing against the outer layer of my mind. It took a moment, then suddenly my mind flared with the memory. "Oh!"

Wonsik and Daehyun watched me, waiting.

"When we were at the site of Min Hyukjin's death, I remember seeing royal guards. One of them hid something under a bush. A small object. I could not make out what."

Wonsik shook his head. "The entire site was searched."

"And nothing suspicious was found? Then it can only mean

they overlooked a certain location. They did not search beneath that bush."

"Maybe we will go inspect, another day," Daehyun suggested.

"I trained Investigator Gu to sweep through crime scenes, to leave no rock unturned," Wonsik said. "But if you are certain—" He paused. "What did the royal guard look like?"

"Like a crow," I said. "Black-haired and greasy. I think his name was Gunwu."

The moment I uttered the name, both men grew tense. At length, Daehyun said quietly, "I think you ought to explain everything to her."

Wonsik remained silent, his gaze still lowered, and his hands gathered before him. "I told you, did I not, that I had a daughter?"

"Yes," I said, growing uneasy.

"I had a son, too. A child who walked out of my life forever." His broad shoulders rose and fell, an unsteady breath escaping him. "King Yeonsan stole my daughter, but she managed to escape. And so the king ordered my son, then a military student, to arrest his own sister or be killed. He chased after her, but before he could catch her, she . . . she killed herself."

My mind went blank, my body numb with cold. All I could do was listen, horrified.

"The guard you witnessed hiding the object, whatever it might have been . . . he is my son." A muscle worked in Wonsik's jaw. "And I have been suspicious of my son for some time now but found no clear evidence tying him to the case."

"What . . ." My voice failed. I tried again. "What led to your suspicion?"

Wonsik let out another wavering breath. His eyes grew red. "My son was the first at the site of the very first murder. During the police interrogation, he claimed he'd found the corpse with a bloody message written on the robe, but that when he returned with reinforcements, the message was gone."

I frowned. "How could it be gone?"

"Someone had smeared more blood over it. I believed it was the killer, that he'd returned to hide what he had written."

"Why would he do that?"

"Perhaps he had written it in the spur of the moment. Perhaps he did not think it through properly, as he clearly did with his following kills. Whatever the case, when my son was questioned about the message, he claimed that the writing had been illegible. But I know my son—I know when he lies; he always fiddles with his right ear. I confronted him many times, but it would always result in us arguing about his sister."

Wonsik ran both hands over his haggard face, and shaking his head, he murmured, "My daughter died when she was fourteen. My son's betrayal nearly killed me. The ones I loved most dragged me through the darkest of hours. Yet in the next life, I would still love them again."

Royal Guard Crow was Wonsik's son.

I tossed and turned, haunted by this revelation. The restlessness became intolerable when dawn arrived with the ringing of the great bell. Rising from the bed mat, I ventured out of the spare room and down the corridor, touching the lattice adorning the hanji screens. All the lanterns had been blown out in the mansion. The servants had retired to their quarters for the night and had not yet risen.

*How can it be?* I thought, striding fast, desperate to shake off the restlessness. *How can such a greasy, vile-looking man be Wonsik's son?*

I paused. The sliding doors to a room had not fully shut. The shadows within beckoned me, promising distraction from the heartache. Stepping in, I looked around; it took a moment for my eyes to adjust to the darkness, barely illuminated by the braziers glowing in the courtyard outside.

It was a library. Tall, open bookshelves lined the walls. Books were stacked, organized by subject: history, poetry, essays, Confucian classics, politics, military, and war. And where there were no shelves, lacquered furniture and precious vases were on display. I paused before one, catching sight of my reflection against the porcelain; my braid had loosened, and my jacket had come undone from the tossing and turning, leaving a collarbone bare. Reaching for the jacket ribbons, I retied it closed and meant to rebraid my hair when my attention drifted.

There was a desk at the head of the library. Covering the table were sheets of exquisite watercolor illustrations, of mountains and rivers, forests and waterfalls. The illustration at the very top had fresh paint, the wet ink gleaming along the mountain ridge. There was a tiny hut at the top of a slope, and upon closer inspection, I noticed two small figures within. Two young boys reading a book.

"Did you sleep at all?"

I whirled around at the male voice, my heart quickening at

the sight of Daehyun. He stood tall, his complexion as ethereal as moonlight, accentuated by dark and stern eyebrows. As he approached, I instinctively took a small step back, but my hip pressed up against the table. Warmth crept up to my cheeks as he joined my side and our gazes met. In that moment, an unsettling intimacy enveloped us in the pre-dawn hour. The world had fallen into a hushed stillness, closing around me and the prince with eyes that offered glimpses into his painted world—of private thoughts and memories and dreams.

"I'm—I'm sorry. I should not have looked."

Nonchalantly, he cleared away the illustrations. "It helps put my mind at ease. Painting." Then he stilled, glancing at where my sleeve grazed his. "Were you thinking of him, too?"

"Whom—?" It took a moment to remember. *Wonsik's son.* The heaviness returned.

"I wish my eyes were wrong," I whispered. "I wish I had not seen Crow hide anything."

"Crow?" He didn't bother to ask for clarification. "Wonsik may be kind and warm to you, but he is brutal, too. He will not hesitate to betray the one he loves if it means bringing justice."

I pressed my palm against my chest, trying to push away the ache. Somehow, I knew Wonsik would ruthlessly pursue the truth, no matter the cost. And I also knew the cost of it would crush him. I did not wish to think of it.

"Your paintings are lovely," I said, changing the subject. "Have you been to these places?"

"Most of them are conjured from my imagination," he said distantly. "From poems I have read."

"Then perhaps, when the Great Event is over, and when everything has settled, you could visit these places. Anywhere."

"I am just here until I am not. I do not think of one, five, or ten years in the future."

"But if you *had* to," I pressed, "where would you wish to venture first?"

He stood quiet for so long I thought our conversation had ended, then he finally spoke.

"Our kingdom is surrounded by the sea, yet I have never seen it . . . ," he confessed, grappling with every word. "I should like to stand before the very expanse that literati scholars have captured in their writings. To witness this vast eternity." There was a beat of silence, and then he murmured under his breath, "To believe that life is far greater than this one wretched moment."

"And you shall experience it, I'm sure."

He looked doubtful.

"We will all die in the end," I said lightly, "but most of us simply do not know when." I would likely never see him again after the Great Event, and this thought emboldened me to spare a few words of kindness. "Whether your days are many or few, daegam, I hope you will embrace each one. I hope you will go visit the sea, and perhaps find a good friend to accompany you. Perhaps Wonsik will go with you."

He let out a single, humorless laugh. "And endure lectures throughout the journey?"

I suppressed a smile.

For a few moments longer, we remained standing awkwardly, me staring at his hand on the desk, and him staring off in a different direction. In the enveloping darkness of the early morning, his proximity felt far too intimate. I nervously tucked a loose strand of hair behind my ear, then sought refuge before a vase, pretending to study it.

"We had several precious ones in my old home," I babbled, acutely aware of his lingering gaze. "I broke at least half of them."

"That does not come as a surprise to me."

"When should Wonsik and I leave?" I asked.

"We are leaving together in an hour or so."

"You too?"

"I am meeting with Yeongho."

I nodded. "Well then, I shall see you later—"

"Wait."

I stilled, my heartbeat quickening as I felt his presence close in behind me. His cool hand wrapped around my wrist, and a crisp sheet of paper slipped into my hand.

"A palace servant delivered it this morning."

I glanced down at it, and everything in me quieted. It was a letter. And even before opening it, my hands had begun to shake. It was as though I could feel her voice lifting from the pages.

*To my sister, Iseul—*

*I have thought little else but of your visit. Please forget my cold words to you. In truth, your presence brought me great comfort, and I hold on to the memory of you as a beacon of light in the darkness, a reminder of all that is still good and lovely in this kingdom. There is so much more I wish to say, but I dare not be seen writing to you.*

*Know that I am resilient, and I will remain so until we can reunite once more. I love you, little sister.*

*I will always love you.*

*—Hwang Suyeon*

My feet moved of their own accord. I wasn't sure what took hold of me, but I embraced him. His hands startled onto my shoulder, as though assuming I'd lunged in attack. I tightened my arms around him, and he remained deathly still. He may have stopped breathing, too. But moment by moment, his muscles eased, and his defensive grip slipped away, and he remained there, embraced by me.

"You did this for me . . . ?" I spoke to his silk robe. "Why?"

He stayed quiet for a long time, then he looked down at me, his brow furrowed with puzzlement. "I'm . . . not entirely sure."

His answer did not satisfy, but I was grateful nevertheless.

Releasing him, I rushed over to the screened window. I reread the letter by the braziers' glow, over and over, unable to look away from my sister's achingly familiar handwriting. Suyeon loved me. She loved me still. She would always love me. Joy burned in my heart, so searing that tears welled in my eyes.

"You are pleased?" Daehyun asked, joining me at the window.

"Thank you for this letter. Truly," I whispered, my voice straining under the emotion. "You are not so despicable after all."

"I suppose I was quite despicable when we first met," he murmured, cracking open the window. The smell of rain swept in. "Hopefully in the next lifetime, we will meet again," he said, glancing down at me. "And in kinder circumstances."

I gazed up and offered him a small smile. "I hope so, too."

# 24

# DAEHYUN

**By the time they arrived** at the inn, the rain was coming down in sheets, drenching them to the bone. Puddles had flooded their quarters, and so they sought shelter in the kitchen.

Yul burst in as quick as the rain shower, hurriedly preparing them bowls of tea. "Tell me everything later," she said, grabbing a tray of rain-catchers. "Wonsik-samchon! Help me bring some more of these! I can't have the rain ruin all the rooms!"

Daehyun crouched before the clay stove and took a gulp of the tea, but he could taste nothing. His mind was elsewhere—on Iseul, huddled next to him, her features softened by the warm furnace light. His attention kept straying to her as she tied her damp hair back, exposing the length of her graceful throat and the delicate freckle under her left ear. He dragged his gaze away. Iseul was becoming a distraction.

"You have done your part," he said coolly. "If you wish, you may return home. Should we succeed, I will bring your sister back to you."

She shot a bewildered glance at him. "You know I cannot."

"Do I?"

"My sister *needs* to know that I am here. I cannot leave until she is free."

His fingers dug into the bowl. He wanted her to *live*, not die—this girl who had embraced him, her warmth still lingering in his memory. A warmth that had seeped under his skin.

"The Great Event might kill us all," he warned quietly. "But if you leave now, your sister may still have a home to return to."

She shrugged. "If I perish, I perish."

He let out a sharp breath of irritation. "Could there be a woman less concerned about her life? Are you so unafraid of death that you would charge straight into it?"

"Of course I am afraid, but what I fear most is regret."

They sipped at their tea, watching the furnace glow bright orange.

"What—" Daehyun hesitated, but he wanted to know her. "What is it you might regret?"

She sipped again, but the cup was empty. "I am still surprised Suyeon chose to write to me at all . . . after what I did to her." Her hands tightened around the cup. "She is trapped in that godsforsaken palace, and I am the one who sent her there."

He was stunned that she thought so. "You did not send your sister into the palace."

"But it is my fault that she is there. We were never supposed to leave the hut, she and I," Iseul whispered. "Yet I ran out after quarreling with her, and she followed me—right into *his* monstrous clutches."

"It is not your fault that your sister was taken," he said matter-of-factly. "It is the king's fault for taking her."

"But if it weren't for me—"

"Sisters bicker and quarrel. They despise and love each other. You cannot stand each other, yet when the other bleeds, you bleed, too. That is family. So do not feel guilty for what occurred. None of it is your fault. Let the king, and the king alone, carry the weight of all his crimes. Do not fall victim to the king's games. He enjoys—nay, he *needs*—to set people against one another, to set people up against their own selves." He glanced down at his reflection in the tea. "He encourages the monstrosity in others to justify his own."

She hesitated, then lowered her lashes as she asked, "Is that what His Majesty did to you? Your brothers . . . ," she began, only to stop. "Never mind."

He stiffened, waiting to recoil, as he usually did. Yet at this moment, he realized he did not mind the idea of telling her his innermost thoughts.

"Do you know how Lady Jeong and her sons died?" he asked, slowly and quietly. "They were like family to me."

"It is public knowledge—your foster brothers beat their mother to death."

He did not flinch; he had repeated the scene in his mind too many times. "They did not know it was her, yet could not live with themselves. They wanted to save me, though. Lady Jeong had been as close to my birth mother as two loving sisters might be, and she'd always wanted her sons to protect me and treat me as family. And so they did."

She glanced up at him, and he avoided her gaze.

"It is also public knowledge," he said, "that I betrayed them. In a sense, I did. My brothers wanted to ensure that I gained the king's favor, so they ran away when soldiers came to arrest them."

"Did your brothers not carry out the king's order? Why would they be arrested?"

"Because the king knew my brothers might try to seek revenge. And so my brothers feigned their escape and ordered me to prove my loyalty to the king by offering to capture them, dead or alive. The king agreed to this; it is his favored tactic, sending family members to capture their own. And so I did. My brothers let themselves be captured, and they told me to survive and seek revenge on their behalf."

"Then that is not betrayal," she said, looking relieved. "You were simply honoring your brothers' wishes."

He fell quiet. The urge to shield his vulnerabilities was strong, but in the gentle glow of firelight, he found a rare sense of security. Or perhaps it was her presence. "I ought to have died trying to save my family."

She shook her head. "My mother was killed right before my eyes, and I ran away. I watched my father be executed while I hid on the hillside. What can we do but watch when the king shows his wrath? We are not generals with a thousand soldiers behind us. We were but mere children, you and I. We were wholly unprepared for such cruelty. And as you said to me, I say to you: Let the king, and the king alone, carry the weight of all his crimes."

A silence settled, at first tense, then one filled with a sense of understanding. As if a page had been turned.

"I did not think, when we first met," she whispered, "that you would one day offer me such wise counsel, and that you would ever think to confide in me." Then she looked up at him with a deep, appreciative look. He noticed for the first time that her eyes were honey brown.

"My heart feels a little lighter," she said softly, as a light smile flit across her lips.

He felt undone.

Before their conversation could continue, Wonsik rushed in, rain dripping off the brim of his straw hat. "A servant came from Official Choi's household. It is an urgent letter arrived for you, daegam."

Daehyun took a moment to read it and whispered, "Your uncle received word from Deputy Commander Park. Everyone is to gather at the House of Bright Flowers in one week's time."

"I wonder whom he is referring to by *everyone*," Iseul murmured, glancing out the entrance. "Do you think my uncle has recruited other officials?"

Daehyun stared at the handwriting. For all his preparation, he had not truly imagined what it would be like to join in a real coup. Not the hypothetical one he and Hyukjin had discussed and theorized over for months.

Iseul abruptly reached for her neck. "I think you need this more than me. Here." She untied a necklace holding a double ring—a garakji, likely her mother's. "Consider this a talisman of sorts that will protect you."

Hesitating, he finally accepted the trinket. "You are superstitious."

"One must believe in something. And when the Great Event is over, and the kingdom rises anew, you must return and give that ring back to me. You had better, or I truly shall haunt you for all of eternity."

# 25

# ISEUL

"You are certain your uncle invited you?"

"Yes," I lied. "He sent me a message saying so."

Wonsik cast me a wary glance, then continued on.

I hurried after him, the swordsman of enormous stature, yet his expression ever reminded me of a mother hen. He had adopted into his circle of care all these feral children, but today it was not myself or Daehyun or Yul he was worrying about. It was his own son. For the past week, he had tailed Gunwu—or as I knew him better, Royal Guard Crow—and I had accompanied him, on occasion. Each time I had followed, I had watched Crow's black hair appear greasier, his face paler, as though something on his conscience drained him of blood. We had observed him drag his feet out of his home in the mornings, had watched as he stood lifelessly guarding the palace gate. Once, at night, he had even traveled all the way to the Red Lantern Inn, lingering outside the yard for a couple of hours.

"Yul told me a few days ago," Wonsik murmured, "that her customers have been complaining of a dark figure stalking them, lurking about the inn. I wonder if it is him . . ."

I still could not wrap my mind around how different the son could be from his own father...

"A week has passed," I said, choosing to voice other thoughts. "Nothing has occurred. What if we arrive only to find the room empty? What if no government official wishes to take part?"

"We will have to see," Wonsik replied, his voice low. "Your uncle and the prince agreed that no correspondence should be exchanged in the meanwhile lest the king take notice, so I am unsure of how things are progressing. We will find out at the House."

"And why, precisely, are the men gathering at an entertainment house? There are so many eyes."

"It is the one place government officials can meet in groups and not garner any suspicion. For what else do men do here but come for drinks and entertainment?"

"What else indeed," I mumbled.

As we continued along the path toward the House of Bright Flowers, we took a long detour and paused before a drama being performed.

"Only a quick glimpse," Wonsik said, "and then we must leave."

The players had to shout through the masks to drown out the noise of the bonfire lighting the scene. The performance told the story of a king from a faraway land who had stolen his uncle's wife—clearly a reference to King Yeonsan and Lady Seungpyeong.

"This is the play Prince Daehyun commissioned?" I whispered to Wonsik.

"It is. Yeongho and his troupe have been performing it in different villages since yesterday, and it is already causing quite the stir." He glanced at me. "Come, we must not be late."

"I hope the play ignites hearts. I truly hope the populace will stand up to *him*." My voice wavered with a mix of hope and agitation as we entered the capital. "Perhaps I will have my old life back, if all goes well. Perhaps I will marry the son of a government official, after all. That is what Father always wanted of me."

After a prolonged silence, when I assumed our conversation was over, Wonsik suddenly asked, "And do you wish to be arranged?"

"Arranged?"

"In marriage."

"What young person wishes it? But it is of utmost importance that I align myself with a powerful family," I said, though I felt strangely indifferent to the notion. "It is of utmost importance and yet . . ." I shook my head.

"Is it so important to you? Why not marry someone you love?"

I crinkled my nose as I looked up at him. "You are far too sentimental, ajusshi."

He shrugged a large shoulder. "When I was your age, I was a rock. I never shed a tear."

"You have indeed changed."

"I became—as Yul likes to call me—an old fart." He spoke with a dignified grimness. "I became old, and I realized power cannot protect us from the greed and wrath of others—and it will not protect us from ourselves. Marry for power, and it will only entangle you deeper in the web of treachery. You will be far happier if you choose the simple life among the mountains and waters. Peace of mind is the most precious gift. And speaking of mountains and water . . ." He glanced around. "When this is all over, we shall continue our investigation in Jangheung County."

"We are leaving the capital?"

"Not yet. The Great Event might occur too soon for me to find the killer in time. And, should we be alive at the end of it, a trip there might illuminate the case for us. Until then, we must take caution—whom we trust in particular."

His lecture trailed off as we arrived before the House of Bright Flowers, an impressive establishment standing at the foot of a mountain. Hanging lanterns glowed like fallen stars, spilling golden light onto crowds of men in luxurious robes and gisaengs in dresses befitting celestial maidens.

A familiar figure shouldered his way through the crowd, halting before us. My heart turned to ice. It was the investigator who served in the State Tribunal—the bureau that had carried out my parents' executions.

"Sir," Investigator Gu said, but his stare was on me. "What brings you here?"

"My eyes still serve me well. I recognized you at once from afar, Gu Jinyoung. We are here following Nameless Flower's trail," Wonsik lied.

"Why, precisely, are you chasing this killer?"

"I was loyal to the king two years ago, and I am loyal yet," Wonsik continued to lie. "I will not stand for a killer who slanders the king."

A look of disbelief weighed the investigator's brows.

"Is that what brings you here, too?" Wonsik asked.

"You wish to see whether the gisaengs know anything about Young Master Baek's death? The young master did frequent this house, but I questioned the gisaengs ages ago. They know nothing."

"I would like to question them for myself—"

"As I said to you yesterday, you waste your time, sir."

*Yesterday*? I glanced at Wonsik. There was a moment in the evening when he had left the inn without telling anyone. Without telling me . . .

"But," the inspector continued, "what concern is it of mine how you conduct your investigations . . . or with whom you choose to investigate?" He cast one last look at me, then strode away. I watched him disappear down the shadowy road.

"That is Investigator Gu of the State Tribunal," Wonsik explained. "You may have seen him at the scene of Hyukjin's death."

"I do recall him," I whispered, and realized my voice was shaking. How easily I could end up arrested, sent into exile, if a man like Investigator Gu realized who I was. I took in a deep, calming breath. "What kind of man was he, the investigator?"

"I was his mentor once." Wonsik urged me forward. "Over the years, he proved himself to be a good and just investigator when he believed the king was benevolent. But when the king became a tyrant, he, too, became corrupt. He wants good for the people but is more interested in protecting his honor and his reputation and his family. Hence why he continues to punish traitors when I know, deep inside, he is against many of the king's policies."

*Should I tell him?* Hesitation writhed in me, then I finally confessed. "Do you know why I am alone? Why I have been without parents for two years?"

Wonsik glanced at me. "I imagine some horrible tragedy befell you and your family. I imagine it has something to do with the purge of 1504."

"How do you know that?" I whispered.

"We all know what occurred in 1504. And for a young woman like yourself, from a powerful family, to have fallen so low—it could only be the king's doing."

I gritted my teeth. "It was all the king's doing."

He placed a gentle hand on my shoulder. "Iseul-ah, we will discuss this at length afterward, when there is no risk of being overheard."

I nodded, my heart melting under his gaze, so warm and full of compassion. "We should hurry, ajusshi," I said, trying to compose myself. "We are already late."

We made our way into the establishment, and a servant led us down the crowded hall, where the shadows were so deep I could not make out any faces. One gentleman stumbled my way, and I ducked to avoid his liquor bottle; I quickly stepped aside to avoid another drunkard, only to brush up against someone behind me. I whirled around and found myself wrapped in the fragrance of musk and smoked incense.

"You ought to have more care, my lady."

I looked up at the prince. Lantern light warmed his eyes and softened the sharp angles of his face. I had not seen him in seven days.

"I knew you would come," he said.

I held his unwavering gaze. "How so, daegam?"

"Because your uncle told you not to." A muscle worked in his cheek as if he were fighting a smile. "When have you ever followed orders, my lady?"

I gave his chest a gentle shove, then stepped around him. "You seem to be in good spirits."

"Of course. Things are coming together," he said.

We proceeded down the hall, and a beautiful gisaeng paused to greet the prince. They both exchanged long, knowing stares, and I felt a painful knot form deep within my chest.

"She is his informant, and a friend of Yul's," Wonsik whispered to me, as though reading me. "Nothing more."

I tried to hide my relief with a scoff, and there was no time to examine my feelings as we had arrived at the farthest end of the house. A pair of fierce manservants guarded the latticed doors.

"Patrol the hall for suspicious characters," Daehyun said to Wonsik as the double doors slid open for us. "Alert me at once if you find any."

"I shall, daegam."

I followed the prince in, and my pulse leaped to see a crowded room. A dozen or so important-looking men sat before a long table, staring at us, among whom was my uncle; he looked mortified by the sight of me. He cleared his throat, then mumbled, "That is my niece. The one I told you all about, gentlemen."

Murmurs rose around me, and a few nodded, as though in approval.

My pulse quickened as I sat before the table, next to the prince. I hadn't thought I would care so much about matters of the kingdom, but perhaps I did, and here I was in the presence of men who could move the heavens and fight for the people. For those like my sister.

Daehyun leaned in to whisper, "That is Official Shin Yun Mu. And to his side, Lord Seong Hui Ahn, Ryu Sun-jeong..." He went on, listing names, but I could not tell who was who. They all looked the same: at least three times older than me and a thousand times more powerful.

"I am glad we have all met today." The gentleman who spoke sat at the head of the table. His beard was thick and black, his brows dark and heavy. According to the prince, it was Deputy Commander Park, the one most capable of overthrowing the king. "We are friends but were too cautious to express our innermost thoughts that have plagued us day and night. It is time to end this reign of treachery and place the king's successor on the throne—the benevolent Grand Prince Jinseong."

Another gentleman spoke, and his voice wavered with emotion. "I, too, have thought of little else. I believe this coup will succeed because of you, Deputy Commander. I told Official Choi that I would join only once he confirmed your stance. I am relieved to see you here."

"With the deputy commander spearheading this great cause, we will surely succeed," my uncle said. "The central government is now filled with resentful officials ready to betray, and it is clear that a catastrophe will happen soon. We must, therefore, move quickly before others revolt, for if we are not first, we might be swept away as suspected sympathizers of the king."

The officials sat straighter, and a murmur of voices coalesced in agreement.

"Since we have lived our whole lives in loyalty," Deputy

Commander Park continued, "we ought to give our lives for our country. We must ensure that we never repeat this history of placing a tyrant on the throne and strive together to distribute the power so not one of us will be stronger than all, which—as we have seen—results in this devastation."

I gripped my skirt tight, feeling the beaming rays of hope. A bright future seemed within our reach.

"And the king's courtesans?" The question slipped out of me. All eyes turned. "What will become of them?" I clarified. "Will they be returned to their homes, their families?"

Uncle cleared his throat, shifting uncomfortably. "A young lady ought not to speak when the elders are speaking."

The deputy commander raised his hand. "Let me give her an answer. I promise you that—"

The double doors slid open, and a new gentleman walked in. "Excuse me for my tardiness," came his voice, quiet and scratchy.

"Ah, Official Wu. Here at last. Come, sit down."

The man's face took form as he stepped into the glow of the floor lanterns, and at once, all the sounds and sensations faded into the background, as if it were only he and I who occupied the space. He was tall and remarkably thin, with hollow cheeks, very long fingers that rose to greet officials, and skin as pale as white worms. I felt ill.

"Maggot."

"Who?" the prince whispered.

Maggot stared back at me.

The deputy commander's voice seemed to blur, dreamlike, weaving in and out of my hearing. "My relative, General Park, is stationed at a military camp in Suwon. I visited him a few days ago . . . We have carefully evaluated our chances of success . . . Of utmost importance is seizing the opportunity . . . One has arrived."

His voice garbled on as cold sweat drenched my face. Each time I glanced at Maggot, I caught him staring at me, and I could not erase from my mind the repulsive manner in which he had spoken to my sister.

Unable to bear his presence a moment longer, I slipped away from the prince's side and hurried out.

# 26

# DAEHYUN

**Among the rumble of outraged** officials, a fist slammed the table. "You mean to say—" The official was visibly shaken. "You wish to plan the coup for *one week* from today?!"

Deputy Commander Park nodded. "We attack on the eighteenth day of the ninth lunar month."

"I am confused," another official asked. "Why the eighteenth?"

"The king," Daehyun interjected grimly, "will be leaving the capital for Kaesong on that very day. It is a golden opportunity; an opportunity, if not seized, that may never present itself again."

More grumbles resounded.

"Listen. Look here, gentlemen," the deputy commander ordered. "The king has over eighty thousand soldiers, but spread out—several thousand are stationed in military camps along the border. So we need to concern ourselves with only the forty thousand or so soldiers still in the capital."

"Do you think forty thousand is nothing?" an official cried, his jowls trembling. "And how many are *we*?"

"When the king leaves for Kaesong, he will take up to ten

thousand military officers and foot soldiers. The capital will be weaker, too, with no king to guard."

One by one the officials shook their heads. "A week is not enough."

"*Ui-hwa-do hwe-gun.*"

Silence fell as the collective memory stirred.

"*Ui-hwa-do hwe-gun,*" Daehyun repeated. "*Turning back the army from Wihwa Island.* In 1388, General Yi Seong-gye of the Goryeo dynasty was ordered to march north with his army and invade the Liaodong Peninsula, despite his great reluctance to do so. But when he saw that his troops were outnumbered, he decided to turn back to Kaesong and trigger a coup. Sometimes, as it was with Yi Seong-gye, a coup is an instinctual decision—plan any longer, and who knows if we will live to see it done. The king's wrath is as fickle as the wind."

"What he says is true," a man murmured. He looked at Deputy Commander Park. "Even the king's most favored, I hear, have recently begun to lose his trust."

Another official sighed. "You may sway me yet if you can answer me this: How do we build an army within a week? Write out appeals and send it to military camps, begging them to raise up soldiers for us? What if this letter falls into the wrong hands?"

"The central five military camps hold troops with superior capabilities, deployed to protect the coast from invaders," the deputy commander replied. "We may not have enough time to build a large army, but we may use the resources already in our possession. One week is enough to mobilize up to ten thousand soldiers."

"From where?"

"Jang Jeong, the former governor of Suwon, will take on the task of mobilizing their four thousand men, together with Suwon Military Official Park Yeong Mun. And you, General"— Deputy Commander Park gazed across the table at a stern middle-aged man, his face tanned and weather-beaten—"the king sent you to serve at the Royal Stable, where at least five thousand soldiers are sent to daily work. And there are several other generals there, too. If you could recruit them, we could easily build a small but significant force."

Faces remained pale, drained of blood. Frightened, wary officials. One finally seemed to utter the sentiment prevalent in this room. "We should only attempt a coup if our chances of victory are high enough to outweigh the serious risk of failure . . . ," he said. "What is the plan?"

# 27

# ISEUL

The sweet fragrance of gisaengs and their laughter crowded around me as I stepped out of the House. Tucking myself in the far shadow of the eaves, I watched the female entertainers welcome their guests.

"You look nothing like your sister."

I flinched around and saw Maggot.

"I heard you were Official Choi's niece," he continued. "Suyeon's sister."

I glared at him. "Why are you here?"

"Why should I not be here?"

"You care *nothing* for the people, I imagine."

The corner of his lips twitched. "You seem to know much about me, young girl, when we have never met before. Or have we?"

"We met once," I said, my voice laced with disdain. "In my nightmares."

He barked out a humorless laugh. "You are an odd one, and you are correct. I care *nothing* for people." He prowled over to my side, peering down at me. "But do you think the men inside care at all, either?"

My brow furrowed. "Of course they do!"

His face puckered into a look of mock sympathy. "Child, you believe in what the deputy commander says? You believe he cares about things such as"—he waved his hand with a flourish—"*justice?*"

"Yes, and if not for the people, then for his sister—"

"His sister, his sister, his sister." Maggot clucked his tongue. "That old hag. The deputy's grief is but a mere display. He needed a reason to justify the—" He glanced around. They were standing at the edge of the House's terrace, far from the crowd, but nevertheless he encrypted his words. "—the *Great Event* and emphasize *his* depravity and wonton cruelty. The true motive is that the deputy commander, along with his three closest friends, all fear they will be next to endure *his* wrath. And the other men? It is because they resent *him* for taxing them. And others yet, like myself? When one horse is about to charge off a cliff, it is the natural course of action, is it not, to switch horses? Besides, the leaders promised to reward us grandly. Do you not wish to know what I asked for?"

After a pause, he grinned as he said, "I asked for your sister."

A coldness crept into my chest, but I beat the fear aside. "The deputy commander promised to *free* the girls."

"Did he? That is not what he told me. He promised to return your sister to the family, but I am in the midst of negotiating. You see, I am Wu Sayong, a senior first-ranking official in charge of the Hanseongbu. Do you even know what that is? It is the bureau that oversees the management of the entire capital. And I hold great influence over many government officials . . .

The leaders *need* me, and they will bribe me with whatever I ask for—"

I had heard enough. "My *uncle* would never give her up to you."

"Your uncle . . . you mean the one who betrayed your parents?"

I stood frozen, shocked speechless. "What do you mean?" I choked out.

"Everyone in court knows. He made an entire spectacle, prostrating himself before the throne, when the king demoted him from the senior second rank to the junior ninth rank. He could not stand the humiliation and blurted out that his sister's husband had been present in the palace when Deposed Queen Yun was executed. That his in-law had begged him to tell no one, and that only the guilty would bury secrets for two entire decades. The king promised to promote Official Choi after this demonstration of loyalty, but never did. So you see, your uncle betrayed your family once for a promotion, and he will betray it again."

My mind grew dark, and I felt utterly alone.

"I do not believe you," I said, trying to convince myself. "I do not believe a word you say."

I hurried down the terrace, cutting through the crowd, and I did not stop running until I was gasping for air. I had, at some point, left the capital and was now on an isolated road, stained red in the light of the dying sun.

Despite my exhaustion, I quickened my steps, desperate to speak with Yul, to know her thoughts. Was Maggot telling the truth, or was he simply toying with me? The inn was only a half

216 | JUNE HUR

hour's walk away, on the other side of the forest. Leaves rustled above me as I entered the woodland, and memories whispered in my head—of Uncle's frequent visits, of his close friendship with Father, of their solemn conversations muffled behind screened doors. As I tread down the path winding through the forest, another memory caught up with me.

Uncle's utter joy over the prospects of my bright future. And his words, odd to me then, now curdled my blood upon recollection.

*It is my redemption*, he had said. *After all these years!*

I fell still, my broken past piecing itself together. Not strangers, not acquaintances, but *family* had betrayed my parents. Uncle had thrown wide the gates to our home, beckoning the thieves to enter—to steal, kill, and destroy.

Strength quickly drained from my legs. I collapsed onto my hands and knees. My parents had died for one man's greed. They had died for *nothing*.

It took a long moment for the sound to register, of hooves clip-clopping behind me. Five riders were approaching. Quickly wiping my eyes, I rose to my feet and withdrew my paedo from its ornamental sheath. I gripped the blade's handle tight, wishing I could plunge it into Uncle's heart.

"Good afternoon, young woman," came a silken, smooth voice.

Dread sharpened in my chest. I had expected them to ride by me. The knife I had only withdrawn out of precaution. Slowly, I looked up.

"I am Senior Officer Yoon," he drawled, a man who grinned

wide, revealing pearly white teeth. A man with an inflamed scab that rippled across his cheek.

I stumbled back, recognition settling cold in my chest.

"I believe we have had the pleasure of meeting before." His hand shot into the air, and in a victorious voice, he yelled, "Tie her up, men!"

"Do not *dare*." I gripped my small knife tighter, its blade hidden behind the fold of my skirt. I glared up at the men before me. How like my uncle they were, those who would descend into depravity to please their king. "You will *not* touch me!" I screamed.

"Aigoo." Scabbed Cheek glanced at his fellow officers. "We have caught ourselves a feisty little she-cat. Arrest her, but do not ruin her face or mar any visible part of her. We have to deliver the goods undamaged."

An officer dismounted and prowled over with a rope. My knife-holding hand sprung forward, and a startled yelp pierced the air as he stumbled back, grabbing the side of his arm.

"The damned wench cut me!"

"Stay away!" I warned. "Come any closer, and I shall kill you! All of you!"

Scabbed Cheek smirked as he slid off his saddle, and with a quick motion of his hand, his sword's hilt flashed my way. Pain exploded in my stomach. I was on the ground, gasping for air, the knife flown from my hand. I forced myself to push past the searing tenderness to search for it. My hand, instead, closed around a sharp rock.

This time, as the officers closed around me, I feigned

compliance. I let them bind me up with a rope, and I let them drag me along, the bloodred sky vanishing as we ventured deeper into the forest. As they focused ahead, I tested my wrists, tied with a rope that was strung to the saddle of a horse. I tripped, half dragged along the uneven trails, and each time I made sure to hold the rock tight.

"Unfortunate," Scabbed Cheek drawled, looking over his shoulder, "that you thought to be *brave*. You tried to save that girl. But you see, I caught her in the end. Now you will join her in the palace where you belong."

"It seems you are mistaken." I slid a note of fear into my voice. "You have mistaken me for someone else—"

"My dear, my dear," he said too sweetly, "how could I forget a face like yours? I have dreamed too often of you." Venom twisted his smile. "I have dreamed of watching you beg for death. You certainly will when I throw you into the king's arms. For alas, his embrace will crush you."

Angling the rock, I began to run its sharp edge against the rope, pausing whenever Scabbed Cheek looked my way. I cut away both rope and flesh. Blood dribbled down my wrist, but the shadows concealed the stain.

"Where are we going?" I demanded, trying to pin his attention on the conversation and nothing else.

"To register you as the king's whore."

I was too focused on my knife to feel much fear. My mind knew only to move on to the next question, to never allow him a moment to examine me too long. "How did you find me?"

"I have been looking for you for quite some time, and as

luck would have it, one of my men happened to catch sight of you at the House of Bright Flowers." Scabbed Cheek rubbed his hand against his knee. "Beautiful young women are difficult to find these days, like pearls in the dark sea. So how glad I am that our paths crossed. The king might finally promote me once I gift you to him."

His lecherous answer dizzied me. Panic grabbed onto my thoughts, threatening to pull me under. But reason wrestled me free. *Focus on the present.* I had finally cut the rope down to a few threads.

Scabbed Cheek frowned. "What are you doing—"

Wrenching my wrists free, I bolted off the trail into the dense shadows of trees, the ground too dark for me to see my way. My feet slipped, and the earth abruptly dropped away. My vision hurtled around; earth sky trees earth sky trees. Finally smashing to a stop, I lay there for a moment, the breath knocked from my lungs. But then I was on my feet again, rushing through the dizzying whirl of shadows, running into trees, tripping over roots. Hooves were charging toward me.

Closer.

Then closer.

A hand snatched me, pulling me behind a tree just as the riders galloped by.

Daehyun.

A wave of relief crashed through me, so violent that I had to steady myself against him. As I pressed closer, his heart beat rapidly against my back. It was then that I noticed a small knife in his grip—the one I had dropped.

Another rider approached, slowly, with a torch raised.

"Can you run?" Daehyun whispered.

"Yes."

He took my hand, and we moved quietly, squeezing ourselves through the trees, pushing past tangles of branches. When we emerged onto a small clearing, I finally became aware of the pain pulsing along my left arm, blazing along my left rib, and with every step I took, my bones cried out in protest. But the soreness numbed again as panic froze over. Movement rustled beyond the thicket, and four officers rode out.

"Found you." Scabbed Cheek grinned, his stare moving to Daehyun, who tugged me behind him. "And who is that? Your lover—?"

"Hold," an officer whispered. "Is th-that not Prince Daehyun? The king's favorite brother."

A wave of hesitation rippled among the riders, and when one dismounted to bow in deference, the rest followed suit, including Scabbed Cheek.

"I beg your pardon, daegam," he called out through clenched teeth. "But you must release this girl into our custody. She belongs to the king."

With deadly calm, Daehyun replied, "She belongs to no one."

"But you are Prince Daehyun," Scabbed Cheek declared, "your loyalty is to the king, and she is—"

Torchlight beamed through distant trees. The earth trembled under the tramping of hooves. Dread coiled even tighter within me.

"Reinforcements have arrived. I thought we would need

them when I heard the girl was with that infamous former investigator, Wonsik." No longer bowing, Scabbed Cheek straightened himself, snatching up his bow and arrow. "When I am asked why Prince Daehyun is dead, I shall tell the king that we killed the prince, thinking him a commoner, for he is dressed as one."

*We cannot escape*, I thought, as Daehyun's grip on my hand tightened. He whispered something, but his voice was drowned out by the noise in my head. I knew how this encounter would end.

The prince would be slain.

And whether I ran or remained, I would ultimately be dragged into the palace, ensnared and consumed.

My sister would not survive this. The sight of her little sister, murdered before her eyes, would truly kill her.

Suddenly Scabbed Cheek flinched, lowering his weapon and glancing behind him.

A tall, burly man stood with a chehongsa officer at knifepoint. "Who among you is the strongest?" he taunted.

The voice was familiar.

"Ajusshi," I choked out.

In one swift motion, Wonsik slashed the officer's throat. Blood streaked across his straw hat and cloak. "Come fight me, and I shall chew you three alive."

Scabbed Cheek cursed, launching arrows that thwacked into Wonsik's shield—the dead man. Another arrow was released. Wonsik nearly buckled as one struck his leg, and the two other officers charged toward him. Breaking off the shaft, Wonsik lunged into the melee, parrying against the flash of blades one moment, and the next, leaping off the side of a tree and in a great robe-fluttering whirl, slashing his attacker, who toppled off his horse.

Wonsik then staggered into position, angling his sword as the next officer charged at him. He waited, only to dash away just as the officer swung his sword, the blade caught in the leafy branches.

Scabbed Cheek knocked another arrow; Wonsik's back was to him.

"Stay here," Daehyun whispered to me. He raced through the shadows, his steps quiet for forty paces or so. He snatched the sword off a dead officer, and just as Scabbed Cheek aimed his shot, Daehyun rushed forward. Steel flashed, and Scabbed Cheek was tossed off his horse, the creature's front hooves beating the air.

All the officers were down, motionless except for Scabbed Cheek, who writhed in pain, his leg twisted into a gruesome angle, a bone erupting outward.

"He needs to die," I said, running forward. "He knows the prince was here with me."

As Wonsik raised his sword, Daehyun turned me aside. A guttural cry pierced the night, then in the ensuing silence, I found myself watching the torchlight, now near enough to illuminate the silhouettes of the chehongsa officers.

"You both need to run," Wonsik said, wiping the blood off his sword. "I will buy time for you both."

His words stabbed me. "Come with us!" I cried.

"Do not let me slow you down."

It was then that I noticed Wonsik's ghastly pale face, the slight tremor to his frame. The broken shaft was lodged deep into his leg, and the side of his cheollik was drenched in blood.

Daehyun gripped his blade tighter. "I shall fight with you."

I picked up a sword, dragging it up with two hands. "I shall remain, too."

"Do not be fools; there is no time for this," Wonsik said, glancing over his shoulder at the approaching storm of men. "Iseul, you have a sister waiting for you. Prince Daehyun, do not waver from the path that you are on. Move the heavens."

"Iseul, run," Daehyun growled. "I will stay—"

"Do not nullify the years I spent guarding your life, daegam! Do not make me break my promise to your mother, that I would watch over you until my very last breath," his voice rasped. And when Daehyun and I still hesitated, Wonsik knocked an arrow to the bow and aimed it at the ground before us.

"Go!" he ordered with such harshness that tears sprung to my eyes. His own eyes turned red as well. "Go. And please . . . do not look back."

Everything was a blur.

Of trees and bursts of open sky. Of an ankle-deep stream that dragged at my skirt, and jagged rocks that sliced at my skin. Of Prince Daehyun's hand locked around mine, our fingers intertwined. And somehow, when I gasped to catch my breath, we were at the bottom of a slope, backs smashed up against roots and soil, his hand over my mouth as hooves trotted on the ground above, torchlight blazing about in their search.

"There!" a male voice shot out. "A strip of fabric. It belongs to the girl's skirt. She went eastward!"

Panic thrummed, but Daehyun held me still, and there was

a calmness to him that told me the discovery came as no shock to him. He must have planted the fabric there.

As the last of the horses trotted off, we did not move. We dared not speak. One wrong decision, and the horde of soldiers would come rushing back. I could still hear them off in the distance, voices calling out to one another.

Daehyun finally lowered his hand from my face and tapped me, pointing ahead at a pile of large granite rocks. Our footsteps light, we hurried over and folded ourselves into the tight yet deep crevasse. There was not space enough for two, so we became one. His arms melded around my back, and I buried my cheek against his torso, our hearts thundering—agonizing—against each other.

The hours that passed felt both short and eternal. The remaining sunlight vanished off the treetops, and as the night deepened, stars powdered the sky. In the silence that followed, broken by the shuffling and flapping of night critters, my mind sank into a cold darkness. My hands began shaking, then my entire body, and my teeth would not cease their chattering.

*He is still alive*, I told myself. *He is waiting for us in the clearing.*

He would be there with his straw hat and cloak, his sword strapped to his back. He would be nursing his bloody knuckles, like the first time I met him. He would look up, with the kind eyes of a good friend. *Nangja*, he would call out, perhaps, *it is all over. Why were you so afraid?*

*He is still alive.* I clenched my jaw. *He is still alive.*

But as time passed, a question crept into my heart, spreading frost throughout me. *What if he is not?*

I shook my head. Surely the heavens would not be so cruel? He had remained kindhearted in a world that was a fist. He had extended friendship to me when he could have left me to die, killed by my own stupidity. He was a father who'd choose to love his son again in the afterlife, the son who had remorselessly walked out of his life. Wonsik was a lantern in this darkened world.

*Please do not blow out his light*, I directed my desperate thoughts to the heavens. *Please, please, please, I beg of you. Please let him live. Please reach down and embrace him, shield him from the raining of swords and arrows. Please protect the kindhearted. Please protect my friend.*

The sky lightened into a miserable blue-gray. Shadows sank, and first light doused the treetops. My head swayed from the weight of a thousand whispered prayers, choking my thoughts like the smoke rising from incense sticks. It took a moment for me to peer through the haze in my mind and to realize that I had not seen a single soldier since the evening.

"Let's go back," Daehyun said stiffly, his eyes burning with grief. "There is enough light to travel now."

"I share your heart," I managed to whisper.

We hurried back across the river, through the forest. We pushed past the tangle of trees, and branch by branch, I caught glimpses of the clearing. Motionless bodies of chehongsa officers were strewn about. At the center of the carnage, a broad-shouldered man lay curled like a child. *I am tired*, his voice laced with the wind. *I need to rest.*

I staggered forward, and as I stared at Wonsik, I remembered.

I remembered the way he would glance over his shoulder,

looking at me as though I were a stray cat lost in a kingdom filled with giants.

I remembered returning to the inn after a long day and him always asking if I had eaten yet, and if I had not, he would personally prepare a table for me.

I remembered his broken heart, and the starry skies as he lectured me.

A sob escaped my throat as I tripped over him and landed on my knees. The blood-drenched earth seeped through my skirt, and Wonsik did not move.

"Ajusshi, please." I tugged at a small corner of his sleeve. "*Ajusshi*. We have returned."

Deep grooves split his flesh, wounds that circled him, as though a crowd of officers had taunted him with quick slashes. The final blow—a sword run through his chest and twisted. How could people be so cruel?

I gripped his hand, as strong and rough as my own father's. And then it came. That surge of grief, my heart splintering into a thousand pieces, shards that dug into my rib cage with every breath I took.

Wonsik was gone.

He would not return in the morning, or by the week's end, or within a few years' time. He would never step into the inn again with his kind eyes and kinder words. He was gone, permanently. Vanished off the face of the earth even though his body lay before me.

"It is all my fault." I could barely speak through the tremors. "If I hadn't walked off on my own, if I hadn't struck that officer, W-Wonsik would not be lying here . . ."

Daehyun stood motionless, shoulders taut. His eyes were that of a dead man. And he would not look at me. Coolly, he said, "We must bury him, lest the king's men discover the corpse. No man is safe from his wrath, even in death." He took a step forward, then halted, his shoulders tensing. The slightest tremble shook him. "We shall return to the inn and find help."

I could not leave. My hand still clung to Wonsik by his sleeve. "How can we leave him again? All alone—"

"Pull yourself together," Daehyun snapped, his voice as brittle as ice. "He is gone, and there is no time to grieve, there is no time to mourn in this *fucking* hellhole." A muscle worked in his jaw, and his brows knitted together. The moment I saw his pain, his features twisted back into a mask. "There is no time for farewells, Young Mistress Boyeon. But there is a killer to be found and a king to be fought. So get *up*."

Dashing away my tears, I bolted to my feet, his heartless words sending molten iron through my veins. "Wonsik is *dead* and you tell me not to grieve?" I stormed over to him, the man who stood before me as an unfeeling rock. My hands balled into a fist, and I struck his chest; he did not so much as wince. I struck him harder, and still not a flinch. "I hope it crushes you, all your unfelt agony and sorrow." I drew out my sharpest words. "And when you die," I whispered, my stare unwavering from his, "I hope no one sheds a tear for you. Not that anyone would."

Slamming past his shoulder, I stalked away, and though remorse pricked at me, I did not turn back. I left him behind, just as I had left Suyeon the day of our last fight.

# 28

# DAEHYUN

**Wonsik was buried that afternoon.** Rocks were stacked to mark where he lay, hidden deep in the thicket where no feet would trample.

"Investigators are searching for Iseul in the village," Yul whispered, standing next to him in the forest. She and Yeongho had followed him to the battle site with a wagon full of shovels, and Yul had cried the entire time while digging. "They seemed to know where Wonsik was staying and will be keeping an eye on the Red Lantern Inn."

Daehyun glanced ahead at Iseul, who sat listlessly before the grave. His grip tightened around Wonsik's journal, retrieved from his robe before the burial. He knew Iseul would want it, but he could not muster the courage to face her.

"What do you mean," Daehyun spoke at last, "that they are searching for Iseul?"

"Investigator Gu received a report that chehongsa officers planned on capturing Iseul this evening, but now a group of them are dead," Yul explained. "So the investigator visited the inn this morning, shortly before you came looking for me. I was questioned along with everyone at the inn. We all swore that we knew nothing about Iseul's whereabouts, that she was a practical stranger to us. So we ought to take caution. We must hide Iseul elsewhere."

"I know of a place," Daehyun whispered, still watching Iseul from the corner of his eye. Watching the way her fingers dug into her skirt, her shoulders stiff. He wished she would cry as before, but she had not shed a tear since his callous words. "There is—" His voice broke. "There is an abandoned hut deep in the mountains."

"The one from Hyukjin's stories?" Yul asked, wiping at the corner of her wet eyes. She cleared her throat. "He told me about it."

"She cannot remain alone there. You will have to stay with her."

"All day and night? My absence would only draw more suspicion. Investigator Gu already has his eyes on me—"

"I can assist," Yeongho said eagerly. He had been watching Iseul the entire time, crouching next to her now and then to offer her words of comfort. "I am merely extra help to our troupe. And I rarely perform at the palace, so my absence would not be felt by anyone. Even the Bureau of Performance forgets that I exist. I can stay with her whenever you need me to, make sure nothing happens to her." His gaze drifted back to Iseul, and gently he said, "She needs a friend. She adored that ajusshi."

An undercurrent of anger prickled through Daehyun. The fool's gentle gaze and kind words vexed him to no end for some mysterious reason. "That is out of the question," he said flatly, and when Yeongho opened his mouth in protest, Daehyun snapped, "You will remain silent, or I shall—"

Yul placed a calming hand on his shoulder. "Everyone is high-strung. But we must not quarrel. We must stick together, that is what Wonsik would have wanted. H-he would have . . ." Yul let out a shuddering breath, her eyes growing wet again as her gaze strayed over to the grave. "He is dead, truly dead, isn't he?" Her voice began trembling. "Y-you know, I despise men like Wonsik-samchon—so infuriatingly noble and sacrificial."

Daehyun closed his eyes for a moment. The sound of grief aggravated him.

Yul could barely speak through her shudders now. Hand over mouth, she waited for her voice to settle. "If W-Wonsik were here, he would tell you to go to Iseul. I am not sure what happened, but both of you can barely look each other in the eye."

He glanced at Iseul one last time, then muttered, "Perhaps it is better that way."

# 29

# ISEUL

**Wonsik is dead.**

Not a moment passed without this reminder. By the fourth day, the excruciating sorrow dulled into a relentless ache, a fatigue that sank into my muscles and bones. I nevertheless endeavored to be of help to Yul. The two times she had visited me at the abandoned hut, she had stayed the night and had spent hours teaching me how to prepare my own meals, and at dawn before her departure, we would forage for greens and wild herbs.

"You knew Wonsik for some time . . . ," I murmured, watching as Yul gathered all that we had foraged, arranging a meal for us out of it. "How is it that you have the strength to run an entire inn and also travel over to keep me company? I would be of no use to anyone if I were in your place."

Yul heaved a sigh. "When the sadness grows unbearable, I try to imagine what Wonsik-samchon is doing right now. He is a ghost unable to pass on to the afterlife, as he was met with an unjust fate . . ." Her eyes were red-rimmed as she marinated each perilla leaf, stacking them one atop the other. Then she glanced out the window at the sunrise, bruising the sky in shades of red and purple. "I imagine he is lecturing a group of ghosts this

very moment, teaching them how to solve their own deaths."
She dipped her voice low, imitating Wonsik's gruffness. "Focus
yourself on the details. The truth is right before you."

A laugh escaped me, which quickly turned into a tearful choke.

We both ended up crying as we set the bowls and chopsticks on a small, low-legged table. My eyes continued to burn as
Yul shared more stories about Wonsik over our morning meal.
When we were wrung dry of both tears and tales, we sat leaning against the wall, her head resting against my shoulder, her
arm linked around mine. She glanced up at me. "And how is the
prince faring?"

I tensed. "How should I know?"

Yul clucked her tongue. "You have spent"—she paused to
count—"three days with him!"

"Three days with an unfeeling rock," I muttered.

I had attempted to speak to him the first two days, and
besides our few awkward exchanges, he had spent the entirety
of his time stationed outside the hut. And when he had left each
afternoon to convene with the coup leaders, I had found myself
too discouraged to even write to him. By the third day, our prolonged silence had become unbreakable.

"Aigoo." Yul jabbed her elbow into my side. "You *know* he has
feelings. In fact, he confessed to me a concern of his. He worries
you fault yourself for Wonsik's death."

I gripped my skirt, an ache digging its heel into my chest. "I
am always too reckless, too thoughtless," I whispered. "I oughtn't
to have left on my own—"

"It is not your fault, Iseul-ah. There is an old saying . . .

Mun-gyeong-ji-gyo. A friendship worth sacrificing one's life for, without any regret. Wonsik lived by that proverb. He would lay his life down gladly for his friends. So, of course you should grieve, but do not let grief consume you." She paused, perhaps noticing my sunken shoulders. "And why should you feel guilty about walking off on your own? You are not the one who arranged this horrific incident to occur."

"I suppose not," I mumbled.

After a moment, she took out a book. "The prince asked me to pass this along to you, but I had forgotten about it until now."

I hesitated, then my hands closed around the bloodstained journal. The one into which I had often seen Wonsik pouring his thoughts into. The weight over me lifted, if just for this moment, as a sense of purpose strengthened me.

"I think he would wish you to continue on with the hunt for Nameless Flower." She then began packing her few belongings. "The investigator from the State Tribunal will be visiting the inn again, likely to interrogate us once more. So you will not see me tonight. Please do not weep over your longing to see me."

Waving Yul away, I finally opened the journal, which was filled with notes. I skimmed past the pages that summarized the victims' wounds, past the names of possible witnesses and the intelligence he had garnered from them. The pages overflowed with so many names and dates, along with a description of the flower found at each of the crime scenes. Then I stopped at the last page of notes, at the quick scribble of handwriting that read:

*Investigator Gu*

The name was underlined in one quick brushstroke, and beneath it:

### Jangheung County

My heartbeat quickened. I went back, reviewing the previous pages, but there was no other mention of the investigator or this county.

A drop of cold splattered onto my nose. I glanced up at the wooden beams and thatch as more droplets leaked through the rotten straw. At once, I worried for Yul. She had, hopefully, caught a wagon ride back to the inn, as before.

Grabbing rain-catchers, I distributed them across the floor, then stilled. A memory seized me. "Jangheung County," I whispered, a chill settling in my bones. Wonsik had said we would take our investigation there—but what was there?

Investigator Gu might have the answer.

Lost in thought, I moved slowly, closing the tattered screen window and readjusting the catchers. Then the door slid open. Yul must have returned. I glanced over my shoulder and stilled.

A man stooped under the low entrance, stepping into the room with rain dripping from the brim of his hat. He threw off his straw cloak and pulled the door shut again, then turned to face me. His face was closed, distant, and expressionless.

"The journey takes more than an hour," I said, aimlessly flipping through Wonsik's journal. "You and Yul need not visit so frequently. I am not a child. I can take care of myself."

"You are in the middle of a mountain," Daehyun replied. "It is best that you have company."

My grip on the journal tightened. The hut was small, making avoidance impossible, and the rain poured like a waterfall, trapping us within the dark hut. I parted my lips to attempt an apology when Daehyun placed a small pouch on the table before me.

"What is it?" I asked.

"See for yourself."

Hesitantly, I glanced inside and was startled to see a vivid assortment of hangwa, sweet confections I had only ever tried during festivals. There were slices of candied fruits, along with taffy-like pieces of sticky yeot.

"A peace offering," he said grudgingly.

I blinked up at him, utterly bewildered.

He took off his hat and sat down before me, his lashes lowered. "I ought to have—" A muscle worked in his jaw as his countenance grew a shade paler. "I ought to have apologized sooner . . . I apologize for my callous words. I never meant to hurt you, truly. But I did." He hesitated for a moment, as though searching for the right words. "I wish I could elaborate on how remorseful I feel, but I am rather inept at expressing my feelings, and so . . ."

I shook my head, holding my trembling hands tight below the table. "I apologize, too," I whispered, overwhelmed with relief and joy. "The things I said, I only said in anger. I meant none of it. Truly."

At last, he looked up at me, and his mask yielded enough for me to catch a glimpse of a vulnerable young man. "I am glad to hear it—that you do not despise me." He gestured sheepishly at the bag. "Taste one. They are from the royal kitchen, and thus, the finest confections in all the kingdom."

"Very well." I picked up a candied yuja, then dropped it into my mouth. A sigh of pleasure escaped me. The slice was crispy and chewy sweet, bursting with memories of sunshine and laughter. "We ought to quarrel more often." I reached into his peace offering pouch and picked up a candied lotus root this time.

"Given our difference in temperament," he said dryly, "there will likely be many more quarrels to come."

As moments passed, the block of ice between us melted into a cautious yet warm companionship. One in which brief conversations were made, but we kept to our corners, myself by the candle I'd lit and Daehyun pacing by the door. It was Wonsik's journal that brought us together.

"I discovered it beneath Wonsik's robe." Daehyun flipped through the candlelit pages as I knelt next to him, my knees accidentally pressing up against his, but he did not move away. "You will continue with the investigation?" he asked.

I nodded. "I want to finish what Wonsik started."

"Hopefully you will find Nameless Flower before the Great Event. Once the king is gone, what reason has the killer to strike again? It will be far more difficult to find him then."

I nodded. "That gives me only two days."

"We will put our minds together—you, myself, and Yul."

I remained near him as he examined the notes, but when I absentmindedly touched my bandaged wrist, his attention shifted toward it.

"I swear," he whispered in a low voice, as though to himself, "the next person to harm you will die by my own hands."

I stopped fiddling with the binding material, unsure that I'd heard him right. "I beg your pardon?"

"The capital is no longer safe for you," he continued. "Your uncle is right: You should leave. He has a relative you can stay with—"

"My uncle?" The mere mention of him raised the hair on my skin. "My uncle cares *nothing* for my safety."

He studied me for a long moment, then slowly shut the book. "Something happened. Tell me?"

"My uncle—" My voice wavered, outrage roiling within me. "My uncle is the one who betrayed my parents to the king."

A frown furrowed his brow. "Your uncle betrayed your parents?"

"My father was executed when a long-buried secret was revealed—that he had been present at the palace during the execution of Deposed Queen Yun. And you know how the king killed officials for merely existing in the palace that day. Such was my father's case."

Daehyun's frown intensified. "Shall I have him poisoned, after all?"

I gently elbowed him. "Nothing must get in the way of the coup. Not even a personal vendetta."

He arched a brow. "How sensible of you."

"My sister is in the palace, have you forgotten? I cannot risk anything interfering with my plans to bring her home."

"Of course," he whispered.

"And there is something else." I briefly held his arm in eagerness, his warmth sinking into my palm. "What happened in Jangheung County? Wonsik wanted to take the investigation there."

"Jangheung?" He fell silent, wading through his memories. "It is where King Yeonsan fell apart."

"What do you mean?"

"Imagine this," he murmured. "A king who feigns ignorance of his mother's execution, while everyone in court conceals her unjust fate, including those who manipulated the former King Seongjeong into killing her."

I leaned in, confused by his words.

"King Yeonsan suppressed his anger, and for ten years he ruled with decency and benevolence, quietly surrounding himself with trusted servitors and growing his power . . ."

I must have leaned in too close, for he paused to glance at me, a glance that slid along my jaw and lingered on the spot below my left ear. I subconsciously raised my hand to hide the dark freckle. My little insecurity.

"After Queen Yun's execution," he continued, his gaze brushing across my lips for the barest moment, "the queen's mother, Lady Shin of the Goryeong Shin clan, was exiled to South Jeolla province—to Jangheung County."

My hand dropped. "What? The king's grandmother lives in Jangheung County?"

"Lived. She is deceased." He flipped through the journal one last time, then returned it to me. "Before her death, a government official by the name of Im Sahong arranged for the king to meet His Majesty's maternal grandmother, Lady Shin. Until then, the king hadn't realized she was still alive."

"And then?" I could barely speak, breathless with trepidation. "What happened?"

"The grandmother revealed Deposed Queen Yun's execution robe, and upon it was the queen's last message to her son, written in her own blood. *Avenge my death.*"

A hand over my mouth, I straightened myself once more. "Nameless Flower also leaves bloody messages on robes," I remarked, heart pounding in my chest.

"It may just be a coincidence. The killer wishes to taunt the king, and so he leaves a message on whatever writing material is available . . ." He folded his arms, then shook his head. "And few know of this—of the deposed queen's bloody robe. And fewer still know of the message left behind."

"But you know of it. And likely everyone close to the king knows of it as well." I pinched my lower lip in thought. "Somehow all of this connects to Investigator Gu. Wonsik met with the investigator the day before his death—they vaguely mentioned this meeting on our visit to the House of Bright Flowers. And the investigator's name is the last thing Wonsik wrote—"

A sizzle, and a gasp of darkness filled the hut.

Rain had dropped through the roof, extinguishing the candle.

Quickly, I rummaged for the flint box and tried to light the candle again, but the fire would not catch. "The wick is too damp," I muttered. Surveying the dimly lit hut, I stumbled about, hoping to find another candle left by Yul—

My face smacked into a solid, warm chest. I retreated quickly, stepped on my skirt, and flailed backward until Daehyun caught my waist. We both collided into the low table and went crashing to the floor. I remained still, completely winded. Then I became aware of who it was I lay upon.

"It is impossible to see anything," I whispered nervously, rising onto my forearms to move, but his hand stilled me, resting on the small of my back. Our gazes locked in the stormy gray half-light, our breaths intertwining. There were moments, I knew, when the earth and stars eclipsed each other. Yet I had never thought it possible that my heart and mind could move in such a way, shifting within the expanse and centering my attention on the man before me. As though seeing him for the first time, I noticed the little details: the shape of his lips, the small and faint scar nicking his right cheek, his luminous dark eyes that yielded under my gaze, revealing the emotions that flickered by, from desire to desire.

His hand slid along my spine, then held the back of my neck, gently drawing me closer. My lips burned, yearning to seal my mouth to his, to taste him out of curiosity—but in that moment, as his heart beat against my palm, a wave of vulnerability washed over me.

*Beware*, a haunting whisper echoed in my ear. *Those you hold dear always die in the end. And he will surely die.*

I could already feel the ghostly echoes from the future, the splitting pain, the days spent feeling lost, not knowing how to exist with all the sorrow.

I refused to ever feel that way again.

"No." My voice wavered, and I moved to stand.

The prince also rose to his feet, and I half expected him to grab my wrist, to drag me to him.

"You needn't look at me in such a manner," he said.

"In what manner?"

"As though I will force you."

"You do not wish to . . . kiss me?"

He offered me a wry smile. "What does it matter what I

wish?" he said quietly, striding up and brushing a loose strand of hair behind my ear. "You said no, and I will receive your word as a royal command."

My throat had dried. I could not form a single response.

"The rain has stopped." Releasing me, he crossed the room, though not soon enough to hide his flushed cheeks. "I shall remain outside to keep guard. Investigator Gu is at the inn. It is best we remain cautious."

The door slid shut behind him, and my knees lost their strength.

Quietly lowering myself, I sat by the door, palm pressed to my thundering heart. *The prince is not going to die*, I repeated to myself, over and over, trying to dispel the rising dread. *It is but a silly omen. He will not die this year. The year is nearly over.*

Gradually, the overwhelming anxiety receded, leaving only a trickle of unease. With a deep breath, I faced the reality of the moment. I had nearly kissed the prince, but more shocking still was that *he* wanted to kiss *me*. I reached for the floor, tracing my finger in the dust as I listened to Daehyun's movement outside the rickety brushwood door.

"Daegam?" I whispered, my heart beating fast. No matter how flustered I was, I could not neglect the task ahead of me. "As I am unable to, would you interview Investigator Gu for me? And then we must also speak with Crow."

"Who is Crow?"

"Wonsik's son. It is the sobriquet I gave him." I continued to trace, wanting to hear his voice again. "Wonsik was suspicious of his son for a reason. Crow might have known about the bloody message . . ." At some point, I no longer knew what I was even saying, my thoughts elsewhere. And when I looked down, I stilled, realizing I had traced out his name.

대현

대현

대현

# 30

# DAEHYUN

*Focus,* he urged himself. *Focus.*

He had forbidden himself from indulging in emotions, for only a fool would daydream when standing on the cusp of rebellion, on the precipice of extinction. Yet no matter his many attempts, he found himself caught in a daze. Servants discovered him staring blankly at furniture and walls, at books that remained on the same page for hours, and each time they would inquire whether he was ill. He indeed felt ill. Everywhere he looked, he found her. Iseul in the bright pink peonies. Iseul in the sound of laughter.

*Iseul.*

*Iseul.*

*Iseul.*

But he needed to focus; he needed to help her find the killer.

"Daegam?"

Daehyun glanced up. "Investigator Gu," he called in greeting, watching as the uniformed young man approached.

"I am afraid you are not permitted here," Investigator Gu said, looking around the Milwicheong Prison in confusion. "I am not sure who allowed you into this courtyard, but you cannot simply walk into the prison block."

Daehyun glanced around, crafting the expression of a traveler enjoying the sights. Long prison blocks bordered the courtyard, and each block held several cells that echoed with the groaning of miserable traitors.

"Daegam," Investigator Gu pressed, "you are not permitted—"

"Am I not? The guards permitted me entrance the moment I declared my title. And as for why I am here in this prison block, the king suggested that I visit this place to see what occurs to those who displease him. Perhaps he wished it to serve as a warning."

Investigator Gu fell quiet.

Strolling down the prison block, Daehyun examined the crowds of traitors held within, the investigator following close behind. "I know former Investigator Jang Wonsik is dead," Daehyun said, glancing over his shoulder. Feigning ignorance, he asked, "Did Nameless Flower kill him?"

"No, daegam."

"I am convinced he did. I heard rumors that Wonsik was closing in on the killer, and as usual, no one knew his thoughts. But perhaps he confided in you? I hear you were once mentored by him."

"Begging your pardon, daegam, but why do you care about this case?"

*Because Iseul cares. Because the coup might fail otherwise.*
"The same reason why other government officials are curious

about Nameless Flower," he replied. "We all wish to gain or remain in the king's good favor—and what immense favor one would receive should they discover the killer's identity."

The investigator shook his head. "Jang Wonsik wanted me to confirm something—to identify an object for him. That is all."

"And what might this object be?"

The investigator did not budge, lips thinned. "I cannot say. It is confidential."

"Indeed?" Daehyun fell still, turning to examine a prisoner grabbing at the straw that layered the cell, desperately chewing at it. "The king is losing patience with you, Gu-dosa. Perhaps we might assist each other so that we might both survive." He dropped his obnoxious act and said solemnly, "You must trust me. Upon my mother's grave, I swear to you that I have information of value."

Investigator Gu glanced at him. Everyone in the capital was aware of his foster mother and how she had died.

"A hairpin," the investigator answered after a long pause. "Wonsik wished for me to identify the true owner of a hairpin."

"A mere hairpin?"

"A binyeo belonging to a royal. By its unique traits, I was able to confirm that it once belonged to Deposed Queen Yun."

Daehyun frowned. "She was executed twenty-four years ago."

"To my understanding, Deposed Queen Yun's decrepit mother had kept it for all those years, then gifted it to her female companion."

"Why was it gifted?"

"Apparently, she wished to apologize on behalf of her

grandson, King Yeonsan, for beating her companion's son, Nam Seungmin—"

"Wait." Daehyun's frown deepened. "I am aware of the one occasion when King Yeonsan visited his grandmother—it was when she revealed Deposed Queen Yun's bloody robe to him. The beating occurred then?"

"Yes, daegam."

How, in all the king's intoxicated iterations of the bloody-robe event, had His Majesty never mentioned this beating of another man? It was as though the king had thought so little of his violent act that he had erased it entirely from his memory.

"Why was this man—Nam Seungmin—beaten?"

"Nam Seungmin often lingered around the residence of the king's grandmother to flirt with a servant girl there. And so, when King Yeonsan visited his grandmother, Nam Seungmin was present, and he must have witnessed something. For he was later caught laughing and saying, 'The king is crying like an infant over his mother's bloody robe.' The king overheard and beat the man, and would have killed him had the man's mother not intervened."

"And the mother received the hairpin as an apology," Daehyun murmured, trying to untangle his thoughts.

"As you know, daegam, the king has a soft spot for mothers, and so he relented and let Nam Seungmin live."

"How do you know all this?"

"I had to interview the king about this incident, as it was connected to another case I was in charge of."

Daehyun rubbed his temples. "And what case was that?"

"The king, a few days later, sent men up to bring this woman to the palace as his courtesan. But she had gone missing since the day of the king's departure. So the king tasked his best investigator, Jang Wonsik, with the search. But then Jang Wonsik sent me instead—a new hire then—to investigate."

"And did you find her?"

"I found her the moment I arrived. She was buried in her own garden."

A chill coursed down his spine. He had heard of the Dead Garden case before.

"I had barely begun my investigation when I was summoned back." Investigator Gu's cheeks paled, and he cleared his throat in discomfort. "It was the fourth lunar month of 1504."

Gu had no need to say more. The purge had occurred then, when government officials were executed daily, and not even those resting in their graves had been safe from the king's wrath—Yeonsan had exhumed the corpses and beheaded their skeletal remains.

"On my return, Investigator Jang Wonsik had already resigned. And thus the case was closed."

"And this binyeo somehow made its way to the capital, it seems? Wonsik did not tell you how?"

"He would not. He refused to, no matter how much I pressed . . ." Investigator Gu's voice trailed off, and he turned to face Daehyun, head bowed. "Daegam, I have told you all that I know."

Daehyun remained quiet, carefully tucking away all he had learned, to be reviewed with Iseul later. "After a round of questioning, I recently discovered that Wonsik was making arrangements to visit Jangheung County. Did you know that?"

The investigator, though his head was bowed, could

not hide the irritation locking his jaw. "I did not. Is that all, daegam?"

"My theory is that Wonsik thought he might find evidence about the killer there. I am not sure how he came to this conclusion, but . . . I find it interesting. Jangheung County, of all the places. Perhaps Nam Seungmin is the killer?"

Investigator Gu chuckled, then quickly recomposed himself. "One oughtn't leap to conclusions, daegam, with so little evidence—"

"The day King Yeonsan witnessed the robe, there was also a message written on it in blood. His mother asked His Majesty to avenge her death." Daehyun tilted his head slightly as Investigator Gu stared at him with widened eyes. "Did you know of this?"

"I . . . did not."

"And now the hairpin of Nam Seungmin's mother ends up in the capital, and so do bloody messages written on robes meant to taunt the king. It seems to me there is a connection there."

Frowning, Investigator Gu rubbed his short beard.

"I will leave you to your thoughts," Daehyun said, then paused. "When you visited Jangheung County long ago, I am sure you wrote a report on your observations. If you should find it, have your scribe copy it for me and deliver it to my residence." Before the investigator could protest, Daehyun added, "And if I come across any intelligence that might be of use, I shall pass it along to you, too."

Daehyun turned to leave, then paused. The prisoner, still devouring hay, locked eyes with him. In the man's eyes burned the same look he had seen in Iseul's. He saw han—a burning pool of resentment, helplessness, and unbearable grief.

"How many men, did you say, are in this prison?" Daehyun asked.

Investigator Gu, so preoccupied with his thoughts, answered without thinking. "Eight hundred men."

Eight hundred men.

Eight hundred traitors.

He glanced back at the straw-eater, his disdainful stare still locked onto his. *Imagine traitors pouring out onto the streets,* an idea whispered into his mind, *and stirring up the hearts of the common people. Imagine the uproar. Imagine the king's forty thousand—their hearts in utter disarray.*

# 31

# ISEUL

**Kingdoms rose and kingdoms fell,** rising and falling on a land drenched in tears. Grief had always existed since the beginning of time; King Yeonsan had simply aggravated it. And I had been too naive to see that life had never been normal, that darkness had always existed beyond my mansion walls.

I saw it everywhere I looked now, this soul-ravaging darkness.

But as I flipped through Wonsik's journal again, I wondered at Wonsik's insistence that I learn how to find the truth. I wondered if the truth could indeed eliminate great sorrow. Pausing before a page, I stared down at the sketch of the flower left at the crime scenes. Beneath it was a note scribbled:

*Baek-du-ong.*
*Used as traditional herbal medicine.*
*Blooms in spring and survives through the summer.*
*It prefers light; it cannot grow in the shade and requires*
*moist soil.*
*Purple in color.*
*Sometimes red.*

I hadn't paid much attention to the detail of this flower—not when I had seen it on Young Master Baek's corpse, nor on Royal Guard Min. It had seemed so inconspicuous then. A flower was a flower, just as the moon was the moon, always present in the night. One could spend an entire month, or perhaps even a lifetime, without truly gazing upon it. Yet as I looked at the drawing now, I studied the flower's drooping bell-shaped head, its six petals with woolly hairs covering the underside. I held the flower within my mind, twirling it slowly by the stem, and within moments, a memory surfaced.

Suyeon and I had paused before a stranger's burial mound. We had watched as a family weeded and pruned the hillock, to keep the tomb in neat condition and to honor those buried there. We had both cried, faced with an agonizing truth that we would never be able to tend to our parents' graves, for we did not even know where they were buried.

In such a manner, we would pause before many more tombs in the following months. My sister would note that there seemed to always be bell-shaped purple flowers blossoming around the mound, greeting us all too merrily. "Creepy grandfather flower," she had come to call the plant, for it was hairy and bent downward, like an old person's bent back.

I glanced down at the sketch again. The similarity between the flower in my memory and the one before me was too uncanny.

A rapping came on the brushwood door, interrupting my thoughts with a rush of excitement. The prince was finally here. Retreating across the room, I inspected my reflection in a small, rusted mirror. I pinched my cheeks and bit my lips until they were rosy. When the knocking came again, I quickly strode over to the door and opened it.

I froze.

A manservant stood before me, a large mole under one eye. He then stepped aside with his head bowed, opening onto me the view of a man who filled my heart with thorns of anger and sadness. Every breath was painful. Here stood before me a traitor.

"If you are looking for the prince," I said, gritting my teeth, "he has not yet arrived."

My uncle did not approach but remained standing a few paces away. "I came for you. I had a manservant follow that innkeeper the other day, and so here I am now." He glanced over his shoulder, and as though on cue, four servants carried over a palanquin, then lowered it by the hut. They pulled open the little door, as though expecting me to step into the vehicle.

"Why did you come for me?" My voice was barely audible. I was struggling for composure.

My uncle was too busy looking around. "What a pity that the daughter of Magistrate Hwang must live in such a place." He then walked over, stopping before the palanquin, patting its roof. "You look pale. I know this is abrupt, but it is for your own good that you leave here. My sister has dozens of servants who will be at your beck and call—"

"*Why* should I leave?"

He frowned, caught off guard by my sharpness. "Hwang Boyeon, you cannot possibly think I would let you remain here." He gestured at the rotting hut. "You ought to leave, before the *event* occurs. It is far too dangerous, and I am duty-bound as your uncle to ensure your safety."

I strode up to him. *Never stare directly into the eyes of your elder*, I had often been told. Yet this elder had done nothing to warrant my respect. "Did you also feel duty-bound to betray my father to the king?" I hissed.

His lips twitched. "I am unsure what you mean—"

I struck my uncle hard, so hard that his face snapped to the side. "May the heavens punish you for your offense. And may your death feel like the slices of a thousand knives." I raised my hand again, but Uncle caught it this time, his grip tight.

"I wanted to spare you the truth," he cried under his breath, giving my arm a violent shake. "But if you are to remain, then perhaps it is better that you know it . . ." He leaned in close and snarled, "You will never see your sister again."

"Do not expect me to *ever* believe anything you say—"

"I wish I were lying, but there is no way back home for any of the king's women," he continued, voice lowered for my ears alone. "They will be distributed as gifts to all the government leaders who join us, and your sister will go to Official Wu."

My knees buckled. My sister—given to Maggot?

"It is the way of things." The faintest look of remorse trembled on his face. "A price must be paid for victory—"

"What do you mean?" a cold and imperious voice cut behind us.

We both looked at the figure towering behind Uncle. So lost in horror, I had failed to notice the prince's arrival.

"Whose decision was this?" Daehyun pressed.

Uncle's entire face twitched nervously. "It was the deputy commander's decision—"

"A decision can be reversed. It must be. Iseul's sister is *your* niece-in-law." Daehyun paused, examining the cowardly, dull, and unremarkable man. "You did nothing, did you, when you heard of Official Wu's request?"

The twitches intensified. "Daegam, what use is there in such confrontation? It is Official Wu *Sayong*. Next to the deputy commander, he holds the greatest influence over the government. Already he has persuaded over fifty officials to join our cause!" He flicked an uneasy glance at me, then murmured, "And the truth of the matter is, the girl—Iseul's sister—will no longer have a place in society. She is . . ." He dropped his voice lower, yet I heard his words all too clearly. ". . . the king's whore. She will be scorned for the rest of her life. But what an honor it is to become the respected concubine of a powerful man—"

Grabbing Uncle by his upper arm, Daehyun dragged the terrified man off into the thicket, with worried servants scampering after them. If cries ensued, I heard them not, my mind ringing too loudly with my uncle's threat. I dropped onto my haunches and stared at my shaking hands, counting.

Thirty-five days had passed since Suyeon's disappearance.

Thirty-five days of being crushed in the king's embrace.

For half of those days, I had waited for the coup leaders to release her. Waiting and waiting like the fool that I was, believing the rebellion would carve out a path to her. But they were all wolves, these men with power, and they were bent on pillaging the king's women once the throne was conquered.

"Iseul-ah."

I hardly noticed Daehyun as he crouched next to me. Specks of blood stained his white collar, his knuckles bruised and raw.

In the distance, the servants could be heard comforting their groaning master.

"We will find a way to your sister," Daehyun whispered.

"There is only one." I dug my nails into my skin, wishing I could bleed, wishing for a pain other than the one clawing at my chest. "Remember what I said—when the person you love is taken, you go into the den of the tiger. You go to the ends of the kingdom and across. You go to where they are." I gritted my teeth to stop their chattering. "I am going to enter Wongaksa Temple, where the courtesans are kept. I am going to retrieve Suyeon myself."

His eyes widened a fraction, then sharpened into a warning glint. "Do not dare. You will not enter the temple. That is an order."

"Do *not* tell me what to do," I snapped, and before the pain could spill over in a stream of vicious words, I bolted to my feet and left. I stalked through the forest, striking branches aside, cursing as I tripped over roots, charging down the narrow trail until I could walk no farther, my path blocked by a wide stream. The reflection of a young woman, trembling with fury, stared up at me.

I screamed.

Damn these men! I would whisk my sister away before Maggot could lay a finger on her. No—I would take with me *all* the courtesans and leave the government officials to protest over their missing rewards. Let the new government collapse for all I cared. I would not let them have their way.

Climbing onto a granite slab, I fell to my knees and cupped my hands into the freezing stream. *I can bring the women home,* I assured myself, splashing my face until the ice water left my bones shivering with determination, *I will do it.* No official would be focused on rounding up the women, not in the midst of a rebellion. I would sneak them out then, in the middle of all the chaos—

A shadow fell next to me. It was Daehyun, proffering a handkerchief.

"I have already made up my mind," I said brusquely, water dripping down my face. "Do not try to change it. Only another captive can closely watch over my sister; that captive must be me."

"If you enter and the coup fails," he said, shoving the cloth into my hand, "you will be trapped. It will be simple enough to enter, but leaving will be near impossible, and if you do, you will be pursued for the rest of your and your sister's lives. Is that what you wish?"

I grudgingly wiped my face. "Then the coup had better succeed."

"Hwang Iseul." A muscle worked in his jaw. "This is a grave decision you are making. One you ought only make after careful consideration. Give me time to speak with the deputy commander first. Minds can be changed."

"He will not change his mind. Maggot is too respected and feared. That man is determined to take my sister, and he *will* if I do not stop him—"

"You have me."

His voice emptied the tumult of thoughts until only he occupied my mind. Slowly, I glanced up to meet his steady gaze. Surely he was only saying this to appease me.

"You ought to focus on your coup," I murmured. "Do not concern yourself with me. I will find a way into the temple, and I will bring her home on my own—"

"Come," he whispered, "sit by my side."

"Stop looking at me like that."

"Like what?"

My heart knotted painfully, but I managed to say in a light-hearted tone, "As though you *care*."

Holding my wrist, Daehyun pulled me to him, until my face was flush against his chest. The warmth of him embraced me, and I could not will myself to push him away.

"Iseul-ah." His voice was impossibly low, whispering against my ear. "You have me, so use me. I am your friend and will do everything within my power to assist you. Let me help you."

Shaking my head, I glared through my tears at the silver emblems decorating his robe. "I thought the coup leaders would surely assist. Now I feel like an utter fool for trusting them. If I lose my sister to Maggot, I will never forgive myself."

"And you will not lose her," he whispered. "But allow me the opportunity to try. I will convince the deputy. If I succeed, you must promise to reconsider."

"The king leaves for Kaesong City in two days," I reminded him, wiping my eyes. "I must enter tomorrow evening, at the latest."

"Then give me the morning."

I stayed quiet, distracted by his thumb caressing the tendrils of my hair. His touch was gentle, almost hesitant, as though he'd never comforted a woman before. Then he lowered his hand down my back. *Something is going to happen*, I thought, feeling the intensity of his stare, the tightening of his fingers against my waist. *Daehyun-gun is going to kiss me.*

For a fleeting moment, a tempting thought danced through

my mind. I could let him this time. I could briefly return to the carefree young lady I had once been, where a kiss was a kiss and I had no need to concern myself with the weight of life and death, or the consequences of entangling my heart with a doomed prince. In that world, I would indulge in the budding affection between us, succumbing to his touches, letting him spread my hair out across the moss. Then I would giggle all the way back home to immortalize the encounter in my journal, recording my confusion over whether it was love or infatuation that I felt. It would become an all-consuming question that would torment me for days.

But I did not live in that world.

In my world, my sister was clinging to a cliff's edge, waiting for me. There was no room to indulge in romantic notions. With silent resolve, I shifted my attention back to the matter at hand.

"I am going to tell Yul tonight. I am going to prepare," I said firmly, "but I will wait on your word. And if you fail . . ." I lifted my gaze, his face alarmingly close to mine. And those eyes, those dark, exquisite eyes . . . "I will not fault you, but you must promise to help me enter Wongaksa Temple. That you will not try to convince me otherwise."

His expression grew rigid as he loosened his grip around me.

"You must promise," I urged, my voice deceptively steady, "that you will not try to convince me otherwise."

His mouth parted, closed, and he struggled for the longest moment. "I promise," he said at last, looking away from me. "You have my word."

# 32

# DAEHYUN

**Wine bottles clinked as laughter** exploded from next door. It was daytime, and the House of Bright Flowers still rumbled with music and merriment.

"You could have any woman, daegam." The deputy commander's voice dipped low as he stared across the low-legged table. "Any courtesan, as many as you desire, and you would hold influence over the government when all this is over. Such a bright future awaits you; do not endanger it over a slip of a girl. Iseul wishes to reunite with her sister? She may do so after the Great Event. A mere trek over to Official Wu Sayong's residence, and there her sister will be."

Daehyun tapped his finger on the lacquered surface, struggling to keep his composure. He had spent nearly three hours in conversation with the deputy, attempting to reverse his decision, yet it had merely come to this: a refusal to free one girl, and a bribe.

"Must I repeat myself?" Daehyun muttered. "Young Mistress Suyeon—Iseul's sister—must be returned home. It is *my* request."

"Forgive my insolence, daegam . . . But the entire future of this kingdom rests not upon you, but upon the government officials who have joined this cause. It is they who I must please."

The deputy's snub did little to offend him, for Daehyun knew who he was—an outcast prince, illegitimate and parentless, and it mattered naught to the deputy whether he lived or died. He was not Grand Prince Jinseong; he was not this kingdom's future.

"If you do not reverse your decision," Daehyun said calmly, "do not expect that I will stay silent."

The faintest snarl flickered across the deputy's lips. "The path to a new government is made of broken hearts. Endure the heartache, daegam. You are young; your heart will heal, and so will hers. But we absolutely need to attempt to keep bloodshed to a minimum, and that means persuading as many officials as possible to join our side, through whatever means—"

"The Milwicheong," Daehyun interrupted. "If I can gather a mob of over eight hundred rebels *within* the capital, on the night of the Great Event, would you then reconsider?"

The deputy paused. His scowling brows lifted, replaced by a look of intrigue. "You mean . . . to break free the traitors from Milwicheong Prison . . . ?" He remained still, his back straight, his stare pinned to the floor in thought. "They would be too malnourished to be a fighting force."

"They would amplify the unrest," Daehyun pressed, grasping onto this thread of hope. "They would be the spark needed to rally the people's spirits. To turn the capital against the king and his soldiers."

The deputy commander nodded and slowly lifted his stare to Daehyun. "It seems to me that you have too much time to spare, daegam, to be worrying about the Hwang sisters. I leave this task to you, then, and will provide you with my personal soldiers. You will infiltrate the Milwicheong when we attack the fort. It should be simple enough, in the midst of chaos."

"Then I have your word?" Daehyun asked, his stare unwavering on the man. "You will persuade Official Wu to leave Suyeon alone—"

"You misunderstand me, daegam. We are called to fight for the kingdom, for the people. Not for two sisters."

*"Deputy—!"*

"I am a man of my word, and I have given Official Wu Sayong my word. It cannot be taken back." With that, the deputy rose to his feet and stalked over to the door, then paused before leaving. "If we fail, we will all be arrested and executed without trial. Iseul will not live to even worry about her sister's fate. So let us focus our minds on what is important: victory."

A sea of dread pooled around Daehyun once he was alone. He felt struck down. Folding his head into the palms of his hands, he stared into the darkness, unable to understand how he could fail to protect yet another friend. Hyukjin was dead. Wonsik was dead. And now Iseul . . .

Crowds flowed in and out of the House as time passed, and he could not will himself to move. When a scratch came at the door, he could hardly turn to look.

"Daegam," came a female whisper.

His heart sank. It was one of his gisaeng informants, and he knew why she had come.

"They are arrived," she said. "Yul and another female companion—"

"Leave," his voice rasped.

"Then . . . then shall we proceed without you? It will take time to apply the cosmetics."

He did not answer. He wanted nothing to do with Iseul's plan.

"I have procured a courtesan's dress, as Yul requested—"

"*Leave*," he ordered again, his voice sharper.

The gisaeng retreated, and he remained still as he examined every other alternative. The most feasible option would be to send Palace Servant Jiyu to keep an eye on Iseul's sister, but she would have to do so at a distance, never close enough to truly keep Suyeon safe. Neither could he entrust the task to another courtesan, for he had no informants among them, absolutely no one he could trust.

He whispered a curse.

Iseul was right. Only she could protect her sister.

When he dragged himself to his feet, he felt a sharp ache splinter through his chest as he made his way down the corridor, to the chamber at the far end. He paused before the latticed double doors. Female voices drifted out, the paper screens too thin.

"Our kingdom has three criteria for feminine beauty," came the gisaeng's voice from within. "And to avoid suspicion from palace attendants, one must look the part. Seulgi-yah."

"Her name is Iseul," Yul's voice boomed. *"Iseul."*

"The first criteria is sam-baek," the gisaeng continued, "which highlights the whiteness of the skin, teeth, and the white of the eye. You possess beauty in the latter two, but your skin . . . you are slightly too tanned compared to other palace ladies. Come closer this way, and keep your face still."

A sunlit silhouette stepped before the screened door, and he knew who it was. He had observed Iseul too often not to recognize the shape of her—her ever-tilted chin, her long throat, her hands primly gathered together.

"The second is sam-heuk, which emphasizes the need for charcoal-black pupils, eyebrows, and hair..." A shadow of a hand reached out, a brush to Iseul's brows. "And the third is sam-hong, which stresses the redness of the cheeks and lips as well as peachy fingernails." The hand dabbed into a pot, then paused. "Damnation. I am out of rouge."

The doors suddenly slid open, and Yul stepped out while whispering over her shoulder, "I will return with another pot—" She then halted before him. Eyes narrowed, she scratched the side of her nose. "Why do you stand here, daegam? Go in."

Brushing past her, Daehyun stepped into a chamber burnished gold in the sunlight. "You ought to lower your voice when speaking," he muttered, striding over to the shade. "Every word can be overheard..."

A chill seeped into his heart as Iseul turned to him, her face molded into a narrow vision of beauty. Her form was no longer dressed in white cotton but lavished in a palace lady's gown—a sheer white jacket that bared her throat and shoulders, and a silk skirt that was the color of bright pink peonies.

"Did you convince the deputy?" Iseul asked.

Daehyun turned away, more shaken than he thought was possible. As he stared out the window, he could see nothing, though an entire garden sprawled before his eyes.

"I thought so," Iseul said as she joined him. "Do not worry yourself. No one will recognize me. Neither the king nor the chehongsa officers, even if they might have seen a sketch of me. Even *I* cannot recognize myself."

He refused to look at her. Refused to acknowledge that he would partake in her reckless decision. But as he stared ahead, he could sense her feelings, as palpable to him as the heat of the sun, as the cold of the moon. She was nervous. The guard he had raised fell, and he turned to her at last.

Iseul was unrecognizable—her full lips thinned into a small pout, her soft brows replaced by dark lines that arced in the shape of willow leaves—yet only one woman had ever gazed upon him in such a way. In a stare that was unafraid, a free fall into the depths of his being. She would always be Iseul, no matter how she appeared, no matter how much she changed.

"Iseul-ah . . ." He faltered, grappling for the words to express himself. "Should anything occur—"

The doors shot open. And as he stared at Yul, stumbling in with panic-widened eyes, he felt dread tighten in his stomach. He had rarely seen the innkeeper in a state of such terror.

"I overheard a conversation, daegam," Yul said, her voice shaking. "Nameless Flower has struck again." She placed a hand over her throat, as if to calm herself. "Iseul's uncle is dead."

# 33

# ISEUL

**Daehyun drew the veil lower** over my head, shrouding my face from the crowd bustling down Jongno Road. Still holding the sides, he peered down at me. "What are you thinking about?" he murmured.

I stared blankly up at him, mystified as to how my uncle could have died. I had seen him only the day before; he had traveled all the way to the abandoned hut. Then between that moment and the hour of his death, Nameless Flower had known of his whereabouts and had moved in for the kill.

"Why does it feel like Nameless Flower is taunting me?" I whispered.

"Does no one come to mind?" Daehyun proceeded to tie the veil ribbon, to secure the jangot from blowing away. "Anyone who might wish your uncle ill, perhaps someone from your past?"

"There is no one but my uncle, and he is dead now."

"I am sorry for his passing—"

"Are you? I am not." Then I frowned, uneasiness thrumming in my veins. "I wish I could continue investigating. I wish I could figure out who Nameless Flower is."

"You may still put your mind to use even from within the

temple." His fingers brushed the underside of my chin, and when at last the ribbon was tied, he reached into his robe. A folded sheet of paper appeared. "It is Investigator Gu's report. But do not read it just yet." He slipped the document into the pouch by my waist. "You ought to focus on the task before you."

I glanced past him, past the pedestrians, at the walled-in Wongaksa Temple, nestled under the distant silhouette of Mount Bugak. Guards were stationed around the compound, as though guarding the palace walls themselves. There truly was no other way to enter the temple but through the gate.

"The time is not yet," Yul called out, crossing the road over to us. Then lowering her voice, she explained, "I managed to question one of the temple servants. The courtesans are not leaving for the Royal Academy yet. They are still being readied." She glanced around, wiping the sweat from her brow. "I will try to strike a conversation with another servant, and once the women begin to line up, I will come find you. For now, you ought to keep out of sight, Iseul-ah. The guards might notice your dress." She gestured somewhere off into the distance. "Wait inside that bookshop; it does not close until curfew."

Exchanging a glance with Daehyun, we made our way over to the shop, crowded with customers browsing the shelves of stacked books. We stood among a group of scholars at the far end. As Daehyun picked up a book, so did I, and I stared at a page as my mind froze around my reality. I was going to enter Wongaksa Temple. I was going to tread into the den of a tiger, hoping the beast would not stir awake, inching my way around his bloody claws, around the skeletal remains of his prey. I was almost afraid to see what had become of Suyeon.

"You are shaking."

I flinched at Daehyun's sudden voice, my book dropping to the floor with a clatter.

"Have a care!" the shopkeeper called out, peering through the open shelves at us before disappearing into the back room.

Taking a calming breath, I finally looked around. The shop was empty, stained red in the dying light. When had the time so passed? I snatched up the book, gripping it tight. It was nearly time to leave. Nearly time to join the captives.

"It is not too late," Daehyun whispered. "You can change your mind—"

"Don't." I stared at my white knuckles as his shadow draped around me. "You promised. Do not dissuade me."

"Look at me."

I did, and at first, all I could see was my own fear. The unknown that awaited me. The uncertainty of whether the rebellion would even succeed. But slowly, slowly, as the dust motes drifted through the rays of light, Daehyun came into focus— the dark slashes of his brows, the aquiline nose crooked ever so slightly to the right, and lips that had thinned into tense lines. For days this man had stationed himself outside my hut, to keep watch over me, and now I would be without him.

His hands held my elbows, and I realized I had leaned into him, my forehead pressed against his chest.

"I will not dissuade you. But whenever you are in need," he whispered, his lips close to my ear, "do not hesitate to send a message my way. I will go to where you are, wherever that might be."

I remained against him in such a manner, feeling his lips still close to me, his hands still gripping my elbows. His intoxicating nearness stirred awake emotions—a blend of dread at the thought of leaving him and the yearning to abandon my resolve. Without thinking, I turned to his warmth. My cheek caressed his, drifting until our lips touched, the kiss no more than a brush of heat, breaths intertwined. His fingers then held my chin, tilting my face upward, his gaze fixed on my lips as he pressed me against the bookcase. He leaned in to deepen his mouth over mine, but he wouldn't. He could not. He pressed a gentle kiss to the corner of my lips instead, tasting me there, and then he moved away.

"You are too flushed," his voice rasped. "The paint will melt."

I raised my hand to examine the jibun on my face, but he caught my wrist.

"Avoid touching. Your makeup will smear, and I have known the king to punish women over the slightest smudge of rouge."

Footsteps creaked into the bookshop. "They are already lining up," Yul whispered, "sooner than I thought. We must leave now."

Disorientation overtook me. My thoughts were a blur as I hurried alongside my two companions, but reality sharpened when we caught sight of the mob huddling alongside the street. They stared at the procession of beautiful women as though witnessing caskets of the murdered. A great weeping of sorrow and fury broke out. They reached past the crush of spears, reaching for their children. They were mothers and fathers who looked like my own, and there were sisters, too, bearing my own reflection.

"Move aside!" guards yelled, brandishing their weapons.

Heartbroken cries continued, rumbling through the marrow of my being.

"Now," Yul whispered, her voice strained to breaking as she hastily untied the ribbon and pulled the veil off my head, "you must go now."

I stepped forward, but Daehyun's hand clung to mine, to the tips of my fingers, holding me to the very end when the current of my decision swept me away.

To Suyeon I would go.

To the girl I had once resented.

To the girl I had always loved.

# 34

# DAEHYUN

"**What have I done?**" **Daehyun** stared down at his hand, and Yul stood next to him on the empty street. "How could I have agreed to this?"

"She would have gone in, with or without your permission," Yul whispered, her concerned stare on him. "Better that she knows we are here for her. It will give her courage."

Daehyun could not move. Horror and despair tunneled through his chest. "I cannot bear the thought—" His voice wavered, and as he struggled to regain his composure, he whispered, "I fear for her safety."

"She is a capable young woman; do not forget that," Yul pressed. "And if you wish to reunite with her, then there is only one thing you must do, daegam."

He finally looked up at the innkeeper, his lips pale and his face drawn.

"You must change the heavens. So go, daegam. Go and move the heavens for her."

# 35

# ISEUL

**I could not find my** sister.

I had searched the sea of faces since entering the Royal Academy, and by dawn, I could no longer tell the faces apart, my mind wandering in and out with exhaustion. When attendants scurried over to assist the intoxicated king off his throne, we were led out onto the dark and empty street, the curfew hours still in effect. I continued my search, dragging my stare to the row of women next to me, behind and before me—still, no Suyeon.

*Do not panic.*

I focused on my feet instead, silk sandals staggering through the gate and into Wongaksa Temple. I had to remind myself of my footing—*left foot, right foot.* Each time I glanced up, fear warped my surroundings; the courtyard swam under my steps, the large buildings blazed in the torchlights, swaying then straightening.

"You," came a tiny voice.

I strained my eyes, a face shifting into focus. A girl with freckles stared at me. We stood in a vast chamber with a high ceiling, with tall, latticed screens and floor lanterns glowing over hundreds of women, collapsed onto their bed mats, exhausted and massaging their aching legs.

"You know me?" I whispered.

"My name is Cheonbi," she replied, holding out a hand. "I'm the girl you saved a few weeks ago."

My mind, frozen with anxiety, couldn't comprehend her words. Then I remembered Scabbed Cheek and the girl he had attempted to arrest. "So you were captured in the end," I murmured, taking her small hand in mine. "I am in need of your assistance this time . . . Do you know a girl named Jonggeum?"

"Usually, I would not know—there are over a thousand women here. I tried to learn everyone's name when I first came but soon found it impossible." She paused. "But Jonggeum, I know."

My heart quickened. "Lead me to her. Please."

She led me out of the main temple, ushering me through a few small gates, and across multiple courtyards, chattering all the while.

"I suppose you are new here?"

"Yes. I am." I could barely speak, my throat constricted by dread.

"Well, hopefully all you will ever know is palace duties. For those like me, who are not sent to the king, we spend most of our days in the palace doing menial chores. I'm part of the sewing department, but I wish I could assist in the Sangeuiwon, where the royal silks are dyed, or the royal kitchen. I despise sewing— but there I am sent, daily."

Finally, we stopped before an establishment bustling with nurses, in their aproned uniform and flowing silk garima crowned atop their heads. I gathered my hands tight, digging my nails into my knuckles.

"Why have you brought me here?" I asked.

"Jonggeum is in the infirmary."

My voice wavered. "What happened to her?"

"She hasn't been herself since she was last summoned by the king. I'm not sure what occurred, and I would not ask if I were you. That is the rule the women here abide by. Never probe into the nightmares of others."

My nails dug deeper, ripping past skin, but the sting failed to deflect the devastation stabbing at my chest. I bolted up the flight of steps, Cheonbi hurrying after me, and upon entering the establishment, I was struck by the smell of women wasting away.

"Where is she?" I stared at the mats laid out across the floor, at the women curled upon them. "Where is my sister?"

"Y-your sister?" Cheonbi blinked, then pointed. "There she is."

At the far end of the chamber, a woman sat with her arms wrapped around her knees, staring down. *Suyeon*, I thought as I quickened my steps. A small part of me had believed I would find her with a book opened at her feet, for she had never been without one growing up. A part of me also expected a scolding the moment she noticed me. *You foolish girl!* she would lash out, concern knitting her brows. *Why have you thrown yourself into such danger?*

But the woman I arrived before was staring blankly at where the wall and floor met.

"Hwang Suyeon," I whispered.

She looked up at me. Her eyes were empty, hollowed out. I tried to look for the spark of her, searching as one might search the pitch dark for a missing loved one—with hands stretched out, desperate to collide into warmth, and finding only more darkness. I scratched at my torn knuckles until my nails slipped against blood. I had found my sister—but she was gone.

"It is me." I shakily knelt down before her, tugging at her sleeve. "Older Sister, it is me, Iseul."

I waited, watching her vacant face. I had never before felt so desperate for a scolding. I yearned for the sister who had fiercely followed the rules all her life, infuriated whenever I had broken them. I missed that outrage. Desperate to spark light into her eyes, I took her limp hand and wrote a word onto her palm.

반정

I studied her again. Nothing. I traced out the word again— the word that had once infused hope through my blood.

*Banjeong.*

There came the barest movement; lashes fluttered. The slightest glow lit up her eyes at the word; a righteous rebellion that would right the wrongs. My sister had escaped somewhere far away, leaving her shell behind, and now she had returned. For me.

"Hwang Boyeon," she murmured, her focus hazy—but it was still there, fixed on me. "I hope that this is a terrible dream and that you are not sitting before me."

"It is indeed a terrible dream," I whispered. "One from which you will awake tomorrow night. It will all be over soon. And you may scold me all you wish, for the rest of our lives."

A long silence drew out as my sister stared down at her palm, at the invisible word I had written. Her eyelids shuddered; her head swayed. "I have not slept in days. Each time I close my eyes, I see them."

I did not ask whom she spoke of. Instead, I shuffled closer, leaning her head against my shoulder. "Then rest, Older Sister," I whispered, the painful knot in my stomach unraveling as I watched the light withdraw from her eyes again. *This is my sister*, I thought, gratitude straining against my being, *and at least she is alive, she is alive.*

I timidly reached out and stroked the ridge of her nose, the same way Mother would when soothing me to sleep. "Nothing and no one will harm you," I whispered, my voice wavering. "Not while your little sister is here."

The weight of her head grew heavier on my shoulder, and it seemed she'd dropped to sleep.

For a long while, I remained still, taking in the weight of her existence. A weight that grounded my spirit. *My sister, my sister, my sister.* The words that had once felt as forgettably light as air now squeezed my heart tight. We were sisters. Two girls who shared pieces of each other, tied together by an unspoken bond, a warm feeling of attachment, that no amount of bickering could easily sever. We were sisters. Comrades born from the same womb.

I glanced at Suyeon for the hundredth time, to convince myself that she was truly by my side. And when realization finally settled, memories unfurled of the long journey I had taken to reach her, of the kind strangers who had become my dearest friends along the way.

Prince Daehyun. Yul. Wonsik...

And had Wonsik lived... I could scarcely fathom the joy he would have experienced upon meeting my sister at last.

Heaving a sigh, I carefully maneuvered my hand so as not

to disturb Suyeon and glanced around. Cheonbi must have left, and none of the nurses were paying us any heed. I slipped out Prince Daehyun's note from my pouch. Wonsik's investigation still remained unfinished and would have to be set aside until this was all over. But I wanted to see the prince's writing. It was all I had of him at the moment.

At first, as I stared at the page, I could not focus. The sheet was crowded with so many words, and when I read it once, my mind spun—confused as to why I was reading about the Dead Garden case, the one I had heard about in passing. What did it have to do with Nameless Flower? But I reined in my attention, and by the time I read the letter thrice, I finally understood.

"The two cases are connected," I whispered, a chill coursing down my spine.

I read over it a fourth time and narrowed Investigator Gu's report into three points:

First, a woman had been buried in the backyard of her house. The culprit accused of this crime had been the victim's husband, a former royal guard who had lost his position because of insubordination. They had a son who had left the county, months later, to free himself from all the gossip about his parents.

Second, the victim had lived within walking distance from the residence of Lady Shin, King Yeonsan's maternal grandmother. She had served as Her Ladyship's companion, and two days before the victim's death, Her Ladyship had gifted her a hairpin. The last person to see the victim had been a visiting friend, a tavern keeper who had sworn the victim had been wearing a golden binyeo.

And third, the hairpin was identified as Deposed Queen

Yun's yongjam. Investigator Gu had interviewed Lady Shin and had learned this hairpin had not been stolen but given as an apology gift by the decrepit Lady Shin.

I flipped to the back of the letter and paused to study Daehyun's writing. The strokes were neat yet bold.

*Not mentioned in the report is the bloody-robe incident I spoke to you about. The victim had a son named Nam Seungmin, who mocked the king for weeping over Queen Yun's robe, and he was beaten for it. Hence the extravagant apology gift from Lady Shin.*

*But I am uncertain as to how Wonsik drew such a firm conclusion that Nameless Flower is connected to the two incidents in Jangheung County. There are coincidences, indeed, such as the bloody writing on the robe, but even this is too weak a connection for Wonsik. It would seem to me that Wonsik knew something else. One final connector to tie the killer, possibly, to the boy who mocked the king two years ago.*

Lowering the letter, I thought at once of Royal Guard Crow, the man who had hidden something away at the scene of Min Hyukjin's death. He seemed to have many secrets. Perhaps one of them would unlock this case one day. But for now . . .

I glanced at my sister to assure myself that she was still there and not a dream. Then a coldness breezed through me. She was not asleep, but staring blankly ahead. A single tear trickled down her pale cheek.

"Older Sister," I whispered, "you ought to rest—"

"I helped a courtesan give birth. She was my friend," Sueyon said, her voice a monotone. "She was already pregnant, carrying her husband's child, when she was kidnapped. And then . . ." She blinked, her eyes as blank as the wall she stared at. "The king killed her after she gave birth. The ojakin disposed of both bodies . . . My friend's and her newborn child's."

I gripped the letter tight, horrified.

"I am leaving tomorrow," she went on in the same eerie voice. "Tomorrow, the king sets off for Kaesong City. All the women are to go, including myself. And if the event you speak of does not occur, then I am afraid of what I will do to myself, Iseul-ah."

Tears welled in my eyes, and I kept my lips sealed, forbidding myself from uttering the words that prickled in my mouth: *How could you think to die? How could you leave me, after all I have done to reunite with you?*

I could not reprimand my sister. How dare I? I hadn't witnessed the unspeakable atrocities she had endured. I hadn't spent weeks in the midst of the captured, anguished women and girls torn away from their lives. I hadn't witnessed the heartwrenching sight of an infant, carried off by the corpse-disposing ojakin. I had no right to dictate what she should feel.

All I could do was hold Suyeon's hand. "It will happen, Older Sister," the words burned in my throat.

*It must.*

# 36

# DAEHYUN

**Wind and darkness tumbled outside** the House of Bright Flowers, and uneasiness stirred within.

"We are a day away from a coup, and Choi Ikjun is dead," Maggot said, flicking a narrowed-eyed stare at Daehyun.

He stared back. Iseul's pet name for Official Wu Sayong was indeed fitting—the man was as vile to behold as the soft-bodied grub that feasted upon decay. Yet his contempt was pinned upon another—the killer on the loose, causing mayhem on the eve of a rebellion. He had searched for Wonsik's son, as Iseul had requested, only to uncover two facts: The young man was missing, and shortly before his disappearance, he had been in search of "a girl named Iseul."

Perhaps it was a good thing that Iseul was secured within Wongaksa Temple . . .

"All we know," Maggot continued, his reedy voice grating at Daehyun's nerves, "is that Official Choi was found in a palanquin, placed on the road facing Gyeongbok Palace."

"Did Nameless Flower leave another bloody message behind?" Official Seong inquired.

"No one seems to know. The State Tribunal moved quick,

leaving behind little to be witnessed, and the king has ordered strict silence over this incident. His Majesty will not even confide in me, a senior first-ranking official. But . . ." Maggot's stare crawled down the long table around which the coup leaders had gathered and stopped before Daehyun. "Perhaps you know, daegam? The palanquin was meant for that girl, Iseul. Why did her uncle end up in it?"

"I suppose Choi consulted you," Daehyun retorted brusquely. "It was your idea, perhaps, that he kidnap the girl—?"

"*Gentlemen.*" Deputy Commander Park splayed his fingers on the table; his stare remained pinned on the map before him. "We will investigate the matter once the coup is over."

"My concern is," Maggot pressed, "that any one of us might be next."

Six other officials were present, and they all exchanged nervous glances.

"We have our private soldiers, do we not?" The deputy stared down each man, as though to shoot down their fears. "Keep them close, gentlemen, at all times. With only a day remaining, we must rein in all our thoughts, all our concerns, and focus our minds upon the Great Event and nothing else."

Maggot slid his hand against his jaw, his stringy beard whispering against his touch. "Of course. You are right, deputy."

"Now." He rapped his knuckle against the map. "Military Official Park Yeong Mun will lead the troops from Suwon and should reach the Han River before the first watch. They are likely marching over as we speak. Once they cross the river"—he slid his knuckle across the sheet—"they will meet us at the military training field here. Soldiers from the Royal Stable Department will also arrive, along with the newly recruited generals and their men from the Hunting Department. They have pledged up to five thousand soldiers."

"So we will have more men than originally thought," Maggot observed. "A total of fifteen thousand . . ."

As the deputy's voice continued to rumble, Daehyun returned his stare to Maggot. It was loathsome, the thought of handing any young woman to this man, let alone Iseul's own sister.

"Daegam." The deputy scowled his way. "It seems you have not heard a word I have said."

"The troops will attack from the northwest Hyehwa Gate and northeast from the Changui Gate," Daehyun replied. "And I will release eight hundred prisoners from Milwicheong."

A muscle worked in the deputy's jaw, then he spoke. "Official Yun Hyungro will go to protect Grand Prince Jinseong. Officials Un Sangun and Lee Gye, along with dozens of other soldiers, will stand by in case of unforeseen occurrences. Others will be sent to assassinate key personnel—"

"And who shall go before Dowager Queen Jeonghyun?" another official interrupted. "We must receive permission to place her son on the throne. It is upon her decision that our entire revolt rests."

"Deputy Commander Park will go, of course," Maggot murmured, sliding his gaze down to the man, who squared his shoulders and raised his bearded chin. "And you tell the dowager, if she refuses to place her son on the throne, that there are other princes who would most gladly become king."

More questions arose from the officials present, rising with panic as the morrow encroached. Questions about the grand prince's wife, about her family members who had refused to join the coup. Questions about key locations they would strive to take control over. And there was one question that was asked over and over.

"Are you certain, deputy commander, that the king will vacate the capital tomorrow? Are you certain, absolutely certain, that he will leave for Kaesong City?"

"We chose the eighteenth for this very reason," the deputy reassured the men each time. "The capital will be empty for our taking."

But no matter how much the deputy reassured each official, the discussion grew more fraught, as though every man were inspecting the thoroughness of his lifeline. By the time the questions and demands died down, the sky had turned into the miserable gray of dawn.

"Daehyun-gun." The deputy lay a cautious hand on Daehyun's shoulder. "You keep to your plan. General Jin will meet you at the Red Lantern Inn in the afternoon for further planning."

Daehyun lowered the brim of his hat, about to set out, when a shadow slid up beside him.

"One moment." Maggot drew him to the side. "The Milwicheong idea, I hear it was yours. With such a mind, you have a bright future awaiting you."

"Indeed?" Daehyun was done with courtesies. "Go on. What do you want?"

His smile only deepened. "What do I want? I only wish for you the brightest of futures, daegam." He took a step closer, and he whispered, "Be careful whose side you choose. The side of a mere chit, who has no connections whatsoever to speak of? Or us—the ones who are soon to rule this kingdom? You must betray or be betrayed. That is the way of the world, daegam."

# 37

# ISEUL

**The day had arrived.**

The eighteenth of the ninth lunar month.

At the break of dawn, attendants poured into the temple, overwhelming in number. They hurried to prepare us for the king's grand procession. Our faces were washed with rice bran water, our hair brushed until it flowed as silk, and our skin glowed with light doses of oil. Soon the scent of sandalwood perfumed the temple.

"How grand will the king's procession be? I can hardly imagine it . . . ," I asked under my breath, powdering my painted face with a silkworm cocoon. "Will His Majesty travel with many soldiers?"

"Oh, many, many soldiers," the attendant replied. "He will be traveling with three defense layers of guards, and the whole procession will be composed of over ten thousand soldiers and over two thousand horses!"

I gripped the cocoon tighter, staring at my reflection in the bronze mirror; a stranger stared back at me. *Ten thousand fewer men to fight. Ten thousand steps closer to victory.*

The mantra continued, whispers in my head, as we were

lined up and led out onto the streets. I held Suyeon's arm to help her walk, and as we proceeded down the crowded road, my gaze drifted eastward. I could imagine the fortress gate, with its grand pagoda eaves, the soldiers making their rounds on the parapet, assuming today was an ordinary day. Perhaps they were complaining about their tired legs, about the heat of the beating sun, about their next meal. But tonight, when darkness descended, the soldiers would peer out over the parapet, blinking in confusion at the approaching sea of torches. Thousands upon thousands of rebels come to reclaim the kingdom.

*Please let us win*, I begged the heavens. *Please—*

The procession turned from its path. We were no longer walking down Jongno Road, and the sight of the fortress wall steered out of view. The procession of women then disappeared, row by row, into Changgyeon Palace. Confusion spun through me as I found myself caught in this flow, drawn through a pair of red gates and into an immense field surrounded by ornate trees and royal pavilions.

"Perhaps the king is still asleep," Suyeon whispered, as though sensing my unease. "Sometimes His Majesty drinks too much to rise the next morn."

I desperately wanted to believe this. "Perhaps what you say is true," I whispered, linking my arm tighter around my sister's. "Perhaps we will depart again soon—"

"We shall not," came another voice. A captive glanced over her shoulder at us. "Apparently the king has changed his mind. The girls at the front of the line, they overheard eunuchs conversing with the court ladies."

"What was said?" I demanded.

She looked at me strangely. "Simply that the trip to Kaesong City has been abandoned. And thank the heavens for that. I would rather not walk to such a faraway city. And your friend here would likely collapse before we reached the city walls."

Shock set in, and I struggled to steady my breath. This could not be. The procession needed to leave by nightfall. The capital needed to be empty. The entire coup had been planned meticulously around this one opportunity.

As I tried to make sense of the situation, another captive leaned in to whisper, "It is because of Nameless Flower, I hear. He left a new blood message on his latest victim, the most taunting one of all. The girl who spent the night with His Majesty overheard the king's entire discussion with an investigator."

My head throbbed, unable to think through the blare of panic.

"The king is determined to find Nameless Flower by tonight," the girl continued. "Remember the policy, where the literate had to submit four pieces of their writing to the government? So that the king could compare documents whenever slander was sent his way? Well, since weeks ago, officials have been comparing them with the killer's writing. They are now down to a thousand or so documents—"

"Well," I finally managed to ask, "what did the killer write this time?"

She glanced around, bit her lower lip, then whispered, "*You shall see me soon, your most loathsome subject, Nameless Flower. And history shall forever remember me as the man who killed the king.*"

Her voice faded as blood roared in my ears. Nameless Flower

knew about the coup, there was no doubt. I needed to warn the prince, but everywhere I looked, there were armed guards and I could not leave my sister's side. Cold sweat drenched my back, and I watched helplessly as the sun moved across the heavens, marking the passage of time into an unknown future.

The sky darkened around us, and the air grew colder as the evening settled in. The curfew bell began to toll, each one lasting for what felt like an eternity, and by the twenty-eighth ring, gates groaned shut, locking for the night.

The guards overseeing us glanced around, confused and distressed. We all were. Everything was going wrong, and at the same time, no one—including myself—knew what was happening.

Complete silence blanketed the capital, except for the occasional footsteps of officers on patrol. The dark trees around us rustled in the mountain wind. A squeaking rodent scurried by.

I closed my eyes. I feared that if I kept them open, staring at the peaceful nothingness beyond the palace walls, I would lose my sanity. Slowly, I counted under my breath. "One, two, three . . ." My heart thundered in my chest as I tried to ward away shadowy thoughts—that there would be no coup, that Nameless Flower would somehow expose us, that we would all end up dead. Fearful imaginings wrapped around my heart like a noose, and I could hardly breathe. " . . . four hundred, four hundred and one, four hundred and two . . ." With every moment that passed, the cold sunk deeper into my bones. Suyeon needed to leave, and if the coup failed, I was certain she would desperately claw her way over the palace wall, and I would follow . . .

Perhaps we would escape the capital and live in hiding

for the remainder of our lives. But, most likely, Suyeon and I would die just beyond the palace walls, faces pressed into the soil, arrows lodged in our backs. Would death hurt very much? I hoped, if it came to pass, that our deaths would be swift—a burst of agony, followed immediately by a peaceful silence.

". . . nine hundred ninety-nine, a thousand, a thousand and one—"

A gasp pierced the silence.

My eyes shot open, and I saw hands pointing to the distant sky. A single arrow blazed bright, then vanished.

"Wh-what was that?" a girl next to me stuttered.

We all remained still, then flinched at a great crashing noise.

"Did you hear that?" a guard whispered, abandoning us to huddle among themselves. "Where did it come from?"

"From Changui Gate."

As far as an hour's walk away.

Another crash fractured the night, rumbling from the northwestern end. Everyone whirled around, confused as more noise clashed from all corners of the capital.

"Damn it!" A guard with a square jaw threw off his military hat. "We've been here all day. Someone go find out what is happening—!" The words vanished from his mouth, and his eyes widened. "What in heavens . . ."

Hundreds upon thousands of torches blazed from over the palace walls. Yells and screams battered against the stone like stormy waves. It felt as though we were trapped in a sinking ship, forgotten in the dank and dreary hold, with no notion of what was occurring above deck.

"M-maybe those are Japanese warlords," a woman whispered. "They have finally invaded Joseon."

"I hear they are rebels," another cried, joy brimming in her voice. "It is our fathers and our husbands. They have come to rescue us!"

A dozen or so women pushed against one another, shoving through the crowd to make their way toward the nearest gate. "We are going home!" they sobbed. Desperation rippled through the mass, and the crowd began surging toward the narrow gate like a tidal wave. Women pushed aside the guards and beat at the locked double doors, screaming, "We are inside! Do not leave without us!"

More shoves and pushes, and soon I could not move, caught in the middle of the sea with my sister, surging toward the red gate.

"Stop! The rebels are not here to save us!" I cried at the top of my lungs, trying to keep the courtesans from pouring out into the main road in their sheer jackets and pink dresses, right into the heart of the violence. "We must stay calm and move as one! If you wish to return home, we must head for the mountains. Tell your companions! Head for the mountains! We must avoid the coup leaders at all cost—!"

A shoulder slammed into my back, knocking me to the ground. I lay stunned, staring at the scrambling feet. Suyeon's scream rung somewhere high above. Sandals trampled my hand. Whimpering, I struggled onto my elbows.

A pair of boots charged toward me—I could not move soon enough. A crushing weight stomped across my back.

Pain exploded across my ribs, and darkness crashed down around me.

"Here, let me assist," came a male voice.

Dirt scratched against my cheek. Someone gave a gentle shake of my shoulder, and I emerged momentarily. A woman was leaning over me, the moonlight blotting out her face.

"We are not losing each other," her voice blared through my aching head, "not for a second time."

The moonlight pulsed. The brightness hurt my eyes, and I was suddenly back at home. Suyeon and I huddled close, watching the blazing glow of a hundred torches invade our mansion, searching for us. Mother gathered us in her arms, her cheeks wet.

*May you never be alone in this kingdom*, she sobbed out a prayer, while a fist banged on our door, *and may you find good friends who will hold you close—even when the kingdom is falling into the sea. Then this mother can die without any regrets.*

On and on, I tumbled into dream after dream, or I lay in an icy pool where memories seemed to blur into nightmares. I surfaced again into the crisp night to the sound of fearful voices.

Women whispered among themselves. "The coup leaders have entered the palace. All the women are running to them."

"We mustn't. If what she said is true, we must run away."

"Which way?"

"To the mountains."

When I awoke, I found myself leaning against my sister. Her face was covered in bruises, and we were not alone. We stood huddled in the yard behind a pavilion among a hundred or so other women. Their powdered and rouged faces had melted under their sweat and tears. Terrified eyes gleamed in the moonlight.

"Where are we?" I whispered.

Suyeon looked at me. "You're awake. Do you think you can run?"

I pressed my aching ribs. "Of course."

"We have escaped into Changdeokgung; the two palaces are interconnected. The route we are to take will draw us closest to the mountain. All the gates have been locked since curfew, so we will need time to escape."

"And have they entered yet? The rebels?" I whispered, my heartbeat throbbing at my temple.

She nodded. "No royal guard dared to stop them—nearly all of them abandoned their post, I heard. Even the king's personal guard ran away to join the coup. Now the rebels have swarmed the southern half of the palace, so we must be quick before our paths cross."

The girl standing before us glanced back. Cheonbi. "We have all imagined escaping from the king and his men," she whispered. "Every night our dreams are of this—of running through this labyrinth and never escaping. But perhaps tonight we shall." She stepped back and waved her hand. "We will move now!"

As the women rushed forward, she remained, waving at the crowd to move faster as she hissed out, "Remember! Maintain this line! The moment we lose our formation, we lose the opportunity to return home!"

Shallow breaths filled the night as a hundred or so women followed Suyeon and me, treading lightly from courtyard to courtyard, passing quickly in pairs through narrow gates. The journey felt endless, as though we had spiraled into a nightmare of never-ending courtyards. My breathing sharpened into pants. I pressed a hand against my side, pain exploding each time my ribs expanded for air. But the pain was minute compared with the terror of being caught.

"We are almost there!" Cheonbi hurried up to join us at the front. "I heard you earlier. Many of us did. Did you mean it? The rebels are not here to save us?"

I nodded. "The coup leaders intend to distribute the courtesans among themselves as victory spoils."

She nodded, growing pale.

Suyeon looked unfazed. "Then I am glad we managed to persuade as many women as possible to stay away from them."

"Who was the man who assisted you?" I asked after a pause. "I heard a man's voice."

"It was a royal guard," she replied absentmindedly. "Come, let us go now."

We ducked our heads low as we crept by residential complexes where royals quaked within. A lone mutt tailed behind us for a few moments, then scampered off into the moon-speckled shadows. Then the courtyards and pavilions grew into a thicket of trees, a walled-in and hilly forest within the palace itself. Women were heaving for air as we hurried down a winding path, past streams and lotus ponds and pagodas, then off the path we went, up a steep slope that left us staggering and clawing at the soil.

"How are you able to keep going?" I barely managed to ask my sister.

She was drenched in sweat, shaking and pale, but her eyes

gleamed bright. "The thought of home gives me strength—
Look. We have arrived."

The women dropped to the ground or collapsed against
the trees, heaving for air while staring at a little red gate that
appeared and disappeared as the clouds shifted across the moon.

"The palace sprawls around the left foot of Mount Bugak,
along Eung-bong Peak," Suyeon said between gasps, "and this is
the gate closest to the mountain. It is isolated enough that we
will hopefully have time to break it down."

I hobbled over, still clutching my side. Every breath sent a
thousand pinpricks through me. Together with another woman,
we pulled off the moss-covered wooden bars. I tried pulling at
the brass handle, but the door barely budged, locked together
by thick chains.

"Here, let me try." Cheonbi, holding a large rock, raised her
arms back, then jammed the rock into the chain. Nothing happened. A few other women offered to try, confident at first, that
either the chain would break or the wood would splinter, but
their confidence wore off after several failed attempts.

"We could climb over," one suggested half-heartedly.

We all peered up at the stone wall.

"We saw several soldiers scaling over them."

"But they were taller than us . . . Perhaps we should have followed the eunuchs, who escaped through the lavatory."

"Escape through a tunnel full of the king's feces?" Cheonbi
grimaced. "I would rather die here."

I winced, reaching for the top of the palace wall, and my
fingertips skimmed the tiles that capped it. "It is not too high,"
I said. "It will take time to get all of us over, but we need to try.

Perhaps if we can find a rock along this wall, large enough to step on—"

"They're up there," came a female voice from below.

My blood instantly turned to ice, and the women around me clamped hands over their mouths.

"I followed her," the voice continued, "as you ordered."

My mouth filled with curses. We were too close to freedom to lose it now. "Have all the women huddle close to the wall, right by the gate and nowhere else," I whispered to Cheonbi. "They must climb over now. Use one another's backs."

"And you?"

"I will distract the rebels, lead them astray if I can. And you must promise to get my sister out first. Drag her if you must."

She nodded, and with that, I grabbed the rock abandoned by the gate. Cautiously, I slid down the slope, the moonlight blocked by clouds and the world nearly pitch dark. I tucked myself behind a trunk once the women were out of sight, waiting to bludgeon Maggot in the face, or at least one of Maggot's men. I would strike, then run away, and perhaps his men would follow . . .

Heavy footsteps crunched up the slope.

Wiping my clammy hand on my skirt, I tightened my grip on the rock, winding my strength up. Praying that it would be Maggot at the front.

Twigs snapped just beyond the tree.

*Now, Iseul!*

I whirled out, heaving the rock forward. But a hand caught my wrist. No matter how hard I wrenched my arm, his steel grip remained on me. With my free hand, I groped about and grabbed his collar, dragging the man forward—to bite him, to bash my head into his, anything—when the clouds drifted apart once more. The shadows crept aside, and I gaped, unable to believe my eyes, convinced I had fallen into a dream. My entire body shook as he gently lowered my arm. The rock dropped from my grip.

"Iseul and her weapon of choice," Daehyun whispered, almost endearingly. "Why did we trouble ourselves with this coup nonsense when we could have sent you in with your deadly rock?"

I had never been happier to see him, and I would have flung my arms around his neck if not for the dire circumstances. And he was also not alone. Behind him stood three strapping men garbed in white prisoner robes.

"Who are they?" I asked.

"Men I released from the Milwicheong Prison. The rest have rounded up an entire crowd outside the palace."

I frowned. "How did you find us?"

A girl peeked out from behind the prince and waved sheepishly. She was a lowly musuri palace servant. "I followed you all the way into the garden and left markers for the prince to find."

Another woman joined us. It was Yul, and my heart soared with delight.

"Where are the rest?" Yul asked.

"The king is missing," Daehyun added, "and the coup leaders are headed this way. The women must escape at once."

"Follow me." I quickly led them up, and as we approached the top, I called out, "They are friends!"

The silhouettes of the women remained tense, stiff with panic, until the prince spoke.

"The three of you kneel," he directed, pointing to the prisoners, and despite their grumbling, they acquiesced. "Women will step onto you to reach the wall. And Yul, you will hoist the women up and help them over." He turned to me. "And where is your sister—?"

"Jonggeum? I forced her over," Cheonbi declared. "She was as light as a feather." Then, stepping atop the prisoner's back, she climbed over the wall and called out to someone on the other side. "All is well! Iseul is here with her sweetheart!"

*Sweetheart?*

No. No, I dared not think of us beyond this night.

I could never return to the capital, not for as long as Maggot lived. His lust would forever be a threat to my sister's happiness. I could never return to the warm embrace of the Red Lantern Inn, to the days when only a wall had separated me from Daehyun . . .

As though sensing my anguish, Daehyun caught my gaze and took my wrist. Slowly, he drew me into his embrace, the warmth of him surrounding me, and every fiber of my soul ached under his touch. With his lips grazing the tendrils of my hair, he whispered, "You must take caution, once on the other side. Nameless Flower is still out there."

I remained still against him, unable to form a single word.

Nothing seemed more terrifying at the moment than leaving his side.

"Yul will guide you and the others to safety." He moved aside strands of my hair, then pressed a kiss onto my brow. "You need to go now." He held my waist, and in one movement, I was up in the air, perched atop the stone wall.

"Hwang Iseul," his voice rasped, his hands gripping tight onto my skirt, "if by any chance we do not meet again in this lifetime, then I will find you in the next—or as many lifetimes as it takes to see you again."

Off in the distance, the footsteps of dozens upon dozens of men marched closer.

"Iseul-ah!" came Yul's harsh whisper. "Come down, now! We must leave at once!"

Hotness blurred my eyes. I clutched the tiles, and as I slid to the other side of the wall, a sob gathered in my chest. I had bid Mother farewell in such a way—over the walls—and had never seen her again.

"Don't die," I whispered to the prince. He looked up at me, holding me with his grief-stricken gaze. What could I say in this moment? What could I possibly say? My voice shook as I spoke. "So long as you live, we'll have the rest of our lives to find each other again. And I will find you again. I promise."

# 38

# DAEHYUN

Daehyun stared down at Wonsik's journal. He had hoped to return it to her, along with her mother's ring, but he had lost the chance to do so. He shoved the journal inside his robe, securing it under the sash band. *I will see her again*, he assured himself, then looked up at the pack of rebels surrounding him and the three prisoners. Dawning a mask of nonchalance, Daehyun watched as Maggot circled the sweating men.

"Dusty footprints on their backs," Maggot sneered. "Such petite footprints, too . . ." He walked over and sniffed Daehyun's robe. "You smell like one of the king's women—of chamomile and sandalwood."

It took Daehyun immense control not to strike Maggot. All that mattered at the moment was that he'd made sure to cover their tracks on the slope and had bribed each prisoner to silence.

"I am not sure what you mean," Daehyun remarked innocently.

Maggot grinned, a predatory smile. "Should a man suddenly be found dead on the night of a coup, would that draw any suspicion my way? What do you think about that, daegam?"

More torches hurried down a hillside.

"The deputy commander has ordered us out of the palace." The soldier panted for air, as did the others behind him. "We have led the search too far north. According to witnesses, the deposed king escaped and was seen heading south on foot. He is likely headed for the Yongsan District. There is a small port facility in operation by the Han River there— Wait!" The soldier held out his hands before anyone could move. "It is the new king's strictest order that we capture Yeonsan and bring him back alive."

This gave Daehyun pause; it gave everyone pause.

"May the new king live and reign for ten thousand years," he whispered, then shoved past Maggot so hard the man spun around and had to grab hold of a soldier for support. "Perhaps you should put aside your lustful intentions," Daehyun growled, flicking a glance over at the vile creature, "and focus on finding the deposed king? What do you think about that, my lord?"

Maggot paled with fury, and in that moment, Daehyun knew he had received a death sentence. And he found himself rather surprised at how little he cared about how his story might end. All that mattered was the future of the young woman escaping into the dark of the mountains.

*Run, Iseul.* He cast one last look up the slope as a drop of rain splashed onto his cheek. *Be safe and be well.*

# 39

# ISEUL

**We traveled through the rainfall,** our painted and rouged faces washed as bare as the river rocks beneath our aching feet.

"Where are we heading?" I called out.

"We need to get the women out of the capital," Yul replied, carrying my exhausted sister on her back, "so we will journey through the mountain to Changui Gate. It is three hours or so away, but for now, we must find shelter. It is too hazardous to proceed in this weather."

Though we ventured along the foot of Mount Bugak, the trail was still treacherous, with sharp rocks and tangled tree roots. Women slipped, mud splashing, knees and elbows bleeding, but we eventually made it deep enough into the mountain to wait out the rain under a large copse.

"The rain will wash away our trail," Yul assured the women as she settled my sister onto the ground. "And we are far enough now from the rebels. Though I do not think they will bother to hunt down a few dozen women in the middle of a coup." She then crouched before Suyeon and murmured, "There is nothing to fear."

"Thank you," my sister whispered through pale lips.

Yul nodded, then glanced around. "Wait here a moment. I will return soon."

*There is nothing to fear.* I repeated this to myself as I stood next to my sister, staring out into the shadowy thicket of trees into which Yul had disappeared. An uneasiness prickled the back of my neck. *There is nothing to fear, Iseul-ah.*

And yet I could not stop staring at the darkness.

"You intend to stay with this group?" a girl whispered, huddling among a few others nearby. "I am leaving for home in the morning."

Another female voice replied, "But will your parents accept you back?"

"I'm certain they will. Our mothers embraced us in their wombs for many long months, raised us and loved us. And so many fathers lost their lives trying to help their daughters escape the palace. They are waiting for us. I know it."

*Some families might embrace their daughters' return,* I thought. *But what of the others?* Darkness seeped into my mind, and I tried not to think of their fates, nor those of the hundreds of women I had failed to lead into the mountain.

When Yul returned, she held a skirt full of bright red berries. They looked poisonous, but I shook my head. I trusted Yul—she was a master forager.

"It is omija," Yul said, distributing the clusters to the women. "It will improve your vitality."

The berries, the little sounds of twigs snapping, the lurking shadows . . . uneasiness expanded then coiled into a tight ball in the pit of my stomach. Something was about to go terribly wrong. Or perhaps I thought this simply because it seemed too good to believe that Older Sister was finally returning home.

As Yul and Suyeon quietly conversed, I sat behind them on the other side of the tree trunk. I didn't wish for my sister to see my needless distress; she had to rest. Subconsciously, my hand moved, and I found myself staring down at Daehyun's transcription of Investigator Gu's report, and at once, the uneasiness unfurled and a memory surfaced. The killer's last words to the king, on the eve of the rebellion.

*You shall see me soon, your most loathsome subject, Nameless Flower. And history shall forever remember me as the man who killed the king.*

Nameless Flower seemed to have known a coup would occur . . . But what did it matter whether he killed the king or not? It did not endanger us or our cause—

I startled when a shadow dropped by my side; it was only Cheonbi crouching next to me.

"Want some?" she asked, offering me a cluster of berries.

I watched as she popped one into her mouth. Red juice dribbled down her chin as her expression twisted as though the berry were sour, sweet, and bitter all at once.

"No," I whispered, gazing back down at the document. At Daehyun's handwriting.

"Is this from your lover?"

I ran my hand over the prince's handwriting, my finger lingering over the words he had circled: *Yongjam binyeo.* I frowned.

"This hairpin once belonged to a queen," I murmured to myself, then glanced at Cheonbi. "Have you ever seen a yongjam binyeo before?"

"Of course. I have dwelled among royals long enough." She popped another berry into her mouth, her face twisting again as she said, "They are long golden rods with a dragon-shaped engraving on one end."

I tensed as a feeling of familiarity pinched at my mind. At the sound of shuffling, I glanced behind us to see Yul quickly gathering up a pile of berries she must have dropped. When she looked up, our eyes locked, and her face turned ghastly pale. She knew something.

I folded the letter and walked over, a memory rolling into my mind—of Yul's hairpin, the one she had quickly hidden from me. The one that was gold with a dragon-shaped engraving. A heavy weight of anxiety stifled me.

"You have a yongjam binyeo," I whispered. "Who gave it to you?"

She grew paler, still picking up the berries.

"That pin is somehow connected to the killer." I crouched before her at eye level. "Wonsik seemed to think so."

"Wonsik-samchon told me to tell no one, that it would endanger the life of anyone who knew."

"I am not anyone. Wonsik would have wanted me to know."

Her hand stilled, and she stared at the berries in her palm. "My parents died in the forbidden territory, as you know..." She plucked a berry off its stem, then placed it into my sister's mouth. "Upon hearing this news, a jester gave me this hairpin, telling me that this would secure a bright future for me. He had promised my father, you see, that he would always watch out for me. My father was once a jester, too, before marrying my mother."

"And . . . why were you hiding it?" I pressed.

"I was scared. The jester had given me such a precious item, and I knew he must have stolen it. He was found dead the next day. This was a year or so ago. I hid it and have tried not to think of it ever since."

I continued to stare at the berries. Among the jesters there was only one who knew the details of the coup . . . I shook my head, refusing to suspect Yeongho.

"How is it that Wonsik came to know about it?"

"He saw me trying to bury it after you'd seen it in my room. He asked to make a sketch of it." She rolled a berry between her fingers, then finally ate it. "Wonsik told me to hide it until the king was deposed and Nameless Flower stopped killing, then to pawn it and keep the fortune for myself."

I took a berry from Yul's hand and popped it into my mouth. Five flavors exploded across my tongue, and I realized then how famished I was. Taking another, I sat next to the two women and stitched together what I knew.

"The hairpin belonged to Deposed Queen Yun," I said, to which my sister stirred, the barest frown flickering across her ashen face. "It was kept by her mother, Lady Shin, who, in her old age, thoughtlessly gave it as a gift to her female companion. The story grows complicated, but in the end, the female companion ended up buried in the Dead Garden case, and somehow this hairpin traveled from South Jeolla to the capital then into the hands of jesters . . ."

"This case you speak of sounds impossibly complex," Suyeon whispered. "But you have never allowed yourself to be constrained by what others might deem impossible."

I held my head, my mind as tangled as the branches above us. A knot of suspicions and coincidences and possibilities, of two cases separated by a chasm of two years, yet somehow connected.

*Concentrate yourself upon the details,* Wonsik would have said if he were here.

I imagined Wonsik sitting next to me on the forest floor, his straw hat shading his gruff features, his straw cloak concealing his sword. *Yeongho speaks with a Southern Jeolla accent. Is that a detail, ajusshi? Or is that a mere coincidence?*

*Never ignore coincidences.* Wonsik's warm and deep voice rumbled through my soul. *Probe them apart until you are absolutely certain that there is no connection.*

*There was a son from the Dead Garden case . . . What if Yeongho is that son? That man ran away a year ago, at the same time another appeared among a troupe of jesters. That, too, is a coincidence.*

*It is, indeed.*

*But even if Yeongho were the son from the Dead Garden case . . .* I heaved a sigh, my head aching. *There is no sure connection between that case and Nameless Flower, besides our theory about the bloody messages on the victims' robes . . .*

*Then I suppose there is more evidence to uncover, until you at last find the path that will take you to the truth.*

I wrapped my arms around my knees. *Did you know, ajusshi? Before you died, did you figure out who the killer was?*

Emptiness stared back at me, and his absence left a hole in my chest.

Wonsik was gone, and I had to find the truth without him.

As I stared out at the shadows again, I sensed that this truth could not wait. That something awful would occur if I left the investigation for another day.

As the cool night faded into dawn, the air warmed, giving birth to a thick, swirling fog that enveloped the earth. It was so dense that my very own feet were hidden from sight as we emerged from the forest. The uneasiness followed me out as well, and I kept eyes on the shadows that lurked between the trees, between the huts, between the groups of people. And what a crowd there was.

Men and women, young and old, hurried down the road. Children ran about, weaving in between the adults, and farmers pushed carts full of mothers and infants. "They're still gathered before Gyeongbok Palace!" the people cried. "The deputy has convinced the Dowager Queen! Grand Prince Jinseong is our new king!"

As we passed, our procession of women garbed in muddy pink silk drew the attention of a few onlookers, their curiosity piqued by our uncommon attire. Yet their interest proved fleeting; no one lingered, beckoned away by the distant shouts of triumph.

The boisterous crowd thinned as we approached Changui Gate, an open wound of fallen soldiers. Arrows protruded from chests, limbs cracked and twisted. Filmy eyes stared blankly up at the sky. Blood everywhere. We quickly stepped over and around the dead, surprised to see only a light scattering of corpses, rather than mounds of them. It was as though most of the soldiers had decided to escape or join the rebels themselves.

We quickly passed them by, out of the gate and out onto the wide, dusty road that wended through tree-lined slopes.

"I think, with the fog, it will be safe enough for us to travel on the main road," Yul said quietly to the group of women. Only a few dozen remained; the rest had scattered that morning, deciding to hide in their respective homes in the capital, certain their family would take them in. "We will journey to the Red Lantern Inn. And there, we shall figure out how to send the rest of you home—"

"I have no home." Cheonbi stepped around a corpse, her eyes beaded with tears. "I know my parents will welcome me back, but not the village. They will humiliate and harass my family, until our home no longer feels safe. I cannot do this to them. I am a ruined woman in this kingdom."

"You know what the royal guards called us?" said another with a freckle under her eye, and more women huddled closer to Yul. "When they thought no one was listening? King Yeonsan's whores."

"Our old lives are gone," a chipped-tooth woman added bitterly. "We may be free, but we are entirely lost. Tarnished."

Yul sighed. "Tarnished? You speak of yourselves as though you were torn silks and shattered pottery. But when I look at all of you," she said, sweeping an arm around at the small crowd, "I see *you*: Hopeful. Afraid. Strong. Most deeply loved. You all deserve a future, and if anyone *dares* to say otherwise, come directly to me, and I'll set them straight. In fact—!" She grew more animated, her cheeks flushing. "It's not you who are tarnished, but *them*! The king, his chehongsa officers, the coup leaders—anyone who would think to blame *you* for *their* crimes! *They* are the ones who should be ashamed!"

Her chest heaved, and when she finally caught her breath,

she straightened the front of her dress and calmly said, "We will figure something out, together. But for now we ought to keep moving."

A faint smile tugged at my lips. Yul was the glimmer of hope all the women needed. She had spoken aloud the words my own heart had struggled to articulate—

I paused. Raising my hand, I strained my eyes against the fog. Shadows undulated, coalescing into the silhouette of a tall, lanky man astride his steed. I lifted a dagger from a fallen soldier's body as the spectral figure pierced the white haze, and I beheld the sight of Royal Guard Crow. His dark hair was loosened from his topknot, greasy strands dripping down his face. He had a sword in hand.

Brandishing the bloody dagger, I demanded, "How long have you been following us?"

"Since you left the palace."

Yul stepped close behind me. "The prince told me you were gone. That you had been searching for Iseul shortly before your disappearance."

"I was," Crow replied, his voice tight as he slid off his saddle. "I've passed by the inn enough times to have seen the girl always conversing with my father about Nameless Flower."

"So it was *you*," Yul bit out. "My customers complained of a dark figure stalking them, lurking about the inn at odd hours."

Crow moved his sword, and my grip on the dagger tightened. "Stay still! Do not provoke me," I snapped, outrage and frustration choking me. "Why is it so irrationally difficult for men to simply leave women *alone*?!"

With a flick of his wrist, he sheathed his sword, then raised his hands, palms out. "Many often find it irrationally difficult to do what is right." In his dead eyes, a flicker of grief appeared as he looked at the women. "I abandoned my father because I could not face my shame . . . the shame of betraying my sister to maintain the king's favor." He lowered his gaze and locked his jaw. "And when Father died," his voice rasped, "I finally visited my sister's grave. I wanted to die there. My conscience weighed so heavily on me. But then I thought perhaps if I assisted with the coup, I could one day face my father and sister in the afterlife."

I frowned. "You knew of the coup?"

"My father never told me," he said, as though sensing my thoughts. "But when one spends enough time at the inn . . . you hear things, see things. I noticed that man named Yeongho. He seemed to take great pleasure in speaking of himself. He would boast to other jesters that the heavens were about to be moved and that he would help move them."

"That damned *fool*," Yul hissed.

"I also overheard him say that Iseul had sneaked into the palace," he murmured, looking at me. "So I returned for duty this morning, to see if I could assist you in any way. I had no idea the coup would occur so soon after."

"It was him," Cheonbi whispered, her finger shaking as she pointed. "He helped your sister drag you away from the crowd, kept you from being trampled."

Finally, I lowered the knife, bewildered. "What do you want from us? Why are you here?"

"You are returning to the Red Lantern. It will be a long journey, and I shall escort you all there to safety."

"How can we trust you?" I demanded.

"If I wished to kill you," he said dryly, "I would have killed you already. And you could not have stopped me."

He made a valid point.

"Let him accompany us," Yul said to me. "A rebellion has occurred, and when there are large crowds gathered, there will be those who misbehave. I should rather not have to deal with them on our own."

When the women reluctantly agreed, I kept watch of Crow as we traveled, the dagger still in my grip. He was once more mounted on his horse, riding ahead—a shadow in the fog that we followed. The women kept a wary eye on him, huddled close together. He was, after all, still a royal guard.

He was also a man I had wished to question for a very long time. I hurried ahead to walk alongside his horse.

"You mentioned Yeongho," I said once I had caught up. "Did your father ever mention suspicions about him?"

"No. My father is not wont to sharing his theories." Crow peered down at me. "He was a difficult investigator to work with, I hear."

"What do you mean?"

"Rumors about my father always found their way to me." He swiped aside a greasy strand of hair. "Other investigators claimed my father was short-tempered. He was egotistical, too, never sharing his thoughts about a case until the very end, when he was absolutely certain of the truth. Apparently, he despised having to ever explain his deductions to others. And he was always chastising the other young investigators for being blind to everything around them."

This sounded both like Wonsik and not like him at all. "Your father was a kind and warm man," I said.

"Was he? I suppose losing one's daughter to the king and failing to do anything about it is certainly a very humbling experience," he murmured. "But his habits were set in stone, it would seem, considering my father told you nothing about his suspicions."

"Your father was waiting to tell me," I realized, "until we traveled to South Jeolla."

Crow nodded, his grip on the reins tightening. "He must have realized something when he spoke to me on the morning of his death."

A chill coursed down my spine. "What did you discuss?"

"It is odd—I was so determined to never confess the truth to him, convinced men like Nameless Flower were needed in this kingdom," Crow said. "But it is his taunting that led to Father's death..."

"What did you confess?" I pressed.

"On the very first victim, there was a bloody message left on his robe. I read it, just before I left to fetch reinforcements, and Nameless Flower returned to smear blood over it. It read: *The king still smells of his mother's milk, for he wept like an infant over his mother's last words to him.*"

I frowned at this new knowledge. The boy who had been beaten by the king for mocking His Majesty's grief was indeed Nameless Flower. The killer had identified himself with the message, written perhaps in the spur of the moment, and realizing his error, he had gone back to cover it up.

"I wanted to aid the killer. I truly thought he was a guardian

of the people. Someone as brave as I wished to be..." Crow
shook his head. "I was a fool. I should have confessed all to my
father sooner—"

"There was one more thing that you hid," I said, a memory
brushing up against my mind. "On the day of Min Hyukjin's
murder, what did you hide under the bush?"

His brows shot up, then he recomposed himself. "It was
nothing—merely a gold pouch full of salt. It didn't seem significant enough to tell my father—but, seeing your face, perhaps
it was?"

My lips had fallen open.

"Yeongho's pouch," I whispered.

Crow frowned. Yul hurried over, asking me if something was
the matter, but her voice faded into the mist as I stood before
the memory of Yeongho: his wide grin, his large ears, his rough
hands clasping mine as he led me to the Royal Academy to see
my sister. *He* was Nameless Flower. The man who had taunted
the king... who had sworn he would kill the king.

"If Yeongho is the killer—"

"Yeongho?" Yul's voice rose with incredulity. "What are you
talking about?"

"Do you know if the prince intends to search for the king?"
I demanded.

"Well, of course," she replied. "He said he would leave to
search for His Majesty after assisting you."

My heart collided against an icy block of terror. "Yeongho
will search for the king, and so will the prince. Their paths are
likely to cross."

Crow and Yul stared at me in bewilderment, but there was

no time to explain. I needed to warn Daehyun. "Where might the king have gone?"

"I overheard that he may be headed south, to Yongsan District," Crow said. "There is a port there. But I'll wager they have already found him—"

"How far is Yongsan District?"

"An hour or so away."

"Iseul-ah." Yul held my arm, her brow furrowed. "I cannot guess what thoughts occupy your mind, but simply answer me this: Is the prince in danger?"

Tremors crept along my legs, along my arms. "I'm ... not sure."

"Your sister has me," Yul whispered, "but the prince is utterly alone . . ."

I hesitated, looking at Suyeon. Torn.

But she offered me a nod. *Go to him.*

"Crow—" I looked up at him, then recalled this was not his true name. "Gunwu, do you know the way to Yongsan port?"

"I do . . ."

"Then take me there."

He stiffened, a look of displeasure twisting his expression, but he nevertheless reached down to help lift me onto his horse. The moment I climbed on, we set off, wind blasting my face.

The distant mountains grew large, surrounding us like dark dragons rippling through the fog, and my head filled with the thundering of hooves as we sped in and out of villages. We finally came to a prancing halt at the sight of the Han River, its dark shores barely visible under the white haze, silhouettes of boats bobbing against a strong current.

"Damn it!" a male voice cursed, shooting through my nerves. A brawny man stalked into sight, peering up into the heavens, his hand stretched out. "It is raining *again*!"

"Sir," I called out. "Have you seen a troop of rebel soldiers? Have they come this way?"

He ran a hand over his scruffy beard as other boatsmen approached. "A long time ago. They have left already."

"They have found the king already?"

"The king!" The men shook their heads, grinning and chuckling. "We could hardly believe it. That the king should quake like a child. He threw a tantrum, didn't he, when we told him no boatsman would dare venture out in such weather. And when we threatened him, he scampered off like a mutt!"

"In which direction?"

He pointed, and my gaze moved along his scarred hand to a forested hill that peaked into a cliff, overlooking the river. "They went that way."

And, I feared, so had the prince.

# 40

# DAEHYUN

A shred of red silk fluttered on a branch.

Daehyun snatched it, recognizing it from King Yeonsan's dragon robe. "He must be near," he whispered, noticing a trail. He then turned his attention eastward. Only moments ago, soldiers had pressed through the short but heavy rainfall alongside him, combing the grounds in search of the deposed king. But now there was only fog, so dense he could barely see beyond his own fingertips.

Raising a wooden whistle, Daehyun blew out a sharp signal. Long moments passed before the silhouette of a soldier emerged. "Summon the men this way," Daehyun ordered. "Follow this track."

The soldier bowed, marking a tree by tying a yellow ribbon around it, then he plunged back into the haze.

Daehyun continued up the hill, following the path of muddy footprints—the desperate, scrambling footprints of a man bent on escaping all his heinous crimes. Daehyun's grip tightened around the scrap of silk as memories of blood thickened around him, of loved ones taken from him so cruelly, of the nights and days he had cried himself hoarse . . .

His thoughts spiraled as his steps quickened, and soon all he could think of was the task awaiting him. It was his duty to avenge the deaths of his loved ones, and he knew well the depths to which he would have to sink to kill King Yeonsan. It would require him to dig a second grave—one for himself. Nothing could spare Daehyun's life after disobeying the new king's order that Yeonsan be captured alive.

But the satisfaction of running a sword through the man . . .

It was too tempting.

He drew his sword as the trail brought him to a clearing. He surveyed his surroundings, then abruptly paused as the fog moved, unveiling the edge of a cliff. He inched closer and peered down. He could not see it, but he could hear the rushing of the river far below, so violently fast that if he were to shove Yeonsan over, the corpse would disappear under the current, and no one would ever know who had killed him . . .

"Daehyun-gun!"

He flinched around. The heady smell of bloodlust vanished as he watched Iseul stagger out from the thicket. He sheathed his sword, his hands trembling, shock rippling through his being as though he'd been snatched away from the edge of oblivion.

"I heard the soldiers mention . . . where you were . . ." She gripped the sleeve of his robe, trying to catch her breath.

He remained still, his hand cupping the back of her head, staring down at the wisps of her hair. He had almost forgotten— there was no satisfaction to be found in vengeance. Yeonsan had purged hundreds upon hundreds of men, and his thirst for revenge had only grown. That agonizing hunger would carve into Daehyun's own soul, leaving him secretive and bitter; Iseul would come to despise him. And that he could never live with.

*The dead are dead.* He knew that was what they would have said—Hyukjin, Wonsik, his mother, and his brothers. *But she is still among the living. Be good to those who are still alive.*

Drawing in an unsteady breath, his attention sharpened on the young woman before him. What had eluded him the previous night, concealed by darkness, now became starkly apparent—the livid scrape on the side of her face, a cut on the bridge of her nose, the blood spot in the white of her left eye.

"It is over." His hand hovered against her cheek, his chest constricting painfully. "You are safe now. No one will hurt you again—"

"Daehyun-gun," she cried quietly. "It is not over. Not yet."

He frowned, then straightened himself. "Where is your sister?" his voice rasped. "Has something happened?"

"Yul is taking care of her. I came because I needed to warn you: Yeongho is the killer. *He* is Nameless Flower. You must have him arrested at once!"

He was shocked, but he was far more stunned that she would have left her sister to travel all this way to tell him. "You care about me."

"You damn fool, of course I do!" She nearly sobbed, and he felt his heart full to bursting. "Yeongho is here somewhere; I'm sure of it. He must be among those men searching for the king. You must have him arrested at once before he harms you!"

"In truth," he said quietly, brushing aside a loose strand of her hair, "I fail to understand why I am in danger. Perhaps you can enlighten me? Tell me everything, from the start, about how you came to this conclusion."

# 41

# ISEUL

Once all was explained, I remained standing before the prince, examining him. He was unharmed. My darkest imaginings had been unwarranted.

"Perhaps I am wrong," I whispered, my head aching as my thoughts entangled again, "but it would still be best to have him arrested."

"I believe you have grounds for suspicion. As soon as the soldiers arrive, I shall give orders to arrest Yeongho. Though, before his arrest, I would hope that he would succeed in assassinating the deposed king, which would be a favor to us all."

"He deserves to be decapitated before the entire populace," I growled. "Why can't the new king now execute Yeonsan?"

Daehyun shook his head. "A king is divinely appointed by the heavens to rule, and as such, we must prove that this revolt against Yeonsan is seen as a righteous act. And so, to ensure a peaceful and stable transfer of power, our new king must demonstrate that he is the benevolent ruler chosen by the heavens. He has no choice but to extend mercy to Yeonsan and have him exiled, alive."

Gods. My head ached. "The people would let the king *live*? After all his crimes?"

"Of course not. The coup leaders will assassinate Yeonsan in due time."

I breathed out in relief, then glanced at the hazy silhouette of trees. "The soldier mentioned you had found the trail. Nameless Flower will be looking for him . . ." I frowned. "How do you know King Yeonsan is still here?"

"Deposed king," he corrected gently. "Do you recall when the rainfall stopped?"

*Deposed king.* I could hardly believe it—that the rebellion had succeeded. It took a moment for his question to register. "Not too long ago," I finally answered.

He gestured at the ground, and I saw muddy footprints along the ridge. "The rain would have washed these prints away." We remained standing close, examining the marks, while the backs of our hands grazed at the slightest of movement.

"The tyrant roams free," he murmured, "and the killer may be shadowing us. This darkness seems without end, and yet . . ." He glanced at me, his touch trailing from my wrist to the very tip of my finger, before intertwining his with mine. "The night is brighter with you here, Iseul-ah." His words settled deep, a warmth that pulsed with both joy and pain. "When this is all over, perhaps I shall take you there."

"Where?"

"To the sea—"

Branches snapped and leaves rustled.

Daehyun reached for his sword.

My shoulders tensed, praying that it was the approach of soldiers. "They have arrived at last. Or perhaps it is Crow. I lost him earlier in the forest . . ." My words drifted off as I trained my gaze upon the lone figure pushing past the forest tangle, waving a hand at us in greeting.

A grinning face emerged.

Daehyun moved to stand before me, his hand still hovering by the hilt of his sword. My blood turned to ice as I stared at Yeongho and the longbow in his hand.

"Has the king been found?" Daehyun called out, his voice calm.

"Not yet . . ." Yeongho's smile faltered, his stare pinned upon me. "Why is she here? I thought she and the other women were heading to the Red Lantern Inn."

"There was a change of plan. Iseul wished to assist with the search."

Scratching his head, Yeongho glanced over his shoulder, then stared at me again. "I saw Wonsik's son among the men . . . He was asking them if they had seen me—" If realization had a sound, I heard it then; a sickening click. "You know who I am?"

Daehyun and I remained still. We could play ignorant, yet I feared Yeongho had already seen the truth in my face, in its pallor, in the wideness of my stare. But perhaps we could fool him, feign that I was shocked over something else—

A shadow darted past. My heart leaped; both men grabbed their weapons, and in one swift motion, Daehyun unsheathed his sword as Yeongho nocked an arrow to his bow. It was merely a rabbit, but it was too late now.

"One move," Yeongho warned, aiming the iron tip at Daehyun, "and I shall shoot you, then I shall shoot Iseul, too."

Daehyun's shoulders tensed.

My mind still raced, searching for a way out.

"Do not doubt my ability." Yeongho drew the bowstring tight. "I come from a generation of soldiers. I served as an apprentice to various armorers and would have excelled in the military examination if the king hadn't thrown a tantrum, ruining my life. So any sudden movement, and I shall launch this arrow."

"Lower the weapon," Daehyun ordered calmly, "or the soldiers will not think twice about slaying you."

Yeongho smirked. "What soldiers? They are now heading westward. I told them that I had seen the king go that way. No one is coming for either of you." He jerked his head. "Throw your sword my way."

"There seems to be a misunderstanding," I called out from behind Daehyun. "Whoever you are, it is of no concern to us."

"Indeed? I killed that arrogant Min Hyukjin, the prince's closest companion, and I am no concern to you?" He let out a single laugh. "Your lies reek of desperation. Now drop your sword, prince."

Daehyun remained immobile, his grip on the sword white-knuckled, and no matter how hard I searched, I could think of no way out for the both of us.

"Drop it *now*!"

A whistle, and I startled to the side when something sharp tore past the hem of my skirt. An arrow lodged right by my foot.

Swiftly, Yeongho nocked another arrow on the bow.

"No—!" The cry escaped me as Daehyun cast his sword away, the blade clanging against rock, then twirling to a stop between us and Yeongho.

"Have you ever wondered how our lives would have turned out if not for the king?" Yeongho called, closing in on the blade. "I would have become a soldier—a general! That was my fate. When I was a child, during my dol, I had reached out and grabbed the hilt of my father's sword. I *will* take my rightful place in this new kingdom, and I will not allow you to hinder me."

Daehyun's head shifted the slightest bit, and I followed his gaze. The thick, smokelike mist was rolling in toward us, obscuring everything in its path. Soon it would choke Yeongho's line of sight; he would lose his aim. And the sword was not too far away to sprint for.

"You are a court jester," I said, sliding a note of confusion into my voice. "What place could there be for you in the new kingdom?"

He barked out another laugh. "I degraded myself so utterly to carry out my plan. One must always keep one's enemy close, and what better way to keep the king close than to become his fool? So, you see, I will go to great lengths to take what is rightfully mine. I will kill Yeonsan and become a king killer. Everyone will know of me; I will be exalted by the people!"

The fog crept toward us with tormenting slowness.

We needed only a little more time.

"Come now, do not look so terrified," Yeongho said. "When you die, you will become a flower. My mother became one."

"Did you kill her? Your mother?" Daehyun called out.

"My father killed her, beat her to death when she wouldn't

let him pawn the hairpin. I was the one who buried her," Yeongho said, his voice devoid of feeling. "And then Mother became a flower."

"What do you mean?" I asked. The veil was moments away now. *Faster*, I begged of the thick haze. *Move faster.*

"Have you ever seen baek-du-ong flowers around burial mounds. They would always grow over the little graves I had created from my target practices. They grew over Mother's grave as well."

I frowned, his words finally sinking in, along with a memory. *Creepy grandfather flowers grow around burial mounds*, Suyeon had once explained, the know-it-all that she was, *because limestone powder is used to build those mounds.*

"You sprinkled limestone powder on the dead," I whispered.

He shrugged. "It is a Confucian ritual, did you know? I read somewhere that the powder allows for mummification. I fancied the thought of a garden filled with my relics, little animals I had struck dead in the heart. A childhood pastime." He sighed. "This is growing tedious. There is a king to be killed, you know."

"And you may go kill the king," Daehyun said. "You ought to hurry before Yeonsan escapes."

"I shall, once I carry out my first task. I always knew I'd have to kill you in the end."

Yeongho aimed the arrow once more, drawing the bowstring to his ear. His line of sight was still in view. It was me; I was his target. "I cannot have my future ruined by those determined to capture me."

"No. No, please. Do not shoot," I whispered, and my

whisper turned into a scream as Yeongho released the arrow. "Do not shoot—!"

It came too fast. The whistling sound. The glinting arrowhead, and suddenly, Daehyun stepped before me with lightning-like quickness. There came a terrible thud as he jolted, his back colliding into me. In that moment, he stood motionless, his tall height folding in on itself. Horror expanded in my chest as I stared at his hands, now stretched out before him, drenched in blood. So glisteningly red. My mind blanked. I shook my head. This was only a nightmare—

Yeongho heaved out another sigh, nocking a third arrow. "I had hoped to kill Iseul first." He rolled his shoulder again, then drew the bowstring tight. "I wanted to see your face, prince, when you stared down at your lifeless beloved. I wanted you to feel out of control and utterly helpless. To know what it feels like to be on the other side of the palace wall—to be one of us, the people, our lives falling into ruins because of your brother." Yeongho grinned as he lined his next shot at Daehyun, who was beginning to sway. "May no mercy be extended to the king's entire family. May his concubines and sons be poisoned, may all the princes who closed their eyes to the king's many sins be slain. Every royal and official will be punished for their inaction—"

A white curtain closed around us.

Grabbing Daehyun, I thrust him aside as a loud whistling shrieked by. I raced into the void, and a breeze blew the obscurity away—Daehyun was bleeding on the ground, choking my name. Yeongho was searching for the sword, and I stood raising its cold hilt in both hands.

Yeongho stilled, and just as he turned his head, I rammed

the blade forward, pushing deeper into his back, scraping past bone and sinew. There was a loud silence. The sword in my grip shook, caught in his rib cage as Yeongho rocked forward. His scream ruptured my ears, and the hilt slipped from my hands as he rose to his feet. He pulled the blade out and turned to me. Cold sweat drenched my face as I staggered back. The metal flashed, swiping for me, and I stumbled to the side. My shoulder collided with a tree. I turned the other way, the forest a blur of panic, and I tripped over a root.

I tried to crawl as the blade rose over me—

An arm locked around Yeongho's throat. Both he and the sword disappeared, sucked into the fog.

I remained on the ground, my body petrified as I stared at the wrestling shadows. Choking, struggling, feet dragging across the earth. And then silence. I waded through the sea of white, as though through a nightmare, my hands stretched out in the hopes of feeling the warmth of him.

"Daehyun?" I cried out, and all that answered me was the rushing river.

The strength drained from my knees, and then I was on the ground, crawling over to the cliff, following the trail of blood that disappeared over the edge. My mind collapsed as I stared at the black waters below.

The prince had stood before me moments ago. I had held his hand. He had whispered my name.

And now he was gone.

# 42
# DAEHYUN

# 43

# ISEUL

I searched the riverbank through the night and into the dawn. Morning dew clung to my skin as I staggered along the shore, my eyes straining, startling at every shadow and rock.

*He is alive. He has to be.*

That was the only thought my frantic mind could hold on to. Death seemed too final for him, too final for a prince whose life had become so interwoven with mine.

*Please, just be alive—*

Something dark floated on the water. I could not breathe again.

"Daehyun." I raced down the slope, tripping, then thrashed through the water. At last, I wrapped my arm around my prince, around the memory of him towering before me in the bookshop, of his hand on my waist, of him whispering my name, *Iseul-ah, Iseul-ah—*

A hand grabbed the collar of my dress, dragging me back.

"Are you mad?" Yul yelled.

She continued to drag me, together with my sister, until I was sitting on the shore, tightly embracing a jumble of empty fishing nets.

I shook my head, my nails digging into the rope, unbearable pain heaving through my chest. He was gone, truly gone. I could not, absolutely could not, believe it; it was incomprehensible. My mouth could not even form the words aloud.

My Daehyun. Dead.

# 44

# ISEUL

*The fleetingness of life* . . . I found myself thinking endlessly of Wonsik's remark. *We mortals exist for but a season, and yet we love as though we are bound by eternity.*

I could not claim to know precisely what love was, but by the second month of his passing, the memory of Daehyun had become a worn-out book. Creased at the spine, the pages stained with tears. A tale that was unbearably painful, yet I continued to return to it time and time again, desperate to keep him alive in my memory. I clung to every fragment of our shared moments. To forget him, I feared, was to forsake him in the frigid depths of the river, his grave.

And so I clung to the ghost of him.

He was the memory I turned to after a long day of caring for my sister, who did well on some days, worse on others. And terrible on the morning we'd received a letter from Grandmother saying she could not take us in again, afraid of what the villagers would say. There was no home for Suyeon and me to return to but this abandoned hut in the mountains, the same in which I had hidden before. And if not for Yul, I feared my sister would have slipped into utter darkness.

Life had not much improved for the other commoners of the kingdom. The people had become buttresses for the extravagant rewards granted to government officials. Land was given to the new elite, and thus land was taken from the people. The elite received tax exemption, and thus the tax burden was increased upon the people. Small and large rebellions continued to break out across the kingdom, led by angry peasants and disgruntled government officials alike.

As for the deposed king's stolen women, the thought of them haunted me the most. They were distributed among the rebel leaders and among the soldiers camped at the kingdom's borderland, like festival treats to greedy children. And it was Deputy Commander Park, rather than Maggot himself, who had hoarded many of the deposed king's women, building a private mansion to house them all.

It pained me to think of the kingdom, and so I focused on my sister's hands. I had crushed bongsunghwa flowers into a paste that I now rubbed onto each of her fingernails.

"When Yul visited this morning," Suyeon murmured, holding her hands still before me, "she told me the deposed king had passed."

I glanced up from where I was sitting. I had been out collecting the flowers, and so had missed Yul. "How did he die? Was he poisoned? Stabbed? Suffocated?"

She sighed heavily. "There were assassination attempts, but they were all thwarted by the soldiers guarding Yeonsan. They protected him out of former loyalties. It . . . it was a natural death. He died of an illness."

I fell dead silent, the disappointment so deep that I could not even move.

"King Jungjong decided not to execute the tyrant in spite of everything," I hissed, my voice trembling. "And now he is allowed to die a peaceful, natural death? Where is his punishment? If I were king, I would have quartered him—"

"Yeonsangun was once our king, so there is the people's former loyalty to consider," Crow called in from where he stood, stationed outside the door. He had offered to keep watch over us, standing between Maggot and my sister as a mountain. "It is simply not the way of our kingdom to kill a man who once received heaven's mandate."

Pain constricted my throat, bitter disappointment like a noose. I beat it away. The kingdom was in ruins, and there was nothing I could do about it. But I had my sister, and I could still gently wrap leaves around her fingers, staining the nails a cheerful orange.

Hopefully Mother's old tale was true—that if the stain lingered, it was a sign that one would find true love by the first snowfall. And how dearly I wished it for my sister, for her to find love, and see the sparkle return to her eyes.

"I will tend to your nails next," Suyeon whispered.

I stilled, an ache twisting in my chest. "There's no need," I said, then mustered a faint smile. "Truly, no need."

On my nails, bongsunghwa stains would fade too swiftly, vanishing well before the first snowfall.

No true love awaited me. Mine had already been found, only to be lost just as quickly.

# 45

# ISEUL

**Maggot died in early spring,** found in a pool of his own blood. Assassinated, surely, by the same dissatisfied officials who had attempted to remove Deputy Commander Park and other coup leaders from office. His death reached Suyeon and me as a ray of light.

With Maggot gone, we returned to the Red Lantern, where Suyeon reunited with other former courtesans, blossoming in the presence of her friends. She seemed to enjoy the work of running an inn with them—together, always together.

The work was overwhelming, and thus a good distraction for us all. With new travelers pouring in every day, I hardly noticed the passing seasons. One moment, there would be green buds shooting up through the snow, and the next, plum blossoms would be fluttering down from branches. Another blink, and I would realize that the time of the year had returned when red leaves would blow into the innyard no matter how frequently I swept, and when the women grew morose.

Chuseok was the festival we most dreaded—seeing the villagers leave for their hometowns to spend time with their families, to cook and eat in celebration of the autumn harvest. Families like the ones we no longer had.

"Why has the Red Lantern turned into a funeral?" Yul said, gathering the dispirited women in the yard. She waved a soup ladle as though it were her sword. "As Wonsik-samchon once told me: Life has been and will always be painful and lonely, and the only way to make this life endurable is that we all work together, for each other. You may have lost your old home, but you have a new home, and we shall celebrate this autumn harvest like everyone else!"

And with that, Yul presented to us an idea that left us all brimming with excitement. We would prepare a lavish feast, just for ourselves.

We poured what little we had—every coin, every warm memory, every longing—into the ingredients we amassed on the week of the festival. We laughed and cried while preparing rice cakes shaped into half-moons, filled with red bean paste, steamed to perfection. By Chuseok morning, we had prepared a feast that tasted of home—bowls of fluffy white rice, boiled fish, radish soup, kimchi and potato fritters, pickled cucumbers decorated with finely sliced ginger.

We all sat around our tables as distinguished guests, and we feasted until our stomachs and hearts were full to bursting.

Unable to stop smiling, I walked into the dark kitchen with two loaded trays. My spirit had never felt so buoyant; my face still ached from smiling and laughing. "This is the last of it, Cheonbi-yah."

Cheonbi was crouched before a basin full of dirty water and

bowls. "Set it down here." She let out a great yawn, then shook her head. "Oh gods, I can barely keep my eyes open. I will clean the rest at first light." She rose to her feet, mumbling, "You ought to rest, too."

I massaged my aching arms as I followed her out, then paused to take in my surroundings. The midnight hour was illuminated by globes of lantern light. A few of the women lay curled on the raised platform, slumbering under the starry sky. The usual hard lines of their faces had smoothed out tonight. I tiptoed past Suyeon and Yul. They sat leaning against each other, whispering and quietly laughing among themselves.

A yawn escaped me as I approached my room. Footsteps creaked from within. Cheonbi must have found her way into the wrong quarters again.

"Cheonbi-yah," I said, sliding open the door, "this is not your—"

My pulse leaped, convinced I was staring at a ghost. The tall, young man before me, his face paler than pale, appearing almost translucent in the lantern light. "Gods." I placed a hand over my thundering heart, now easing at the sight of Crow. "What are you doing here?"

"Nothing." Silver glinted, then disappeared into Crow's fist. "I—I should leave."

"Where were you last month?" I asked. "If you were here, you could have frightened away the deputy commander. He tried to arrest me, perhaps to interrogate me over Maggot's death. And if it were not for Investigator Gu, I suspect I would have been tortured—"

"I should go," he murmured once more, and tried to shove the silver into a pouch, but it slipped from his fingers and hit the floor with a metallic ping. He glanced around frantically. "Damn it, where did it go?"

The silver came rolling to my feet. It was a double ring, tied with a red string. Picking it up, I smirked. "Have you finally found yourself a sweetheart—"

There was a flower engraved into the silver.

A flower with five petals.

Just like Mother's.

I rushed the ring to the lantern light, uneasiness prickling my spine. Inscribed inside the first ring was the name Kim Jungim, and in the second, Hwang Heejae. Shaking my head, I brought it closer to the light, my whole body shaking. Perhaps I was imagining the inscription. I had to be.

"How could . . ." My breathing shallowed, my chest constricting, for the names of my parents remained. "I gave it to him. It was with him. He had it . . ." Fog seeped into my skull, clouding my mind, and my world swayed back to a year ago. I was on my knees, staring at the trail of his blood, disappearing over the cliffside. My ears filled with the terrifying noise of the devouring river, the sound that kept me up most nights.

I sucked in air, but my lungs would not fill. My head grew light. "Where did you get this?" I barely managed to ask.

Crow ran a hand over his face, then shook his head. "It is better you not know—"

"Answer me!" I cried. "Where did you get this ring?"

Footsteps rushed in, and soon Yul and Suyeon stood next to

me. They were speaking to me, but the river roared too loud in my ears to hear.

"As you must have heard, Yeongho's corpse was found a while back . . ." Crow's voice was muffled, bits and pieces reaching me through the noise in my head. "We all thought Daehyun-gun would be found in that area . . . The police finally found him farther down recently . . . A fisherman had buried . . . thought it would be best to return it to you."

I placed a hand over my stomach, feeling sick. On and off throughout the year, I had clung to an impossible hope. A hope that would have me racing through the market, convinced I had glimpsed him, only to find myself accosting a stranger.

"I apologize for being the bearer of such sad news," Crow whispered, running a hand over his haggard face. "I had hoped you'd never find out, but perhaps this is for the best. We shall give him a proper burial. A place to rest your heart upon."

One by one, the memories of the prince fluttered awake, like candle flames in the darkness of my thoughts—his half smiles, his quiet acts of kindness, his warm hands that had steadied me throughout, and his voice. I had missed his voice the most; deep and melodic, especially when he would call my name: *Iseul-ah*. No one had ever uttered my name with such intimacy, as if it were a secret meant for us only.

Pain tightened my throat as those cherished memories, carefully guarded over the months, now vanished, leaving only a curl of smoke. "H-he is dead," I stuttered, my heart writhing in pain, "he is dead—"

"He has been dead for a year," Crow reminded me cautiously.

I shook my head. "I still can't comprehend it, even now," my voice trembled as I stared down at the ring, "that he is truly gone . . ."

Wonsik's steady voice echoed in my head. *Focus yourself on the details.*

Though my heart still twisted in pain, and my hands still shook, I nevertheless raised the ring before my eyes.

*Focus on what is true. Do not be swept away by feelings.*

I turned the ring, then a thought glinted into my mind. "I gave the ring to Daehyun-gun." My voice rasped, and slowly, a frown knitted across my brow. "We were wary of you up until the day of the coup. Why would the prince suddenly confide in you?"

"I'm . . . I'm not sure what you mean."

"How would you know this ring belongs to me," my voice sharpened, "unless *he* told you so, and *after* the coup?" The moment I uttered those words, a horrible thought descended, and the ring felt like ice in my palm. "He is still alive, isn't he. And he ordered you to play along."

Crow mumbled, then made for the door. At once, Older Sister blocked his path.

"*Why* do you have this ring?" I demanded. "Why has he suddenly ordered you to return it?"

"I told the prince I was a horrible liar . . ." Crow played nervously with a loose thread from his sleeve. "He will be leaving soon, traveling somewhere far away, and thus he wished to return the ring to you."

A cold detachment settled over me. I almost felt as though I were inquiring about a stranger. "And where is the prince now?"

"Speak!" Older Sister snapped.

"I do not know where, at the moment. He has been moving from province to province to evade arrest. But I do know where he will be in thirteen days."

"*Where*," I whispered, my voice cold and unforgiving.

# 46

# ISEUL

**Thirteen mornings later, we saw** the blue sea glittering along the horizon.

"Thank heavens," I whispered, shuddering.

The merciless journey was nearing its end. We had traveled for as long as there was light in the sky, and twice through the night, determined to reach Mokpo sooner rather than later. Every traveler along the way had attempted to dissuade us, assuring us it would be impossible to reach the port in thirteen days' time. But here we were.

I watched the changing scenery, from the expanse of green fields and rolling hills to the muddy streets with their endless rows of shops, and gradually, to the southern port that glowed purple under the setting sun. We both dismounted and looked around. The road was empty except for the crush of soldiers loading a string of convicts onto a vessel.

"Do you think we are too late?" I asked.

"Daehyun-gun informed me he would take the last boat out, to avoid the crowd." Crow glanced up at the sky. "Let me go find a boatsman. You stay here and guard the horses."

Tethering the reins, I took in deep breaths, trying to steady my nerves. I had come all this way, and I knew what *not* to expect. Old feelings would not reignite. Familiarity would not rush in. The bond that had tied us together had stretched thin. I had come to bid him farewell. That was all.

"Iseul." Crow jogged over, shaking his head. "The last of the boats to Jeju have already left. The next one arrives tomorrow. And that vessel there is reserved for the military and for convicts."

"So he is gone," I whispered.

"He is gone. But I know where he is to stay on Jeju—with a distant relative, a military official there. Write him a note, and I will find a courier for you. It is too dangerous to travel all the way there yourself. Jeju is a penal island, full of criminals—"

Crow was still talking, but I could not hear him over the disappointment knifing through my heart. I hadn't realized until now how desperately I had wanted to see Daehyun again. To see living proof that he was alive. To finally see past the haunting fog, to stop hearing the terrifying sound of rushing water.

"You are absolutely sure?" I whispered as we stepped into an inn. "He is truly alive?"

"Who else have I been talking to these past several months? A ghost?"

"I know you are not—"

My shoulder knocked into a gentleman. The brim of his tall hat was lowered, and he stilled as I mumbled an apology.

"I know you are not lying," I continued, "but I simply cannot fathom that he is indeed alive."

"Well, perhaps it is better this way, to consider him dead." Crow waved a hand, then called out, "Jumo! We are in need of a room!"

My face blazed as I glanced around. Heads had turned our way, eyes taking in the sight of my daenggi hairstyle, that of an unmarried woman. I smacked Crow in the chest.

"We agreed to be siblings while traveling," I hissed, stepping close to him. "We need two rooms."

"I am not staying here tonight. I traveled for thirteen days to reach Mokpo, so I am not leaving until I taste fresh seafood. And I have a few military friends stationed nearby. I'll return by dawn."

The innkeeper appeared, led us to a room, and Crow left shortly after.

Expelling a sigh, I finally collapsed onto the floor and could not will myself to eat the meal Crow had ordered for me. Sadness made me tired. Curling up on the ground, I watched the paper-screened door, stained violet in the setting sun. My consciousness drifted in and out as I watched shadows deepen, and lanterns were lit, casting a warm glow across the door. I must have drifted off, for my eyes opened long enough to glimpse a gentleman's silhouette, hesitating outside my door. I rubbed my eyes, and he was gone. The fatigue dragged me back into its dreamless depths.

By the early morning, I awoke more tired than before, and the thought of returning to the capital gnawed at me. I had traveled thirteen hellish days to reach Mokpo. I had nearly fallen off my horse in exhaustion multiple times. My knuckles were torn and bloody from scratching myself awake. All for what?

Sunrise painted the sky in vivid shades as I stepped outside. The sea shimmered gold, yet the exquisite sight did not move me with awe. Instead, it saddened me. Of all the islands, why had the prince chosen the farthest one from me?

Footsteps crunched across the dirt, drawing my attention. I turned and noticed a gentleman crossing the yard, his hat tilted to shield his face, his black robe billowing in the salty breeze. As he neared, his steps faltered, our heights almost aligned by the veranda I stood upon. And then, slowly, he looked up. A breath caught in my throat. I had etched his countenance into my mind, painstakingly retracing the contours from memory in a desperate attempt to find comfort in his death . . . and now, that same face stared back at me.

"Good morning," Daehyun whispered, dark eyes peering into mine. "It has been a while."

I nearly laughed, outraged and stunned by the casualness of his tone, as though we were two acquaintances greeting each other after a brief excursion. "I have half a mind to truly make you a dead man."

He reached out to gather my hands in his, but I snatched them away, agonized and offended by his presence.

"What is the matter with you?" I whispered harshly, wishing I could shake him. To snap him out of the daze he seemed to be in. "You hid from me with such ease for an entire year, and now you come back?"

"With ease?" His brows knitted together for the barest moment, then his face smoothed out. "You cannot fathom how difficult it was."

"Then you ought to have stayed away," I snapped, retreating from him. I couldn't bear to be close. The sight of him filled me with freezing water. "Go on," I said, trembling. "Go and live your life, and I shall live mine as far from you as possible, as you clearly desire."

Before I could leave, his gruff voice stopped me. "I will tell you everything, if you wish to know."

"I do not wish to know," I lied.

"I was carrying Wonsik's journal; it was tucked inside my robe," he said, his voice low and hesitant. "The arrow punctured the book and wounded me, but the injury was survivable. Crow eventually found me."

"Where did you go after—?" I started to ask, but caught myself. I sounded like I cared for him still.

"My friend Hyukjin had a sister, Court Lady Sonhui. She was released from duty and went to live with her aunt in Wonju," he explained. "I stayed there for the first few months until I was recovered enough."

This time I did laugh. A cold, humorless laugh. Daehyun was alive and had hidden the truth from me; this alone had cut off feeling to half of my body. To learn that he had spent all those months with another woman cut off what was left.

"Nothing occurred between us," he reassured me.

"Of course not," I replied, and quietly added, "now I understand why you stayed away."

"You cannot mean that. You cannot truly think that I would—" His voice broke, and a hint of a crack began forming on his mask. "I would waste entire days deliberating over whether to seek you out. You, and you alone, occupied my every passing thought. Have you already forgotten my affection for you? What . . . what I would do for you?"

"What you would do for me? You *abandoned* me. You, who know the pain of losing those dear to you. How could you be so cruel?"

"What else was I to do?" The rim of his eyes grew red, his immense control unraveling, thread by thread, revealing his devastation. "I am a wanted man. How could I dare approach you? How could I dare endanger you?"

"What danger? The deputy was angered by your involvement in Suyeon's escape, but surely not enough to kill you. And Maggot died!"

His jaw tightened, and his eyes lowered, as if avoiding my gaze.

"Maggot was assassinated. He is gone and . . ." I stilled, watching the way his expression grew taut, the way his hands retreated behind his robe. Suspicion crept in. "You killed him?"

He remained silent, his head still lowered, the brim of his hat obscuring his features. "I killed a high-ranking official, a member of the new ruling power. I would have taken the lives of a hundred more if it meant securing your happiness. Do you understand now?" he said quietly. "That is why I must live as though I am dead. Dead even to you."

I covered my face briefly, trying to hide the sudden surge of tears. Despite him being just five paces away, it felt like an insurmountable chasm, a raw wound torn open.

"I cannot," I whispered, my voice barely audible, and retreated into the solace of my room. Once alone, a shuddering sigh escaped me. Daehyun, in his own twisted way, believed that his death was the best outcome for both of us.

And yet . . .

I found myself remembering the days I had spent by the riverside, by what I had thought to be his final resting place. How many hours had I sat quietly on a rock, my mind tormented by visions of his painful end? I didn't know how to chase away this lingering grief, this sadness melded into the hollow of my bones.

As tears dripped from my lashes, I looked down, fiddling with a loose strand of my sleeve. None of this was Daehyun's fault. My sister lived, she laughed, because Daehyun had chosen exile. I owed him proper thanks—and a farewell.

"Iseul-ah," came his deep voice.

His shadow pooled around me, his broad shoulders blocking out the light. My heart raced as he stepped closer. His pleading gaze burned the back of my neck, and when I continued to remain motionless, I half expected him to leave. Instead, his arms encircled my shoulders, trembling as though shaken by the simple warmth of human contact.

"You need not forgive me, but please understand." His hoarse voice brushed the tendrils of my hair. "I would have burdened you to choose—between your sister and myself, between a life of a free woman and that of a fugitive."

"I never wanted your sacrifice."

"You did not want my sacrifice, and neither did I want yours."

"And yet here you are now."

We stood there, locked in an embrace, as the angle of sunlight shifted, casting long shadows that crept toward the corners. In the distance, the cry of seagulls mingled with the rhythmic sound of waves crashing against the shore.

Closing my eyes, I allowed my thoughts to drift amid the ebb and flow of memories, images that felt distant, like they belonged from a decade ago. I summoned them to life: A prince with a silvery blue robe, glowing like moonstone as he'd pointed his arrow my way, and an encounter that ought to have ended in enmity that had shifted like the current at sea, at the whim of fate. He had grown into a friend who carried my burden, and my sister's, too.

My hand lowered to his sleeve.

"It was not my intention to accost you," he finally said. "I had planned to depart this morning, but then I wanted a glimpse of you. Just a glimpse. And when I saw you standing there, the woman who haunts every corner of my dreams . . ." His voice faltered, heavy with unspoken words. Then he shook his head. "I don't know what I was thinking. Tell me to leave," he urged me desperately.

I knew I ought to bid him farewell, yet my hands would not release his sleeve. "And if I do not?"

After a long, tense moment, he leaned in, pressing his forehead gently against the curve of my shoulder. "Then I will be yours," he confessed, his voice a soft caress, "and I shall be your ruin."

I turned in his arms until I was staring up at him. He was alive, his heart bounding under my palm, strong and resilient. For the first time in over a year, I studied him. Daehyun was no longer so polished and pristine, but scarred and roughened, blending into the rugged landscape. He was changed and yet not.

"My ruin?" I murmured. "What is it that you would ruin? My life with Suyeon? My sister is happy and well loved at the inn with Yul. My freedom? What is freedom if I cannot share it with my dearest friend? And what bright future? I have long ago stopped caring so much about what could be tomorrow."

Tomorrow, the kingdom could sink into the sea.

Tomorrow, all the elders we trusted could betray us.

Tomorrow, the fog might consume everything we loved.

But I had him today. And he had me.

"This is your last chance. Tell me to leave, or I will not fool myself into letting go of you again—"

I lifted onto my tiptoes, pressing a kiss to his cold cheek. I watched a wrinkle form between his brows, his eyes widening the slightest bit with surprise. "Do not leave, Daehyun-gun. And do not die again."

He stilled, searching me for a long moment, then hesitantly caressed my cheek. "Call me Kyung." His voice had dropped into a raw whisper. "Yi Kyung is my birth name."

"Yi Kyung . . ." I tasted his name, a name I would hopefully call for many years to come. "Kyung-ah."

A small sigh escaped him. His hand held my waist, drawing me closer and closer, until I stood flush against him. When his mouth touched mine, it was the gentlest of pressure, the lightest brush of warmth. Then he moved away.

"Are you quite certain about this?" He hesitated again, his voice a rough whisper. "You would brave a life with me?"

"I would brave this life," I murmured against him, "and a thousand more."

A hint of a smile tugged at his lips, then he dipped his head low. His tongue drew across my lower lip, and when my mouth parted for him, he held the back of my neck, angling my mouth closer, and finally deepened his kiss over mine. In that moment, everything disappeared. The walls of the room dissolved into mist, the cacophony of morning birds grew silent. It was only us,

Kyung and me. Our hearts melding into one thundering beat, into one impulsive decision.

To Jeju, I would go.

To the island of rock and wind and strife.

It would not be the life I had envisioned for myself, but I felt no fear. Life had taken me to strange and frightening places before, and even in my darkest and loneliest hour, I had always found treasures hidden in the deep. And I knew I would find them again.

# EPILOGUE
## Kyung

**It took eight years for** the last of the main coup leaders to die off. With them finally gone, Yi Kyung dared to leave Jeju Island with Iseul, for they had long wished to pay homage to Wonsik at his grave. He had been dead for nine years now.

"This day was so long in coming," Iseul said, gracefully mounted on a horse as Kyung led the creature by its reins. "I thought we would never return to the mainland."

"I thought many things would not happen," he replied, gazing up at his wife. "But it did."

"Sometimes I catch you staring eastward, in the direction of the palace. Do you miss your old life?"

"My old life . . . I admit that I miss it to some extent. I yearn for the harrowing nightmares and the web of treachery that enveloped those days."

"I *mean* it. Speak truthfully."

"You know my answer. I am happy wherever you are."

Her tense shoulders eased. "I have grown fond of Jeju, I must admit."

"Then in Jeju we shall remain. We've made a good life for ourselves there, albeit far from your sister."

"It is, but she has made a good life for herself too. Half her letters are always bursting with exciting stories about travelers."

"And the other half, about how good Yul has been to her," he remarked, pulling the horse to a halt when they reached a stream. "We will let the horse rest here—"

"But if you wish to return, I will follow you without hesitation," she vowed. "Perhaps the king will forgive you and grant you a rank in the government. He has lifted the banishment from many of the officials he was once forced to punish."

Once, King Jungjong had existed as a puppet upon the throne, his royal authority tied to the immense power the coup leaders had held over him. But His Majesty was free now, and there were large-scale reforms occurring throughout the kingdom, with land distributed more equally among the people, and plans to grant government positions to even intelligent peasants. Kyung knew that, if he so wished it, he could carve out a good position for himself in the capital.

"You are still a prince, after all," she murmured. "Surely it must weigh upon you that you cannot make your mark on the annals of history."

"I have no desire to be remembered by history, and a return to the palace will likely invite my death. I think you know this, too."

"I know," she sighed. "But I'm suddenly filled with so much doubt. I keep thinking you must surely want more than our quiet little life."

A smile played at his lips. "Our life is anything but quiet," he said, but she did not hear it.

"Just tell me. What do you truly want in life?"

He tethered the reins, then reached under Iseul's skirt, holding her ankle, steadying her as she swung over and dropped before him. He gazed at her honey-brown eyes, greenish-gray in some angles, eyes that had darkened slightly over the years. Eyes he still felt lost in. "All I desire," he whispered, tenderly caressing her hair, "is to live a peaceful and honorable life, and above all, to be remembered well by you once I'm gone. Then in the next life, perhaps, you will not pass me by."

"I would never pass you by," she replied softly. "And should I find you first, I do hope you will not greet me with an arrow."

Chuckling, he ran a hand over her shoulder apologetically, then drew her in for a kiss as the horse drank from the stream. When wind blew and red maple leaves danced across the forest floor, they continued their journey. They traveled across a land once marked off as the forbidden territory, but now the road wended through flourishing rice paddies and rebuilt villages, over small mountains and through valleys bursting with autumn foliage, early frost, and silver grass.

"Yul-ah!" a distant female voice cried out. "They are here! I see them!"

Kyung gazed ahead, and he spotted the golden thatched roof of the Red Lantern Inn, and soon a figure materialized in the distance. It was Iseul's sister, running down the road, her apron billowing around her.

"Iseul-ah!" She waved her hand frantically, joyfully. "Hwang Iseul!"

As he watched the two sisters run into each other's embrace, he felt a fullness in his heart, a delight he could never have imagined for himself at the age of nineteen. He had imagined, then, that his life would crumble like dry bones.

Young Daehyun had not known that the prophecy of his death would not be a story of how his life would end, but of how it would begin.

# HISTORICAL NOTE

Many of the cruel and brutal acts of King Yeonsangun depicted in this book were taken directly from the Veritable Records, a history account written by officials, so sacred that not even the kings were permitted to rewrite what was witnessed and recorded.

For example, it is documented in the Veritable Records that on March 20, 1504, two princes were indeed ordered to kill two of the former king's concubines, Gwi-in Jeong and Eom, the ones involved in King Yeonsangun's mother's execution. Prince Anyang and Bongan were the two princes. Under the king's threat of death, Anyang and Bongan were made to kill the two women, one of whom was their own mother.

Another recorded event was King Yeonsan's ban on the Korean alphabet, hangul / 한글 (also known as the vulgar script, eonmun / 언문). This ban occurred on July 20, 1504, the very day after someone sent a slanderous letter to the king. Then, on July 25, the king ordered that every literate person write and submit four pieces of text to their government offices. King Yeonsan attempted to use these texts, hiring literate women to go through hundreds of thousands of writing samples to identify the anonymous writer, just as we might take fingerprints of people in an attempt to match it with the culprit.

However, for the sake of plot flow, I altered the timeline of when the coup occurred. According to historical records, the coup leaders began planning after Lady Seungpyeong's suicide on July 20, 1506, and it was executed with very little bloodshed on September 18 of 1506, but I decided to shorten the timeline by a few weeks. I decided that rather than adding filler scenes to match the historical timeline, I would rather shorten the timeline to tighten the plot.

Another detail I feel is important to point out is that Official Wu Sayoung (aka "Maggot") is a fictional character loosely based on the real historical figure Gu Suyoung (구수영). Other characters, like Deputy Commander Park, were actual historical figures, and it is recorded in the Veritable Records that he *did* take King Yeonsan's concubines for himself, and even had a separate house built for them.

While striving to stay as historically accurate as possible, I dived through as many records of King Yeonsan's reign as I could find, and some discoveries absolutely shocked me and required me to rewrite the outline of my book. The biggest shock to me came when I learned that the coup leaders weren't the honorable heroes I had hoped them to be. These leaders may have liberated the populace from tyranny, but they also made the common people pay a steep price for their freedom. In fact, there are claims that the kingdom of Joseon was worse off after the coup than when the populace had been under King Yeonsan's reign.

The reason for this is due to what is known as "Gongshin chaekbong," 공신 책봉, which refers to the traditional practice of giving honorary official rank to individuals who made significant contributions to society. After overthrowing King Yeonsangun, the "Gongshin chaekbong" was bestowed on 117 government officials for their contribution to the Jungjong Rebellion (중종 반정), though there is speculation that more than half of those who'd received the reward hadn't actually helped out in the coup but were given this reward for simply being related to the coup leaders.

This reward included various benefits, such as tax exemptions, promotion in rank within the government, large parcels of land, ten soldiers, twenty servants, monetary wealth, a horse, and political benefits for the recipient's family. However, only around fifty individuals were granted this same reward for their contributions to the founding of the Joseon dynasty in 1392, in stark contrast to the 117 who received it after the rebellion. This vividly illustrates the opulent nature of the coup leaders of the Jungjong Rebellion. For these reasons, the rebellion was only half successful, as the coup leaders managed to overthrow the king, but they failed to create a system in which the common people could prosper.

Researching this book, in many ways, was a deeply unsettling experience. The more I delved into the king's atrocities, and the extent of the coup leaders' corruption, the more uneasy I became, questioning my decision to take this dark period as the subject of my work. However, I was reminded by readers that books that confront disturbing historical events are crucial.

It is imperative to confront history because it repeats itself when ignored.

So if you have reached the end of this book, then thank you for bearing witness to this tragic chapter in Korea's past.

Thank you for not looking away.

# ACKNOWLEDGMENTS

Thank you, Emily Settle, for always challenging me to grow as a writer, and always inspiring me to step outside of my comfort zone. I wouldn't be the writer I am today if not for your guidance.

To my agent, Amy Elizabeth Bishop, you are my rock in this publishing world. Thank you for always advocating for me, and for always being such a huge encouragement to me.

Many thanks to my publishing team at Feiwel & Friends, including my fantastic publicist, Chantal Gersch; my copyeditor, Tracy Koontz; proofreader, Lindsay Wagner; and cover artist, Yejin Park; executive managing editor, Dawn Ryan, and senior production editor, Avia Perez; my designer, Aurora Parlagreco; and production manager, Allene Cassagnol. I'd also like to thank Lauren Abramo for her work with translation.

Thank you to Sarah Mughal, my adviser in all things political and angsty; Joan He, for always being open to answering my random questions; Eunice Kim, for being my Korean history research buddy. Thank you to Geehae Jeong, Cristina Lee, Kess Costales, and Sharon Hur, for being the best cheerleaders. And a special thank you to Musa for the incredibly insightful feedback.

Thank you to the Canada Council for the Arts for the generous financial support.

My eternal gratitude to all the librarians, booksellers, reviewers, and readers who have supported my works. Your enthusiasm allows me to keep doing what I love: exploring Korean history through fiction.

To Mom and Dad, thank you for instilling in me a love of stories; I wouldn't even be an author without you both. I also want to thank my in-laws, Mr. and Mrs. Tung, for helping me out with the kids. What would I do without you both!

A special thank-you to my husband, Bosco; your brain is my secret weapon, and your kindness and love are a constant source of inspiration.

I'm grateful for the many resources that made it possible to write this book, especially:

- Kang Haewon, Goeun Lee, Lyndsey Twining, and Jeongsoo Shin's "An Annotated Translation of Daily Records of King Yeonsangun, Chapter One (the 25th Day to the 29th Day of the 12th Month of 1494)"
- Dag Tanneberg's *The Politics of Repression Under Authoritarian Rule: How Steadfast is the Iron Throne?*
- Anna Tolman Smith's "Some Nursery Rhymes of Korea"
- Lu Gwei-Djen and Joseph Needham's "A History of Forensic Medicine in China"
- David M. Robinson's "Disturbing Images: Rebellion, Usurpation, and Rulership in Early Sixteenth-Century East Asia—Korean Writings on Emperor Wuzong"
- David W. Kim's "Royal Taoist Sogyeokseo: The Political

Encumbrance of Confucian Sarims in the Gimyo Literati Purge (1519)"

- Edward Willett Wagner's "The Literati Purges: Political Conflict in Early Yi Korea"
- Mina Kyounghye Kwon's "'Bak Cheomji's Sightseeing' from Kkokdugaksi Noreum, a Korean Traditional Puppet Play"

I'd also like to offer my many thanks to sillok.history.go.kr for providing full access to the Korean translation of King Yeonsangun's Daily Records.

And last: I thank Jesus, my lord and savior, for always being my place of refuge.